P9-EKE-828

Please turn the page for more reviews....

The World Below

A NOVEL

SUE MILLER

BALLANTINE BOOKS • NEW YORK

To the memory of Marguerite Mills Beach,
my own beloved storytelling grandmother.

ACKNOWLEDGMENTS

I'm grateful to the Radcliffe Institute for Advanced Study and the Bunting Fellowship program for the gift of time and a tiny aerie-cum-computer that allowed me to finish this book; to Perri Klass for answering my many questions and for guiding me through the Neonatal Intensive Care Unit at Boston Medical Center; and to Doug Bauer for his generous help.

PART ONE

One

Imagine it: a dry, cool day, the high-piled cumulus clouds moving slowly from northwest to southeast in the sky, their shadows following them across the hay fields yet to be cut for the last time this year. Down a narrow dirt road between the fields, a horse-drawn carriage, two old people wearing their worn Sunday clothes seated side by side in it, driving to town for their grown daughter's funeral. Neither of them spoke, though you could see, if you cared to look, that the old woman's lips were moving ceaselessly, silently repeating the same few phrases over and over. It was her intention, formed over the long weeks her daughter lay dying, to rescue her grandchildren from their situation, from their motherless house. To take all three of them back to the farm with her. She was rehearsing what she'd say, though she wasn't aware of her mouth forming the words, and her husband didn't notice.

Imagine this too: later in the afternoon of the same long day, the two older grandchildren, the girls, laughing together. Laughing cruelly at the old woman, their grandmother, for her misguided idea.

But perhaps it wasn't truly cruel. They were children, after all. As thoughtless as children usually are. What's more, they'd spent a good part of this strange day, the day of their mother's burial, laughing. Laughing nervously, perhaps with even a touch of hysteria, mostly because they didn't know what they ought to feel or think. Laughter was the easiest course. It was their way to ward off all the dark feelings waiting for them.

They'd been up before dawn, long before their father and little brother were awake, long before their grandparents started in to town, almost giddy with the number and variety of their chores. The meal after the church service was to be elaborate—deviled eggs, ham, scalloped potatoes, rolls, three kinds of jellied salad, pudding, and butter cookies—and they each had a list of things to do connected with it. They worked in the kitchen in their nightgowns, barefoot, as the soft gray light slowly filled the room. When the housekeeper, Mrs. Beston, arrived, she chased them upstairs to get dressed.

They had ironed their own dresses the day before because Mrs. Beston was so busy. They hung now on hangers from the hook behind their bedroom door, smelling of starch, smelling just slightly still of the heat of the iron—that sweet, scorchy odor. As they pulled them on over their heads and then helped each other plait their long braids, they were convulsed, again and again, by lurches of laughter that felt as uncontrollable as sneezing. Sometimes it was wild, almost mean. It fed on itself. Just looking at each other, or at their sleepy little brother, Freddie, who'd come in in his nightshirt, his hair poking up strangely, to sit on their bed and watch them, could set it off.

Maybe this explained it then—why, later in the day, when their father told them of their grandmother's notion, they couldn't stop themselves: why they gave way again to the same ragged hysteria. They laughed at her. They laughed at her and their grandfather's having clopped into town with horse and buggy; their father had had a motorcar forever, it seemed to them (it had been seven years). They laughed because she had only eight teeth left in her head and therefore smiled with her hand lifted to cover her mouth—they could both imitate this awkward, apologetic gesture perfectly. They laughed because she wore a ridiculous straw hat shaped like a soggy pancake, and an old-fashioned dress, the same old-fashioned dress she wore to all ceremonial events. They laughed because she had thought their father would so easily give them away.

"They are still children," is what the old woman said to her son-in-law. "They need a childhood." The two of them had gone together into the parlor after they greeted each other, and when she told him it was private, what she had to say to him, he shut the sliding pocket doors. It had been such a long time since anyone had pulled them out that a thick gray stripe of dust evenly furred all their decorative molding.

They sat not really looking at each other, the new widower and the dead woman's mother, and the grandmother forced herself to keep talking, to try to explain her plan to him. She wasn't a good talker, even in the easiest circumstances, and none of this was easy, of course. She hadn't imagined very much beyond her first state-ment ahead of time either. It was really her entire argument.

What's more, her son-in-law had always made her shy. He was a large, almost handsome man with slicked-down hair, getting burly now as he approached forty-five. He was a salesman, of vulcanized rubber goods, and his way of dealing with the world came directly from that life: he wanted to amuse you, to charm you. When he was courting her daughter—Fanny, her name was—he had flirted with the grandmother, and this had made her tongue-tied and silent around him. Once, after she'd served him a blueberry cake he found especially delicious, he'd grabbed her and waltzed her around the scrubbed wooden floors of her farmhouse kitchen. This had so unnerved her—his energy and strength, and her helplessness against them—that she'd burst into shameful tears.

That's what she felt like doing now, weeping, she was making such a mess of getting this said. It had seemed so clear to her as she moved through her solitary days while her daughter was dying and then since. The children needed her. They *couldn't* be left alone through the week any longer. The girls couldn't be asked to be so responsible—taking care of themselves and then their little brother too. It was too much. It was simply too much. They needed a home: someone to take care of *them*. She would offer to bring them to town on Fridays to be with him for the weekend. Or he could come out and stay with them on the farm. Oh, they'd be happy to have him!

All this planning had kept the image of her daughter—wasted, curled on her side, rising to consciousness only to cry out in pain— from her mind; though she'd spoken to Fanny often, another version of Fanny, as she'd made her preparations: as she'd shaken out the extra bedding, as she'd set out the framed pictures of her in the unused rooms she'd made up for the children. "Oh my dear girl," she had whispered. "They will be fine, you'll see. They just need someone to tend to them for a change, that's all, and I am the one to do it."

Her son-in-law waited a moment now, out of kindness and sorrow, before he answered. Then he cleared his throat and said that he saw things somewhat differently. His older daughter was almost sixteen, the younger thirteen—not really children at all. They were big, good girls. He needed their help, he said.

Of course, this was exactly her point. She didn't press it, though. She sat silently and nodded, just once, furious at herself. She was giving up. This easily.

And they were, he continued gently (very gently: he was fond of his mother-in-law, this cadaverously skinny and stern old woman), *his* children, after all.

She stood up and turned away from him, but not before he saw her mouth pull down, grim and defeated.

It had taken Fanny several years to die, of cancer, though no one had ever spoken the word in the house or in front of the children. And the truth was, as the grandmother would have admitted if she weren't wild with a grief that turned in like self-blame, that Fanny had been so unusual a young and then a nearly middle-aged woman that the girls had been in charge of the household long before anyone had guessed she was ill. So much for needing a childhood.

The girls were named Georgia and Ada. Georgia, the older, could remember even in the years when her mother was well, coming home from school for lunch, a privilege of the town children, to find the house silent, Fanny still in her housecoat, lying on the sofa in the parlor reading, just as she had been when Georgia left. She'd look up, surprised and dizzy. Her face was round and full, with fat, childish lips and a baby's startled blue eyes: a pretty, oddly unformed-looking young woman. "Why, Georgia," she'd say, day after day. "How *can* you be back so soon?" And then she'd rise and ineffectually pat at her hair or her robe. Often she was barefoot, even in winter. "Well, we'd better go see what we can scratch up for you girls to eat, hadn't we?"

It was a disgrace, really, though the children didn't care; they'd gotten used to it long before. In the kitchen, the breakfast dishes were still on the table, the grease congealed, the skin of the syrup pools lightly puckering with the unseen motion of the air. Upstairs, the beds would gape, unmade. When the baby, Freddie, came, Georgia's first task at noon would often be to take him up to the nursery to change his drooping diaper. "Oh, you pooper," she would say. "You big flop maker. Look what you've done now, you wicked boy." She would keep a steady stream of this insulting talk flowing, so that he would lie still in fascination and amusement and make her job easier, but also so that she wouldn't gag—she never got used to the piercing scent of ammonia, and worse, that she released each time she unpinned his sagging, weighted cloths.

It was a little while after Freddie came—Georgia later thought it must have been then that her mother had first become ill—that they began to have regular help, finally. Mrs. Beston. Her name was Ellen, but no one ever called her that, not even their mother. Mrs. Beston, always and only, though their father sometimes called her

Mrs. Best One when she wasn't around to hear it. She was tall and raw-boned and strong. Entirely without humor, and yet endlessly, bottomlessly cheerful. She arrived Monday mornings, just as their father was leaving for the week. "You must take these children in hand, Mrs. Beston," he'd say, pulling on his coat. "They're spoiled rotten. A daily whipping, I should think, and gruel for supper four nights a week at the minimum." The children, sitting on the stairs waiting to say goodbye, would look at each other with wicked grins.

"Oh, Mister, don't say that!" Mrs. Beston would cry uneasily.

"No, no, we count on you, Mrs. Beston. Lock them in their rooms. Send them to bed with *no* supper. Hang them up by their thumbs till they promise to obey."

"Oh now, Mr. Rice!"

"I'm off now, Mrs. Beston. By Friday, I have every confidence, you'll have instilled in them the fear of the Lord."

But she didn't. She forgave them everything. Everyone, to her, was a *poor dear,* most of all their mother. *Mrs. Rice, the poor dear.* It was only slowly that Georgia came to understand that this was more than peculiarly expressed affection, that Mrs. Beston was referring to something specific, something sad and wrong about her mother.

She was supposed to leave by three-thirty or four—she had her own family to get home to and cook for—but often she stayed after her chores were done, just to do a few pieces in the puzzle with them, just to play one more hand of Slapjack, one round of War. When she did leave, the house was clean, the laundry was done if it was laundry day, and—after their mother was really ill—there was always something prepared in the kitchen and the girls left with instructions on how to warm it and serve it. Though by then Fanny didn't have much appetite, Ada or Georgia would always take a tray to her room before they served themselves and Freddie at the kitchen table. And after dinner one of them would go to fetch the nearly untouched tray back down. Both of them were good at keeping track, both of them always knew whether she'd eaten more or less today than yesterday, though they never commented on this to each other.

But they'd all gotten skilled by this time at never acknowledging what they knew, at pretending they didn't see what they saw. Everything conspired to encourage them in this—Mrs. Beston's determined good cheer, their father's strained, sometimes desperate gaiety, their neighbors' polite silence about what was happening in their house.

And their mother: well, hadn't she always been this way? Indolent, half the time in bed anyway, reading or just daydreaming? Oh, she was sick, they certainly knew that, but they all expected—or pretended to expect, and then forgot they were pretending—that she'd be herself again by spring; or then by summer, when they'd drive over to Bucksport and have lobsters at the pound; or surely by fall, when they'd need to go shopping in Pittsfield for new school things.

Late one afternoon the summer her mother lay dying, Georgia came out onto the screened porch off the kitchen. Mrs. Beston had gone for the day, but she'd left Fanny's sheets soaking in a galvanized metal tub of cold water. The blood had colored them evenly a beautiful shade of deep sherbet pink. They looked like snow-covered mountains at sunset. Caught by surprise at the sight, Georgia stopped short and gasped. Her heart was pounding. But then quickly her mind performed its familiar, useful trick: they were having chicken stew for dinner that night, and what she told herself was that the blood was of course from the slaughter of the chicken, somehow spilled onto these cloths.

There was a world of knowledge that she had to ignore to hold on to this thought, starting with the fact that the chickens were slaughtered out behind the henhouse, but she was practiced at it, it was all accomplished in seconds. She started to whistle as loudly as she could, "Where E'er You Walk." She went outside into the overgrown yard where the lupines and lemon lilies were slowly being choked out by weeds, and began savagely to pluck them, singing now, ignoring the occasional cry of her mother, audible even through the windows she insisted stay shut.

She wanted her father, Georgia thought, yanking at the flowers. She wanted him home right now. But he was out on the road for two more days, until Friday, driving his usual circuit of general stores and hardware stores in a radius of several hundred miles. He carried samples of his wares in his motorcar, and the car had come to have that rubbery odor permanently, an odor Georgia would find reassuring even into her old age.

Avoiding the screened porch, she went around to the front door of the house and brought the flowers inside. In the kitchen, she found a pitcher for them. Ada followed her in from the parlor and they harmonized loudly until their mother had fallen asleep again; or at least, perhaps hearing them, had stopped making noise.

The pattern had been the same even when their mother was well: their father was gone from Monday till Friday. On those days they had their lazy, slatternly routines without him—improvised meals, what their mother called "picnic dinners." It was fun, they thought of it as a kind of game. On Friday mornings, they bustled around frantically, cleaning up. "Good Lord, this place is a pigsty!" their mother would say, as if she'd only just noticed, as if some large group of messy strangers had sneaked in and made it so while she wasn't looking. Usually their father was home by the time they got back from school that afternoon.

Their weekends together were the center of the family's life. There were rides in the Model T when the weather was fine; there were real picnics and visits to their grandparents' farm; there were sleigh rides and sledding and skating in the winter, and an endless round of charades, games, theatricals. There were big elaborate breakfasts both weekend days, and on Sunday a long, late dinner.

Of course, there was the unfairness that neither parent attended church, whereas the children were made to go for the whole morning—the nursery class for Freddie, Sunday school and then the ser-mon for the girls. They didn't get home sometimes until twelve-thirty or one. "Give your parents my regards," "Say hello to your parents," the other grown-ups, the churchgoers, would say, in what you would have thought was a slightly mean way. "Oh, yes," they'd say on their way to pick up Freddie, on their way home across the town green. "Oh, we will!" they'd call as they ran the length of the hedge of mock orange with its dizzying smell in early summer, as they turned into their walk and thundered up the three wooden steps in their good Sunday shoes.

"We're starved!" "We're dying!" they'd cry out from the front door. Often their mother would stay upstairs—you could hear her washing up—but their father would come down right away, hand-some in his shirtsleeves, and take them to the kitchen and fix them butter-and-sugar sandwiches, *to tide you over*, he would say. When their mother appeared, she would be wearing her Sunday best, just as if she *had* gone to church. She would be flushed and smelling of lavender, and their father would cry out some silliness: "What is this vision, this apparition of beauty that appears? Girls, girls, you have a beautiful older sister you've been hiding from me!"

It was strange, Georgia thought at the service, how little she felt now. Perhaps she had gotten used to the notion of death, her mother's death anyway, because of the long illness. She watched her grandparents at the end of the front pew. They didn't look at each other, but she saw that their knuckled hands were tightly entwined on her grandmother's lap. The old woman's shoulders made a stooped, dragging line down. Her dress was shapeless, and shiny from ironing, the lace collar turned a brownish yellow with age.

Afterward, the grandparents didn't stay for the buffet Mrs. Beston had set out in the dining room while they were at church. Instead, they shyly summoned their son-in-law to the front porch. When he had said his goodbyes to them, he sent the girls out to see them off. He had told them by now about their grandmother's plan, and as their grandparents drove away, the girls' laughter started again, so wild and uncontrollable—at their grandparents' peculiar old hats, at the splayed horse, the listing buggy—that they had to go around to the meadow at the back of the house to calm down before they could show their pink, glistening faces once more.

But that night Georgia dreamed of her grandmother, holding her dead mother across her lap—like a Pietà—and weeping inconsolably. And when she woke in the dark in the bed she shared with Ada, Georgia's face too was wet with tears.

Two

It was my own grandmother who told me this funeral-day story, one among many. For it was her story. She was Georgia, the older daughter. She grew up to be a charming woman—small and pretty and always in motion—and she loved to tell the stories of her life to me and my brother. She had a quite particular way of talking when she did, just that much *off*, rhythmically, from her ordinary use of language. It was a little like the narrative voice of the Brothers Grimm, or some of Rudyard Kipling's children's tales. When my father read us those stories aloud, I can remember more than once meeting my brother's eyes, the exchange of a glance of recognition, a sly smile. If we'd spoken, either of us, we might have said, simply, *Gran.*

Georgia lived to be eighty-eight. She outlived her husband by decades, and all of her children but one, my mother's only sister, Rue. When Rue died her solitary death in France a year ago, it fell to me, to me and my brother, Lawrence, to decide what to do with Georgia's house.

Lawrence said he didn't care, though it's possible he was just being kind to me. "I could use the dough," he told me on the phone. "Who couldn't? But if you want to hold on to it, that's all right by me. Except it has to pay for itself. No way can it actually *cost* me anything."

This wasn't a concern, because for all the years since my grandmother's death the house had paid for itself. It was in West Barstow, a pretty town about fifteen miles from the Connecticut River in southern Vermont, with a view across the lazy hills to the ineptly named Green Mountains in the distance—from here they were blue, a steely faraway blue. After my grandmother died, Rue had had no difficulty in keeping the house rented four or five months of the year as a vacation home, and for the last few years there'd been a year-round tenant. In fact, when the attorney notified me that Rue had left the house to me and Lawrence, he also told me that this primary renter, a retired academic, had offered several times to buy it from Rue, and when he'd heard of her death, he asked that his offer be extended to her heirs.

I didn't know what I wanted. I could have *used the dough* too, of course—in all likelihood more than Lawrence, who did quite well, thank you, at a job in Silicon Valley, the exact nature of which I was incapable of understanding, just that it had to do with money, not technology. And probably selling the house would have been the most sensible option. It was too far away; it was old and in need of regular maintenance. The problem was, I had a deep attachment to it, even though I hadn't seen it in so many years, not since my grandmother's death in 1988. I thought of it as *home*—at least more than I thought of any other place as home. In a way, I'd grown up in it, and even now I sometimes dreamt of the house, safe and unchanged from the way it had looked in my adolescence; and of my grandparents, not visible but palpably *there* somehow, inside it, waiting for me. So after I got word that we owned it now, after I talked to Lawrence and realized he was leaving the decision to me, things seemed, in my mind, to complicate themselves.

Part of my confusion was my sense of having reached the end of some kind of road in my life in San Francisco. I'd been divorced, for the second time, a few years earlier. Now in conversations I sometimes heard myself refer to the man I'd lived with for twelve years as "my second husband," words I could not have imagined, in my youth, that I would ever have reason to utter. And you would be surprised, people do look at you, hard, when you say this, as they don't when you say, "My first husband." Everyone's allowed one marital mistake, it seems, but two is over the top.

What's more, my children, who had fixed my life in the city for all those years with their attachments, their schooling, their passionate interests, were launched now. No longer attached. Scattered widely, in fact—except for the oldest, Karen, who had wound up back in San Francisco.

Though it struck me that the divorce had dragged them all back a bit emotionally: they were, I thought, slightly *pissed* about it. They'd loved Joe and relied on him, as they hadn't their own father, who'd pulled a disappearing act years earlier—and now I'd upped and lost Joe for them too. I might have been imputing these thoughts to them, but I felt they'd come to see me as a certain kind of person, really: a sort of loser. I felt I worried them, uncoupled. They asked me more often, and with deeper concern, how I *was,* what I was *up to.* I imagined their e-mail and phone calls to each other. "Are we going to have to take *care* of her? *How* old is she now?"

But I might have read them this way in part because I felt like such a failure myself. I'd taken Joe and our steady deep friendship for granted. I'd been shocked and wounded when he announced he'd fallen in love with someone else. And then even more shocked by his surprise at my reaction.

What he'd assumed was that it wouldn't matter all that much to me. He'd assumed a disaffection on my part, a restlessness as deep as his own. "You can't tell me you've been *happy,*" he said. We were sitting in our fancy kitchen. I'd been cooking a meal when he made his announcement. I hadn't been able to respond at first, I was so stunned. I remember that I carefully and deliberately turned off first the burner and then the oven, as if they, and not his news, were what represented the imminent danger to us both. Then I went to the table, filled a glass to the brim with wine, and sat down.

"I would say content," I told him. I'd finished half the glass by now.

"*Content?*" he asked, his tone conveying his utter disgust with the notion. He pushed his chair back and stood up. He crossed the room and leaned against the granite counter. He ran his hands through his hair—with Joe, always a sign of deep agitation. The expensive sharp knives gleamed in a row behind him. Everything seemed thick and slow to me. He was talking. He didn't understand, he said. How could I, why would I settle for such a thing? Why would I imagine that *he* would settle for such a thing?

It was a good life, I said. A decent life.

That wasn't the kind of life he wanted.

We talked some more. He got angry, his voice rose. This was good, actually, because it allowed me to get angry back. It allowed us both to yell. Eventually I threw a few things. Glasses, to be exact, with the satisfying explosive noise they made as they hit the tile floor. At some point I stormed into the living room and he followed. There, I actually threw a chair. To my great surprise, it too broke as it landed, as though it were only a movie prop.

A man unnerved by the slightest violence, Joe left the house. But after several hours, hours in which, unbelievably, I fell into a deep sleep on the living room sofa, he came back and gently woke me up. He said what he wanted was for us to be friends, forever. We sat around in front of the fireplace and had a great deal to drink, talking about this, about how it would be accomplished. We both wept. At some point we decided to burn the broken chair. "I never liked the fucking thing anyway," he said.

We did. We burned it, and then because in the drunken moment it seemed utterly reasonable—and also funny—we burned several other objects too, objects that seemed emblematic of our marriage, including a worn old sign from an inn we'd stayed in without the kids when we were first in love—since torn down—and all our letters to each other.

It was the kind of scene that should have ended in our making love, if not in our reconciliation, but it didn't. We went to bed separately; Joe slept in the guest room. In the morning we were both hungover and cross with ourselves and each other about that, and each a little angry too about the things we'd destroyed in our drunkenness. I remember pulling some of the bundled papers out of the ashes to see if I could save anything. In the center of each page a few scorched phrases were still legible, but that was all.

Later on I did feel what he'd called on me to feel that night—a kind of shame at my own contentment, at my willingness to settle for what he clearly thought of as *so little*. Later on I wondered: What was wrong with me? Why wasn't I hungrier, greedier? Why hadn't I wanted more sex, more friends, more interesting talk? It was like a kind of adult *parallel play*, what I'd been happy with.

But the thing is, he had been happy too, at least for some of the time. Often in the months after we separated, my mind ran over the years of our marriage, looking at us here, and then again here. It seemed to me he'd loved the harried, frantic early part best, when the children were teenagers, when there was always a drama, there was always noise or music or an activity to do with one or two or three wired, lively kids. They were mine from my first marriage, there when he met me and part of who I was then, in an important way.

I remembered his coming in once from a jog on a chilly, wet evening in December. Every room in our tiny house was ablaze with light. Fiona had a record on—the English Beat, singing "Stand Down, Margaret"—and she was dancing by herself in the living room, a kind of frenzied jumping up and down. Jeff was playing a computer game in his room, yelling when he scored. Karen was in the kitchen with me, reading me the conclusion of a paper she was writing on Emily Dickinson. I was doing something or other about making dinner. The house was warm, it smelled good. We'd been married less than a year. I looked over at him, my almost brand-new husband, his skin and beard glistening wet from the foggy cold. His color was high from his run, but his face was suffused too, with a kind of visible, sated pleasure. He touched my hair as he passed through the room on his way to a shower, and it seemed to me at that moment that I felt a kind of electric charge running through his fingers into me.

When all that energy and life went away, as it gradually did, of course, he didn't have the memory of us alone together—or of me alone, of who I was without the noise, the kids—to sustain him. It was all a blank to him, I think. A silent, empty kind of life. He wanted out, and he found a way by falling in love again. The woman he married after we divorced had two little children already, and they've quickly produced one more of their own. Sometimes I can feel happy for him.

When I got news of the house then, my grandmother's house, it seemed connected to all this in a way I couldn't have given words to and maybe didn't understand. A kind of answer, perhaps, though I wasn't sure to what. In the end I decided not to decide anything right away, just to go east and *see*. See the house and see what happened. I arranged for a half-year sabbatical from my teaching job; I was long overdue anyway. I rented my own house out for the fall months, which was surprisingly easy: the real estate agent had a family with three teenage boys no one was eager to have crashing around in their home while they were gone. I told her I didn't care, which was almost true. I let the real estate agent in Vermont know that I was coming just after Labor Day. The tenant would have to leave by then.

My daughter Karen had said she'd pick me up and take me out to the airport. I was in my bedroom at the front of the house when she drove up. I stood still and watched her getting out of the car. She was about three months pregnant, just beginning to show.

She'd always been the less conventionally pretty of my girls, tall and big-boned and slightly ungainly, but the pregnancy had already softened the way she looked.

She wore a big man's shirt today, crisp and white, over black leggings. Her long dark ponytail fell halfway down her back. As she came up the walk, she stopped to bend over and talk to a neighbor's cat, making a kind of music even of this—she was a composer: a solitary, eccentric life—though the man she was married to, Robert, was the essence of stability: a lawyer. An estate lawyer—he made a great deal of money—and adoring of her in a way that would have made me slightly claustrophobic.

She let herself in, calling out *hello,* and I answered her. As I shoved the last few items from the bathroom into my bag, I heard her walking through the other rooms of the tiny house. She appeared in the bedroom doorway.

"Where's all our stuff?" she said. I looked at her. She, of all the children, always wanted things to stay exactly the same in our lives, and she was vigilant and critical of me in my role as guardian of all that: her past, her history.

"Oh, all that junk!" I said. "I chucked it."

"Mother!" she said, and then was silent for a moment, thinking about it. "You did not," she said.

"You're right."

"So where is it?"

"It's in the basement, of course. Put. Away. We've got teenagers coming in here. You know what they're like. Having been one."

She shifted in the doorway. "I don't think I was that kind of teenager, was I?"

I thought of her at that age, so careful and sober and responsible, always trying to get me to be stricter with the other two. "No, you weren't," I said.

Her hands lifted to the faint curve of her belly then, and I felt I was seeing her train of thought: *What kind of child was I? What kind of child will I have?* I felt my heart squeeze for her.

On the way to the airport, she quizzed me repeatedly about various arrangements I'd made for my absence, as though she were the parent and I the child, at risk of leaving loose ends. She wanted to come in with me to the gate, too, but I pointed out that I had just the one bag, a bag with wheels at that. Reluctantly she pulled up alongside the departure curb and got out. Her hair had begun to escape in wisps from the ponytail, and she was slightly flushed as she embraced me.

"You look so pretty," I said to her, gently stroking her hair back over her shoulder.

She laughed. "You say that 'cause it's your job to think so, Mom."

"I say that because it's so true, Karrie."

She made a face and I walked away, into the terminal. When I turned to look back as I stepped onto the escalator, I saw her still standing there, her hand raised to shadow her eyes, looking big and girlish and almost frightened. I had a twinge of regret for what I was leaving behind, a twinge that vanished almost immediately.

At any rate, it was gone by the time I buckled myself in on the plane. And though I knew the flight would be long and boring, I felt excited, as though I were stepping into some new, unknown world that would change my future, my fate.

I flew into Boston, where I'd leased a car. I stayed there for two days, most of that time in a room near the airport in the Bostonia Hotel, in bed with an old lover, Carl Olney. I had called him a few days after I heard about the house, and it might have been the case that his availability was a small part of what drew me east.

Availability I say. In truth, he was not available at all. He was married, which I'd known very well when I called. But I asked anyway, and he said yes. I asked because I knew he was kind of a rat—he'd certainly been a rat with me in San Francisco years earlier—and it seemed to me that might be useful to me now. I asked because he'd always been an enthusiast about women, about sex, and I was in

21

need of enthusiasm. I hadn't had a lover in the two years since Joe, and our lovemaking—our companionable, rather functional love-making—had been only very occasional for some time before we separated. I asked—I *risked* asking, a fifty-two-year-old woman—because I yearned to be touched passionately again, to feel another's body, another's skin, pressed against me in need and hunger, and I thought that Carl, who'd known me when I was young and pretty, might see through all the changes in me and still want to press his body, his flesh, against mine.

Carl's body had changed too—he'd grown a little round paunch just below his rib cage, and a bald spot was widening at the back of his head. At first he was apologetic about himself, but we quickly adapted to each other and found our old rhythms again, if not our old frequency; and eventually we were able to joke about the sense of hungry sorrow with which middle-aged lovemaking begins.

I'd called Carl because I'd missed sex, but I found I had missed more simply lying next to someone and talking in that desultory postcoital or precoital way. You could speak of anything then, which I'd forgotten. I told him how hard it had been for me to call him. How all the things that had once seemed to me potentially charming about myself now felt like liabilities—certain expressions, certain habits. He talked about his marriage to a difficult woman, something I would normally have discounted, but I'd known Carl's wife in San Francisco before they married and she *was* difficult. He said he was doing better now "with the fidelity thing." When he said this, I happened to be lying naked on top of him, and I started laughing. After a moment, he joined in.

We laughed about the hotel too. Our room was small and taste-ful and pretty, but it looked out over the expressway. The flow of traffic and its noise seemed to come from the world of cheap road-side motels, so we made jokes about our $250-a-night cheesy flop-house.

The whole thing felt illicit, as it was, and slightly tawdry, as it also was, but I have to say that this was part of its pleasure for me. I had an odd sense of betraying Joe too, but I tried to enjoy that. I did enjoy it, in fact. *Take that!* I thought at least a few times as Carl and I heaved and jolted. I could have done with even more, really, though I was swollen and felt well used after just the first night.

I'd been about to leave on Friday morning, literally almost out the door, when Carl started in again, kissing me, pushing my skirt up, sliding his fingers into me. I was still wet from the night before, from my eagerness now, and his fingers in me made a light, slipping noise. We made love one last time, partly dressed, sitting on the edge of the bed, my skirt pushed up around my waist, Carl making enthusiastic yelps. I was so pleased by all this activity that I didn't even try to find my panties again before I left. Let Carl discover them, picking up his scattered clothes—a kind of calling card.

I got into the leased car with my thighs still wet, still sliding smoothly against each other as I moved. From time to time as I drove north, I became aware of the faint odor of sex rising from my lap. Once or twice I slid my hand under my skirt and let my fingers play over my own swollen flesh. I was excited by the thought of how I'd spent the last two days, but that was only part of it. I felt a kind of general eagerness, the sense one has only rarely in life, of starting anew, of a new adventure beginning, and it roused me sexually, this excitement. My first husband had sometimes said of me that I thought with my cunt. Unbelievably, he meant this as a compliment, and perhaps more unbelievably, at the time—a very different time—I took it as one. No longer. For some reason I remembered this abruptly now and it sobered me. It stopped me.

To distract myself, I turned the radio on: NPR, talk of the current political state of affairs. I listened responsibly until the signal faded. Then I turned off the radio and drove on in the silence of the rushing road. I'd swung to the north now, and the highway had emptied out; it had been a long time since I'd driven on such empty roads. The woods, touched with the earliest hint of fall color in the flare of a maple here and there, pushed in on either side of the blacktop.

It was midafternoon when I arrived. I'd made several stops along the way, once for lunch, once for wine, and then again for groceries. The air outside was so cool by now that I'd had the heater on for the last hour or so.

The town, once I got past an ugly little mall just to the south, seemed unchanged. The cemetery was as neatly groomed as ever, flowers and flags planted here and there on the old graves with their tilting stones. The frame buildings on Main Street still leaned together as if for warmth. It was quiet this afternoon, no one around. A large yellow dog slept in the road. He got up slowly and moved when I honked. I turned right at the only stop sign in town and drove downhill, toward the river—and suddenly there it was: the house, with its white clapboards, its steeply sloped roof with the curling wooden shingles, its sagging black shutters that hadn't been closed ever, in my memory. A low slanted sun blazed in the windows at its front.

The yard was slightly overgrown, the driveway two narrow dirt paths in the tall grass. The splayed blue asters under the burning windows were still in bloom. When I opened the car door, the chill of the air struck me, and then the old, old smell, some combination of pine with the farm life in the fields that started just outside town. I stood, simply breathing, for a moment. I crossed the damp grass. The key was on the lantern to the right of the doorway, as I'd asked the real estate agent to leave it, and I let myself in. A musty, familiar odor greeted me as the door swung open: mostly woodsmoke and ashes. For years I had thought it was my grandfather who gave the house this odor; he was the one who tended the fire, and that smell was embedded permanently in his clothes. It was only after he died that I realized it was the smell of the house too—along with years and years of certain perfumes, certain teas, certain kinds of cooking odors.

As I stepped into the hall, I was immediately startled by something I sensed in the room to my left. I turned to look, and stood, probably gaping.

It was utterly changed.

What I remembered best of this room—this front parlor—were the years it had served as my grandmother's bedroom. She'd moved down here the last decade or so of her life, when the steep stairs became too difficult for her. It had been papered then, and thickly curtained for privacy from the street.

Now it was reclaimed as a living room, with front-parlor furniture. But it wasn't just that that had caught my eye—it was everything else. The walls were stripped to plaster and painted white, the windows were half-shuttered in white too. I noticed now that the floor here and stretching back to the rear of the house ahead of me had been sanded and refinished. The old dark stain was gone and the pine was now a light amber color. The new surface gleamed dully.

The place was transformed. It looked like the summerhouse it was, not the dignified old residence of a country doctor. I went to the back parlor and found the thermostat. It clicked as I turned it up, and then after a few seconds I heard the distant rumble of the old furnace starting. I looked around, taking in the pared-down quality of this room too. I was thinking that my aunt Rue must have replaced most of the old furniture over the years; when I suddenly realized that the pretty chair I was looking at *was* my grandmother's: a wicker rocker. She'd loved to sit in it back here when the room was still papered in repeating palm branches. The chair had been painted black then, or perhaps dark green or brown, I couldn't quite remember. Now it was white, with big bright-pink tulips printed on its cushions.

Slowly I walked back through the rooms that led from one to another, taking everything in, doing a kind of inventory. The old floorboards creaked as I made my way around. A few pieces were just the same, unchanged, unrenovated. Others—most—were transformed by paint or reupholstering or slipcovers. Everywhere it was the same: things had been lightened—sanded, painted white—and then the shocks of color added: green-and-white striped curtains, a wild flowered slipcover, fuchsia pillows, light straw rugs.

I went back through the kitchen, past the back storeroom and two steps down into the little addition to the house that had once been my grandfather's office. Here too the dark old cabinets and curtains were gone, the no-color walls were white. What had been a somber, gloomy office—though that was not how I thought of it then—had become a pretty, airy space.

I felt a pang of loss. My grandmother had always kept this room just as it was when my grandfather died, and in that form it had had a magical quality for me—and for my brother too, I think. He used to study there when he was home from college. I can remember going in to sit with him. He'd be at the rolltop desk, the light from the green-glass lamp falling white on his hands and his books, leaving his face in shadow. He and I would talk for hours; he never seemed to mind my interrupting him. Behind him in the dark shelves were the chemicals, the instruments, the organs. The white enamel scale still stood in the corner of the room then, with the metal arm that swung out on top of your head and told you your height; and the odd chair, a little like a dentist's or a barber's, where Grandfather had performed tonsillectomies or tooth extractions. My grand-mother had been his assistant in the early days, she'd told us. She'd administered the ether, which you gave then by dripping it onto a gauze mask laid over the patient's nose. As I looked around now, I was remembering my grandfather's framed degrees that had hung on the wall, and next to them the huge chart of the human body—male, of course. There had also been, peculiarly, a few stuffed ani-mals set high on top of his shelves—a badger and a great blue heron. Their fur and feathers were already, even then, moth-eaten and dull. Both were gone now. Sold, or perhaps just thrown away.

I assumed the renovation had been Rue's choice. Though maybe she'd paid someone to do it. She'd lived in Paris all her adult life, and I didn't think she'd come back at all after the trip for her mother's funeral. I hadn't kept in good touch with her. The news of her death had startled me and then made me feel guilty for not having written her, not having cared enough.

The truth was, I hadn't liked Rue. For years when I thought of her, I pictured her alone in her apartment on the Right Bank, looking censoriously out her window at anyone passing, anyone who might be making some kind of social mistake, as she saw it. At some point, I realized where this image had come from: a photograph I'd seen of the Duchess of Windsor, her face seamed in bitterness, peering out from *her* window in Paris in her old age and widowhood. After I made this connection, my brother and I started calling Rue "the Duchess." One or the other of us would have had a note to report from the Duchess, or a Christmas card, or, unexpectedly and often unaccompanied by any explanation, the gift of some piece of family history: a bunch of photographs, a stack of six monogrammed coin-silver spoons tied with a ribbon. By the time of her death, she had faded in my mind to the slight pinch of dislike I felt when I heard her name—or nickname.

I went back to the front hall and up the complaining stairs. There had originally been three bedrooms under the sloping roof in this, the oldest part of the house, but one had long since been turned into a large bathroom. Its door was open, and within it you could see another door, which gave onto the two attic bedrooms in the extension beyond. These small rooms had been mine and Lawrence's when we visited and then came to live. There was another, steeper stairway that descended from between them into the kitchen. Lawrence and I used to leave its door open at night: our rooms were unheated, and what we said was that we wanted the benefit of the rising warmth. But I think too that we were comforted by the nighttime sounds of my grandparents moving around, talking intermittently and peaceably below us.

The same revising touch at work downstairs was evident up here. The wide floorboards, brown then, had been painted a light blue-green. And I could see that our dark old nightstands were now a pretty gray.

A faint scorched odor was spreading in the house from the heating ducts. I opened a few windows to air things out and then I went back downstairs, back outside, and started to unload the car: groceries, booze, and the single suitcase I'd brought with me—I'd mailed myself several other boxes of clothes and books and things I thought I might want, so that I wouldn't have to lug them around. The air was even chillier now, and somewhere in the distance a dog was relentlessly barking.

While I put things away in the kitchen, I started a small pot of coffee in an electric percolator I'd found set out on the counter. When it was done, I sat down at the dining room table with my cup. The coffee was terrible—it made me wonder how long the can had been sitting around—but I managed a few sips as I watched the light through the pinkish maple outside the window. It had been years since I'd seen trees this color. I was struck with a kind of grief, looking out the window—as though, even though I was here now, looking at it, this world was already lost to me.

Ridiculous, I thought. I got up and took my cup to the kitchen sink. I dumped it out and went back to the front hall, where I'd left my suitcase. I lugged it up the steep stairs and began to unpack slowly in the room that had been my grandmother's when I was young, putting my things away in her old bureau. The drawers were lined with paper that might even have dated from her day; it was browned and crumbling with age at the edges.

I nearly jumped when the knocker on the front door sounded. On my way down the stairs, it was struck again, four times, loudly.

I opened the door.

An old woman stood on the granite block step outside. She was tiny and slightly curved over, so that she had to look up and a little bit sideways to see me. It made her seem sly, and I had a quick odd moment of what felt almost like a child's fear of her. She introduced herself—Mrs. Chick—and only then did I recognize her. Of course. *Mrs. Chick, Chick, Chick,* we'd called her as children, imitating the way you call hens in. She lived two doors down.

Mary Chick, she told me now when I tried to call her *Mrs.* She'd brought over sticky buns for my breakfast tomorrow; she'd made a double batch and didn't need them all, she said. She handed me the heavy packet in aluminum foil.

I thanked her profusely. I offered her coffee. She said she didn't mind. I hung her coat up and led her back to the kitchen. I took down a cup for her and filled it and then refilled my own—though I didn't really want any more—nattering on pointlessly all the while about this and that: my trip, the ease of the drive up, the way things in town looked exactly the same.

"Well, I suppose they might, to *you*," she said.

We carried our coffee to the back parlor, and I turned on a few lamps, still making nervous chatter, the more nervous now because of her silence, because of her eyes moving shrewdly over everything.

In the faint *whoosh* of air that rose when I sat down, I smelled sex again, and I wondered if Mrs. Chick had noticed that as I walked in front of her. Whether she would even recognize it if she had. As she set her cup down after the first sip or two of coffee, she said, "Changed a bit, idn't it?" and nodded, a quick flip up of her chin.

"The house?"

She nodded again.

"*So* much," I said. "I know it's lovely, but I can't get used to it."

"Your grandmother would spin in her grave to see it."

We both surveyed the room. In the warm lamplight everything looked fresh and welcoming. "I don't know," I said. "Maybe she'd like it."

Her mouth pulled straight, as though insulted. "Oh, no, not her," she insisted. "'Where's my . . . ?'"—she looked around—"'Where's my rocker? Where's my old sofa? Where's my down puff?' Oh, she had to have her old things."

I looked at her, smiling so gassily at me. My grandmother had never liked her; I remembered that now. It was a comforting notion somehow. "Do you have any idea what happened to all that stuff?" I asked.

She sniffed. "Your aunt took some, I know that. Silver and the like."

"Oh. Well, we got some of that too, actually. Lawrence and I."

"Hm!" she said.

"Do you think she sold the rest? What's not here?"

"She did, some. They had an auction, I'm told. It was over to Rutland, and I didn't go, but some did. She only sold what was worth real money, I think. Some more silverware. Some rugs, they say. You know, those old Oriental ones she had. And some rag ones too, apparently. Those are worth something now. We used to think they were just a good way to use up our old clothes." She smiled grimly, and I smiled back.

There was a little silence. She shifted, and her chair protested. "You going to stay on, you think?" she asked at last, with the little glance sideways and up. Her ears were slightly outsize and pointed at the tops, I saw. Maybe she *was* an elf. A gnome.

I shrugged. "I just don't know," I said. "It would depend on so much."

"I suppose your family might not like it," she said in a leading tone.

"Well, there's not much family left at home to consult." I set my coffee down. I just couldn't drink it. "None, really."

"Well, but I imagine your husband might have an opinion or two."

Ah, here it was. The gossip had reached even this far corner of the country, apparently. All right then. "As it happens, my husband and I are divorced." I tried another smile at her. "So even if he did, it's not an opinion, or even two opinions, that I'd have to listen to anymore."

"Hah!" she said, it seemed, for a moment, appreciatively. She stopped to lift her cup and have another swallow of coffee before she said, musingly, her eyes gone distant and flat, "Now, if I recollect, you divorced the first one too?"

"Why, what a good memory you have!" I tried to keep my voice innocently enthusiastic.

"Some years back," she said.

"That's right."

"There were children there, I recollect."

"Yes. Three."

She turned her head. "None from this one, I imagine."

"Three seemed enough to me," I said. "Sometimes it seemed like too much." I was trying to change the tone, trying to include her in a kind of tired-parent joke.

She didn't bite. "Well," she said, "I guess that's the way you do it now." Her mouth made a tiny bundle of righteousness. "I've been married for sixty-two years come February. Only one way to do *that*."

"Amazing," I said. I stood up. "You know, I'm awfully sorry," I said, "but I'm afraid I've got to keep at it, or I'm never going to get unpacked."

When she'd left, I went directly to the kitchen and threw away the heavy packet of sticky buns. I wouldn't have eaten them anyway—all sugar and butter, not what a middle-aged woman still afflicted with vanity needs—but it gave me pleasure to close the lid of the trash can over them. I took the back stairs to the second floor two at a time. Wild with irritation, I went into the bathroom and washed my face. As I scrubbed, I was thinking of Mrs. Chick's sly sideways look.

Abruptly I recalled that my grandmother had always made funny stories of her visits, her *descents*. She'd amused us all with her retelling of Mrs. Chick's self-satisfied judgments. *"'They say,'"* she would imitate. "Who? Who says, Mrs. Chickadee? Who besides you?" *That* was the tone I needed to take, the attitude I needed to strive for.

But it seemed such an effort. And suddenly I thought I'd made a mistake, coming here. This world was too small, too insular, too full of judgment and history for me to fit into it in any way. Hadn't I been in flight from it when I chose to go to college in California?

Hadn't I deliberately stayed on to live at the other end of the country, in a place where people were allowed to reinvent themselves, over and over if they wanted?

Of course, I hadn't thought of it this way at the time. At the time I stayed because I'd fallen in love with Peter, my first husband. Because I'd entered his seductive world completely. Because when I came back to visit my grandparents, it felt like time-traveling to me, and I wanted to live in the *now*, the now of Peter's life, with him. He was a political scientist. He'd been my instructor my junior year, and I felt singled out by him, *chosen*, recognized in some deep and important way, when he asked me for coffee, when he touched me, when I moved in with him and began to share his life—a life full of his political convictions, of meetings he chaired. Of articles he wrote and interviews he did. Of people turning up suddenly to spend a week or a month on our couch, a week or a month in which it seemed the talking and the drinking and the dope and the music never stopped.

We were married in my world, my old world, back here in West Barstow, in the Congregational church at the top of the green with the sun streaming through the clear glass windows and all the early-summer flowers in the churchyard glowing like jewels in its clean light.

My father and I had come east a week ahead of time to help organize things and to have a visit with my grandparents before I began my new life in the West. I had looked forward to this time when I was still in California, but once here, installed in my room above the kitchen, I was almost crazed with impatience, with my appetite and need for Peter, with my eagerness to be gone. When he arrived, two days before the wedding, I picked him up at the station in my grandfather's car. We stopped in the parking lot of the wildlife management area—many jokes about this—and made love frantically for hours, climbing and draping ourselves this way and that over the seats. When we got to my grandparents', late for dinner, we were so clearly postcoital—our hair in disarray, my lips swollen, my face chafed; I'm sure we even smelled yeasty and sexual—that no one bothered to ask what had happened to delay us.

After the ceremony, we took the train to New York, where Peter had academic meetings to attend. As we rolled and ticked along, he stared out the window at the hilly rockstrewn fields, at the old villages we were passing through. At one point he said, "You must feel sometimes as though you came from another country, Cath."

"No, not really," I answered.

"Well," he said, "it's not the same country I came from."

I finished putting away my few things, and then I stood in the upstairs hallway, looking from room to room. I went back through the bathroom to the rooms that had been mine and Lawrence's. There was one window in each space, in the dormer. The light leaking in now in what had been my room was dim and melancholic—a soft gray rectangle.

I thought of my life in San Francisco, the bright light falling into the kitchen there late of a fall afternoon, the cheerful loud noises of my Hispanic neighbors performing their eternal car repairs in their driveway. I thought of Joe, of the way he used to call out from the front door when he arrived home in our happier days, of his habit then of bringing me small gifts several times a week—four cookies in a white box with a bow from a bakery he liked on Green Street, or a pair of antique earrings, or a book I'd expressed interest in, or a little brown paper bag of some spice neither of us had ever heard of from the Syrian market. I thought of the children. Of Karen, so happy, but so unrealistic, as I saw it, about how she'd manage everything once the baby came. Of Jeff, who'd written from Ecuador of standing on the equator and jumping from one side to the other. Of Fiona, in college in New York and in love with the city. All this life. All this past. Mine.

None of it had any connection that I could feel to the hungry, lonely girl who had come to live in this room.

Three

I came to stay at my grandmother's for the first time when I was seven. Lawrence was nine. It was my mother's first breakdown in the eleven years since her marriage, but the family was so well prepared that it seemed they'd all been expecting it for a long, long time.

She'd gotten us up in the night. My father was away. He was often away when we were small. He was a lawyer. He dealt with business mergers, and he frequently had to travel at a certain stage in the negotiations to help work out issues of seniority and of salary schedules.

Mother made us get dressed. She herself was wearing an old wool coat, tweed, and galoshes over which her pajama legs belled out. She was very gay, very happy and excited, so we didn't protest too much, though Lawrence has told me since he knew right away that something was wrong. It was as if at that moment, as he woke from his thick sleep to her urgency, he could see how everything was going to be with her from then on.

We went for a long walk in the pitch black of our suburban neighborhood. At first it all seemed very orderly, very well planned, in spite of the hour and the deep stillness of the dark streets. "See, children? Now here we turn left," she'd say, pleased; and we'd turn left. But it didn't end, and it didn't end, and Mother seemed increasingly desperate as we flagged. Certain things *had* to be done certain ways. We couldn't stop! We couldn't rest. Down here we had to go right. Wasn't it right? Maybe it was left. She began to moan a little to herself as her uneasiness and uncertainty grew.

It was Lawrence who finally broke away, who rang someone's bell—by now the sky was turning a pale pink—and told the frightened-looking woman who opened the door that we needed help, that something was wrong with our mother. The woman came out in her robe, came down the walk and tried to talk to Mother, but that was no good, we could all see that right away. Mother began to get shrill and angry. "I cannot—I cannot tolerate your stupid, stupid *interference*! You mind your own goddamn business, why don't you? You ... *interference*. You ... *stupidity*!"

A little while later the police came, driving up slowly alongside our odd procession, smiling and affable. We all got in. Mother thought they'd come to help us get to where she needed to go, so she didn't protest. And after that, everything unfolded as if according to some master plan. We went to family friends and spent the day, not even having to go to school, to our delight. That afternoon my father came back early from his trip and took us home, and the next day we all got on the train in downtown Chicago to go to my grandparents'. Our rooms at their house were ready for us, and we began going to the village school just a few days later.

What I remember of the strange night that triggered this change in our lives was the long walk between the widely separated streetlights on the grand, leafy Oak Park streets, each light the oasis that called us forward, that we had to pass through to plunge again into the blackness ahead of it. That, and my mother speaking to the kind woman who tried to help, using a tone of voice and words I'd never heard before. And the police, appearing so suddenly next to us— the gentleness, the friendliness of the big men in their uniforms and the way their car smelled inside: leathery, male, reassuring.

I can call up, too, the magical ride on the train, where we had our own sleeping car. Lawrence and I shared the berth above our father. We slept with our heads at its opposite ends, and in the morning we leg-wrestled for a while before we got up; and the porter called me "little missy" as we stepped off the train onto the platform, which Lawrence and I found hilarious.

I don't think I ever asked about my mother once we were settled at my grandparents'—it seemed somehow we were not supposed to. I thought of this later, when I was a parent myself, of how impossible it was for me as a child to *bring something up* in what seemed like a cautionary void. "Wait until they ask," "Wait until they want to know," the books and advice columns say. But my theory is everyone always wants to know, even when they don't have an inkling of what they want to know about. I explained everything to my children, long before their questions could have been framed. Mostly the divorce and their father's absence from their lives but also the meaning of swear words, the reasons people were so often unkind to one another, pregnancy and child-birth, sex and all its intricacies. Karen used to say that she was the only person she'd ever met who'd learned what a blow job was from her own mother. Better me than some others, I thought. She wasn't so sure.

We stayed with my grandparents that first time for the whole school year, swaddled in thick *not-knowing*, safe. My mother went home from the hospital in April, but it was thought that her transition back—to us, the unspoken goal—should be gradual. And it was thought we should finish out the year in one place. So we stayed on with our grandparents in their enchanted village. Mother came east to be with us the last few weeks of school, and then we all went back to the Midwest together—my grandmother too, to help Mother manage for a while. She didn't linger long. Mother seemed calm. She seemed, as everyone kept saying, "herself" again. Herself, but somehow different too, I thought.

I'm not sure what her treatment was, but I suspect electric shock therapy or insulin therapy. And she was medicated even after she was back.

Still, she could be easily upset. "What are *you* looking at?" she said to me abruptly, angrily, one day.

"Nothing," I answered. A lie. I'd been staring at her.

"Well, just keep your big fat cow eyes to yourself," she said. But she went on with what she was doing—sewing—and the next words she spoke to me were unremarkable and normal, something about what she was making.

She had seemed *taken over* when she was ill, and after that first breakdown (it was her second, actually, she'd had one in college also, though Lawrence and I didn't know this until much later), this came and went more frequently, so that she'd slip into sudden anger or wildly coarse or threatening language for a few seconds at unpredictable moments in our ongoing lives. It was like having a tic. Like Tourette's. We learned, all of us, to ignore it, to turn away and go on as though it hadn't happened: the rage, the hurtful, child-ish words, sometimes the hitting.

And it didn't affect the love Lawrence and I had for her, except perhaps to intensify it. You read sometimes of abused children weeping in court to be returned to a parent who has beaten them or burned them with cigarettes. It seems almost incomprehensible that this should be so, but I understand it. Our attachment to our mother was deeper, wilder, more profound after she was ill. Those moments when she laughed, when she was relaxed and easy around us, are lit with a golden lantern in my memory. It was years before I let myself understand that what had seemed so special to me were what passes in most households as the most ordinary acts of parent-hood: the table set, the beds made, the question asked about school, the smile when affection was offered, the willing touch of a hand to another's hair or cheek, the food cooked and served.

I still don't know what was wrong with her. No one ever gave it a name to Lawrence and me, and I suppose that the name—the diagnosis—changed over the years anyway, as psychiatry and medicine altered the way people like my mother were looked at and thought of. At the time, though, we felt to blame. It seemed she had wanted something from us, from Lawrence and me, that we couldn't give. Something you might call, simply, *more*. It was probably the least of her symptoms, I realize now, but it was the one that most touched us, this need of hers to be the focus of our attention; the *apple of our eye*.

It is hard for a mother to achieve this; usually the reverse is true—the adoring parent, the unconscious child. But we tried, Lawrence and I. We strained to give her what she might feel was enough. And somehow angered her even with that, when she had the need to be angry.

My first morning in West Barstow was cold and damp. A mist hung low to the ground outside, as if being exhaled by the earth. Frost silvered the blades of the lushly overgrown grass. I made myself some more of the horrible coffee and sat in the chilly, bright living room with thick wool socks on, wondering what I'd do with the day. When I'd pictured myself living here, I'd always been outside in sunlight, walking, raking leaves; or driving down dappled country lanes, stopping to buy blackberries here, apple cider there. None of this seemed likely today, overcast as it was. I would have to improvise projects for myself.

In my other life—what I was thinking of as my *real* life now—I would be at work already, in the teacher's lounge with Emily LaFollette, with Ellen Gerstein, with Carole McNamara and Bob Willburn. I would be having my last sips of coffee and listening to their talk before we all headed down to chapel and the start of the day. We'd be discussing whether Liddy Dole would suffer in the primaries because of her husband's erectile dysfunction ads. Did this make her, somehow, politically laughable? Whether fat substitutes were carcinogenic. Whether Potrero Hill was safe at night. Whether Bob really needed to raise his kids Catholic now that he had them, just because he'd promised to before he did. I missed it, I realized, even the most tedious aspects: Bob's terrible dirty jokes, Emily's ability to reproduce verbatim long and uninteresting conversations between her and her kids or her husband, Ellen's ongoing bitter divorce.

The school was private, a girls' school, one that clung to such traditions as the uniform, the formal standing greeting to the teacher at the start of class (though the girls knew how to bray it just enough too enthusiastically to show their contempt for the very notion of what they were doing), and chapel—of course no longer specifically religious. No, more a time for a quick homily of moral life from our headmistress, and sometimes just for announcements. I'd taught there for twenty years, in part because it meant my own girls could attend tuition-free at a time when I had no money, in part because I could work there without the teaching degree I would have had to get for public school—which paid better—and in part because I got used to the rhythms and routines and it was easy work. Time-consuming during the school year, but easy. I liked the girls too, most of them. And literature was a way of talking with them about life, of making them think about who they were, about what choices they might have.

If I moved to Vermont, there was no guarantee I'd find anything comparable. Probably not in a private school nearby, in any case. Was there, in fact, a private school nearby? I didn't know. I had enough money not to have to worry for a while—Joe had been generous when we divorced—and if I sold my house in San Francisco I'd actually be quite comfortable. But I couldn't imagine a life without work of some kind. To come here would be to start over, to invent myself anew. There had been moments, thinking about this in San Francisco, when I felt eager for it, even impatient. Now, sitting in my grandmother's living room with not the least idea what to do with just this overcast day, I wasn't so sure.

I had been slowly taking in the room around me as I thought about all this—sipping gingerly at the coffee and noticing again the changed light in the house, even on a day as dark as this one, appreciating the well-chosen bursts of color, the spare quality—when suddenly I thought *Enough of this*. I took my cup back to the kitchen and poured the remaining coffee out into the old soapstone sink. I went back upstairs and got dressed, washed my face, and put makeup on. It was ten-thirty by now, still as dark as a much earlier hour outside, but it wasn't really raining, not yet. I decided to go for a walk.

I'd learned to be a respecter of motion, even of *going through the motions*, after Joe moved out. I'd been motionless for some time then, and just the memory of that could terrify me—my blankness, my ability to sit unmoving for long hours, looking out a window, listening to street noises or the tic...tic...tic...tic of a clock dropping seconds. I remember being grateful that school was in session then, that I was forced to get up each day and perform in that context anyway—and I performed adequately, if not well; but I had enough goodwill built up from having done it well before so that even the girls went along with my charade. They continued to work, to behave for me, whereas with a newcomer with as little energy as I had there would have been minor rebellions. Note-passing. That barely masked rudeness and disobedience that signals the imminent arrival of classroom chaos.

I collapsed once I got through work each day. When I bothered to eat, I did it standing in the kitchen, never even turning on the expensive appliances, just making odd meals from whatever was left of my dwindling supply of groceries: peanut butter on stale crackers, or cereal, or canned soup. I stopped cleaning. When friends called and suggested doing things, I made up lies, reasons I couldn't. The thought of it: getting in the car; driving to the theater or a restaurant or a museum; parking; then talking, looking, eating, smiling—all that seemed like insurmountably difficult *labor*.

An accident in the car brought it to an end, this spell of blank misery I was in.

I was on 101, heading north for home from a meeting at a fellow teacher's house. I was in the passing lane, almost pulling alongside a car going slower in the traveling lane, when I saw a jerk speeding toward me from behind and to the right—also in the traveling lane. I knew he was going to pass me on the right and cut in. I knew it. I could tell by his assaultive speed in the rearview mirror and then also by instinct. I slowed, to give him room for his maneuver.

And he did, he cut in sharply in front of me from the right, with barely enough room to make it in the space I'd left. But he'd cut too hard, he was going too fast; his car began to fishtail lazily—in memory, almost gracefully—left, right, left. In response, I began to brake, to swerve too. Everything was happening very fast and very slowly at the same time: I was aware of his long slide sideways in front of the car I'd been trying to pass, of that car's swerving and braking too, of my own braking with all my strength, steering sharply to the left, away from whatever was going to happen with them; of hitting the guard rail, then hitting it again as I slowed and turned and came to a stop in the ripping of metal, the screaming of my own tires and brakes and others'; and what I'd been thinking as I responded, as I acted, was passionately and violently *angry*, more than anything else: Not *me*! Not *me*! Not *now*!

I sat in the momentary stillness—before several other cars began braking and skidding and hitting each other; seven of us were involved by the time it was over—and in those few seconds I heard my own laughter, silly and slightly hysterical. Girlish-sounding. What I felt, aside from the sense of my own body at work—pulse, breath, nerves—was an overwhelming relief and gratitude to be alive.

And that was it, really. I made an appointment with my doctor that afternoon, and he referred me to a psychiatrist. I got pills, I had about a dozen sessions with her. All of that helped. It was useful to me, yes. But secondary, I felt. Secondary to my yanking the steering wheel, to my pulling sharply left as I braked, to my wanting so desperately and reflexively to be in life, to be still *moving* and *doing*, those wonderful verbs.

Downstairs now, I found a vinyl slicker, crackled with age, in the front hall closet under the stairs. I pulled it on and went out.

The air was utterly still, heavy with moisture. A car hissed by up on Main Street, its lights on. I turned up that way. I walked past the post office and then the four or five small stores—a pharmacy, a hardware store, an antiques store (open only on weekends the sign said, and by appointment), and a general store, which, I knew, sold newspapers and staple grocery items and coffee and magazines. ("Run up to Grayson's and get me some yeast," my grandmother would say. "And here's a penny for the great trouble I'm putting you to." The penny would buy me something from one of the squat glass jars of candy that sat at child's-eye level in front of the cash register.)

The mist was beginning to feel more like rain. There were no other walkers around, though an empty car idled, its radio squawking faintly, in front of Grayson's. I walked up to the green that opened off Main Street. It was the site of my social life in my adolescence, the place where kids gathered after school to smoke, to flirt, to watch the older boys drive by in cars and pickups. It was lined on its three closed sides with buildings, the tall white Congregational church where I'd been married the first time prominent among them. There had been elms in the old days, perhaps a dozen, arched thickly over the grass. Now there were three big maples flaring a light yellow-orange through the gentle rain.

I started my walk around. As I passed the graceful, silent houses, I stared at them. I could still feel it—the same charm, the same pull the town had for me when I'd come here before, something that had to do with the pull of my grandparents' lives too, the promise of some ordered and old-fashioned way of living that I knew full well

I sentimentalized: a world I had created in my imagination, where words like "lilac" and "fidelity" had a similar weight and power.

It had started to rain in earnest. I put my hood up and walked faster, back toward the shelter of my grandmother's house. I was almost running as I cut across the lawn to the side porch—the rain was pelting now—so I didn't notice the car pulled up behind mine in the driveway. But then I heard its door slam and turned to see a woman running up to and then past me. She stopped once she'd reached the shelter of the porch and turned back.

She was smiling and gesturing upward as I approached. "Not a very nice welcome for you," she called. She was fortyish, and pretty. Or not truly pretty, I saw, but well groomed and cared for in a way that was attractive and appealing. Hair of that elegant but clearly tinted ashy blond, makeup that was muted but carefully applied, expensive wool slacks and a silk blouse under her jacket. The only false note from my urban perspective were the ugly gray rubber shoes she wore. But I envied her them. My feet were wet and cold.

"Hello," I said, as I stepped onto the porch and flipped my hood back. "I'm Catherine Hubbard. Cath. You're . . . ?"

"Leslie Knox. Just a sec, I've got a card."

I recognized her name: the real estate agent who managed the house. We'd written and e-mailed back and forth.

And then I noticed the boxes, the three cardboard cartons of clothes and possessions I'd sent to myself from California. "Oh, these came!" I said.

"Yes, I told the guy it was okay to leave them, I hope you don't mind." She had found the card and handed it to me. "They looked fine to me." She laughed. "And I sure hope they are, now that I'm responsible for them."

"Yes. Thanks," I said. "Well, it's nice to meet you." I pretended to look at the card and pocketed it. "Would you like to come in?"

I led her inside, taking my parka off. I hung it on the doorknob to drip.

She stood, just in the room, looking around. "I always forget this is *such* a pretty house," she said. "I have to say, if you ever do decide to sell, it'll show fantastically."

"Please!" I said. I was startled. We hadn't really talked about this. "I'm a long, long way from that!"

"Oh, I know. I know. Ignore me if you can. It's just the broker in me talking. I never stop thinking in those terms."

"Will you sit down?" I gestured at the couch. "Can I offer you coffee? Or actually I have juice too."

"Oh, no, thanks so much," she said. "I was just driving by and I saw the UPS guy about to leave, so I hailed him down. And then I thought I'd wait a few minutes, since your car was here, to see if you turned up. I just wanted to say hi and be sure you were settling in okay."

I told her now that my boxes had come I'd feel more settled, and we talked of the importance of having your own things around you. She produced for me from her vast purse an information packet about the surrounding area, "part info, part Welcome Wagon kind of stuff," she said. She was chattering about it as I flipped through the material. The whole time I could see her eyes move restlessly and appraisingly around the room. But I talked back, grateful and interested-sounding, I think.

Finally she came to the point: how much she'd love to show the house—could I bear it? when I'd just got here?—to a couple coming up from New York next week. Not that she'd say it was on the market, just to give them an idea, an idea of what some of these old houses could look like with a little TLC. And maybe to get an idea, too, of the response to this one. That never hurt.

"But I thought we had a buyer if I wanted to sell. A potential buyer."

"Oh, Eliasson. Yes. Well, but you don't want to just hand it over, on the other hand, do you? I mean, it'd be nice to have the sense of others, waiting in the wings, as it were. We'd like to get what we *can*, after all."

Yes. Yes, I saw that. Though I wanted to remind her...

Oh, yes, she knew. It wasn't for sale. No problem. She'd make that clear.

She'd moved back to the door now, and she turned to look around one last time. "It's just it's such a great story too, you know. This house"—her hands circled—"in the family for generations. Both your grandparents living here into their old age, and so forth."

"But none of that's true!" I protested.

"No?"

"No, it wasn't in the family for generations. Not at all. My grandparents bought it sometime in the twenties. They moved here from Maine. I don't have any idea who owned it before then."

She laughed. "That's still enough generations to make a good story for your average New Yorker. Your grandparents, your parents, you, your children..."

I didn't bother to argue any further.

As I stood watching her cross the yard, I wondered why I'd recoiled so instinctively from her version. Maybe, I thought, I was just reluctant to think of myself as standing in for a generation, such a small quickly-summed-up part of the story, so easily over and done with.

And then I thought, no. No, that wasn't it. The truth was I didn't want to think of any of us that way: my grandparents, my mother, me. Or to have our life here used as a selling point—all that pain and sorrow and joy—to make the house itself more appealing. We weren't the house's *story*, none of us. That was what I objected to. That, and the fact that the story was so much more complicated than she could know.

I went back out on the porch, and one by one I slid the heavy cartons over the threshold into the house. From the kitchen, I got a knife to slit them open. Though I'd packed them only a week or so earlier, I felt a kind of childish eagerness to get at what was inside—to arrange the things I'd chosen to mark the house as mine for however long I'd stay.

I spent several hours at it, setting my few framed photos on top of the upright piano in the dining room, standing the books up on my grandfather's shelves. I got out the little espresso machine, the beans and grinder, and made myself what I thought of as a *real* cup of coffee. I lugged the clothes upstairs, hung them up, or put them in drawers. I claimed the shelves in the medicine chest with my cosmetics and my drugs, throwing away the Mercurochrome I found there, the rusted bobby pins in a little cup, the ancient-looking bottle of aspirin.

I got waylaid by an old box of photos I'd sent myself—I planned to spend some long solitary evenings by the fire putting them into albums. Here was my life for twenty years or so, now that that life was over—photos of the children at various stages, photos of Joe before and during our marriage.

I picked up a picture of my father and his second wife, Rosalie, standing in the overgrown abandoned vineyards behind their adult community just outside Calistoga a year or two before his long dying began—a series of cruel little strokes, each one waiting to arrive until he'd just begun to recover from the one before, until he'd just begun to be hopeful, as if to say, *Oh, no, you don't!* I came to think of them this way, actually: animated with willful malevo-lence. I was furious at his death, and inconsolable for weeks after-ward. During this period, when I would sometimes stand cooking dinner or cleaning up with tears dripping off my face, Fiona said to me one night, "Well, it was his own fault, really, Mom." And then, in response to my incredulity: "I mean, he could have stopped smoking and then he'd probably still be alive." I stepped forward and slapped her then—I, who took pride in never hitting my kids.

In the picture, my father looks healthy and strong, and Rosalie, with her great mass of obviously dyed black hair, is in the midst of saying something to him animatedly.

They moved west when he retired, to be near me and Lawrence. I was glad later that he'd died before Joe and I divorced. He once said to me, "It's good for me to see you so happily settled. I always worried, after you got divorced, that your mother—you know, her illness—might have maybe damaged you in a way, for love."

An assortment of others: many of Jeff giving the camera the finger, his favorite pose for years. Many of my garden in the backyard, taken to help me plan changes in it. A few of me, when someone wrested the camera from my hands. Here's one in which I'm turning from the sink, talking, apparently—my mouth is open in an unattractive way. It was at a period when I had my hair short, a big mistake, and the apron I have on makes me look shapeless and thick. What you see in this picture is a woman whose husband might leave her, who might find herself at midlife casting about in her past for answers to her future. I tore it in two pieces, then in four, and threw it away.

The last time I went to my grandmother's, the time I went to stay, I was fifteen. My mother had managed it finally, her own death, and she'd done it well, I came to think when I was older, in that none of us had had to find her.

In the months before it happened, she'd had an increasingly intense preoccupation with Egyptian hieroglyphics. As part of this, she found an educational conference she wanted to attend at the Oriental Institute at the University of Chicago: two days of scholarly papers. My father thought about it—she'd asked his permission, essentially—and then said yes. She'd been all right for a while, though I think my father was worried about her near obsession with this glyphic language, the notion of signs and symbols that spoke to her. Still, she arranged it all competently and seemingly calmly, and this reassured him. She booked a hotel for two nights, with a view of the lake, near the university—so she wouldn't have to make the long commute back and forth each day, she said. That made perfect sense, too. Fine, then.

When she called him the first night, all was well, apparently. But she didn't call the second night, and he couldn't reach her. Still, she'd sounded so buoyant the night before that he didn't worry. He hoped she was out with other people, people she'd met at the conference. He hoped—he always hoped this; it's the disease that affects those who love people who are ill—that this would be a turning point for her, that things might be different from now on. She would make friends, she would have a life in the world that compelled and occupied her.

The hotel called him at work the next day. When they'd gone to her room after checkout time, they'd found her. She was a person with access to many pills, and this is what she'd used.

My father gave me my choice, my freedom. I could stay with him, which he recognized might be rather a lonely life with Lawrence off at college now and his own work as a lawyer so consuming; or I could go to my grandparents' and live with them for the two and a half years until I too began college. I made my decision with a dazzling selfishness and speed it takes my breath away to recall—though it was useful to keep in mind when my own children reached that age. I chose my grandparents, where I felt safe, where the air seemed lighter, clearer. Where people spoke to each other in seemingly harmless and transparent ways. And left my father to his solitary life.

My grandmother made the connection for me more than once—how I'd come to her after my mother's death in just the way she might have gone to her grandmother after *her* mother's death. Now wasn't that a strange coincidence? Two young girls, motherless like that at nearly the same age? She said then, and she wrote to me later, that she thought some of the pleasure she took in having me there, aside from her love for me, aside from the connection it made with her own sad daughter, was that she felt almost as though she were able at last to offer comfort and help to the girl, and then young woman, she'd been herself when the parallel events happened to her. "Who knows how things might have turned out for me if I'd done what you did—if I'd gone out to my Grammy

Parsons with Ada and Fred after Mother died. Of course, Grammy died together with Grandfather just a few years later in the influenza epidemic. Fit as a fiddle one morning and gone the next. And all that lovingkindness gone along with them. So you just can't know, can you?"

She wrote this to me in my first year of college in California, where I'd gone to get away from my history and the confusing bonds of attachment and guilt and need I felt—for her and my grandfather, for my father, even for my mother. And standing there in my dorm room, hungrily reading the letter, I felt again the yearning for her, for them, that I never outgrew.

I remembered a moment from the spring of that first year I'd lived with them, four or five months after my mother died. I was lying on my bed in the attic, watching a sudden storm come up. The sky blackened, the birds stilled, the trees heaved and shuddered, showing the silvery undersides of their leaves. A wooden chair came skidding drunkenly across the yard, stopped, then hurried on. Suddenly my grandparents appeared in the yard below me, fore-shortened and legless from my vantage—I could hear their voices before I saw them, and my grandmother's laugh. They began to take the wildly flapping laundry off the line: the towels, the white sheets. They worked together quickly, with practiced skill, both holding a sheet, folding it, walking toward each other, away, then in again: the big white belling cloth first halved, then quartered and calmer, now disappearing to a compact bundle between them. They finished—they moved offstage—just before the sky ripped open with lightning and thunder nearly simultaneously, and the pelting of the fat drops began to accumulate to a dull roar on the roof above me.

But I had seen it—their quick mirroring dance, the arms lifting at the same time as they approached each other, lowering as they stepped back, the magic of the wild white cloth growing smaller and smaller between them on the dark grass—and what it looked like to me from my lonely perch above them was the purest form of love.

Four

Georgia's old grandmother had been right: the children grew up fast after their mother's death—Georgia faster than either of the others. It wasn't that her burden increased. Actually, she was freer now than she had been, so much of her time had been taken up in the care of her mother during the week. And she felt it, it was a relief not to be waked in the night by her mother's groans or wild wails, or by the bell that signaled she needed help.

But she also felt lost and alone. Because however odd Fanny had been when well, however ill she grew, however much maturity she needed from Georgia; still, she was Georgia's mother, and her existence, on whatever terms, meant that Georgia was still a child. And Fanny had struggled, within the demands of her illness, to remind Georgia of that, to try to continue to be maternal—and perhaps because of that was actually more maternal as she was dying than she'd ever been before. She touched her daughter frequently, she stroked her bright braided hair or her soft hands. Her voice, when she spoke to Georgia, often deepened with tenderness. She said, "I'm sorry for you, dearest, you shouldn't have to do this," as Georgia helped her up the stairs or into the bath or, later, carried her chamber pot in or out. For as long as it was possible, she made an effort to connect with the running of the household, to select meals, to discuss with Mrs. Beston the schedule of her duties for the day, to suggest activities or playmates, especially for the younger two—and to arrange, when she could, for Georgia's freedom.

In the later stages, she tried to protect her children from her illness. The last four or five months of her life, Dr. Holbrooke came almost daily at her request to give her morphine so her pain wouldn't scare the children—she didn't realize how terrifying her drugged, slow thickness was in itself. And the summer she was dying, she insisted the windows to her room be closed, in spite of the heat, so her cries wouldn't float out into the yard where Mrs. Beston tried to keep the children occupied in those long, empty waiting days.

Now Georgia felt abandoned and particularly responsible, more responsible than when she'd had far more to do. It is true there might be a vast, peaceful silence when she waked in the night, but, at least at first, she felt this as her sorrow, her burden. She was in charge of it—the peace, the black nothingness. She was alone.

It was a life not without its pleasures, though, and slowly Georgia learned them. She came, over the long months, to feel a real sense of pride in running her household well. In having stiff fresh-smelling sheets on the beds each week, the new holes neatly patched with darns. In using the dust mop daily, even under the beds, letting Freddie whack it vigorously on the edge of the front porch between rooms. In polishing the few silver pieces they owned at least once a month. And she herself cooked the dishes that the two other children and her father especially loved: Indian pudding, lemon pound cake, corn chowder, baked beans, blueberry pancakes, soda biscuits.

Gradually her life changed to conform to her new role. Perhaps to avoid the lonely wakening at three or four in the morning, she began to stay up later and later when her father was away. Long after Ada and Freddie were in bed, she roamed the house. She took a delight she couldn't have explained simply in sitting in chairs she normally didn't use. *Here I am,* she would think, looking at the darkened room from this new perspective. *This is me, seeing this. Feeling this.* The world seemed, at these moments, to be arranged, fitted, exactly around her.

She liked to watch the empty town green at a time when everyone else was safely asleep, intensely aware of her separateness. She read, sometimes until well after midnight. There was a mantel clock in the parlor with a glass case etched with flowers, and hearing it strike those few isolate notes in the dead span of the night made her feel a rich, melancholic sense of her own solitude.

In her senior year of high school, she fell in love with Bill March, who lived on the opposite side of the green. It was their arrangement to signal each other with a candle at ten o'clock precisely, he from the dark attic bedroom of his house, she from what had been her mother's sewing room. She loved seeing him there in his white nightshirt in the flickering light, his face a pale blur, so much more romantic than the tall, solid Bill she knew by day, with his square jaw, his occasional stammer. He told her he went to bed directly after this, filled with thoughts of her. But Georgia stayed up. She was restless with thoughts of him, yes, but she also worried about her future: how could she think of marrying, ever? Of leaving her father? Who would take care of everyone? She felt middle-aged at these moments, already a spinster.

At other times, though, she began to seem more a child than she had in her childhood, to go backward. There was, after all, no one there anymore to remind her that she was a young lady now, that there were certain decent ways to behave. Mothers in town and other older women commented on this, that it was a shame, a disgrace, really, the way she still raced Freddie and Ada across the town green after church, shrieking and carrying on. The way she jounced when she walked, you had to look away, you truly did. The way she'd been seen in a tree in the Marches' front yard and you could look right up her dress and she didn't seem to have the least idea.

She played wild games in the house with Ada and Freddie too, their own three-person versions of Hide and Seek or Sardines or Kick the Can that went on long after the younger children should have been in bed. One night, Mrs. Mitchell, hearing what she described to anyone interested as "blood-curdling screams" coming from the Rices' well after nine, went over to see what was happening, whether she could help. A silence fell in the house when she banged the knocker, and after a long minute or two, Georgia—panting, flushed with excitement and damp with perspiration—opened the door a crack. No, she said. No, nothing was wrong. She was terribly sorry if Ada or Fred had been a bother; she'd speak to them right away. And then, much too quickly, she shut the door again, hard, right in Mrs. Mitchell's face.

The wildest play, though, was aimed at their father, at diverting him, at lifting his burden of grief. During the week they planned their surprises: their theatrical productions, their scavenger hunts, their patriotic tableaux or concerts, their minstrel shows, their living room parades, once with their cat, Napoleon, dressed as a baby pushed in a carriage at the head. Friday nights were frantic, sometimes, with gaiety. And when their father laughed, when he gave himself over again to his family's life, to the possibility of finding some pleasure there even without Fanny, Georgia felt complete, she felt rewarded: she, *she* had made this possible, through her efforts. Surely this would be enough forever.

It was all, anyway, she was aware of wanting.

And so, after she graduated from high school, she did not, as she had planned earlier, go to the university along with Bill March—or even to normal school, as many of her friends were doing. She stayed home, she undertook more of the household chores, more of the cooking, and they were able to get by with having Mrs. Beston come only twice a week.

It was just as her grandmother had said it would be: her girlhood was done.

But as illness had trapped her in this particular box of happiness, so illness rescued her, too. For several months in the third winter after her mother's death, Georgia had a cold, with a cough that never seemed to ease. Finally her father insisted she go to the doctor, and, as he would be out of town the day of the appointment, he arranged with a friend to drive her into Pittsfield. The doctor was their family doctor, the same man who'd cared for her mother. He knew Georgia well, of course, though he hadn't seen her in three years. He welcomed her in; he invited her to sit down. His office smelled sharply of soap and disinfectant, and of something else, too, something more pleasant. Wintergreen, perhaps.

In the time since she'd last seen him, Dr. Holbrooke seemed to have changed somehow. Changed completely, he would have said. He'd been to war in France. As a doctor, to be sure, but that, perhaps, made it worse. What Georgia thought, as she sat down in the wooden chair opposite him and looked at him across his desk, was that he'd become old in the meantime, but somehow without altering much physically. She looked carefully: surely there must be something she could attribute it to. It's true there was a bit of gray where there hadn't been in his dark hair. There were a few more lines around his brown eyes, and his mouth seemed drawn down. Perhaps those regular features, the largish nose, were a bit more chiseled. But most of it was just the sense of a man weighted by some knowledge, some sorrow, he hadn't possessed before.

If she'd known how to ask, and if he'd been in the habit of articulating his thoughts to anyone, what he might have said to her was that he'd learned how temporary man is. Man, or life. Something he'd known, in some sense, since he lifted a knife to cut open the yellowed flesh of his first cadaver in anatomy class. Something he'd known when he visited Georgia's mother every day while she was dying, when he passed the three children stopped in their games or their outside chores, to watch him, to nod back as he lifted his hat to them, the two pretty *jeunes filles* and the sturdy little boy; when he mounted the stairs behind the bustling Mrs. Beston; when he entered the airless room and his wasted patient greeted him with an unearthly cry, a rictus of joy and pain lifting her skull's face. He'd known it, yes, but then he'd had sufficient time—sufficient leisure, really—to consider amply each death, each loss. To count them. To hold himself accountable for them. This, he knew now, had been a gift.

For now he thought of death differently: as a vast disinterested scythe, cutting us down carelessly, brutally. Leaving half a man to die here and half a man to live there. Leaving him standing in the blood of both to decide which fate for which half, and why, and how.

Without knowing any of this, Georgia felt sorry for him.

And he felt sorry for Georgia. She was much thinner than she should have been. She had no color except for the two hectic patches on her cheeks. Her ears, which were large anyway, seemed too large now that her face had narrowed. The pretty young girl watching him from the meadow as he entered the house, standing across her mother's grave from him, tearless and brave—she'd become this frayed, harried-looking young woman, her hair badly pinned up at the nape of her neck, her nostrils chapped, deep circles bruising her eyes. Still, the word that leapt to his mind when he looked at her was *valor*. He found her more beautiful than he could have said.

They talked for a while in his office before he asked her to undress. As he inquired and she told him about her life—her routines, her diet, her sleep habits—he felt a sense of cold, energetic outrage welling up to replace the dispassionate distance he'd come to keep from his patients.

She didn't mean to arouse his sympathy. Never for a moment did Georgia feel sorry for herself. There was something nearly callous, actually, in her inattention to emotional nuance, to the effect her life and her words had on others. I felt it occasionally much later, when I lived with them. She was nearly congenitally buoyant and always a bit surprised when others were not.

Now she had no sense of the impact of her sad story, no sense of the harsh judgments the doctor was making with every detail she offered. Cheerfully, she went on. "I should be ashamed, I suppose," she said. She'd just told him that she let Ada and Freddie read at the table at supper, that nearly any book you opened in the house would slide its load of crumbs onto your lap. "The mice actually eat them sometimes: the books!"

"Shame doesn't enter in," he told her. He raised his hand as if to sweep the notion away, and she saw how long and elegant they were, his hands. Prettier than her own, she thought, looking down at her chewed-off nails.

The doctor had never liked Georgia's father. He'd been shocked, actually, by the arrangements made—or not made—during Fanny's illness: that an invalid should be in charge of the house-hold, that the children were left alone with her at night. As he made notes now on his patient's case, he was already beginning to think in terms of rescue: what could be done, even if this young woman were not truly ill, to extricate her from the unsuitable demands of her situation, from the way that cavalier, shallow man, her father, was robbing her of her youth and health.

She in turn was moved, thrilled by his concern, his gentle voice asking questions, his eyes on her, amused and kind. Even the fact that he wrote down what she said, as though each detail of her ordi-nary life were of great interest to him, thrilled her. Solicitude! It was nothing she was used to. She felt it as a balm poured over her. She turned and preened under it. She told him more than she'd meant to, more than she'd told anyone, even Bill March, about the exact state of things at home, about her lonely, proud life.

Then, the undressing. For her, it was, of course, difficult, but probably no more difficult than the notion of undressing before any other doctor would have been. Any of them would have been a man, after all. Oh, she'd noted he was handsome. She'd loved his tender attentiveness to her. But he was old, to her. He was thirty-nine at this time, and she was just nineteen.

She sat in her white cotton petticoat and chemise on the examining bench, and when he asked her to, she slid the wide straps down off her shoulders and eased her arms out. The chemise was bunched at her waist now, and her shoulders curved forward, as though she were trying to hide her breasts. She *was* trying to hide her breasts.

He was faced the other way while she did this. When he turned around to cross to her, he was already lifting his stethoscope. He didn't meet her glance.

For him, this was a moment of almost breathless suspension, a moment in which he recognized what he felt for her, what he'd felt for her even when she stood in the field those summer afternoons nearly four years earlier, the sun lighting her from behind—stopped, watching him as he went into the house. Counting on him, as he felt it, to be able to do something, to help her—which, of course, he could not. He found her inexpressibly lovely now, with her pale face, her pale skin—her nipples and nostrils touched with the same faint pinkish hue, the dimmed blue tracery of veins in her breasts, the smooth sheen of the skin of her incurved white shoulders, the weighted pull of the pinned-up brown hair, the wisped loop of it fallen loose, straying freely over her back. He lifted the stethoscope. He touched her flesh, hot with fever.

He examined her silently, gravely, his eyes always averted from hers. She breathed deeply for him. She coughed. She felt his cool dry fingertips as he tap-tapped against her hollow-sounding chest.

When he was done, he stood on the other side of the office to inform her that he thought she should take a tuberculin skin test, that it seemed possible she'd been infected somehow. She'd gotten dressed again, and her hand rose to her bosom when he said this. It rested where his fingers too had touched her. He leaned against his oak file cabinet and looked at that hand, work-roughened but still so young. He was thinking about her breasts, her lungs beneath them. She agreed to the test, trying to sound lighthearted and unafraid, but his words had been like a blow to her.

As she unbuttoned her sleeve to expose the flesh of her arm to him to be scratched, he was talking. She would have to come back again in three days to have the test read—Saturday. Was there someone who could bring her again then?

Her father, she said.

Though a part of her understood what it meant as soon as it began to rise—the reddened swelling on her forearm where Dr. Holbrooke had tested her—Georgia hoped she was wrong, she hoped perhaps it wasn't quite red *enough,* quite swollen *enough* to indicate anything serious. By Dr. Holbrooke's grave face when he looked at it on Saturday, she saw that she'd been wrong to indulge this hope.

And then it was all happening too fast for her. He was telling her father she couldn't live at home any longer, that she needed to rest, to gather her strength to fight the illness. She needed further tests: fluoroscopic examinations, sputum slides. He wanted to send her directly to the sanatorium from his office.

"Oh, no, not today!" she cried. She looked to her father for help and saw that none would be coming. There was something already fixed and sorrowful, closed off to her, in his wide, boyish face.

She looked at the doctor. "I just can't today," she pleaded.

He smiled gently back. "Why not?"

Why not? There was too much to do. And she began to list her duties: the school clothes that needed mending, the rugs to beat, the Sunday dinner to fix tomorrow, the trip to buy groceries planned for this afternoon, after her appointment here. But as she spoke, as the image of each task rose in her mind, it was not so much they but the unspoken pictures she was barely conscious of that pulled her: her long delicious nights alone, the close air of the bedroom she shared with Ada, the way it looked by lamplight, the wild freedom of her solitude, the gleeful preparation for Friday night, the gargling sound of her father's motorcar pulling into the shed. How could she give any of it up? How could she go away? She just couldn't, not today.

When she was done with her public list—her list of chores—he smiled kindly at her again. "But you see," he said, "this is precisely why you have to go."

He had made all the arrangements, it turned out. He had done this because he wanted to be prepared in case the test was positive to fend off any protests by her father. He wanted to be ready to present her going away, if that's what was required, as a fait accompli.

As it happened, her father was quietly grateful that it could all be taken care of so easily, so quickly. He turned to his daughter, and he too began gently to insist: she had to go, there was to be no questioning, no arguing about this. It was something she must do for all of them.

Holbrooke watched him speaking to his daughter. All the ease and joviality were erased from the man's wide, fleshy face. He looked stricken, actually. Ashy. For a moment only, then, the doctor allowed himself to think of the other man's losses, of the fear he must be experiencing. To feel sorry for him.

There are only a few pictures of Georgia at the sanatorium, taken by friends, I suppose, or by Ada or her father when they came to visit her; and then, later, at the end of her stay, by the man she married—her doctor. Dr. Holbrooke. My grandfather. The difference between her image in these pictures and those of her in her earlier life is a revelation. In the old days she wore long dresses, white in the summer, dark plaids or stripes or solid colors for winter. She kept her hair parted in the middle, pulled back into braids or, later, in a bun at her neck, fastened often with a long, drooping ribbon. She had a radiant, open smile: a girl's smile.

The san remade her. Of course, the way other women looked and acted changed too, with the end of a kind of national innocence; everyone, after the war, was moving into a newly made world. But clearly my grandmother embraced the change eagerly, chose it. Her hair in the san pictures has been cropped and blows in loose curls around her face. Sitting in the sun in a cure chair on the open terrace has lightened it, so that in these faded photographs she looks suddenly blond. She wears the new narrow skirts of midcalf length and a long baggy sweater jacket. A scarf is flung carelessly around her neck. She is laughing in several of these pictures, she is self-consciously flirting with the camera. She looks the way I remember her looking later in life too: confident, poised, self-contained.

She said not, though. She said she was nervous as a cat, wild with constant strained emotion. "I was kind of crazy, I think," she told me once. "We all were. And of course, everyone was in love, even the ones who were dying. Even some of the patients we thought of as the old folks, strange to say, had their romances. *Romance.*" She weighted the word oddly. Then she smiled, what seemed a sad smile. "It was how we managed to get by from day to day."

The way I used to think of it, her stay in the san, the way she described it to us, was as if it were a long voyage on a boat—that same forced intimacy of the small private world within the larger one. The enormous emerging importance of people you might not pay a moment's attention to if your life were your own.

She felt that—that her life was not her own. And she hadn't brought anything with her to help her remember her old life, her arrival was so rushed. It wasn't until the third day there that her father and Ada arrived with several boxes of things they had packed for her. In them, the quilt from her bed at home, pieced by her grandmother. Her clean monthly cloths, folded and wrapped discreetly by Ada in a wool shawl. A few dresses, a few sweaters, quantities of the necessary undergarments. Her three-month baby picture in her mother's arms, her mother "fat as a pig," in her own words. Cookies made by Ada and her four-year diary, which she was in the last year of.

She had been a faithful diarist, and she would feel an ache whenever she opened these pages to the empty days she'd missed when she was first sent away and then when she wasn't allowed to write in the san. Her first entry after the almost monthlong blank:

April 14. A lovely day, but chilly. News: I'm ill, the doctor says, and must stay here, in Bryce Sanatorium, until I get well. I worry about Ada and Fred, but Father says not to, maybe he'll marry some nice widow to take my place, ha-ha! I cried for several days at first, but then he and Ada brought all my things and lightened my spirits. Still, I've been gloomy since then.

On the same day three years before:

Lovely day. After school I weeded and turned over the vegetable patch. Father will bring the seeds home on Friday, so it's good to be ready. Mother had a bad night. Mrs. Beston left Spanish rice for supper. Fred wouldn't eat it.

Two years before:

Strangely warm today. We ate lunch outside at school, though we kept our coats on, and John Mitchell sat with me and asked me to go bicycling with him. I am cutting down an old dress of Mother's for Ada to have—the soft brown wool she wore for best in winter. At first Ada said she didn't want it, but now she sees how pretty it will be, she does.

And the year before:

A gray day, wintry and sullen. Winnie told me she is engaged! To Harold of course. It's still a secret. She will marry in the fall if he doesn't have to go to war—and surely it will be over by then, with all our boys headed over! She would like me to be maid of honor. I've said that I will be pleased to. She's already planning it out. We're all to be in apple green taffeta, she thinks. Not my best color, but I don't complain, I am so happy for her.

Georgia's father married again just after she was released from the sanatorium—as it happened, the widow he'd joked about had been real. A little over three months after that, Georgia became engaged to my grandfather, and they were married too, after a scandalously short engagement. Looking casually at this history, you might have thought that she'd arranged a life that repeated itself, that she was again offering herself as a caregiver to a much older man. But that wasn't the nature of the relationship as I remember it.

My grandfather did seem very old to me when I was a girl; he was in his seventies then. But in spite of this, it was he who seemed the caretaker in the family: he was always completely protective and solicitous of my grandmother. It was as though she were a fragile blossom, as though she could be easily damaged. Which seemed strange to me. For she was—everyone who knew her said so—the most flirtatious, the most playful, the most energetic of women. He was the one who seemed vulnerable: frail and shaky.

My grandfather was white-haired and tall. He bent slightly forward from the hips when he walked, and he walked stiffly. His hands trembled, rising to any task, though in its execution he was always steady and precise. In the evenings he read, Hardy or George Eliot, occasionally Raymond Chandler, but mostly his favorite, Dickens. At some point his breathing would begin to thicken, the book would slip from his hands, and his head would drop forward. "Give him a poke, lovey," my grandmother would say, passing through the room on her way to some duty. "It's too early for bed, and he's not in it."

And my brother or I would cross the room and gently, almost fearfully, shake his shoulder till he woke.

"Ah! Thank you, my dear," he'd say, and pick up the trembling book again.

But still, it was he who hovered gently around her, who reminded her to rest each day. Who took us out, away, so she could do so, always with the same line: "Your gran needs her beauty sleep."

But what could I know of them then, or of their marriage, really? My old grandmother, my very old grandfather. I saw only what they wanted to show me, what they chose to show the world. And they were as careful about this as they were about what they wore—about *dressing* each day, for instance. It mattered, I think, that my grandfather arose each morning and put on a jacket and tie, even long after he retired. That my grandmother wore a dress—or a skirt and blouse—and stockings and shoes with a moderate heel. Every single day. (These stockings were held up by a girdle or a garter belt, never panty hose. You could glimpse this elaborate arrangement every now and then if she sat awkwardly, and you saw these things pinned on the line in the summertime—businesslike, glaringly white: no-nonsense. Though there was something humorous, I always thought, in the way the tabs danced so gaily, so promiscuously, in the wind.)

It mattered, I think, because appearances, surfaces, counted for so much with them. Because this was where they lived, for the most part. Because, it seemed to me then—and it does now too—they didn't have the habit of examining their lives, of looking under the surfaces for what was dark or difficult. Their days together were predictable and ordered from the moment they got up. My grandmother made a full, hearty breakfast every morning: freshly squeezed orange juice—though she allowed herself the frozen kind when it became available—bacon and eggs, or pancakes, or muffins, or waffles, with maple syrup. She moved around her kitchen as she moved through life—as a hummingbird moves: a rush in one direction and a focused stillness about her work at that station. Then another rush, and the concentration on whatever needed to be done next.

And all the while she kept up a light, easy chatter, a kind of perpetual warm invitation to her view of the world. Ah! she'd just remembered: she'd had a funny dream in the night, had anyone else? How many pancakes, by the way? Lawrence? John? Cath? Looky here, Lawrence shouldn't let his grandfather show him up that way, surely he could do as well, squeeze a few more in. Now, her dream, if she remembered it rightly, was one of those pickles—you know them—where you end up in your nightie right in the middle of the town crossroads. She'd waked up with a start, she was so embarrassed.

"Which nightie was it?" my grandfather asked.

"Why? Whatever difference would that make?"

"It would make a difference to me," he said.

My grandmother laughed, and we did too, though we didn't know why. "Aren't you ashamed," she said, touching him lightly on the shoulder as she leaned forward to slide a stack of pancakes onto his plate.

Darker events than these took place in our house, and it was my pleasure, mine and Lawrence's, to soak up what seemed the light, the air, the sense of play that was the atmosphere in my grand-parents' house, that surrounded my grandmother even when she was busiest at what was clearly her work. And if we didn't notice the charged quality in a silence that fell between them occasionally, if we chose to disregard a sudden burst of impatience on her part toward him, or a long hard look from time to time, who could blame us? We had every reason to find it perfect—their life—to think of it as a safe haven, a refuge. For us it was.

"Oh, your grandfather!" she would say. "His big idea was, he wanted to lock me up in a castle with a big moat around it—the moat to be called tuberculosis, you understand—and he the only person supposed to cross the drawbridge. Well! Little did he know!"

And we'd all laugh, my grandfather too.

It was only later that I thought, *What? Little did he know what?*

Five

Of course I idealized them. I took the pieces I knew of their story and made from them a great and uncomplicated romance, a thing of deep and enduring fidelity and devotion, which I heard in my head in my grandmother's rhythmic, storytelling voice. Why wouldn't I have been eager to believe in it this way, growing up as I did? And as my life went on, and filled up with what seemed to me its own sordid adult complications, I didn't revise that view. Instead, I idealized them even more. I wanted to. I wanted there to be a world where things were simpler and cleaner and finer than the world I seemed to have landed in as I started making my own way in life.

Occasionally I still hear about my first husband, Peter, or read about him. He was famous for a while as a political activist; even now he's still unearthed from time to time—dug up, as it were, from where he's buried himself in his present life—to comment on those times, the times in which he had his fleeting fame. Once I was watching a television documentary on those days and there he was, both young and old. Young, much as I remembered him, but with that pall of the ridiculous—hair, clothes, manner of speech—that falls over those we knew then, even over ourselves, when we look at old photos or films. It's not there in memory, of course. There we are only who we were, young and beautiful and passionate. But in the record that's been made, we wear the absurd uniform of the time: hairy, wildly patterned, deliberately frayed and worn, hippie. We speak in ways we've come to mock in this more ironic age.

But I wouldn't have mocked Peter in this documentary. Everything he was saying—about life, about the government, about Vietnam—was what I believed then.

The older version was a shock. He's heavy now. Those mournful, delicate features have become doughy and thick. His hair is scooped back smoothly on his head. It looks wet. He wears rimless spectacles. In this documentary he spoke of the fate of Jerry, of Abbie and Rap. He spoke of his disillusionment with political answers, of the importance of self-actualization and living mindfully.

I don't mean to suggest he sounded stupid. To me, he didn't sound stupid. He just sounded lost. He sounded, really, wrecked. Destroyed by what had happened in the passing of all that time.

At the time we separated, he said I was what was destroying him.

I had just had Fiona. I was in a daze of nursing and sleep and child care. My episiotomy was swollen and sore. My body was immense and slack. I still looked pregnant, actually, in a baggy, softened way. But that wasn't all he had to complain of. There was the way I kept, or didn't keep, the house. Every time he went to use the toilet, there were dirty diapers soaking in it. I had spilled a sack of flour in the kitchen and it took me three days to clean it up—three days in which the two older children played in the powder as though it had been arranged for their pleasure, like sand in a sandbox. The house was tracked with it, the furniture bore little white handprints. I didn't care, and this, to him, was unforgivable.

I didn't care about much, actually, except making it through each day. For days there was no coffee in the house, nothing for dinner except what I fixed for the kids: peanut butter and jelly sandwiches, macaroni and cheese. Someone had scribbled on the living room walls with Magic Marker. I didn't care. He said living with me was like living with a zombie.

I felt a sorrowful sense of betrayal. He had forgotten the first two births; for each of those he had been a zombie with me. He'd get up in the night, then, and change the baby—Karen or Jeff—and bring it to me in bed to be nursed. Sometimes we talked companionably for a little while before we slept again. Sometimes we slept leaned together while the baby nursed. In the mornings we all had breakfast in bed. I remember those as the happiest days of our marriage.

This time around he had no patience for that. We had just moved back to California, after his stint as a postdoc in the Midwest. He was anxious to prove himself to his mentor at San Francisco State. What's more, the timing of Fiona's birth couldn't have been worse. Peter had a full month to go until the end of the semester, the busiest month of the year in terms of his workload: papers to grade, exams to prepare, final conferences, planning for the fall. All of this gave him a clear distance and perspective on me and the children and what we had done to his fine and interesting life.

Here's how it ended.

One sunny afternoon, I decided I'd take the children out to the park just down the hill from our house. Out of guilt, primarily—I'd had three naps already that day, I'd given them Cheerios for both of the meals they'd eaten, they'd been squabbling and fighting with each other all afternoon. All right, I said, around three. All right. Here's the story. We're going out. We're going for a walk.

I found some shoes for all of us. That took awhile. Responsibly—noticing how responsible I was being—I put an undershirt and a tiny sun hat on Fiona. I bounced her carriage down the front steps and we all went out into the glaring midafternoon light.

The children were wild with the sense of release. Possibly also with excitement—I bought them each an ice-cream bar when the truck pulled up beside the playground. And then I bought them another, the thought being that maybe I could get away with just fruit and milk for supper. Sticky, sweaty, they ran and swung and dug in the sand. I'm not sure what time we headed home—I didn't have a watch on—but most of the other kids and mothers had left, and we cast long pointed shadows on the sidewalk.

The children were whiny and fussy now, though the baby was sound asleep. In the front hall they started to fight, grabbing each other's hair, hitting. I squatted with the baby tucked up against me and tried to separate them, yanking wherever I could get a hand on one of them. Jeff had a metal Matchbox truck in one fist. He hit me in the face, across the mouth. I cried out in startled pain, and suddenly they froze, staring at me. I tasted blood, then felt it filling my mouth, rolling down my chin. The baby's undershirt had a big splotch on it, then three splotches, then a single, widening stain. Karen started to cry.

I grabbed a clean diaper from the stroller and pressed it to my mouth. My voice shrill, I ordered the two older children to their room. In their terror, they obeyed me.

I laid the baby on our bed and went into the bathroom. There was a deep clean slice across my upper lip, already swelling open from underneath. I washed it with soap. I pressed a towel against it. The baby started her scratchy cry. When I bent over her to check her diaper, drops of blood started to land on her again. I changed her, biting down on a towel. When I was done and she'd quieted, I went back to the bathroom and found one of Peter's styptic pencils. The bleeding finally slowed to an ooze of thickened blood.

I carried the baby to the kitchen. I gathered up some bananas, some apples. I took them to the children's room and propped myself up against Karen's pillow to nurse Fiona while they ate the fruit. I sang softly to them for a long time: "The Wheels on the

Bus"; "I Bought a Goat"; "Mr. Rabbit, Mr. Rabbit"; "Clementine."
The sun streaked sideways into the room and then turned pink and
faded. The children lay tangled together. The baby had fallen
openmouthed and stunned with sleep away from my breast. In
a minute, I thought, I'd get up and run a tub for Jeff and Karen. In a
minute I'd get out their clean seersucker pajamas. I'd read them
a story and tuck them in and pick up a little before Peter came
home.

And then suddenly his dark shape was in the doorway, the hall
light bright behind him.

"Jesus Christ!" he said, and in three steps was upon me, grabbing
the baby. *What the fuck . . . ?*

Karen moaned and turned on her side, tucking her hands
between her thighs. The baby had started to cry. "Shhh, shhhh . . ." I
began.

"Get out here!" he said. "Get the fuck up."

He had the baby, he was under the hall light. Blood was all over
her. She looked horrible, I saw that. The cut must have opened
again while I slept. There was even blood on her face now too. "It's
not her," I said. I was shutting the door behind me on the dirty
sleeping children.

"What the hell is going on here?" he said. He was handling the
baby roughly, trying to find the source of blood, and she had begun
screeching—a dry, ratchety noise.

"Here," I said, trying to take her from him, to comfort her.

He thrust his elbow hard into me and I stumbled and fell. My
head hit the door frame and I cried out. He looked down at me piti-
lessly, at my swollen bloody mouth, my open blouse, my heavy
breasts, my dirty bare feet. In his face I saw that it seemed possible
to him that what he thought had happened could have happened—
that I could have hurt the baby, badly, and hardly noticed, or perhaps not even have cared.

How do these things change? That what you loved you come to
hate? That it is gone, all the love? In any case, it all poured out from

him—how he couldn't stand it anymore: my dazed incompetence, my unconsciousness, my miredness in my body, in the children. I took my turn too, of course. He'd abandoned us since the move to California. There was no car, no way to shop for anything, no money with which to shop anyway. The baby, in case he hadn't noticed, was two weeks old. How could I not be mired in her? What did he think I ought to be doing instead?

At one point he said, "I didn't want any of this," and that seemed so deeply offensive to me—these were our children!—that I told him to leave. We went round a few more times before he did. My lip was bleeding again now, I'd nursed the baby once more. But finally he picked up the car keys and started toward the door.

"Leave the car," I said. That's how I knew it was over. My practicality. My hardness.

He was startled.

"I've got three kids. I've got shopping and doctors' appointments and errands. You leave the car right here."

"Jesus Christ," he said. But he left the key and walked out. There were apparently other places he could go to spend the night, something that couldn't have been said for me.

In fairness—ah, in fairness! which came much later—it was a hard time for him too. Everything else had fallen apart in his life. The war was over, Watergate was resolved, Nixon was gone, Saigon had fallen and been shamefully abandoned. The glory days of the academic political scientist were past. His youth had run out. Now he was an assistant professor hoping to get on the tenure track, hoping desperately for what he'd once scorned, a middle-class bourgeois life. The arrests, the magazine interviews, the cocktail parties, the all-night strategizing, the TV appearances, the access to the famous and the infamous, to women, to drugs, to free meals—they were done, all done.

When we'd met, he was just beginning all that, and I was along for the sexy, sexy ride, adoring and pliable. A smarty-pants. One of those clever girls who corrected Stokely Carmichael's language when he said the only position for women in the movement was prone. *Surely he meant supine,* we said, allowing ourselves that momentary frisson of superiority without apparently noticing the meaning of what was being said or the way it was received among our boyfriends and lovers: as a damned good joke. Well, when the laughter died, I was alone with the kids.

Over the few weeks after Peter left, we agreed: I'd go east for the summer and he'd move back into the rented house on Alabama Street. By fall he would have found another place to live, and I'd return and we'd figure out how to get divorced. I was twenty-seven years old, and I felt my life was finished. Wrecked.

We made it to Vermont in six days. I drove when the children slept, usually until one or two at night. Then I'd pull into a rest area and nurse the baby and sleep myself. When dawn broke I'd start the car and drive for a few more hours until they woke. We'd stop for breakfast, we'd play ball, fly kites, sightsee. We poked around in Las Vegas, saw Mesa Verde National Park, the Museum of Science and Industry in Chicago, the Indiana dunes. I did more with them than I'd done in months. They were happy. After lunch they'd nap and I'd drive again. We'd have a long picnic dinner somewhere by the side of the road, then get back in the car for the night.

What I didn't let them see was how terrified I was: of what would become of me, of what would become of them. I kept that to myself. I let it flood me as I drove at night. I let the frightened, obsessive thoughts rise and rise again. I would have to work: what could I do? I couldn't even type. Who would care for the children? How could we pay for things? Who would care for me?

We arrived at my grandmother's house in early June. She came out to greet us in the cool evening air, her hair pinned up in a bun at her neck, wearing an apron over her sweater and skirt, wearing her old-lady shoes with the moderate heel, and stockings. The lilac by the front door was just starting to bloom. My grandmother smelled of sachet and maybe vanilla, of everything clean and comforting. When she held me, I started to cry.

That was the last extended stay I had with her, that long summer. A summer in which my bottomless appetite for sleep seemed finally satisfied, in which the children adapted quickly and easily to all her routines, learned to say *please* and *thank you* and to carry their plates to the kitchen when meals were through. In which we all napped deeply for several hours after lunch and then went down to the pond behind the cornfield to wade and catch tadpoles and play with the other children. In which I walked with the baby for an hour after supper, in which I cut my hair and rode a bike and lost weight, in which the baby began to sleep through the night, in which the lights in the house were all out by nine and I woke to sunlight, to the smell of breakfast cooking, to the sounds of Karen and Jeff and my grandmother in the kitchen, and the chucking cries of the baby in the fold-up crib next to my bed. I got well, it seems to me. I recovered from all that had happened, to me and to the world. The cut on my mouth turned to a deep scab, and then a red scar, and then to the white line through my lip I carry to this day.

In the fall I went back to the little house in San Francisco. For the first several years Peter supported us in a sporadic way. Lawrence helped me too, and I had a series of part-time jobs with flexible hours. I did plant care for Barbara's Botanicals, staggering into verdant office lobbies all over San Francisco with Fiona in a pack on my back, to prune, to mist, to water, to mulch, to do tasteful seasonal underplanting. I worked at home for a catering company and became well known among a certain clientele for my dacquoise, for my lemon pound cake. I worked for a tutoring company helping high-school kids write their college application essays and term papers.

It was through one of my parents at the tutoring company that I heard about the temporary job at the Frye School for Girls. I worked as a substitute for a semester, and then when a real opening came up a year later, I applied for it and got it. Karen and Jeff were in school all day by then, and Fiona was in kindergarten, so it wasn't too hard to manage. Suddenly I had a real salary, and we felt rich. In that same year the owner of the little house decided to sell it. My father loaned me the down payment, Lawrence co-signed the mortgage—by now we rarely heard from Peter—and it was ours.

It would be fair to say that I loved my life in this period. I loved the children with a kind of consuming adoration—for everything they said, for their very physical beings: their voices, their bodies, their turns of phrase, the way they moved, the way their minds worked. I loved the house. I loved its being mine. I loved walking into it at the end of the day, I loved painting it and rearranging it. I liked my work, and the feeling of independence it gave me. Nothing else mattered much, especially not men. I went out perhaps two or three times a year. Once or twice I started affairs—my lover Carl, who later moved to Boston, was in this category—but they were all short-lived. They seemed like static, like complication and interference in my otherwise full and happy life.

I met Joe four years later. Karen was almost thirteen by then, musically gifted, we'd discovered. I decided, in a flush moment, to buy her a piano; up till now she'd been staying after school to practice on their piano each day.

Engle and Sons was a deep jumble of elephantine grand pianos. The showroom was cool and dark; it smelled of dust and wood. The uprights, the elderly man with the eastern European accent told us, were in the back room.

While Karen tried them, setting her music up in her precise and careful way on one after another, I could hear him arguing with someone in the office he'd retreated to—arguing about money, a loan. Arguing with his *son. Papa*, the other man's voice kept saying. *Papa, you always; Papa, you never.*

Karen did scales. She thrummed around in the bass notes, did arpeggios up high. She was quick and dismissive, as though she'd been doing this all her life, as though it were her job to rate pianos. *Ugh, this one feels so awful.* I was reading price tags and eavesdropping. Fiona was noodling around on the grands in the front room, bits of "Chopsticks" or "Heart and Soul." *Ick, buzzy!* Karen said. The son wanted money, some investment that was sure to pay off. The father had heard it all before and didn't have it anyway. Business was slow. Look at it out there. Nobody was buying. Everyone wanted a bargain. And what about his own old age? What was he supposed to live on?

The son was good-natured and persistent. He'd heard it all before too. "Tell you what," he said. "I'll throw in my firstborn child."

"To have a child," the old man said, "you first need a wife."

"This is a nice one," Karen said. "It's only one thousand two hundred dollars." She struck a dramatic chord, the beginning of the Beethoven sonata she was memorizing for a recital, and moved on to the light runs that followed. I sat down on one of the benches to listen. In a moment the old man and the son came to the office door, drawn by the music. The son stood behind the old man, tall, with a neatly trimmed black beard. He made his father seem wizened and frail. When Karen was finished, he burst into wild applause and whistles.

That was Joe.

Karen was flustered. She hadn't known anyone was paying attention. But then, in a moment of grace uncharacteristic of her, she stood and solemnly bowed, her face radiant. Her shy pleasure made her, for the moment, beautiful. Joe used to joke that he fell in love with her at first sight, that falling in love with me took a little longer.

What shall I say of Joe? That I felt rescued by him from something I hadn't been conscious of needing rescue from? That I trusted him? Both were true. I never considered that I might be rescuing him. I never thought about how safe and comforting a package I offered him: a happy woman, a woman with a house, with pleasant, bright children, with a job, with an income, with friends and habits.

He moved in. We married. We built an addition on the house, what the architect called the master-bedroom suite. Joe's investment—in a vineyard in the Sonoma valley—did very well. When the time came, the children were able to go to colleges I could never have afforded. Joe invested in a restaurant in the city. We began to know food people, wine people. We redid the kitchen and had dinner parties and weekend luncheons that lasted into the evening. Joe was busy. He had dozens of friends. I didn't notice at first how much more he was staying away overnight north of the city, how distracted and distant he seemed.

I'd met her, of course—Edie, the woman he married after we divorced. I'd watched him charm her over dinner at a friend's house with the stories that always worked, the same stories that had worked on me. Stories of his parents' flight to South America from Poland just as the Second World War started, of their arrival in San Francisco speaking no English, with no money, his father trained as a piano tuner. How he'd taken Joe along to translate when he went to rent his first store.

"It's so hard to grasp," Edie had said to me that night. "That absolute dislocation from your past, from everything that was familiar. And what a burden on a kid. Poor Joe. To have to bridge it all for his parents. That sense of exile."

"Oh, Joe," I'd said dismissively. I'd heard this same story once too often, and I'd seen Joe once too often be unpleasant to his father or mother about the very things he'd described to Edie—their dependence on him, their sometimes faltering English, their harping on what was forever gone. "He always plays that refugee card," I said. "And it almost always works, too."

Later, when Joe told me he'd fallen in love with her, that he wanted us to separate so he could be with her, I thought of that dinner party, how I'd made our old friends laugh with my remark—they knew Joe so well too—and how I must have sounded to Edie: so unloving, so unpleasant and hard a person. This would be part of the way she thought of Joe, of course. That he had a wife who made fun of what mattered to him, who mocked his history and the meaning of his parents' lives—their having made their way in this new world, their having to live at such a painful distance from all that meant home and comfort to them.

That wasn't who I was, I wanted to tell her. I loved him longer and better than he loved me. I loved his father and mother, I loved what they'd made of their exile. It was I who sat with his mother through her long dying, when she spoke again only in Yiddish and Polish, when she seemed to be swimming back in time to a place where she finally belonged. It didn't seem alien or foreign to me, that swimming. It seemed how it must be, how we are. It made me think of the borders we all cross, the distances we've all come from what feels like home. Who lives at home, in America, now?

When I was living with my grandmother for the last time, that summer after I left Peter—or he left me—we sat up late one evening on the side porch.

Well, not really late. It was perhaps all of nine. But it was August, and dark at nine, though the moon was out, bathing everything in its clear, virtuous light.

I had just come from tucking the older two children into their beds in the hot attic space. I'd pulled a sheet over each of them and kissed them by their damp ears where the hair was still wet. In the bathroom, under the old yellow overhead light, I rinsed the grit out of the tub and put their brightly colored plastic playthings in a basket.

Now I was sitting in a rocker in the dark, like an old lady—like my grandmother—listening to the night sounds, the nocturnal birds and insects that started calling only now. And I was thinking, suddenly, about going back. How I would have to go away, to go home, in just a few weeks. Thinking about how it would be to be living alone with the children. How chaotic the house still was, some boxes still unpacked from the January move. How terrible it would be to see Peter again. How far it all seemed from this stillness, this order, this deep peace.

I sighed. "My life must seem so strange to you," I said to my grandmother.

It was a moment before she answered. "Oh, I don't know," she said then. She rocked some more. She was so small that her feet lifted off the ground on each tilt back. "Really, when you come to it, everyone's life is strange, isn't it? If you just tell it flat out."

"Well, but I mean my marriage. I mean, three kids, and then getting divorced. It's so unlike what you and Grandfather had."

"Of course, that's true."

That wasn't enough for me. I poked at it. "It must seem very … alien to you. Our giving up. Very … I don't know. Newfangled or something. Very modern. In a bad way."

When she spoke again, her voice was kind. "I don't feel you didn't try hard enough, Cath, if that's what you're saying."

"I suppose it is."

In the silver light, her white hair almost glowed, surrounding the faint pale circle of her face. She had taken her glasses off, and in this light she was beautiful again, perhaps even more beautiful than she'd been as a young woman. After a moment she said, "You know, I'm not so old-fashioned maybe as you think."

"I suppose not." Up on Main Street, an unmuffled car blatted past, trailing music.

"Have I told you ever about the time I was in the san," she said suddenly, "before I married your grandfather?"

"A little." And she had. But the way family stories come at you as a child is necessarily always incomplete, for how can the adults ever really explain what the world was like for them then? Its different shape. How it felt. The grown-ups in my life when I was young were generous with their stories—of course my grandmother in particular. She explained to me whatever I asked her about and more. In that sense there was nothing that was not available to me to know. But knowing is different from understanding.

This is what I knew: my grandmother had had TB. She'd had to live for a while in a sanatorium. But to me as a child it was like saying, "She had chicken pox," "She had mumps." I understood nothing of the mortal fear, of the sense of contamination and damage that the diagnosis brought with it. The feeling they all must have had—my grandmother, her father, her sister and little brother—that their family's life was being forever altered—and made shamefully visible, at the same time, in its alteration. And that's what she wanted me to understand tonight.

"It wasn't long," she said. "A little under six months, I think. Probably about average for a stay in those days. And as it turns out, I probably didn't need to be there even that long." She pronounced it *probly*. "Maybe didn't really need to be there at all. Your grandfather told me that. Later. He waited to tell me. And then I was so mad at him he was sorry he did. Hah!" she cried.

I couldn't see her face, turned away from me in the dark. I couldn't tell if there was any pleasure in her cry.

After a moment, she went on. "But that's how it happened, and suddenly there I was. I was just a young girl, really. Young and foolish. And I was so unhappy at first." Then she described it to me for the first time, going in as if to a prison, having to be stripped and washed, having to lie motionless, without speaking or reading or writing for three weeks after her arrival, the exacting routines and diet, the feeling she had of being shamed, lost, abandoned. How she'd wept, the first days there. "I can't tell you, really, how unclean I felt. How much I felt I'd failed at everything I'd tried to do in my life up till then."

How slowly, then, she'd stopped weeping and entered her new life. How that became what mattered to her. "That's what happened," she said. Her voice had changed now. "It happened to all of us, I think. We started to care about that world, and a very peculiar world it was. And I s'pose I should have been more sensible or smarter, but you know, there was a way, I'd have to say, in which I'd been kept sort of *more* young, *more* unaware of what goes on in life, by my mother's dying so early. You would think it might have made me grow up fast, and in one way I guess it did. But it also kept me young. I just closed up at a certain age, I think. I wasn't sensible or smart." She shook her head. She was frowning. "Anyhow, that's how I was when I went into the san. Kind of goony and young. A babe in the woods. And the san ... well, it was a place that existed out of time, I guess you'd say. People were just yanked up, don't you know, as I was, out of their ordinary lives and ways and plunked down there. We all felt that shame, I think. Oh! and so many of them had no hope, really. So there was a kind of—I suppose you'd say maybe a ... greediness about life, about all we'd missed or would miss or had left behind. Or might never get back to. It made people wild. Reckless." She smiled. "It made us quite *modern*, as you would say. People fell in love. Everyone. Everyone had their romance." Her voice was suddenly bitter, and I felt a kind of shock, not so much at what she was saying as at her tone. She must have sensed this, because it was gone when she spoke again. Her voice had softened, and I had to lean forward to hear her under the steady sawing of the crickets. "We behaved scandalously, really," she said.

I didn't answer.

After a moment, she spoke again, more loudly, more normally. "And then, when you recovered—if you recovered—it was like going back to a different world from the one you lived in at the san. Having to unlearn ... oh, a great deal. Going back to the old rules, the old ways. Not easy.

"It was as though" she rocked forward and smiled directly at me—that radiant, inclusive smile, "as though we were magically transported to the future, where the rules we knew were smashed to smithereens. Or different, anyway. And lived there for a while. Lived there just long enough, I suppose, to get used to it. And then the spell was broken, and all *that* world lay in ruins, and we had to find our way back to our old life.

"It was doubly hard, you see. First we were sent away. And then, just when we got used to that, just when we figured out how to find some comfort there, then we were sent back. And I suppose I've always felt it, in a way. That sense that I've lived another life. Or several other lives, maybe. Far away. Somewhere I could never get back to. Somewhere not just far away, but gone. It changed me," she said. "Living that way." Her rocking had stilled, and now it started again. After a few moments, she said, "So you see."

Well, yes, I saw. Some of it I saw. And this was enough. Enough so I didn't ask about what I didn't see, though I understand now she may have been inviting me to—even wanting me to. But I didn't. I didn't inquire about what she meant by *romance*. By *scandalously*. I'm not sure I even thought about those ideas then or made the connection with what I'd been told of her life earlier by my aunt Rue, the Duchess. No, the gift she was giving me was enough for me in that moment: the gift of her parallel failure, of her loss. The healing gift to me of her own shame. I didn't think of the gift I might have given her, of asking for more or letting her say it all to me. Instead, I sat silently next to her and watched as the moon rose and whitened, and in the dark yard the fireflies blinked their silent songs.

Six

It was a judgment. A judgment had been visited upon them, and the signs of that judgment were there for all to see: the visiting nurse to check Ada and Freddie to be sure they weren't infected too. The instructions to Mrs. Beston for cleaning, for sterilizing or burning everything that had come in contact with Georgia. The sense among the neighbors and the town that nothing in that house had been quite right for a good long time; way back before the mother got ill, things were run very peculiarly over there.

They all had stories they remembered now and passed around. Ada heard the gossip; she felt its sting and passed it on to Georgia when she visited her at the sanatorium for the first time. And Georgia felt even more cut off from what she had loved. With all she'd given up in her own life, she'd done a bad job, apparently. She'd fallen ill, she'd exposed her family.

Her failure, her failure, her failure.

Her first weeks in the san were spent in a kind of bereavement like none Georgia had ever felt before. She wept for everything she'd lost: her life, her pride, her reasons to go on from day to day. She wept at last for her mother too—for her mother's illness, her mother's death. None of this, none of this would have happened to her, she felt, if her mother had lived. She wept because she missed her father and Ada and Freddie, who were to be allowed to visit only once a month. She wept because she was friendless and alone, and she was frightened that she wouldn't live. Or if she did live, that she would never be able to marry, to have children and a normal life. She wept because she'd never lived with rules before, and here rules hemmed her in every hour of the day. She'd had to take off all her clothes to be bathed with brown soap when she first arrived, though she frantically explained that she'd washed herself, even her hair, before she went to the doctor's. Nonetheless, *those were the rules*. She had to lie in bed day and night through the first three weeks, not permitted up even to go to the bathroom. This was a scorching humiliation for her—there were five other women sharing her sleeping porch.

She was not allowed for these three weeks to read, or to write, or even to talk to anyone. Her rest, the first step in her recovery, needed to be absolute. The fifteen minutes they'd let her have with her father and Ada by her bedside when they came for the first time was seen as a great and generous exception.

The result of this was that when she was finally permitted to get up and move around a few times a day—to the bathroom, to her locker to get a fresh nightgown—she was elated. She was dizzy and weak from lying still for so long, and one of the nurses had to help her the first few times she rose, but even so she felt *on the mend*, as her mother would have said. And it was true that her cough was better, nearly gone.

But by now she'd begun to run out of tears anyway. Her natural energy and curiosity were taking over slowly. She felt herself coming to life—she thought of it as *waking up*—in this strange new place.

She remembered the turn, the moment when she noticed this in herself. She was in bed. The women who shared her cure porch were talking. Talking! When they were supposed to be resting their lungs, lying silent and still, as Georgia obediently was—watching the gray rain drip through the gray-green needles of the pine trees that brushed and scraped against the screens. The foggy air seemed to have floated right onto the porch, to be hanging as a mist around the shadowy figures in each iron bed, around each piece of furniture. Nothing seemed real. Georgia's nose was very cold. She kept reaching out from under the covers to touch it, amazed, but then her hand would turn cold too and she'd have to put it back, to slip it against the heated flesh where she'd unbuttoned the top of her nightgown. She had three heavy blankets pulled up over her chin, plus her grandmother's quilt from home, washed at the san and smelling of carbolic disinfectant. *Drip-drip-drip* went the rain, and the needles shuddered and bounced with the watery blows.

"They threw her out," the woman named Mrs. Priley was saying. "We won't be seeing *her* again." There was deep satisfaction in her voice.

Who? Georgia thought.

"They never!"

"What could they do? They found them together."

Georgia turned on her back and looked up at the beadboard ceiling. Who? she thought.

"But when did they get the chance?"

"Stayed back at lunch, is what I heard, and then—the fools!—made such a racket someone went up to see who was dying."

"I wouldn't sneeze at such a death myself." They laughed, like naughty girls—though there wasn't one of them under thirty years old, Georgia thought—and it was by their laughter, the sneaky dark tone of it, that she understood they were speaking of what men and women did in bed together. An image came back to her: her father coming downstairs in suspenders and a collarless shirt on Sunday after they'd been to church, pink as a nicely cooked roast and smelling of shaving soap; and then the butter-and-sugar sandwiches he'd fix for them, the white crystals glinting like tiny diamonds on the pale yellow chunks of thickly spread fat. Biting into it, the opposing textures, the melting sweet grittiness.

Dying, you called it when you lay together. Well, she hadn't known that. Though sometimes when she felt Bill March's hand on her back, on her arm, she had felt a little that way, as though she were dying—a plunging, lurching feeling inside her. But she didn't like it so well when they'd kissed: the surprising wetness and taste of his mouth, and then his rubbery lips.

"Who?" she said aloud now, and the women turned to her, startled.

"Why, it's a little owl, come to visit us at rest time," Mrs. Priley said. *"Who, who, who."* They laughed again, but not unkindly.

After this Georgia found herself hearing things, seeing things around her that drew her interest, that made her hungry to know more. That made her want to live in this place, among these strange-seeming people. Her very lostness, her sorrow, gave her a peculiar energy, a kind of desperate attentiveness to what was in front of her.

Sometimes one or two of the mobile patients came in to talk to them on their porch, bringing gossip, notes from other patients, news. This one had upped and left, sick as she was—told the doctors off and then packed her bags. Someone else had died, and they'd tried to take the body out in the night so no one would notice, but his fellow patients stayed awake and sang hymns when the muffled footsteps passed in the hall. That one had sneaked onto the women's ward two nights ago, bringing champagne someone had smuggled in to him.

Slowly certain names became familiar to her. Miss Farraday, a nurse everyone was frightened of. Mr. Bethke, a patient who argued and broke the rules constantly. She learned that Miss Shepard, who had the bed next to hers, was thought to be "cousining" with him; and twice when she woke in the night and looked over, it seemed to her that Miss Shepard's bed was flatter than it should have been: flat enough, perhaps, to be entirely empty. Though in the mornings she was always lying there, waiting with the others for the cups of thick warm milk to be distributed.

Sometimes now she dreamed of people she'd heard of but hadn't met yet, and in their facelessness, in their vague but urgent sexuality, they were more compelling than anyone she'd known in her past, anyone she could conjure from memory.

And indeed, when Ada and her father came for their second visit, Georgia was startled that their news and the names they mentioned—even Bill March's—seemed less vivid to her; seemed themselves to come from a dream she might have had once, a peaceful, nostalgic dream of that old life.

She was allowed to take her afternoon rest on the terrace now, on one of the cure chairs set out in neat rows facing west, and the touch of the sun warm on her face, the stir and smell of the air, and the long view down the lawn and over the dark hills made her feel in the world again.

But what a changed world! What a mysterious one!

Once she came back onto the sleeping porch after one of these rests and interrupted some procedure being performed on Mrs. Moody. Her shirtwaist was lowered, and Georgia saw the white flesh of her back. There was a deep red incision line running along the curve of her shoulder blade, and a stubby pink tube emerged horribly, obscenely, from the swollen, open wound in the flesh within the curve. Everyone—Mrs. Moody, the doctor, and the nurse—froze when she came onto the porch, and they held themselves that way as though having their picture taken until she quickly withdrew again. She never spoke of this to anyone, she never understood what she had seen, but her revulsion and terror at the sight became part of how she thought of her own disease and made her more determined to get well, to do everything they told her. To obey every oppressive rule.

The fourth Saturday Georgia was at the san, a cold evening in April, she was allowed to go to a musicale put on by the patients. This would be her first evening up, in public. She was giddy with delight. She thought about it, only it, for several days ahead of time. After supper, she put on a clean dress, one she hadn't worn at all here before, and let Mrs. Priley pin her hair up in a new and more grown-up way. The women on her porch all admired the effect when it was done. She looked older. She looked like a Gibson girl. Georgia turned and preened for them. She felt mothered, basking in their praise and then walking in their gossipy midst down the long dim wooden corridors. It would not have occurred to her that there was something slightly prurient, something of the amuse-ment of the initiated dealing with the initiate, in their attentions. It would not have occurred to them how in need she was of what they were so casually, and with such mixed intentions, offering her.

The musicale was held in a room called the library, though it held few books and those mostly of a pious and uplifting nature. No one read them, except to launch jokes about them; the room itself seemed mostly to be a kind of waiting area where patients were allowed to gather before they were let into the dining hall next door for meals.

Georgia had begun to take meals there only in the last week, since being allowed out of bed some of the day. It was the first time she had seen the general population of the place, and she was shocked at the degree of illness of some of them—she felt she didn't belong there. Thin and pale as she was, she felt, by contrast with them, large, horsey, ruddy. She felt well. On the second day she was at lunch, one of the women at her table had begun to cough so violently that she pushed her chair back abruptly and fled the room. You could hear her under the gentle din of clinking, scraping spoons as she hurried away down the long hall, the cough now combined with a horrible retching noise. Not one person spoke of it. No one stopped eating.

The upholstered chairs in the library were pulled into a kind of rough row tonight alongside a deep sofa that faced the stone fire-place. A piano had been centered in the front of the room, between the fireplace and the sofa. The wooden dining room chairs were lined up in four or five rows behind these choice seats. Georgia and her friends came in and made their way to the back. You could see everything better from here, Mrs. Priley told her, and Georgia understood that by this she meant the other patients, not the performers. And sure enough, as the others began to arrive in clusters and groups, the older woman, who seemed to have assumed some kind of responsibility for Georgia, leaned over and whispered names and relevant information to her. This one was just up, that one had been away for a few months—see the newfangled dress? Stay away from that gent, he went after all the new girls. This one had just had two ribs removed and they said it had helped, but look how bent he was! Still, they said he'd be leaving soon.

As Mrs. Priley talked, Georgia's eyes moved around the room. No one was truly old, she saw, but few seemed to be as young as she was. Even so, they called back and forth, they laughed and teased and rearranged their seats. As though they were in the fifth grade, she thought. She'd never seen grown-ups behaving in this childish way before, and after the initial shock a part of her was perversely delighted. Perhaps outside her proper little village, other ways of being, other ways of living, were possible.

There was even, Georgia realized, a kind of *flirting* going on among them, the kind of playful touching she knew from the beginnings of her romance with Bill March and from foolish games she'd played with others before she chose Bill. And yet many of these women wore wedding bands. She thought of the overheard conversation she'd awakened to from her trance of sorrow, and then of other conversations she'd ignored or half attended to in that trance and since. Noises she'd heard in the night. Laughter. When Mrs. Priley got up to speak to someone else, she looked around her more carefully.

Here was Rosanna Moody, Mrs. Moody, whose naked, wounded back she'd seen, who'd told Georgia she had three young ones at home. She was standing, talking animatedly to a tall, slightly stooped man with unruly red hair wearing an old-fashioned tweed suit. Two bright dots flared in Mrs. Moody's cheeks, and her hands were in constant motion, her fingers lightly dancing on the man's sleeve, fluttering at her own bosom; and then back to his elbow, as if beckoning, as if saying, Here, I'll touch *for* you. Her laugh was bright and sharp, rising above the waves of voice, laughter, voice, that rolled around the room in bursts and ebbings of sound.

Georgia noticed the men's hands abruptly, how they were everywhere, touching the women. How they rested at the back of women's waists as they guided them to their chairs. How they dented the bare flesh of an inner arm at the elbow or just below the cuff of a sleeve. She saw one man, perhaps as old as her own father, grip Miss Shepard's shoulders and turn her, pulling her slightly backward at the same time—almost against his front—as he leaned forward to point something out to her: *See? Over there!* His face nearly sat on Miss Shepard's shoulder; she looked as though she had two heads momentarily. Georgia would have sworn she saw their cheeks touch, just for an instant. It made her breath rush in; a momentary strange hunger invaded her. She looked away quickly.

Now the first performers arrived, a man carrying a violin, who walked to the front of the room, and a plump woman who sat down with many elaborate readjustments at the piano bench.

After a moment or two of tuning, they launched themselves into a series of Stephen Foster songs. You could hear the man's deep breathing, sibilant in his nostrils as he moved his upper body slightly with his bowing. They closed with "Aura Lee," a song Georgia's father had sung for them sometimes. She felt a pang of homesickness.

After them, a young woman, perhaps younger than Georgia, came to the front of the room and stood by the piano. She carried no music with her. She was extraordinarily thin, and she wore a butter-colored dress—an unwise choice, Georgia thought, for it made her bloodless skin look unhealthy and blue. Her black hair, which was caught up at her neck and then fell to her waist, glistened with a luxuriance that seemed, by contrast with her skin, almost obscene. Georgia felt, abruptly, that her own hair in the arrangement she'd allowed Mrs. Priley to fix for her was cheap and artificial. She felt embarrassed for herself.

And then worse as the music began. The girl had announced the pieces before she sat down, several Chopin preludes. Georgia had heard that name, Chopin, but never his music. As the girl began to play, Georgia was startled to a pure attentiveness by the music's shocking swing from piano to forte, by its emotive, swaying rhythms. It seemed to her to be speaking—*singing*—of things she'd felt without knowing them, of a life she'd always yearned for without understanding it, a life that connected to the stillness, the solitude of her father's house at night. She sat motionless, held, tears pricking her eyes, until the music was over. As she applauded the dying girl—someone her mother would have called "that *bit* of a thing"—she had the overwhelming sense that she'd wasted all her opportunities, that she'd done nothing with her life but drift around staring out the windows or making batches of muffins or darning socks and stockings. If she herself should die tomorrow, what would she have accomplished?

Nothing, she thought.

And then was shocked at herself, revolted and confused by this new and strange way of thinking.

At the intermission, there was punch and cookies. A man came up to Georgia and offered to add "a little bit of flavoring" to her punch from a flask he held up quickly, but she shook her head. "Oh, I couldn't," she said.

"Suit yourself," he answered in an offended tone, and moved off.

Mrs. Priley began to introduce her to people, sometimes pulling her away in the midst of one conversation to start another. At a certain point, Georgia heard her own excited voice rising to be heard above the general hum around her, and she suddenly wondered at herself; so quickly, she'd become one of them! It confused her. She excused herself and went to sit alone. Slowly the others too drifted back to their seats.

There were two more performers after the intermission. The first was the san's director, Dr. Rollins, the man who'd examined her on the day she arrived. He sang ballads and drinking songs in a voice that seemed deepened, almost muffled by his thick beard.

Then a young woman recited a long poem by Tennyson. There was polite applause when she finished.

A silence fell. In it there rose a growing confusion. Was it over? Was this the end? And if that was the case, why didn't someone say so? They were a group of people used by now to being directed—herded, really—from one place, one activity or nonactivity, to another. The room began to buzz with their angry passivity. Someone ought to take charge. Who would it be?

And then a sharp cry pierced the air, a wail, and quickly another, continuous and blended with it. It seemed to stab at Georgia's heart. Bagpipes! she knew it almost instantly, though she'd never heard them before, only read of them. Nearly as one, everyone in the room turned—and Georgia did too—to see where the wild music was coming from.

And here was the piper, walking slowly up the side of the room in the aisle formed between the chairs and the window wall that opened onto the terrace. The swollen sac and the prickling array of pipes made his shape seem exotic to Georgia, atavistic, as he moved, almost in silhouette against the dying light outside, toward the front of the room. There he turned into the lamplight and became flesh, three-dimensional. She saw that he was not a man. He was a pale boy, probably several years younger than she was, tall, with a thatch of thick dark hair falling over his forehead. For a moment now his pumping cheeks flattened, and Georgia saw the shape of his jaw, the light-colored, almost feral eyes under his heavy eyebrows taking the measure of the room. When they met her own, she felt seized; she was unable to look away, even when Mrs. Priley leaned toward her—she was enveloped again in the woman's lilac perfume—and said, not troubling to lower her voice at all, "Seward Wallace: I heard he's been at death's door and back again."

Others nodded in morose agreement as the tragic music started once more. Georgia bent her head to shut herself away within it.

The next day, at rest hour, Miss Shepard reached over from her bed and handed Georgia the weekly patient newsletter, though this was against the rules; Georgia was still not supposed to read. It was folded back to expose this bit of doggerel:

> *Georgia Rice*
> *Has come to Bryce*
> *To set the hearts a-flutter.*
> *But just whose hearts*
> *Receive such "smarts"*
> *Our lips will never utter.*
>
> *They're male, they're pale;*
> *they have the "rale."*
> *They may not last for long.*
> *But now she's here*
> *They're of good cheer.*
> *If they die, it's in mid-song.*

Passing it back silently, Georgia felt a thick blush flooding her face, heard the light pounding of her heart in her damaged chest.

Seven

It wasn't until mid-October, after I'd found my grandmother's diaries—in fact, in a burst of curiosity fed by her diaries—that I made my pilgrimage to Maine to trace her life there. It took the better part of the day on the winding two-lane highways that cut laterally across New Hampshire and Maine. The leaves had begun to drop by then, and there was a faint tone of desolation under the vibrant colors of the fall landscape, the bare bones of things emerging.

Bryce Sanatorium still stands—or rather the building that was Bryce does—high on its hill in almost the exact center of Maine, but it has changed its function (hotel, insane asylum, meditation center) and even its appearance over and over again through the years. The array of outbuildings is long gone now, and the jury-rigged upstairs porches, on one of which my grandmother lay nearly motionless for a full month, have been torn off. In fact, the old shingle building may look now very much the way it looked at the turn of the century, before the sanatorium boom, when it was a private female seminary, owned and run by the very virtuous, very Christian, Misses Bryce.

But the steep hill leading up to it, a meadow in one of the photographs of my grandmother, full of tall grass and blurry, wide-topped flowers—daisies? Queen Anne's lace?—is now a painfully groomed lawn. In the middle of it sits a conference center sign, and there's an asphalt parking lot, full of late-model cars, where there was once a wide gravel turnaround. (My grandmother never forgot the crunching sound of her father's car, backing up, driving away, and—when he reached the bottom of the hill—the deep hoarse google of his farewell horn.)

The conference center that owns the building now gutted it and completely rebuilt its interiors. You can imagine it, I'm sure—the plush carpeting on the floors, the muted, tasteful southwestern colors, the indirect, subtle lighting everywhere. It was hard not be disappointed, seeing it—and then amused, really. My long trip, and this blandly tarted-up building the end point.

In my grandmother's day, the interiors must have been ornate and dark; the tacked-on cure porches would have robbed almost every window of light. The hard floors in the long corridors would have been worn wood. Maple, perhaps, or pine, paler in the center where the mahogany stain had been scuffed away by all the years of passing feet. In the hallways, shaded sconces would have leaked their brownish light. Only in the grand rooms on the first floor would there have been air and sun and a sense of the wide vistas the hill commanded. Only there, and from the sleeping porches themselves, where, over the spring, Georgia lay and watched the birches fill in, watched the maple trees turn a tender, acid green and obscure the spruces—all but the dark pointed tops along the far ridge.

By the middle of June, she was required to exercise for an hour or more in the late afternoon, and a few weeks after she'd begun her first shy walks out with Seward (Seward did what he liked, in defiance of the schedules set for him), they went into these spruce woods, where the heavy dark boughs made a canopy above them, where they could wander freely over the rust-colored needles. It seemed enchanted to Georgia the first time she saw it, a new world opening out to her suddenly as the undergrowth fell away in the thick, deep shade. It felt like coming on secret, spacious rooms hidden in the woods.

"Oh, it makes me want to be a child again!" she said to Seward. "To bring Ada here and have a pretend tea party. Or a dance!" she cried, spinning away from him.

He leaned against a tree, watching her twirl. After a moment, she stood still in the middle of the clearing, her arms out, rocking a little in dizziness and pleasure. He stepped forward, lifting his hands. "Surely we don't need Ada for that," he said.

Without hesitation, she walked into his arms and let him waltz her slowly, gravely, over the soft whispering needles. She could hear his breath wheezing in his chest, and his hand holding hers felt hot. She kept her head turned a little to the side, away from his steady, asking gaze.

Slowly they shuffled to a stop. He let her go. "Georgia," he whispered, his head bent to hers.

Again and again over the last few weeks they'd come to this moment. And stopped, like this. It thrilled Georgia—his very tone thrilled her—but there was something intensely uncomfortable about it too. Perhaps it was that she knew they were already reputed to be cousining—though they hadn't even kissed yet. But something about that, about what seemed its inevitability given the gossip, given the world they were living in, terrified her; it would have been so impossible a notion for that other Georgia, the one she seemed to have utterly left behind. The one who had flirted so gaily, so carelessly, with Bill March, confident that she was in command of their situation, confident that in any case he would never ask her for more than a kiss. It would have been inconceivable, really. She was almost certain he wouldn't even have wanted it.

Here, in this new world, it seemed there was nothing that couldn't be imagined—and tolerated, and openly discussed—between men and women. In fact, it was through just such a discussion that Georgia had recently learned exactly what sex entailed. Her diary for the momentous day reads:

May 20. Sunny and cool. Delicious bread pudding for lunch. At rest on the porch, I heard a detailed description of the sex act, which was always a little unclear to me heretofore. Well! It changes my view completely.

Who would have spoken of it so openly, so graphically in front of her? Mrs. Moody? Miss Shepard? And what did it change? She sounds only a little startled, actually—she must have guessed at some of it, anyway. There is even, perhaps, a quality of amusement in her entry. She was, as Mrs. Priley sometimes told her half admiringly, a cool one.

The coincidence of this access of information and the beginning of her relationship with Seward, though, confused her in her feelings for him—made him seem almost dangerous. And for it to be presumed that that's what they were up to! For it to be thought that the purpose, the aim, of their tender, fumbling attraction to each other was to lie coupled in the way she'd learned of, this, this seemed to her almost insulting, and certainly embarrassing.

"You're a lovely dancer, Seward," she said, now brightly. "Were you made to take lessons, as I was?" She stepped away from him again, waltzing on her own, going backward with her arms up to hold an imaginary partner in dancing class. "One-two-three, one-two-three," she sang out, swaying deeply on the downbeat, twirling up on the last two counts.

Georgia's transformation was complete by now. She was unrecognizable as the girl who'd arrived at the san three months earlier. Her long hair had been cropped off, and what was left curled in thick waves around her face, exposing her slender neck. Ada had brought her new clothes, since she'd outgrown her old ones on the diet rich in milk and butter that the patients were kept to. The skirt she wore today was nearly straight, ribbed, and ended midcalf. She'd buttoned her long sweater when they'd entered the woods, where the air was suddenly so much cooler. A wide stripe near its hem circled her hips like a low-slung belt.

Seward watched her for a moment, and then he began to cough. It went on, and Georgia stopped in the middle of the clearing. The air was twilit under here, though it was only around four in the afternoon on one of the longest days of the year. Seward was turned away from Georgia, hunched over, one hand resting on a tree. She saw that with the other, he held a glinting silver vessel to his mouth, a sputum cup or flask. He wore a black suit today, as always, and, bent over as he was, he looked suddenly like a frail and angular old man. You wouldn't have guessed at the fierce energy he normally conveyed. She went close to him and, after a moment, touched his convulsing back.

He yanked himself angrily away. On the ground around the tree under him, she saw a spray of glistening blood droplets, their deep red color shocking against the orange needles.

"Go!" he said fiercely. And when she stood, open-mouthed and confused: "Go! Get the hell out of here!"

That evening after supper, Georgia found a note in her mailbox. She stood in the dim hallway, with people passing behind her, talking and laughing, to read it.

Dear Georgia,

I am sorry to have shouted at you today, but I couldn't bear it, your seeing me like that. Especially after you had turned away from me once again.

I say I am sorry. That may not be true, for I am still angry with you too. Why? Because over and over you seem to encourage me. You seek me out. You launch conversations. It was you, after all, who suggested the walk today, after I'd told you about the woods. And then when I touch you, or speak tenderly to you, you become at once all nerves and gaiety.

I think you've misled me about your feelings. You've allowed me to believe you may care for me when you don't, when what you feel is pity, or a kind of bemusement at your ability to stir feelings in me so easily. This is intolerable to me. I'd rather not see you at all than to feel myself made light of in this way.

Of course you have some voice in this matter too. In case I've misunderstood you or misjudged you, I want to give you the opportunity to correct that. There's to be a movie tomorrow night, as you know. I won't be there, but fifteen minutes after the start, I'll be waiting outside, just below the terrace, in the apple trees. If I am wrong about you, you will come. If I am right, please stay away. I will be no more wounded by your absence than I've been already by your presence.

Yours,
Seward

It was only a few weeks before these events that Georgia had had a visit from her father and Ada and Freddie. It was late in May, only the fourth visit she'd been allowed with them, and she'd looked forward to it for days. It was on this occasion that Ada had brought her the two new outfits, storebought and—to Georgia's eyes as she held the things up—strange. But Ada had assured her this was the new style. She was wearing a version of it, and Georgia had to agree, it looked fine on Ada.

What's more, it was sensible, their father pointed out. No more of that tripping over long skirts, no more layers of underthings, no more corsets.

Of course, neither of the girls had ever worn corsets, so this made them both whoop with laughter. Their father sat there watching them, and it seemed to Georgia he might actually have blushed.

Then, as if he were following a train of thought, he turned to her. He said, "I've wanted to wait until we were together with you again to tell you all something, my dears."

They were sitting in a corner of the living room. Miss Duffy, one of the women on her porch, was playing the piano, "The Lost Chord." Georgia's father's voice was so uncharacteristically grave that they sobered instantly and waited.

"I'm planning to get married again," he said.

After a few seconds' silence, he went on.

"This is someone you haven't met, Georgia, but Ada and Freddie have, and I know when you do come to know her, you will love her as much as they do."

There was a sense of suspension. No one spoke. Georgia could feel an odd breathlessness squeeze her chest. Her father's gaze was steady on her. In his hands the straw hat he'd been wearing earlier turned and turned.

"Is it Mrs. Erskine, Pop?" Ada finally asked.

"Well, of course it *is*." He looked over at his slender younger daughter and grinned suddenly. "Good Lord, Ada, you speak as though I were dragging home a different woman every night of the week! Of course it's Mrs. Erskine." He lifted his hat to his heart. "My one and only."

Freddie saw something strange in his older sister's face. He slid closer to Georgia on the settee. "She's awfully nice, Georgie." His voice was soft and private. "She gave me a kit for a tetrahedryl kite and I glued it all myself."

"Did she, Fred?" Georgia tried to smile back. She couldn't look at her father, though she had a thousand questions she wanted to ask him. *What about me?* she wanted to say. *What about me?*

"Will she come to live with us?" Ada asked.

"Have I raised a gaggle of geese?" Their father's voice was pitched for fun now, and Ada and Freddie smiled in anticipation. "A pack of pachyderms? Of course, my girl. This is what marriage means. She will live with us and be my wife and your mother."

"And what will we call her, Dad?" Fred asked. "Will we call her our mother?"

"I'm sure she would like that, Freddie, but we'll see. Maybe the girls, because they're older, will call her something else. But we'll figure all this out in due time."

Georgia could feel his eyes upon her again, could feel him waiting for her to respond in some way, to ask a question of her own. It was unkind of her, she knew, to stay so silent, so turned away from him and his news. But something thick and dull and shocked within kept her mind from working.

Freddie and Ada, though, were eager enough to make up for her muteness. They peppered their father with questions—about Mrs. Erskine's dog, about her car, about which rooms in the house would be hers.

Finally, in a moment of silence that fell, she drew a deep breath and managed it: "And when will you be married, do you think?" She felt her heart in her throat.

He looked at her gratefully. "We'll wait, of course, until you can be there, my dear. Until you're well."

The very thing, she thought later at her rest—and bitterly—that might slow her recovery. For why should she labor to get well only to come home to a wedding? To come home to a house that was no longer hers? To come home to be displaced, replaced, made useless and unnecessary?

Georgia went with them for a walk around the grounds before they left. At the bottom of the meadow, there was a small pond, skimmed with bright-green algae and partially overhung with the delicately traced foliage of two old tamaracks. They took turns throwing stones across it. Georgia's stones fell short of the other side consistently, landing with deep reverberant *plunks!* in the murky water.

"You've lost your arm here, Georgie," her father said, and she remembered that sentence as she waved to them, as the car grew smaller toward the foot of the drive and then honked and turned left, toward home. *My arm, my heart,* she thought.

There was no place to weep, no place to be alone. Georgia returned to the living room and gathered her new clothes up. She carried them to the sleeping porch.

The women there were excited, delighted for the diversion. New clothes! They were something to share, a form of news, really, from the outside world. They insisted Georgia try them on. It was Mrs. Moody who offered to cut her hair in the new style. Someone found a stool, and their nurse, Miss Farraday, loaned them a bed-sheet to drape around Georgia's shoulders. She unpinned her hair and let it down—*your crowning glory* her mother had called it—and watched as the long bolts of it slipped and whispered to the floor.

When it was done, she stood in front of the hall mirror. She hardly recognized herself, but that seemed right to her, somehow, since the terms of her life seemed to have changed so absolutely too. She stepped barefoot toward her reflection in the stylish clothes, her eyes glittering.

Mrs. Moody, standing behind her, saw Georgia's tears in the mirror and thought they were for her shorn head. "Oh, lovey, there's no need to cry," she said. "Everybody feels that way at first with a new haircut, but it'll pass. You do look grand, you know."

"I know," Georgia said. She spun around and hugged the older woman. "Of course you're right." She stepped back, her hands still on Mrs. Moody's arms, her chin trembling slightly. Then, as though she were on stage, as though she were playing a part—Georgia: the new version—she slowly took a deep, elaborate bow, and the little group of women looking on from the open porch doorway all applauded her.

Dr. Holbrooke came to visit only a couple of days after her father had been there. In fact, when she was called downstairs, Georgia had the fleeting thought that perhaps it was her father, come back to tell her it was all a mistake, that he'd changed his mind about Mrs. Erskine.

There were four or five strangers in the living room when she entered. Georgia recognized Dr. Holbrooke at once, of course, but he did no more than nod at her, so she assumed he was there for someone else and sat down to wait for her visitor to claim her—please, let it be her father! let it be him! She was looking out the window, intently scanning the grounds, expecting at any moment to see his bulky, energetic shape in shirtsleeves, when she felt a presence next to her and turned.

"It *is* you!" Dr. Holbrooke said. "I didn't know you at first."

Her hand went up to her bare neck, as it had over and over in the last few days. "Yes, I cut my hair all off. Well," she said, and stood up awkwardly. She extended her hand, and he took it, but instead of shaking it, which was what she'd intended, he stood holding it in both of his and looking down at her.

"You look very well," he said at last, letting her go. "I'm so pleased to see it."

"Thank you." She dipped her head. "I've tried my best to be a good patient."

"It shows. It shows," he said, nodding. "Your new haircut is very fetching too, if you'll let an old man say so."

"You're hardly old!" she said. She felt the heat rise to her face. "But I do thank you. And who are *you* here for?" she asked.

"You, of course," he said.

"Oh!" She couldn't help it, she sounded disappointed. "Oh, well. What an unexpected . . . treat."

He laughed. "You're kind to say so. Perhaps you were hoping for someone more dashing."

"No, really, I thought it might be my father, that's all."

"But he was just here, wasn't he?"

"Yes, he was. Two days ago. How did you know that?"

"Why don't we sit?" he said. "Over here by the window, perhaps." As Georgia followed him, she caught his scent. He smelled of wintergreen. But more than that: he smelled somehow *well*. He smelled of health, in a way, she realized, that was noticeable and foreign to her now.

"You're still my patient, did you know that?" he was saying as they sat down. "I stopped in with Dr. Rollins to see how you were doing just before I sent for you. He told me your family had been in to visit. That must have lifted your spirits immeasurably."

"Of course it did," she said obediently.

"Things are well with them?"

"They are," she said. She talked a little about Ada and Freddie. She didn't speak of her father or Mrs. Erskine. Holbrooke seemed politely, mildly interested, though his amused, intelligent brown eyes were steady on her. He was wearing a rumpled blue-and-white-striped seersucker suit today, a summer suit, and it made Georgia think of the times he had come to the house the summer her mother was dying, of her relief when he got there at the end of the day—the tired-looking but handsome doctor in his light, wrinkled summer clothes, occasionally flecked here and there with what she assumed was blood, come to put her mother to sleep for a few hours.

He asked about her life at the san, about what her routines were these days, and she told him: her pleasure at being up and around, and, blushing, the joy of the first real bath she'd had.

"Water is … well, you miss it awfully, don't you, when you just have sponge baths. I *do* love a bath," she said soberly, and he laughed, in delight it seemed, which made her laugh too, though she wasn't sure why.

Then her face grew serious.

"What I'm wondering now, I suppose," she asked abruptly, "is how things are with me?"

"What do you mean?"

"Well, if you are still my doctor, I'm wondering about my illness. I feel so well at this point, I'm wondering whether I couldn't be thinking about going home soon." A half-formed notion had occurred to her: that if she could get home now, quickly and unexpectedly, she could somehow stop her father's marriage. He would see, simply, that there was no need to go through with it.

Holbrooke leaned forward. "I know how you must miss them all..." he began.

She shook her head. "It's more than *that*," she said. "They miss me. They need me, truly they do. It seems that things are simply falling to pieces without me." At the lie, she blushed. "Of course, I can't pretend to have been a particularly good housekeeper, especially not to you, to whom I've confessed just the opposite. But I did more or less hold things together at home for my father." She was so intent on her purpose now that she didn't note that at the mention of her father, his mouth had hardened and the warmth had drained from his face.

After a moment he said, "I suspect it's for exactly that reason that you wound up in here."

"Yes, but now it's done its work. It's made me well. I know I am. Look!" she cried, lifting her hands dramatically. "Look at me! My fever is gone. I'm fat as a pig. I've stopped coughing, almost entirely. I'm well: won't you say it?" She leaned forward and smiled flirtatiously at him, unconsciously copying the behavior she'd so carefully observed all around her at the san. "After all, you're like a fairy godfather to me—all you have to do is touch me once," and here she reached over and lightly, playfully, rested her fingers on his arm, "and I'll be cured."

"My dear girl," he said, in a voice she wouldn't have recognized as his, "that's hardly within my power." His face had changed utterly. He looked almost frightened of her, of her touch.

Georgia felt stung, rebuked, as much by his tone—so suddenly formal, so cold—as by what he said. She was abruptly ashamed of herself. She turned away from him quickly to look anywhere else, out the window where the sun slanted across the terrace. And there was Seward Wallace, standing motionless by a cure chair in his black suit, with that dark thatch of hair falling across his forehead, staring back in at her, a strange expression on his face.

She cleared her throat. "Well. I wonder if you can't tell me, then, when . . . how long it will be till I may hope to be released."

He shook his head. "I can't, really," he said. He too was looking out the window. Now he turned back to her. "This is something we have to monitor, Dr. Rollins and I. There is a host of factors that concern us, which we look at when we make such a decision." She met his gaze. The light, amused look was gone from his eyes. He was her doctor now, only that. He said, "Sometimes a person can seem quite well while being potentially very fragile. It's very difficult, very difficult to say."

"So you can't even suggest to me when I might be able to go home."

"I'm afraid not," he said, more gently now.

"How disappointing," she said. She was, she discovered, furious at him. *As though it were his fault she was ill.* Still, she couldn't help the chilliness in her tone. She stood, and he quickly rose too. "Well, it was kind of you to stop in to see me," she said. All she wanted was to escape him, escape herself, escape the room. She extended her hand again, and this time he shook it.

"It wasn't kindness," he said, as though he wished to prolong their talk, to begin again.

"Yes, it was," she said firmly. "It was terribly kind. And I must go up now. And rest. To speed my all-too-poky recovery." She meant to be light, she meant to mock herself, but even she could hear that she'd failed, that she sounded bitter.

Well, what could she do? She *was* bitter.

"Goodbye, then," she said, and he answered, and she turned and walked away, leaving him there among the other visitors and patients.

Seward Wallace spoke to her for the first time the day after this visit. They were gathered in the library, waiting for the bell to ring for breakfast, when he came up to her, smiling in a way that seemed artificial to Georgia, entirely too toothy.

"You've transformed yourself, I notice," he announced.

Georgia took a step back from him, from his booming voice. "Well, Mrs. Moody cut my hair, if that's what you mean."

"But you're wearing a different kind of clothing too, aren't you?" There was something accusatory in his tone. He seemed angry.

Though perhaps, Georgia thought, it was his eyebrow, the strong, dark, single eyebrow, thinned only slightly in the middle above his nose that made him look intense and uncompromising, even in repose. "I suppose I am." She shrugged. "But I outgrew all my old clothes. They didn't fit anymore."

"Ah!" he said. "Still, you look very different."

"Well, yes. I know I do."

"I'm Seward," he said abruptly. "Seward Wallace. I know your name: Georgia Rice."

"Fine," she said. "Then I don't have to bother to introduce myself, a thing I heartily detest."

He didn't return her smile. "Did you do it for him?"

"I beg your pardon?"

"For him. The man who visited you yesterday. Is it for him you've so *altered yourself*?"

His tone was unpleasant, Georgia thought, as though he were describing something contemptible. What cheek, really! "Where on earth did you get that idea?" she asked. "He's my doctor, that gentleman. Dr. Holbrooke."

He was silent a moment. "I see," he said. "You know him quite well, I take it." His voice was stiff.

"Well, of course I do. He's been our family's doctor since I was a girl. He cared for my mother in her illness. For many years."

"I see," he said.

"I should think so," she said, and walked away.

Though she wasn't angry, she thought, as she ate her breakfast: coffee with yellow cream, oatmeal and syrup and milk, eggs and bacon, and thick slices of buttered toast that you could sprinkle, if you wanted to, with a mixture of cinnamon and white sugar kept in tin shakers on the tables. What she thought was that he should be made to realize he'd been rude. You simply couldn't go around speaking to people that way.

As she conversed with the others at her table, she could see Seward Wallace across the dining room, eating silently, glancing occasionally her way.

It was Freddie he reminded her of! she thought abruptly. And with that she felt a wash of tenderness toward him. He seemed so young, really, so awkward.

And so, when he spoke to her again after the meal, almost unable to lift his eyes to her face, and asked her if she would walk out with him the next day, she consented.

When she thought about this time in her life later on, it seemed to Georgia that she had let Seward *come after her,* as they said in the san—that she'd fallen in love with him—because she felt alone and abandoned and she seized on him for comfort.

But still, she did love him. Didn't she?

Sometimes when she talked about her time in the sanatorium to me, she seemed to be saying that none of it, none of what she felt and thought then, was quite real.

She spoke to me only glancingly and indirectly of Seward, of course. It's mostly from her diaries and the letters she kept that I know anything at all about him and his relationship with my grandmother. (And from my aunt Rue, of course, who had her own version of the story.) But once I had its general outlines— the story's—I began to rehear and reinterpret various of my grandmother's remarks or asides to me over the years about her life then.

What I know for certain is that Seward was more than two years younger than she was, sixteen or seventeen to her nineteen, and that he'd been ill already for several years when she came to love him. His promising life was torn in two when, at fourteen or so, a freshman at Andover Academy—a scholarship boy whose father had been a newspaper editor before he too succumbed to tuberculosis—Seward bent over on the football field in the middle of a game and coughed up nearly a cupful of bright red blood. He was taken immediately to the infirmary, and his family was asked to remove him the next day.

His sisters, one of them a teacher, one of them not well herself, had to take in boarders to put him in the san. He'd been there ever since except for a month or so shortly before Georgia's arrival. He'd left then without the doctors' permission—run away, essentially. His sisters had had to beg and wheedle to get him back in again, he told Georgia in one of their first conversations. *"Whingeing,"* he said, "the great gift of my family," and she could hear in his voice that he loved his sisters with the easy, contemptuous love that you're allowed when you're the family pet. He'd told her he was the youngest, the only boy.

She had smiled then, and looked away, her eye caught by a motion in the distance. They had been lying side by side that day in the slatted cure chairs on the terrace. High in the air over the tree line, two hawks had lazily floated on the wind, tilting themselves this way and that to stay aloft on its currents.

After a moment she said gently, "But the doctors wouldn't have kept you out if you were truly ill?"

His mouth twisted into its characteristic bitter smile. "But of course, I *was* truly ill. And it's their pleasure, it seems to me, *to keep you out,* if they feel like it. *To lock you in.* To tell you everything you may and may not do."

Georgia shifted under her light wool blanket. "But surely it's all in the service of making you well."

"Do you truly believe that?" he asked, as if such a thing weren't possible, as if she couldn't be so simple.

"Of course I do," she said. "Of course I do or I wouldn't be here."

"Then why do as many *not* get well as do?" He turned to look at her. "Think about it and you'll see I'm right. They've no idea what works and what doesn't."

There were other chairs on either side of them, all lined up neatly in a row in the sunlight. Murmuring voices, lazy conversations rose from here and there down the line. Somewhere to the left, someone was coughing.

"But some do get well, Seward. You know that as well as I do."

"And some, who cure equally hard, die. Look at Mr. Briscombe. There was no one who worked harder at it than he did."

She was quiet a moment. She had liked Mr. Briscombe, a short, stout balding man who showed to anyone who would look a single worn photograph he carried of his children, seven of them, all indistinguishable, even male from female, all exactly like smaller versions of him—but with hair, of course. He had given her a book, *The Song of the Lark,* by a writer he thought she ought to know, a woman named Willa Cather, and Georgia had loved it.

"On the other hand," she said finally, "look at me. I'm already better. I know I am."

He did look at her with his surprising light eyes, and then he looked quickly away. The wind, which smelled unaccountably salty that day, whistled lightly in the trees.

Could he be right? Georgia was wondering. Surely it was inconceivable that the whole structure of their lives here was falsely premised. She saw Dr. Holbrooke's amused eyes, Dr. Rollins's gentle bearded face. Grown-ups, after all.

No, this was just part of Seward's darkness, his need, as she saw it, to oppose everything.

In fact, Seward was the first angry person Georgia had ever met, the first person she'd known to express rage at the hand he'd been dealt in life; and she, who was incapable of such an emotion, was drawn to him at least partly on this account. It would have been unusual then in a person his age, this degree of self-confident anger, this argued contempt for the adult educated universe, a universe that Georgia herself, even though she was the older, would never have questioned. It made her admire him, though she still felt the tender, protective pull toward him that his age and his situation demanded.

These were all new feelings for her. Her love for Bill March had been based on the great safety she felt with him, on his familiarity, his predictability. He had been an old friend—a playmate, really—from youth. He was handsome in his thick-jawed way, steady, slightly humorless. When she had imagined marriage with him, which she had allowed herself to do from time to time, she saw them leading a life together that would be a continuation of the lives they had led in their parents' homes.

The attraction Seward had for her was connected to none of that. To nothing safe, or predictable. To nothing permanent. The bond had to do with his illness itself, and then with his anger against it. And with everything that seemed to her exotic in his history: the journalist father, the exclusive boarding school, his having run away from the san.

With a host, too, of small things about him she would have been embarrassed to acknowledge the power of. The catlike, almost feral green of his eyes. How his long bony fingers looked playing the piano or holding the bagpipes—he was prodigiously musical. His shambling, touching walk. The way he held his shoulders hunched slightly, as though to hide his skinniness. The deep resonance of his voice, surprising in someone so young. A kind of burning, dark energy he conveyed.

In fact, it's possible it was his dying itself that attracted Georgia. For there was a phenomenon so common in the later stages of tuberculosis that the doctors had a name for it: *spes pthistica*, a kind of surge of life and false vitality that, oddly, often directly preceded the final decline. It served to exaggerate certain characteristics of Seward's, to make them more or less *who he was,* for that time, in that isolated place.

The day of the movies was blustery and rainy. Even during the rest period, the women on Georgia's porch talked, speculating about the evening. What the movie was reported to be. What each person thought she might wear. Whether Mr. Bethke, notoriously fickle, would come after someone else now that Miss Shepard was in the infirmary, doing so badly. Their voices rose from here, from over there, disembodied and muffled through the wet, foggy air and the thick bedding tucked up over their chins.

"I wouldn't let him get close to me," Miss Duffy said. "He's the kiss of death. She's about the third one he's loved and outlasted." Outside, the rain roared dully against the roof and into the wind-whipped trees.

"Watch out, Georgia, you may be next," someone called.

Georgia hadn't been talking, partly because she still tried to follow the rules, and partly because she couldn't speak of what she was thinking of: Seward, Seward.

"Oh, Georgia has other fish to fry," Miss Duffy said.

"Georgia has *littler* fish to fry." They laughed.

At the movie, Georgia sat by herself in the back row. Mrs. Priley beckoned her forward with a questioning face, but Georgia shook her head, pointing to the empty chair beside her, and Mrs. Priley nodded, assuming, Georgia hoped, that Seward would be coming to sit there.

Miss Duffy, who accompanied the movies, was warming up on the piano. There was the usual calling back and forth across the rows of chairs, the usual changing and rechanging of seats. ("May I sit here?" Mr. Huls asked eagerly, and Georgia said, "I'm sorry, but I was asked to save it.") Then Lewis Lunt, who worked the camera and had one withered leg, began to lurch around the room, turning off the lights, and it grew silent, but for the rippling piano and the occasional seizure of laughter or coughing.

The movie was *Tillie's Punctured Romance*, a Mack Sennett comedy. Charlie Chaplin was starring, playing a scheming city slicker, and Marie Dressler was Tillie, big and sweetly, awkwardly funny, somehow touching in her hopeful ugliness. About ten minutes into it, they'd come to a scene in which Chaplin and Dressler were precariously balanced on a log fence, flirting and alternating falling off, then scrambling up to their perches again. This was the moment, Georgia thought. She coughed, one burst. Then another. Then a long fit. She stood up and left the room, coughing all the way down the hall, in case anyone was listening.

She opened the front door of the building and stepped out into the wet black uproar outside. She circled around to the back of the san, the terrace side. Her feet and clothes were immediately soaked, so she didn't think about where she was stepping, just jolted across the flattened hillocks of grass to the cluster of twisted old apple trees. She didn't look back even once to the terrace windows, behind which the movie's gray light leapt and flickered. She was straining to see Seward under the trees. It seemed he wasn't there, and she was thinking she might turn back; then his shape separated itself slightly from the thickest trunk. She had the odd thought that it was as though he'd been part of the tree and were emerging from it. An image from her high school mythology book rose in her mind: Daphne turning into a laurel tree to escape Apollo's love. She ran to where he was and stepped in under the down-bent thick branches.

As she straightened beneath the leafy tent, his arms encircled her, she felt his breath hot on her cheek, her neck. And then, for the first time, he kissed her, his lips hard, pressing into hers, his entire bony body embracing hers. He smelled of his illness, of the brown soap they used at Bryce, of mentholatum, of rain, of flesh and fever heat. Georgia rose to her toes to push her body against his in hunger and terror and a kind of willed abandon.

Her diary entry for this day reads:

Dreary all day. The movie at night. I stole away and met Seward as he had asked me to, amongst the apple trees in the pouring rain. We went to the little gardener's shed together. Soaked. We took off our wet things. I belong to him forever now.

Eight

My grandmother gave me a diary once. A four-year diary, like the one she'd kept in her youth and young womanhood. It was on my birthday the first year I lived with them, and I remember her carefully explaining its virtues to me—how, if you kept it religiously, you could look back and get a picture of yourself living your own life: the way you'd grown or changed over the years. If she was disappointed that I didn't really use it, she never said so.

When she explained it, she told me about the journals she'd kept, about how strictly she'd held herself to the daily task when she was young, even when she didn't feel like it, even when she was sick and exhausted and wanted only to sleep, to sleep forever at the end of each busy day. She drew a picture for me then of herself, the only one awake in her father's house. How she had loved that, the delicious sense of being aware of herself, as she wasn't in the course of the day. Aware of her feelings and of herself as the one feeling them. And then she said dismissively, "Oh, you know how it is when you first think of yourself as at the center of your own universe. Maybe even somehow its creator. That was me all over."

It was then too that she told me about the prohibition against reading and writing the first weeks at the san, and how looking at the blank pages that stood for that time in her diary hurt her. "Though maybe those empty slots were just as good as words in some ways. Some things just feel empty, I suppose, and that time—those first weeks in the san—they surely did to me."

It hadn't occurred to me then that her diaries might still exist. Though if I'd thought about the way my grandparents lived—the careful preservation of everything: string, wrapping paper, corks, old clothes, old furniture—I might have wondered, anyway. As it was, it was almost by accident that I found them.

The first weekend I was in Vermont, I got sick. I could feel it descending Sunday afternoon, an afternoon I *did* spend driving down country roads, stopping in one place to pick my own apples—I remember standing on the wooden ladder, reaching through the gnarled, scaly branches, feeling a kind of pride in the way I was embracing my new life, stepping out into my new world. And then in the car, on the way home, it began: the dry throat, the tight chest. I could tell it was going to be bad. *Amazing*, I thought with a kind of detached wonderment, as though it were happening to someone else. *Amazing. It arrives. It descends.*

By the time I got home, I was feverish, and I went directly to bed. Through the night I slept and woke, getting up to take aspirin and drink water whenever I felt the fever and chills begin again. And one of the times just after the fever had faded, while I lay there in my grandmother's bed enjoying that welling gratitude you experience at simply feeling *better*, I started to think about illness itself. About how fearlessly we get sick now. It's innocent, our sickness. We're used to its meaning nothing. Miserable as we may be, we know *it's just a little flu, it's just a cold*. There's no sense of mortality connected with the experience, none of the terror of death that was part of falling ill when my grandmother was young. "Fit as a fiddle one morning and gone the next."

I pondered childbirth, which I'd so thoughtlessly undertaken three times. Always with fear of the pain, it's true, always with the anxiety that I would not endure it well, that I would somehow shame myself before the assembled multitudes in the delivery room (and why were there always so many people in there? to this day I don't understand it) but never with the idea in my mind that I might die in the process. Or *from* the process, later. Never.

Polio, I supposed, was the last of the illnesses that might have frightened me that way, and my memories of it were vague. It was the putative reason for our trips east each summer, for our long stays away from my father at my grandparents' house. West Barstow was, we understood, somehow a cleaner place, a safer place than home. A place where we could play freely with the other kids and swim in the dammed-up river and run out together in the evenings with clear glass jars to catch fireflies, all without fear of infection.

And then suddenly that fear was gone too—banished: the iron lung, the wheelchair, the thick hinged braces. It seemed there was nothing that could threaten you that doctors couldn't cure.

How different life was for my grandmother! How full of terror she must have been at every fever she had, every cough, every flushed cheek. How frightening were childbirth and infancy; she lost one child before he was a year old. Death lurked everywhere—death, and blame.

And then to have my mother succumb, as she saw it, to dementia, so long after she thought that job was well done. How terrifying it must have been, the remoteness of my mother's tranced face in her adolescence, her bewitched conversations about the instructions she had received and her need to proceed in certain ways. (That first time, in college, it was renunciation—no food, no bathing, no brushing her hair or teeth, no changing her clothes.)

And how tiny, how weak, my grandmother's arsenal was against anything. Bed rest. Rich foods. A daily nap. She herself took one all her life, just after the lunch dishes were washed and put away. The whole house fell silent in order not to disturb her sleep. I chafed under this regimen when I lived with them. I remember my restlessness in my hot room under the eaves in summer, sweating, listening to the buzzing of the hornets in their nest outside the window, idly touching myself sexually while I waited for release from the stillness and heat. "Well, thank goodness that's over," my grandmother would say briskly when she reappeared smelling of rosewater, her hair neatly repinned—ready for battle, as my grandfather put it.

She told me she used to send my mother to her room when she spoke of the voices directing her. "I'd tell her, 'I don't want to hear another word about it, Dolly. There's nobody talking here but you and me, and until you can see that plainly, I want you to sit up there and think hard about it, and I don't want you to come out until you've calmed down.' Poor girl, as though she could help any of it."

This fear, the fear that I'd pass this contamination, this disorder, on to my children, did cross my mind often, especially in their teens, which I'd learned by then was when schizophrenia frequently makes its first appearance. But each of them progressed through that period, sometimes angry or odd but clearly *healthy*. It gave me, I must say, a certain distance on whatever difficulties they did have, a distance that sometimes made them wild with irritation. "Don't you even *care?*" Karen yelled at me once, when I didn't get angry over Jeff's missing a curfew.

How to explain? I didn't, really.

Toward dawn, I slept. I woke in daylight, fevered again, to the noise of the knocker.

I decided to ignore it. It was just someone being neighborly— maybe the charming Mrs. Chick. Or a delivery. They'd leave a note, I told myself. They'd come again.

And then I heard people in the house. I was startled for a few seconds, but then I recognized the voice doing most of the talking:

Leslie. Leslie Knox, the real estate agent—of course!—leading the New York couple in. I thought of the dishes I'd left out in the kitchen—too late. Quickly I got up and opened the curtains, threw the clothes scattered around the room into a drawer, and put on my robe. I climbed back into bed, flapping and smoothing the covers over me. An orderly sickroom: the most I could be asked to offer, I thought, in my condition.

They took a long time downstairs. I could hear Leslie's voice rising and falling, the murmur of a question every now and then setting her going once more. When they arrived at the top of the stairs, I called to her. She appeared in the doorway, groomed, coiffed, a black-and-white scarf knotted flamboyantly over the shoulder of her tweed jacket.

"Oh, poor thing, you should have *phoned*!" she said, when I explained I had the flu.

"I forgot you were coming, honestly," I croaked.

She insisted they didn't need to look in the bedroom at all. "Oh, no, no, no, no. We're just getting the *idea* here, since the house isn't even on the market. I'll just shut the door, how's that, and we'll poke around super-quick up here and get out of your *hair*." The door closed behind her and then opened. "What do you need? I'll pop by later with soup and stuff."

Nothing, nothing, I assured her. She clucked some more, and I could hear her after she'd shut me in. "Can you believe it? And here we are. Oh, well, we'll just take a quick peek around. Now this is the bath. Huge, isn't it? Because it was converted, of course, from an old bedroom. You could do a lot with this space, not that it doesn't already have a certain country charm...."

After they'd left—the front door banging and Leslie's voice rising from outside now—I got up to get more aspirin. I stood in the bathroom a moment, looking from there back into the attic rooms, trying to see everything as the New Yorkers might have. It was then I noticed that the narrow door in what had been Lawrence's room—a door that led to the attic storage area—had been left open. I went to close it. Once there, though, I stepped on impulse into the attic. It was dark and cold. I reached my hand out, swung it in the thick air, and caught the pull chain. The feeble light went on, and I nearly cried out. There, placed on two trunks, staring at me gimlet-eyed and unfriendly and nightmarishly larger than I'd remembered them, were the great blue heron and the badger from my grandfather's office. I stood, my hand on my pounding chest, staring back for several seconds.

When I'd calmed down a little, I looked around. There were four or five old trunks shoved back under the eaves and some laundry cases stacked up in a corner. There were the animals, of course, and my grandmother's treadle sewing machine and her trim but buxom dress form. There were two drunken-looking chairs with broken legs, one a Queen Anne with a dusty needlepoint seat. There were some rolled-up rugs and smaller scattered rolls of what looked like wallpaper. There were various cardboard boxes of stuff, one labeled, for instance, FRAGILE: ORNAMENTS.

So this was where it had all gone: what the Duchess hadn't sold, what didn't fit in the new decor. I felt a kind of warm, growing plea-sure of possession, of appetite. It was all still here, then—my past, my mother's past, my grandparents' life.

When I'd shut the door behind me and gone back to bed, I lay there daydreaming of the treasure for a while before I fell asleep again.

A few days later, recovered except for a periodic sag of fatigue, I carried the heron and the badger out to the hall. In daylight they looked particularly pathetic, like very old, very sick animals, but I wanted them downstairs somewhere anyway, reminding me of how things had been.

The trunks, I discovered, were all locked—against the tenants, perhaps, or thieves. I explored the house for likely keys. There were none, only extra house keys and skeleton keys for the inner doors.

In the end I took a screwdriver upstairs and used it to pop the locks, feeling a vandal's recklessness as I heard the mechanisms yield within.

The first trunk held woolens. An old suit of my grandfather's, sweaters, a few thick blankets I remembered from childhood—late in the summer, as the nights began to grow cold, they'd emerge, smelling of camphor. As they did now, the heavy fabrics, when I lifted them out. In the very bottom was one of those fox stoles elegant women like my grandmother wore in the forties and fifties, the fox's head still attached, the lower jaw fixed with springs. To keep the stole in place, you arranged it so the fox, who in this case was slightly cross-eyed, bit his own tail. "It's not enough that he's dead," my grandfather used to say. "He's got to look idiotic for all eternity too."

"Mere commentary," my grandmother would say. She said this to him often, and it always made him laugh in response.

I put the woolens back and turned to the next trunk. It was full of papers, mostly bank statements, check registers, tax forms, and bills, all arranged in labeled folders: HOUSEHOLD, AUTOMOBILE, HOBBIES, CHILDREN, WEDDINGS. I set these last two files aside to look at more carefully later.

Another trunk held linens: pressed napkins and pillowcases and runners and tablecloths, delicately browned over time. The remaining trunks and the laundry cases contained more linens, some legal documents, bundles of letters from their children and grandchildren, neatly sorted—I recognized my own handwriting in one stack, my mother's in another. Here was a dissecting kit; a tarnished clarinet, carefully taken apart and laid in its case; a tackle box, the flies arranged in rows, like colorful botanical specimens. The Christmas ornaments, as promised, old-fashioned and simple.

The last trunk held elaborate old undergarments and nightgowns that must have been my grandmother's as a young woman. I lifted up a chemise, a long full petticoat with a crocheted hem. It occurred to me that these were just the kinds of things that Fiona would wear, not as undergarments but as clothing. And she was coming to visit Columbus Day weekend. I put them back. We could go through them together then.

I was tired by now. I took some of the packets of letters with me—mine among them, of course. It wasn't until Fiona's visit a month later that I ventured into the attic again.

She came up on the train from New York on Friday. I drove to Rutland to pick her up. I hadn't been on a train in years, and just being in the station made me nostalgic. Fiona herself was wildly excited by the trip, chattering away practically as she stepped onto the platform about how awesome it had been, the view into all those towns and places you'd never see otherwise. "But I mean their *backsides*, Mom," she said.

I hadn't seen her since early in the summer, when she'd been home for a few weeks before she started a job back east. She'd gotten thinner, and her hair had grown out quite a bit from the virtual crew cut she'd had the year before. She looked lovely to me. She was small and sprightly and had her father's delicate skin and features. She wore a big sheepskin coat that flapped open over the shortest possible skirt, black tights, and big boots. She carried a backpack that she heaved into the rear of the car before she got in.

When she'd fastened her safety belt, she turned sideways to look at me behind the wheel and said, "Tell all, *s'il vous plaît*."

I laughed; this was so typical of her. She was my last child and by far the most outgoing, the sunniest. Life, she clearly felt, had been arranged for her pleasure. She was open and curious and interested in everyone. As a little girl, she used to drag home the most unlikely playmates; in high school, her friends included the nerds as well as the popular kids. "Fiona casts a wide net," we used to say after meeting yet another of her adoptees.

"No, you tell me," I said. And she did. Some of it anyway. By the time we got home I knew about the piercing place she'd gone to for her ears (PAIN OPTIONAL, the sign said), about what you could play on the jukebox at her favorite bar (*"Lili Marlene";* "Ain't Nobody Here but Us Chickens"), about the boy she'd dated in the summer, the boy she was dating now, and uh—oh, yes!—about her courses.

We went into the attic the next morning, and as I had hoped, she was wild about the old underthings. Together we pulled out the pieces of white cotton, and as she claimed them—the eyelet camisoles would be lovely tops, the nightgowns with crocheted straps and bodices the most delicate of summer dresses, the hem-stitched petticoats long pretty white skirts—as she cried out over them and pulled one or two on over her jeans and sweater, I thought of my grandmother in her youth, the pinned-up heavy hair, the pale smooth skin, the trim small body, putting on this one or that. They would be pretty on Fiona too, even though it was an odd combination—Fiona, with her multiple earrings and geometrically cut hair, her unplucked eyebrows, her wine-red lipstick, wearing the pretty underclothes of another era as summer finery.

We emptied the top tray in the trunk and lifted it out. We worked our way down through the second level. "More, more. I'm a greedy girl," Fiona said, reaching for the handles of the second tray and lifting it out.

We looked in. No more clothing. Just a quilt, old and faded. "Phooey," she said.

"But it's lovely, Fee. Look." I bent over it. And as I lifted it out, three or four things slid out from its folds back into the trunk, thunking the bottom as they fell.

"Qu'est-ce que c'est?" Fiona said, peering in. "Hey, books!" She reached down and scooped several up. They were small, leather-bound, in black and dark red. She opened one. I could see the pale ink, the rhythmic cursive writing.

"God, they're diaries!" I said. I bent into the trunk for another one. It was a square brown book, a young girl's diary, clearly; the handwriting inside was childish. I recognized the name on the fly-leaf as belonging to one of my grandmother's aunts. Interspersed with the short entries were faint drawings done in pencil: houses, long vistas, flowers.

I bent down again and lifted out a set of small thin notebooks, tied together with ribbon. I undid them and opened the top one. It was my great-great-grandmother's, Sally Parsons, the woman who had come by wagon to rescue Georgia after her mother died and rode away empty-handed. The ink in these had faded to pale brown, and some of the pages were breaking apart at the edges. The diaries ran for seven years, 1869–1876.

"Oh, I get it!" Fiona said abruptly. "It's *weather*!"

"What?" I asked. I looked over at her. She had been reading through the book she had picked out first. She was sitting on a trunk under the weak light of the single bare bulb, wearing a long white cotton slip over her sweater and jeans and heavy boots.

She grinned at me. "See, I couldn't figure it out at first. Every entry says, 'Lovely day,' 'Lovely day,' and I was thinking, Now *here* is the cheerful type! and then there's one that says 'Cloudy day,' and another, 'Gray day.'"

"Whose is that one?" I asked.

"The diary?" She flipped back to the front. "Georgia Rice. And then she's added *Holbrooke*." She looked up at me. "Gran."

She lifted the book and read aloud:

"January 12. Lovely day. John in the office all day. Maudie Osbourne came over and we went together to call on Laura Kendall. She's getting better, but hasn't gone out yet. I knitted in the evening. John read aloud chapters 8 and 9.

"January 13. Lovely day. It snowed a little this evening, John out most of the day, driving from here to there. A long time with Mrs. Wood, but the baby came fine in the end. Didn't she yell though, he said. You would too, I told him. I finished a sweater, started on leggings. John read. I'll be glad to be done with Hardy."

Fiona looked up and grinned. "Well, Anaïs Nin she ain't."

She looked down and was about to start again. "Fee," I said. I couldn't bear it. She looked at me, startled. She could hear the discomfort in my voice. "Don't read any more, honey," I said. "It just means too much to me."

"Oh! Well. Of course, Mom. I was just having fun. I wasn't thinking anything about it."

"I know. And I'm sure they are fun. They'll be fun. But I guess I'd just like to have time to take them in first."

"Well, sure."

"Do you mind?"

"No. No, of course not. I have my treasure," she said, scooping up her pile of underclothes, "and you have yours."

And while she gathered her hoard together and chatted to me about each piece, I made a little pile of the books and sat with them on my lap, as though it were nothing to me to wait.

Of course, I read them all. I was a greedy girl too. And then I read them again, and again. It was all I did for several days after Fiona left. And slowly pieces of the puzzles began to fall into place. Not all the pieces, not all the puzzles. But the one story among all the others in the trunk that I wanted to understand, those few years of my grandmother's life, this shifted and sharpened and pulled into perspective. Some of it. Enough for it to become imaginable to me. Enough for me to begin to make a long narrative of the disparate stories she had told me over the years, and to pull in even some of the stories others had told me. Rue, for instance. Or my grandfather. Or my mother, the few times she had spoken clearly of her past or her parents.

Later on, when I understood the story more fully, I wondered why my grandmother had held on to her diaries. I would have destroyed them if I'd had such documents. I would never have wanted my children—or their children when they came—to know the way I made the decisions that resulted in their lives, to know the way I thought and felt when I was young.

But then my diary would have revealed all that, as my grandmother's, initially anyway, seemed not to. My diary would have been more about the person that went through the days than it was about the days themselves—their weather, their events—as hers seemed to be. And yet tonally I could feel her in that careful record. I could imagine her voice expanding the compressed version I was reading, I could imagine her way of telling the story. What I felt, I think, as I read and reread the diaries, was that I was somehow coming to know her, to understand what her deeper thoughts were under the quotidian of the surface. What I felt was that understanding these slender books would somehow let me piece together too what lay under the later loving surface of my grandparents' lives together.

I suppose in our contemporary lives, our cumulative e-mail might constitute a kind of diary: that informal, moment-by-moment description of life as it goes by. And sometimes when I'm looking through my sent mail on the computer—to see what I've told someone about a date or a time or an event in my life—I'm struck by that sense of a record made. My computer letters from Vermont to my children and friends, for instance, certainly would have worked that way. Especially my notes to Karen. By now, because of some episodes of early contractions, she'd been sent to bed by her doctors for the remainder of her pregnancy—nothing to worry about, she assured me. But I could imagine her boredom, her restlessness, so I wrote to her often, sometimes several times a day, reporting whatever struck me or interested me in what I saw or read or did. As I think about those notes now—what I wrote, what I said—it seems to me they danced across the surface just as my grandmother's diaries did—Anaïs Nin she wasn't, and I wasn't either, of course. Who is? Not even Anaïs Nin. Still, on occasion I would actually feel a vague sense of loss as I trashed them. But what would have been the point of keeping them? Who would care, ever, to reconstruct a life from such details? It would have taken someone as obsessed with me as I was with my grandmother to make any deep sense of these notes of mine. And as far as I knew, there was no one so obsessed with me. No one likely to be either. No one with any reason for such an obsession. My children understood my life. There was not that constant division between the surface and the depths of it; and I'd been careful to explain the differences to them when there was.

I had my reasons for mine with my grandmother. For one thing, she was a woman who'd grown up in another time—another universe, really. Understanding who she was and what she was to me depended on understanding that unfamiliar universe too. And then of course there was the mystery lying between us, the mystery of my mother, of her illness, which I'd spent my life worrying at the meaning of. All this fed my appetite for what could be extracted from the accounts of my grandmother's seemingly ordinary life.

I set myself up in my grandfather's study. I laid everything out neatly in a kind of time line: the diaries, her relatives' diaries, the letters from my grandmother and from others to her, the files of bills and receipts, the financial records. As my life unfolded in Vermont, as I lived it and wrote about it to friends and to the children ("Karen, dear, it's a fine day today, just what you might imagine New England in the fall to be"), I was living her life too, it was running steady as a buried stream under mine.

And my life? I complicated it, of course. I looked for ways to attach myself here, for that was the point, wasn't it? To see if I could. To see what there was to attach myself to.

I discovered a few movie theaters within driving distance that showed what my kids used to call "fillums"—anything other than action and violence and spectacle. I bought the village paper. I bought the regional paper. I went up to the bulletin boards at the town hall, at the post office, at Grayson's, for information. I gave myself assignments. Set myself *in motion*. I began to attend a reading group that met weekly at the library. I went to a cider festival, a baked bean dinner. I helped serve at a church potluck. Slowly a few people began to greet me by name as I moved about the town. I had Leslie and her husband over for dinner to thank her for her kindness to me while I was sick—she *had* brought me soup, and flowers too.

I had coffee several times at a little shop on the green. I spoke one day to my high school boyfriend, Sonny Gill, when I stopped to refuel my car. He was as he'd come to be very quickly after high school—thick, graceless, his face deeply seamed with what looked like worry but probably wasn't: he seemed singularly cheerful. And very loud, which surely he hadn't been then. I didn't remember it anyway. Several of his teeth were gone. He still smoked. "Don't be a stranger," he said when I left.

I got a paying job too, of sorts. I went to the town paper—a weekly—and offered myself as a writer. They didn't really need anyone, the man at the front desk (the editor, it turned out) said. Except (laughter here) to do sports—the implication being that I wouldn't qualify as a sports writer. This irritated me, this assumption, so of course I said I'd do it, and we agreed on a trial column: I'd cover a crucial football game the next Saturday for the Barstow Catamounts, to be played away, in a town just the other side of Rutland.

When I got home, I called Samuel Eliasson to see if he'd go with me.

Samuel was my tenant, inherited from Rue along with the house, the man I'd forced to move out so I could move in, the man who wanted to buy my grandmother's house. He was living for the time being in another big rental house on the green, the Gibson house. He was a tall man in his seventies with a head of silver-white hair, and I'd run into him several times by now—the first time when he introduced himself to me at the potluck. Since then, he'd stopped over once to say that if the house presented any problems or complications I couldn't manage, he'd be glad to try to help. That he knew it rather well by now. I liked him for the flattering, courtly charm that elderly men sometimes offer to women my age. And in this case, I thought that since he'd been a college professor, he might know something about football. I didn't, really. Jeff had played soccer in high school.

We went. We had a good time. There were no bleachers, nowhere to sit, so you meandered up and down the sidelines with the action, trying to see through the flailing bodies to figure out what was going on. Early on, it started to rain. Slowly the boys on the field were covered with mud. By the end, you couldn't see their numbers, let alone the color of their uniforms. I screamed myself hoarse. Barstow won.

We stopped in Rutland for supper on the way home, and Samuel helped me make sense of the scattered notes I'd taken. Over the next few days I wrote the column. I submitted it to him first. He sat opposite me in my grandmother's back parlor, a tall, lanky old man, his long legs stretched out in front of him, grayish tennis shoes on his feet, and peered through his half glasses at my rough draft.

"Well, see, Cath, this is a form that needs to be completely predictable," he said. "Nobody wants anything new, anything very personal." He laughed. "Nothing even very interesting, really. So the description here: the weather, the crowd"—he shook his head and looked over his glasses at me—"out." He looked like a stern old headmaster.

"Yessir," I said.

He suggested more violent alternatives to all my verbs: *hit, pounded, hammered, squashed, sacked, flattened*. "Those are really *de rigueur*," he said. He added a string of corny adjectives, always preceded by an article: "the burly O'Connor," "the speedy Evans," "the indomitable Reed." "There!" he said when he was done, when he handed it back to me. "Now *that's* sports writing."

They loved it. I was on, for $25 a column. When I wrote the next one—by myself this time—I kept his editorial advice in mind and doctored my own language as I went.

We took Fiona to a game with us the weekend she was in town. She was charmed by Samuel, by his way of speaking. "Imagine saying 'I'm completely at your service, madam.'" She was cleaning up after our supper, hers and mine, and imitating Samuel, his answer when I reminded him of the following week's game. "Think of it, Mom. No guy I date will ever, ever, say that to me."

"I'm not *dating* Samuel."

"Did I say you were? Very touchy. Should I say ... too touchy?"

"You should not," I answered. "He's old enough to be my father." I did the math. "Well, almost."

We worked side by side at the sink for a few minutes. Then she said, "Speaking of fathers. Or of people who ought to be older than they are. I saw Joe."

"Did you? In New York?"

"Yep. There on business of some sort. He called and we had dinner."

"Was it okay?"

Fiona had been the most angry of the kids at Joe about the breakup. She had been very angry, actually, and this was so unlike her that we were all a little frightened. And secretly relieved too, I suppose. She acted out for all of us. Called him an asshole, slammed doors. For a while after he moved out, she refused to see him, *to be reasonable,* as he put it.

"I *am* reasonable," she said. "This jerk is abandoning me. He's saying 'go fuck yourself,' and I'm saying to him, 'No, excuse me, excuse me, *you* go fuck *your*self.'"

"In whose world does this pass for reason?" Karen had asked.

"Oh, it's just the language you object to," she said. "Get over it. Think about what I'm saying. You know I'm right."

When she finally did consent to see Joe, she was sarcastic, unpleasant. She rode him mercilessly. She wasn't interested in meeting Edie either. Joe had somehow imagined, I think, that he could have us all. Not quite all together, but all within his emotional purview anyway, all still somehow his family. Fiona was the one who said *no*, clearly. No. He'd walked out on her and was not to be allowed to forget that.

She shrugged now. "I suppose. It was a little polite, if you know what I mean."

I laughed. "Let me see if I can imagine that. You. Polite."

She smiled back. "Well, I mostly meant him, actually. He was polite. Careful, I would say."

I waited a minute before I asked, "And did that make you feel triumphant, dear?"

"It didn't." She sighed. "It made me sad, really."

I said nothing.

Her back was to me now, her long neck elegant but somehow also vulnerable. She was putting the tops on the jars and bottles left out on the counter. She said, "He showed me pix of the kid. Mariel."

"She's cute, isn't she?"

"All kids are cute, Mom."

"Not so. Though you, of course, et cetera, et cetera."

She crossed to the refrigerator and began to put the cream away, the bottled water. When she turned around, she was frowning. "Wasn't that the Cuban boat thing, you know, with all the criminals? The *Mariel*?"

"That sounds right."

"Anyway," she said.

"It's still a nice name."

"I said so." She leaned against the counter, facing me. "I also said, 'So what will you do when she's not so cute and little anymore and you want new babies to go goo-goo over? Begin again?'

"And he got all stiff and said, you know, *This was his child, how could I speak that way?* And I said, 'Well, I guess 'cause for a long time I thought of myself as your child too.'"

"Oh, Fee," I said.

"Yeah," she answered glumly.

In spite of my defensiveness with Fiona, the truth was that as the fall wore on I found myself looking forward more and more to my Saturdays with Samuel. The long drives to the games reminded me of drives I'd taken here and there with my grandfather as a teenager—drives designed, in all likelihood, to let my grandmother have some solitude. Samuel even looked a little like my grand-father, white-haired and handsome, with not a sign of balding. He had the same strong beaky nose, the same olive palette to his skin. He towered over me, even though he was beginning, like my grand-father too, to stoop a little. He even dressed a bit like him. Oh, not as formally; Samuel was an academic type, after all. Corduroy pants, tweed jacket, and, almost invariably, the old tennis shoes. But he did wear the jacket every time we were together, and whenever we did anything special—and the games were apparently special to him—he wore a tie, too.

And as we made our way on those Saturday mornings to one town or another in a wide circle around Barstow, we talked in the same desultory and yet somehow deeply satisfying way I'd talked with my grandfather.

What of?

Books, I remember. He loved Edith Wharton, which I found sur-prising. Except, he told me, for *Ethan Frome*.

"Same here," I said.

He sometimes brought a couple of books to loan to me. Occa-sionally history—I remember reading *Changes in the Land* with his careful notes, all but illegible to me, in the margins—but he loved contemporary fiction too. I first read Penelope Fitzgerald when he introduced me to her. "Such witty economy," he said admiringly, as he handed over two thin volumes. "A hard act to pull off."

Of course, it's easier for me to recall what he told me than what I told him. What would I have felt compelled to fill him in on? My situation, yes. I know I described that generally, mostly by way of letting him know how confused I was about the house—the house he wanted. Wanted for his own. "If I came here . . . I don't know," I said to him, "it would change my life. My work, my friendships. I suppose at least some of my bad habits."

I remember that he laughed at that. "Surely you have no bad habits," he said.

I must have spoken to him about the children: Fiona, whom he would meet; Jeff, so far away, so happy being so far away and what that might mean about his future; Karen, who was discovering and reporting to me via e-mail from her bed about the astonishments of daytime TV, a revelation to her.

And Samuel? Well, he talked to me about his work, I remember, though I had to prod him to get the details. "What *kind* of writing?" I asked.

"Oh, it's just a small project, I don't know that I'll ever finish. The kind of thing an old professor undertakes when he's retired."

"And what kind of thing might that be?" This was very early in our friendship, I remember, when I still found myself impatient with his slowness, his indirection.

He heard it. "I'm sorry. I'm not trying to be evasive." He smiled. "Though it may be that it comes naturally. Certainly my wife would have said so." His expression, at that moment, with those words, was suffused with a kind of rueful regret. He was a widower, and I'd noticed this complicated sorrow on his face whenever his wife was mentioned. "It's essays. On the death of a group of towns in Massachusetts in the thirties. I've written, I would say, three and about a half so far. It's taken two years." He smiled.

"So, what's your . . . *angle,* I guess?" Hearing myself, I grimaced. "Nasty word, isn't it?"

"It's a modern word. And it's a question a publisher would ask me, I imagine, if it ever got to that stage." He was silent a moment. Then he said, "That may be the problem. I don't think I have one. I just want to record it. The towns' histories, some of what happened as they died. You know, stories."

"It sounds suspiciously like a book."

"It may be, I suppose. Depends on what gets finished first, it or me. It's essays, for now."

He spoke of his fondness for my grandmother's house. "I found a real pleasure in its shotgun arrangement," he said. "The way each day I had to walk through all the rooms to get to the few I used. From bedroom to kitchen, where I ate, and then back to that little room off the kitchen that I used as a study when in residence. No room went unvisited, as it were." He paused to look out the window. We were driving past a little waterfall. "I miss that at the Gibsons', where I don't have any idea what's going on in most of the rooms." Now he grinned at me. "Why, there could be others living there with me, for all I know."

This charmed me, and I smiled back at him.

It was his wife, it turned out—with my aunt Rue's permission—who'd done the redecorating. I asked him once what his wife was like. We were driving home; I always drove. I was the hostess on these trips. I picked him up, though he would never let me pay for the treats we usually bought—soft-serve cones at the Dairy Queen, beer at a country inn.

He was silent a long time. I didn't look at him. Finally he said quietly, "She was a fine person. Discerning, I would say."

"Now *that's* a lovely word. Discerning."

"Yes. And true. True of her. Discerning of beauty. Of what was right.

"I think she was often unhappy with me," he said, after a moment. He cleared his throat. "Well, of course she missed the opportunity to work, to have that kind of life—that was hard for many women her age, you know. To see life, and the opportunities of life, change so dramatically just after you'd made all your choices—difficult. It made her doubly critical of *my* choices. But I think, even aside from that, she found me ... well, a little sloppy, I'd say. That I'd settled for something so unambitious, so unlikely to do the world much good. An old professor, at what was really a teaching college. Not even a university."

We drove along in silence for a while. He broke it.

"But of course, what I felt was that I was in the world, that I couldn't afford her delicacy." I nodded. "And she felt, I suppose, that I'd sold my soul somehow. And finally, I think, she came to feel that the academic life was not much to have gotten in return."

He turned to me. I felt his attention and looked over at him. He was smiling.

"That was it, the bedrock of our argument with each other." He looked away.

I didn't know what to say, what he was telling me.

"I miss her," he said. His voice sounded scraped and tired, suddenly. "I miss the argument itself."

"Yes," I said, because I didn't know what else to say.

Even this somehow reminded me of my grandfather. When I thought of those comments and the way Samuel had looked, making them, I remembered the moments between my grandparents when some bitterness that stayed submerged most of the time would suddenly surface. I remembered my perplexity as a child over this and then, when I was an adolescent, my sense of embarrassment—mostly, I think, for my grandfather, shamed as he seemed by something in it.

It made me think about my marriages. If Peter and I had stayed together, or Joe and I, would the price have been the pushing under of whatever enraged or disappointed each of us in the other? Or would we have come to some forgiving peace that included the anger?

Or was that forgiveness at all, if the anger still lived there underneath the peace?

When Samuel spoke, I wanted somehow to comfort him, though I said nothing. I suppose I was afraid to seem to be criticizing his wife.

We talked about the diaries one day. The diaries and the other material. I told him about my compulsive reading and rereading.

"Ah, you've got the bug," he said.

"Is that what it is?" I asked. "Is that what it feels like to you when you're doing research on something?"

"Very much."

"Without the personal connection, though."

"No, absolutely with it. I think if you don't feel connected, if you don't feel that what you're figuring out is going to answer something personally for you, then you don't do it. *I* can't imagine doing it, at any rate."

"So what was answered personally for you by writing about railroads?" I was referring to his most famous book, *The End of the Line.* I'd looked it up in the town library, where there was an inscribed copy. "Large-hearted" it was called on the jacket copy taped inside. "Magisterial and comprehensive." In the photograph cut from the jacket and taped there too, he was perhaps in his early forties, a seriously ravishing man in a theatrical pose: squinting into the middle distance, a half-smoked filterless cigarette raised partway to his face in curved fingers. A tweed jacket, naturally, but the shirt under it open at the neck. It pleased me to see he'd been vain then; that he wanted the world to see his image shaped in this romantic way. Later I wondered what his wife had thought of this photo—the vanity apparent in it.

"Aha!" he said. "You've been poking around in *my* past too."

"Well, I assume you want people poking around in that part of your past."

"Of course it was written to be read, yes. But not the way a diary is."

"But a diary isn't, is it?" I asked. "Written to be read? By anyone but the diarist, I mean."

"No?"

"No. Absolutely no. You write it for yourself."

"Then why do you hold on to it?"

"To look back over your own life. To see how things were for you at a set time, how you felt about them and understood them then."

"And then why don't you, at a certain point in old age, let's say—if it really is just for yourself—destroy it?"

"Oh, who knows?" I said. I thought he was being difficult. "Maybe you're too ill. Or tired. Or you've forgotten it, with everything else that presses in."

"But what presses in more than the past when you're old?"

"I don't know. The notion of dying, maybe?"

"Ah, but that's what makes the past press in."

"So what are you saying?"

"Just that I can imagine your grandmother imagining *you* reading her diary."

"No." I shook my head. "No. I honestly don't think that. If you could see them. While they're not very intimate, they're really ... private, somehow.

"No," I went on. "What *I* imagine is that it would be like killing your past, like killing yourself, in a way, to destroy it. And so you just don't. You don't get around to it. You might tell yourself you would tomorrow. Or when you knew you were nearly gone. But it's so hard to believe that ever, I would think. That you really are going to be *gone*. And then you *are* dying, and it's too late."

"But you see, I think all that is true, and I also think at some level your grandmother must have intended you to read them."

"But Rue inherited the house first, remember. Not I. If she'd found them, they would have been long gone."

"But she was so much less likely to."

"To ...?"

"To find them. Even to look."

"How do you know that about Rue?"

"You forget, I dealt with her through the mail for some years. A less sentimental woman, at least on paper, I've never encountered. *She* wouldn't have been poking through things, looking for her past. When Maggie wanted to redecorate, she figuratively washed her hands of everything. We could have thrown it all away, as far as she was concerned. 'Sure, do what you like': that was her tone. Which was lovely for us, of course, to be able to make it ours, more or less. But that's how she was about it. It was Maggie who felt we couldn't chuck anything, and it was I who hauled most of it to the attic, at her behest."

"So *you* put it all up there."

"Well, some of it was there already. Your grandmother's dress form, for instance. Charming." He smiled. "It made me think of the professor's house."

"What professor?"

"*The Professor's House.* The Cather novel."

"Oh." I nodded, feeling stupid.

"There's a dress form in an attic in that book, actually several of them, I think, and the eponymous professor, who more or less hides away from his own life up there, is, as I recollect, comforted by them."

"Yes, I remember it," I said. After a moment I said, "And is this you? Are you the professor somehow?"

He laughed. "No." Then his face fell. "No, I was quite happy downstairs."

When we got back that afternoon, I invited him in. I made us warm cider, with a shot of bourbon—the game that day had been chilly, and by the end, sunless—and we went back into my grandfather's study. I showed him the way I'd grouped the documents I had. I wanted his approval, I think: *yes, this is exactly the way a historian would proceed.* But he seemed unamazed at any of it, except for the diaries themselves. Those he lifted almost reverentially, opened carefully.

Afterward I asked him to make us a fire in the back parlor, and we sat, sipping the cider and eating crackers and cheese for a while. I wondered if he was thinking of similar darkening fall afternoons spent here with his wife. I wondered what they might have been speaking of.

I was talking about my deepening sense of my grandmother's life, in particular everything that I had come to understand about tuberculosis and the shame and fascination of the san, and what a revelation that was to me. "That's what the task of the historian must be—is it? To explain how life *felt* as it went by. Not just what happened, but how differently it signified: what happened."

"Yes, that's apt," he said. "I've often thought of it as like anthropology. Like explaining the rules of another culture, another country. Which it seems to me the past is, in some sense."

He thought for a few moments. The fire hissed.

"I'm sure there are countless other things that would be as revelatory if you knew of them. If you were looking for them. They'd change the ground under the story."

"Like what, do you think?"

"Oh, well. Let's use my wife as an example. She was a believer. Religious. And that was always present in her life in a way I sometimes lost track of, since I'm not. Or at least not in the way she was. For her it was, I would say, the central invisible fact of her life. And yet you could write her life's story without including it if you didn't know specifically about it. It was simply underneath everything else. As it may well have been for your grandmother. Probably was, in point of fact."

"Do you think so?"

"I can't know, really. But she was a churchgoer till the last. I remember that. We used to see her there every Sunday in the summers we were up before she died, in one or another of her hats. Many hats." He smiled at me. "You will remember them."

"Yes," I said. I stretched my legs out, toward the fireplace.

"Now maybe she went for the sociability, or just because she'd always gone. But maybe, just maybe, she was a believer. A true believer. And then, if that was so, it would raise other questions. You'd have to know, for instance, what kind of a believer. Did she see each moment of her life as given by God: here, a test to rise to, there, a moment of grace? Or did she just assume him as a benefi-cent presence? Somehow, maybe even casually, in charge of every-thing."

"I see," I said. "Yeah. Well, all that would make a difference, wouldn't it?"

"It would. But it's not something she's likely to have written about explicitly."

"No," I said. "No, I don't think I've come across it. Explicitly." I'd been staring into the fire, as one does. Now, because he was silent, I looked at him. He was watching me, frowning.

"What?" I asked.

"Oh, sorry. I was just wondering, I suppose. What you would say the central fact of *your* life is. The one that I can't see."

"Maybe you see it all," I said.

He laughed and shook his head.

"No, really. I'm a thoroughly modern woman, after all. Maybe what you see"—I raised my arms—"is exactly what you get."

As he set his mug down, he said, "Now that is something I very much doubt."

I smiled. We sat in silence for a long moment. A log shifted and scattered sparks on the hearth. "It must feel odd to sit here with me," I said at last. I gestured around with my cup.

"No. In what way—odd?"

"Oh, I mean that it was yours for so long. I've stolen it out from under you in some sense."

"Well, you've hardly stolen it."

"Yes, but you know what I mean." I sat up straighter. "Come on, Samuel, I'm saying I'm *sorry*."

"Don't be." He smiled. "If I'd had my way, I'd have stolen it all out from under *you*. But we'd still be sitting right here."

"What do you mean?"

"Oh, just that I would have offered *you* the drink."

I grinned at him. "You should have got to Rue before she died," I said. "Bad planning."

"I tried. Believe me. No, actually I think she had some sense of obligation to you. To hold on to it for you."

"Did she say that?"

"I inferred it. What she said was that there were others—other heirs—she'd have to consult. I went so far as to check to see who these others might be—I thought I might try approaching them on my own—but of course it was hers and hers alone. There were no others. So she was either thinking of you as an heir, even though you weren't technically, or she was just lying to put me off."

I was remembering Rue. "It's really very strange if she did think of it that way. We hadn't been in touch for a long time. I didn't much like her. I lived with her once," I offered. "One summer. In Paris. She took me in."

"That doesn't sound so evil. Very auntlike, actually."

"Well, she meant to remake me, I think. I was more her project than her guest. She disapproved of the way I was growing up. And to a degree, she succeeded. In remaking me, I mean. New haircut, new way of dressing." I shook my head. "I came back here completely unsuited to be a high school senior in rural Vermont. But I suppose it was helpful later—to have seen that other world. That other way of being." I smiled at him. "I was *very* chic in college." I thought of myself then, wearing skirts and little heels when everyone else was in blue jeans.

"I can imagine," Samuel said. "You're still chic."

"Ah, but I'm in rural Vermont again. That helps enormously."

"Nonsense. You'd be dazzling wherever you went."

"Well. Thank you," I said, after a little pause. I was embarrassed, suddenly. I hoped I wasn't blushing. Was this a kind of pass? Or just an older man being courtly, being kind to a slightly younger woman? I couldn't tell, I realized, and it made me uncomfortable. I thought of what Fiona had said on her visit earlier. *Was* I, in some sense, dating Samuel? Had *he* seen this as a date? Was that why he sat on now, as the windows grew dark?

"More cider?" I asked.

As if he had read my mind, he stood up. "No," he said. "No, it's time for me to be getting home."

After Samuel left, I heated up some soup for supper, thinking of him. Was he interested? Was I?

And then I thought, *No*, that I was misreading everything. That I'd been right earlier; what seemed like interest was just a kind of courtliness, Samuel's way of being polite. Still, carrying my bowl of soup back to my grandfather's study, sitting down at the old desk and beginning to read through my grandmother's diaries once again, looking for references, specific or oblique, to religion, I found myself thinking of Samuel from time to time—just his face, and the way his smile lifted it suddenly from its melancholic cast.

There were only a few entries in the diary concerned with belief or nonbelief. Georgia wrote of churchgoing, of course, and, yes, what she wore to church too. Occasionally she named someone she'd encountered there. Sometimes she mentioned the topic of a sermon—the prodigal son, or the signs of God's goodness around us.

She wrote about an argument she'd had with Bill March once about whether God intended the Allies to win the war.

I cannot think He would take sides in such a question which seems to me an argument only between men. Bill says I am wrong, that He is always on the side of right. It made us unhappy to disagree, so we stopped speaking of it.

She was troubled, more than once, by Seward Wallace's doubt of God's existence.

Seward thinks I am foolish to pray for his recovery, or mine, that if there is a God, He is so cruel that such a thing couldn't possibly matter to Him. I do not know if this could be, but I do not like to think so.

On New Year's Day, 1920, four months after her return home from the san, she wrote:

So ends this year, a year of so much turmoil and change in my life. So many hopes and fears and joys and sorrows. I wish that I could better apprehend our reason for being on this earth and that I could set a better example for Ada and Fred. That I could be better prepared to live, and so to die too of course. G.L.R.

Two weeks later, she married my grandfather.

PART TWO

Nine

Colorado. It was Seward's dream. In Colorado the air was a rinsed blue, cloudless and dry, above the towering Rockies. He had a postcard that showed its magnificence. Thousands, he told Georgia, had gone out there and been cured. And then stayed on, to start a new life in a place where you could do anything, be anything. Couldn't she picture them there? How it could be?

They were lying together in the dusty toolshed, on the narrow cot kept there for the gardener to nap on. It was after dinner, almost time to return for their nightly rituals: the thermometer, the mugs of thick milk, and then the long restless wait for sleep on the cure porches, the sky still faintly light till nine or later.

Georgia's head rested on Seward's chest, and within it she could hear the whirring, the ticking of his breathing, as well as what felt like the overemphatic slow thud of his heart on each beat. They were dressed. They had never been undressed in each other's presence after that first night; there was always too much risk of being discovered. Their lovemaking had become a matter of unbuttoning a bit here and there, of sliding Georgia's skirts up to her waist, of pushing fabric aside. Seward hungrily stared at Georgia's flesh where it was exposed, but Georgia had no wish to see Seward's body. She could feel its thinness—the bones of his pelvic cage driving into her as he lay between her legs, the hard arch of his ribs sheltering his weakened lungs, the knobs of his spine under her hands when she held him, the pronounced ridge of his clavicle where her fingers rested now. It broke her heart to touch him through his clothing, to unbutton his shirt and rest her hand on the working oven of his chest, to feel his heart shake his body.

But it wasn't only this that kept her from wanting to look, and she knew it. It wasn't just his unbearable boniness, the mark of his disease. It was also the sex itself. It was the sheer embarrassment of it. She didn't understand it, truly, what it was all about. The parts she enjoyed and would have liked lingering over—the teasing beforehand, the gentle touching—these were always rushed now, too soon over. And then there was all that desperate huffing and puffing, and—so quickly afterward!—Seward's pained cries, one, and then another, and another.

She held him then, she loved him for his crying out, for his need of her, for the way he lifted himself from her when he was finished and looked so hard at her, seeming to see her most clearly then, to wish to burn her face into memory. And she loved this too, perhaps most of all—the lying still afterward and dreamily talking.

But in between . . . well, it sometimes seemed so silly. And his stiff member an odd kind of joke really. Georgia thought of it as like some kind of helpless animal, the way it poked at her, sometimes so blindly that Seward asked her to touch it, to help him put it into her.

His voice rumbled under her head now. He was spinning an elaborate story, a variation on a story he had told her over and over—a story they had told each other, for Georgia had added her embellishments sometimes, and sometimes her corrections. They would go out by train, in their own sleeping car, and watch the wooded green of the East fade as they came to the plains, those vast grasslands. And then they'd see them, rising like a row of low, distant clouds on the horizon line—the Rockies! Only they wouldn't believe it initially. Mile after mile what they would at first think were clouds would sit, motionless but increasing in size, in grandeur—until their eyes would make the translation: not clouds, mountains! Blue, white at the peaks, just like the postcard.

And then their life there. A little hut, a shack, really; they would need no more. A stream nearby, where Seward would catch fish for their dinner. The dry thin air, easy to breathe, shrinking the lesions on his lungs, giving Georgia her strength back.

In one version he'd spun, she would be well almost instantly— she really was well, Seward had insisted, it was just these jackass doctors who didn't know it—and she would, perhaps, give piano lessons to support them until his recovery was complete.

Georgia had laughed, then, and reached down to flick the pine needles off her skirt; the women on the porch had such an eye for these things.

"I couldn't possibly do that, Seward," she said.

They had been in the clearing that day, resting on the soft ground. Georgia was leaning over Seward, propped up on her elbow.

"Why not?"

"Why not? Because, you dunce, I don't play."

"Of course you play. Everyone plays. And anyone can teach beginners."

"But I *don't* play. Not a note. I can't read music, except vaguely. 'Dah, dah, *dah*': here it goes up. 'Dah, dah, dah': here it goes down. This many beats to a measure. Just from singing in choir, though, not playing."

He had looked at her, then, as though seeing something new and startling in her face. "You don't play," he said.

"I don't."

"But that's so strange. So surprising. What an odd way to grow up. Not playing."

Georgia had laughed again, but she was hurt—pained in the way she often felt in the san. For everything she didn't know, hadn't even guessed at, until she arrived here. For her sense of being always *too late*. She stood, slowly, and bent over, dusting her skirt. After a moment, she said casually, "Really, it's strange of you to think I necessarily would have. To think everyone grew up exactly as you did. Like a blinkered horse who thinks what's in front of him is all there is to the world."

"Oh, a horse now, am I?" He sat up to watch her.

"You are. No sideways vision at all."

She had hoisted her skirt then and refastened her garter, pulling the white stocking taut on her leg. She'd gotten so plump that a little roll of fat pushed over the top of it as she yanked it up.

"I don't need sideways vision to see what I see now."

"Oh?" She smoothed her skirt down. "And what's that? What do you imagine you see?"

"I see you, Georgia." He had stood up, too, and come to her. Now he bent and lifted the hem of her skirt. His hand scrabbled up her leg. She felt his fingers on the skin above her stocking, and now his thumb sliding up into her step-ins, where she was still moist. "I see just what I want. You." He had walked her backward slowly until she rested against a tree, and then he began to kiss her again.

This was how all difficulties were resolved between them: more kissing, more touching, more lying together. But sometimes Georgia thought about the ways in which it seemed that Seward hardly knew her. How could he love her, as he said he did, when he seemed so incurious about her, about how she had lived before the san? He knew nothing, really, of what her life had been, of what had been important to her. Sometimes when Georgia offered an opinion, he would dismiss it, but so casually that it seemed as though he felt it wasn't possible she could really think that.

How had he come to be so sure of himself at seventeen?

Maybe, she thought sometimes, it was the way he had been raised, with a houseful of women adoring him, his mother and his older sisters. He was the one they had all had hopes for, the one who would go into the world for all of them and do something glorious and astonishing, the one who would make up to the family for their father's death. And perhaps, somewhere in there, they even thought that eventually their positions would change, that he would be the one, increasingly over the years, to take care of them, to allow them, one day, to rest and watch his dazzling progress: Seward, the guarantor of their comfort into old age.

Or it might just have been his illness, she thought, which seemed to have had the opposite effect on him from what it had done to her. She was in awe of his quick anger, his defiance, while at the same time she felt a maternal superiority to it—to him, really—which was part of her love and her tenderness for him.

Now he was speaking of his impatience with his sisters. Georgia listened and watched the light through the dusty windows of the shed. He was irritated with their reluctance to concede that Colorado was a good idea, with their slowness in pulling together the money it would take—"It's nothing, really!" he said to Georgia—to send him there and get him settled. Though they had been working on it: writing letters, trying to find what they thought of as an appropriate situation for him.

He began to talk of how it would be if Georgia came with him, of how that would reassure his sisters, ease their minds about his situation. If he could tell them about her, it would probably free up the money more easily too.

Georgia felt her familiar response to this: a kind of lazy pleasure at the fantasy, a wish to linger in it, but also the anxiety that came with the knowledge that while for her it was no more than idle dreaming, for him it was something like the hope of salvation.

"So, shall I?" he asked.

"Shall you what?"

"*Tell* them," he said impatiently. "Tell them you'll come with me." *Thump* went his heart, under the rattle of his chest.

She turned and lay on her back, staring at the cobwebs above her. "I don't see how I can, Seward."

He sat up abruptly and swung his legs down. His back was to Georgia. After a moment, he said, "Then what, I wonder, are we talking about?"

She touched his back. "Seward," she said. He didn't answer or move. "We're talking about what *may* be. What *might* be."

"No. That's not so, Georgia. I'm talking about us. About what ought to be." He coughed. He stood up and went to the low, dusty window. He rested his hands on its sill and coughed again, his legs braced. After a few moments he fell silent. And then he said, "I will go. I'll go, whether you go with me or not."

"I know you will."

He turned around. His eyes blazed. "And you don't care. You won't come."

She was sitting up now. "Seward, how can I come? I have to stay. I have to stay until I'm well. Until my father marries. And probably for a while after that. For Ada's sake, and Freddie's."

He shook his head violently. "You're wrong. You're dead wrong, Georgia. You are well, first of all. You're well. And your father will marry no matter what you do, and Ada and Freddie will like that just fine. It won't make the slightest difference to anyone whether you're there or not."

She didn't answer. She didn't look at him. She was waiting, waiting until she could leave.

"You're frightened, aren't you?" he asked softly.

For a moment she couldn't respond. She wasn't frightened, not at all. But, she realized abruptly, that was because she didn't truly imagine doing it—going with Seward to Colorado. She'd never imagined doing it. It wasn't real enough to frighten her. Finally she said, "I suppose I may be, yes."

"But Georgia, what could be more frightening than staying back? Staying here through another cold, damp winter? Not trying, not grabbing at this chance." His fists clutched as he said this. "You've seen the stories." Stories he'd shown her, worn newspaper articles he'd saved and folded and refolded: miraculous recoveries, lives begun anew. "It's a new world, Georgia, and we could be part of it."

She shook her head slowly. "I need to settle things here first, Seward."

"Can't you think of me? Can't you put me ahead of all that for once?"

The bell calling them in began to ring rhythmically, and it occurred to Georgia that she didn't believe in any of it, that she never had—not the new world he spoke of, not her going there. Most of all, she realized, she didn't believe Seward was going to live. He was dying. He was dying and he didn't know it, and that was part of why she loved him: his brave, insistent ignorance, his refusal to see what was there. It was part of who he was.

But she *did* see it. This was part of who she was—her hard-hearted *seeing*. She felt this and felt, too, a kind of self-disgust at her own practicality, her clearheadedness.

She stood up and smoothed her hair. "We have to go back now," she said. "It's time." The bell clanged a few times more and then fell silent.

He didn't answer.

"Seward," she said. "I love you. I do love you." She moved close to him. "You are so very dear to me," she whispered.

He closed his eyes and coughed. Once. She could feel him straining to stay in control of himself. "But you won't come with me," he said finally.

"I can't. I can't come. Not now. Not right away."

"Ah! Not *right away*." He was mocking her, a bitter smile on his face.

She went to the door and opened it. "I should go."

"Go then."

"Seward."

"I'll stay. You go." He laughed. "We'll try it this way."

"Seward," she said.

"Go!" he barked.

She stepped outside and closed the door. As she started out of the little clearing around the shed, she could hear the coughing begin again, long and wrenching, as though it would never end.

Dr. Holbrooke came the next week to visit, his second trip to the san since he'd sent her there. It was late in the afternoon. He was alone in the library when she came down, sitting in front of the west-facing windows with the sun at his back, so she couldn't see his face as she stepped quickly across the room toward him, as he stood to meet her.

"Oh! I'm so glad it's you!" she said, extending her hands.

"Are you now?" he said. "I wonder why." He took her hands, half shaking one, but holding on to the other too. Up this close his face was clearer; she could see him. He looked absurdly happy, and younger than she'd seen him look before.

"Because I've been wanting to talk to you," she answered. "Let's go outside, though. It's so dim and dreary in here, don't you think?" She opened one of the long French doors to the terrace. "Here"— she gestured to the chairs set out in rows, as though the terrace were the deck on a mighty ship and the rolling meadow below a deep green sea—"come, cure with me," she said.

He laughed and sat down. There were four or five other pairs of people clustered here and there on the cure chairs, idly talking. It was the long free period before dinner, after rest. Seward was in the infirmary again, as he'd been once before this summer.

As Holbrooke swung his legs up onto the chair, he said, "Ahh, I feel better already."

Georgia sat down sideways on the leg rest of the chair next to him. She leaned forward toward him, resting her elbows on her knees.

"Now," he said. "What is it you wanted to talk about with your doctor? He's listening."

Georgia looked at him a long moment. For some reason she thought abruptly of Seward's bluish flesh, the bones seeming to jab at him from within.

"Colorado," she said, freighting the word with the dreams they'd spun about it.

"Colorado?" He frowned. "What about it?"

"Just: what do you think of it? For TB, I mean. As a solution. A cure."

"You're not serious."

"Well, I'm wondering. I've read such extraordinary things about people recovering there. Beginning all over."

"And you're thinking of it for yourself."

"Well, yes. I am. Wondering about it, anyway."

He shook his head. "Speaking as a physician, I can't see there'd be any benefit for a patient like you."

"But how about...? Well. I've a friend. A friend here who's quite sick. Much sicker than I am."

"I see. All right." He put his hands together, fingers touching, at his chin. "I think at this point that what we can say is that it's little more than a romantic notion."

"But what about the cures you read of?"

He shook his head. "No doubt some patients have gotten better. But that would have happened elsewhere too, in all likelihood. And some have died. And that too would have happened elsewhere." He turned his hands and held them up to her, flat, equal.

"But the sans there, they must be as good, anyway, as those here."

"Oh, I imagine so."

"And so, being there would increase a person's chances of getting well."

"Not over being here, no."

Georgia frowned. "But these do increase our chances, don't they? Being here? Isn't that why I am here, after all? At your suggestion."

"They do. Indeed they do. But not for all. You see, what we know how to do with TB is to temporize with the bug. We give the body its own chance to fight it off, to encapsulate it. Eventually there will be a cure, I've no doubt of that. But in the meantime, we can only keep those alive whose bodies want to help them to stay alive. And some bodies are less cooperative than others. Some bodies fight less well, even when they're given all the help a place like this can give. And for those bodies in particular, I wouldn't suggest the rigors of a long trip out west and then all the effort of setting oneself up out there."

"But why has it such a reputation then? Why do people go?"

"I don't think they do as they once did. Oh, before we understood the disease as we do now, it seemed to make sense. Fifteen or twenty years ago, I would no doubt have answered you quite differently, and that's when most patients were making that pilgrimage."

"And some, curing."

"To be sure. But some not. And even then I imagine the trip itself killed some." He shook his head again "No, I wouldn't recommend it. And if I were you, I'd advise your friend that she should stay right here."

"He," Georgia said. Her eyes were steady on Holbrooke now.

He looked startled. "He?"

"That *he* should stay right here. My friend is a gentleman. A patient here."

"Ah!" he said. "I see." He looked away. "Well, it's very good of you to be so concerned for him."

Georgia could feel herself blushing. "He's very ill."

Holbrooke stared at the distant line of dark spruces for a while. Then he swung his own legs down and sat up. He was facing Georgia now—their knees almost touching—but still he didn't look directly at her. After a long moment, he said, more or less to the terrace, "You seem quite well, yourself."

"No different than I've been for a while."

Now he did look at her. "Perhaps you should be beginning to think of going home." He said this questioningly but brightly, as though he expected her to seize on it, as though it were a gift he had to offer her.

"Oh, surely not yet!" she cried. Her eyes met his, and he was startled to see that she looked frightened, even appalled, as though this were the thing she wanted least in the world.

In the end, the two things happened within several days of each other, Seward's departure for Colorado and Georgia's return home.

The sisters, it turned out, had saved the money for Seward long since but first wanted to try a surgical procedure, artificial pneumothorax, the deflating of the lung in order to rest it. If it worked, and it had worked for some, there would be no need for Colorado, perhaps no more need for Bryce. Since Dr. Rollins didn't perform this surgery—or any others, for that matter—they had been putting Seward off while it was arranged for a doctor from Boston to come and work on him. Once Dr. Rollins had set this up and it was announced, several other patients signed up for the procedure too, to take advantage of the doctor's visit.

There was a hum and buzz in the sanatorium as the great day approached; some stories passed around about miraculous recoveries, others about fatal perforations. There were those who were skeptical of the whole thing, those who were jealous, those who were greedy and impatient.

Seward's surgery was unsuccessful. He described it to Georgia afterward, the doctor loud and jolly at the start, a fat man, Seward said, with a wide, carefully groomed mustache and strangely small and delicate hands. After the first attempt he'd fallen silent, except to murmur, "Difficult, difficult." Twice more he tried. It was a wide needle, Seward said. "It's like having a nail ever so tenderly inserted in your side." The doctor could find no soft tissue, no unscarred area. "He's the first medicine man who's ever said 'I'm sorry' to me," Seward said. "I was so struck by that I actually thanked him for it."

They were sitting in almost the same spot Georgia had sat in a few weeks earlier with Holbrooke. Seward had been released from the infirmary, but he was weak still, tired. He hadn't suggested a walk, their euphemism for finding a place to lie together—the shed or the soft bed of needles in the woods. Once or twice as they were speaking he had drowsed and waked, without seeming to notice his own absence, and this frightened Georgia. She was holding his hand, she didn't care who saw.

She hadn't told him anything of Holbrooke's visit, of what he'd said about Colorado or the risks of the trip out; or of her last examination with Dr. Rollins, when he'd pronounced her as well as she could be; and the subsequent telegram from the san to her father to ask him to come to fetch her. She had heard from him two days earlier: he would come for her a week hence. None of this had she mentioned to Seward.

She'd stayed silent because she thought Seward should go to Colorado. She thought so in spite of the risk. Because he wanted it so badly, because it gave him hope, and she saw, with Seward, that it was hope—and rage and defiance—that kept him alive. What else could be, with lungs so destroyed by lesions that there was no room for a needle to slide in?

In some odd way, too, unconnected with what she knew was real, she still entertained the belief that she would join him. She believed at one and the same time that he would die and she would lose him and that he would recover and she would go to live with him. She was adept at this, living at once in the worlds of hope and despair, of life and death, because of her mother. Her mother, who had spoken only weeks before she died of taking Georgia to Bangor to buy her new slippers. The old ones, she said one day when she was particularly alert, were a disgrace. They made Georgia look like a slattern.

And Georgia had held on to that until almost the end. Of course her mother wouldn't die. Her slatternly slippers had not yet been replaced.

Now, with Seward, she was more conscious of the impossibility of her position but no less capable of holding to it, believing in it. He had never seemed so beautiful as now to her either, the hawkish nose so sharply defined, the dark single brow, the pale deep eyes, deeper now than before. His wide, full mouth was the only flesh left to him, it seemed.

He smiled sleepily at her. "When will you come, do you think?"

"After the wedding," she said.

"Riddles," he said. "And when will the wedding be?"

"After I'm home. Maybe late summer."

"Late summer in Colorado," he said dreamily. "I wonder what that will be like."

"It will be wonderful," she said.

His eyes closed. His breathing scraped, and then a cough chuckled lightly out of him. His hands felt hot and dry in hers.

His sisters came for him the next day, a surprise they thought would delight him. He tried to find Georgia to say goodbye, but she was having her bath, along with the others on her porch, a prolonged and even festive social event.

When she was dressed again, smelling strongly of the brown carbolic soap, she went downstairs and outside. She was standing on the terrace when Mr. Cooper saw her and rose laboriously from his chair, trailing his cotton blanket. "Oh, my dear, did Seward Wallace find you?"

"Just now?"

"Within the hour. He was looking all over for you."

"No. I haven't seen him."

"Ah. Well. He's gone now. He left, with his sisters. I'm sure what he wanted was to say goodbye."

"He's left?" She looked at him in disbelief.

He nodded eagerly. "Yes, they took him away."

"But I didn't know of it! I never heard anything of it at all!"

"No, I think he didn't either. They descended and spirited him away, as it were."

"But, he's not gone. Gone—to Colorado?" She heard the word suddenly in all its lonely ringing.

"Oh, I couldn't say that. If that was the plan, perhaps he is. But I don't know." He could barely contain his excitement. His lips quivered.

Georgia stood dumbstruck, looking past him. Her hand had risen to her opened mouth.

Mr. Cooper leaned forward and spoke more intimately. "I'm sorry, my dear, to have been the one to tell you." A lie. He would delight in repeating what he'd said, what she'd said in response to him, over and over in the next week.

"Perhaps he left a note. He must have," she said, already turning.

"Perhaps," he said vaguely, and watched her moving quickly away, into the library, the dark center of the san, a ghostly figure in her white summer clothes. "She looked positively *spectral*," he would say later in each of the many accounts he gave of it.

Seward had written her a short note, all he had time for; and when Georgia's father came to pick her up it was folded and tied with his other notes to her under her clothes in one of the laundry cases she had packed things in. The handwriting, rushed, wasn't as shapely as the writing in his other letters. Even so, by our standards, it was calligraphic.

Georgia—This note will have to do for goodbye for now. I will be waiting for you, thinking of you, every day, hoping that the wedding is arranged quickly and over soon and that you are on your way to me.

Your devoted,
Seward

She kept these things in her underwear drawer at home, where she felt they were safe. But Ada, wounded by the changes in her sister in the weeks after Georgia's return—by her new reserve, her snobbery, as Ada saw it—opened the packet one day and read through them all as a kind of revenge. Then she told a few of her own friends what she guessed of Georgia's secret life at the san. Since none of them was close to Georgia, though, it hardly mattered except as abstract scandal; it didn't have the right shocking deeper meaning.

No, it wasn't until years later that Ada finally found the perfect listener: Rue, my aunt, Georgia's daughter. Rue, the Duchess, who was angry at her mother for a long list of offenses anyway, and who seized on the news of these letters as gratifying evidence of her mother's betrayal of her father, of her perfidious coldheartedness.

How strange it was to be back at home! To be sleeping in the double bed with Ada under the light blankets that smelled of sachet, not carbolic soap. To feel another body so close and have it not be Seward's, have it not mean what it had meant so recently. Ada wanted to snuggle—she was happy to have Georgia home—but Georgia was almost shocked by her sister's touch, shocked and somehow embarrassed. After a few minutes, when Georgia lay rigid in her embrace, Ada turned away, hurt.

Strange too to wake to a day without routines: no milk, no regulated meals, no bed checks or appointments or thermometers or nurses or rules. She dressed late, the first morning, and ate breakfast after ten o'clock. She and Freddie played three long games of Parcheesi. When he was hungry, she fixed him lunch. Ada came home about then and made herself a sandwich too, and then Georgia went upstairs to take a nap. She had been told she must do this daily, indefinitely, and get plenty of sleep at night to keep her strength up. It was important not to get worn down again.

When she woke in the hot, musty room, she didn't know where she was for a moment. From outside she could hear children's distant voices and the start-and-stop whir of someone mowing a lawn nearby. She licked her lips and lay there awhile, looking carefully around at the objects in the room. Ada had rearranged things a little, put her collection of dolls, for instance, on top of the dresser they shared. A small thing, among other small things, but looking at them Georgia felt displaced. She felt displaced generally, she realized. It all seemed to have gone so smoothly without her. Much of that was due, she knew, to Mrs. Beston, who'd come four or five days a week in her absence. But Georgia had noticed too how Ada took charge easily now, commanded both Freddie and her father in a way Georgia herself had never dared to do. She had even carelessly directed Georgia in the setting of the table last night. It wasn't that she minded, Georgia told herself, so much as that she felt superfluous. And though Ada would undoubtedly gradually step back and let Georgia resume some of her authority, she knew this would scarcely matter. Within a month or so her father would have married and she would owe it to Mrs. Erskine to keep herself superfluous.

She got up now and washed her face. She looked at herself in the mirror. There had been so few mirrors at the san and no privacy at any of them. One caught glimpses of oneself only. Now Georgia looked, hard. *My brown beauty,* Seward had called her. And she was, brown. Her skin a honey-brown from lying out in the sun, her hair brown touched with a sun-struck gold, thick and flyaway at her chin. Her eyes, brown with flecks of green. At the san, in her bath, she'd noticed that even her nipples had browned. Somehow she felt this to be the result of Seward's touch, the sign of their sin on her.

Seward! she thought. How far away, how gone he was! What could she do with her life here that could connect to Seward? That could make any sense of what she and he had done together? What they'd promised each other? She thought of the way he smelled, she thought of his hungry eyes on her, the way his long fingers felt on her legs. A screen door banged downstairs.

She went back to bed.

When she woke again, it was late afternoon; she could tell by the sun in the western sky out her window. She heard voices below her in the kitchen, and when she came down the back stairs and stepped onto the old linoleum, Mrs. Beston cried out and crossed the room to seize her, to hold her face and look at her, to touch her hair and make her turn around and around and be admired. "You're a new gal!" she said, with tears in her eyes, and Georgia felt that someone, at last, had seen her, had understood that everything was changed in her life.

They had a little party for her a few days later. It was to be Georgia's introduction to Mrs. Erskine, and she was both impatient and reluctant to have it happen. Once she'd seen Mrs. Erskine, she knew, it would be real, there could no more be the fleeting sense she allowed herself every now and then that things could just *go on* as they always had.

Mrs. Beston arrived that day "at crack of dawn," as she said, to clean and get things in order, and Georgia went upstairs right after lunch, to rest and then to dress carefully, to spend a long time fixing her hair, wetting the flyaway strands and pinching them into place.

Mrs. Erskine came in the early afternoon, her car loaded with food, and flowers from her garden, and a cut-glass punch bowl and twenty-five matching cups, all wrapped in tissue in a huge box. She was a slender woman, handsome, Georgia thought as she stepped around the car, with frizzy, prematurely white hair, which she wore pinned into a chignon at the back of her head, under the drooping brim of her straw hat.

She came up the porch stairs and embraced Georgia lightly and gracefully, touching her cool cheek to the younger woman's for just a moment. "Finally," she said with satisfaction, as she stepped back. "Though I feel I've known you forever, your father's so crazy about you." Her voice was light and musical, which seemed strange to

Georgia, she looked so mature, almost matronly. She couldn't have been more different from Georgia's mother.

Georgia's father had come out onto the porch too, and now he stepped forward and, taking Mrs. Erskine's hands, he kissed her, one of his noisy big busses that got the kiss accomplished while making a joke of it too, Georgia was relieved to note. They all laughed at him, even Mrs. Beston, who'd come out to help unload the car.

Mrs. Erskine was dressed for the party, in a silk print dress and white shoes, but she unpinned her hat and put an apron on and started to work right away. Georgia tried to help, but Mrs. Erskine and Mrs. Beston told her to go away—what a disgrace, to get help from the guest of honor!—so she went and sat on the front porch swing, listening to the clatter of dishes in the house, the footsteps going back and forth, the voices speaking and laughing. At one point she heard Mrs. Erskine call her father. "Davis?" she said in her girlish voice. "Davis, I'll need help with this table."

"I'll be there in two shakes," he called back from upstairs, and in his words Georgia heard a lightness that hadn't been there in years, since long before her mother died—a lightness she'd never succeeded in bringing to his life, plainly. And she was glad for him—she was! she thought, as she swung slowly back and forth by herself on the porch.

Who came? Several of her parents' old friends and some neighbors. Mrs. Erskine had invited her own sister and brother-in-law and their family, so there was a boy Freddie's age and several slightly younger children, all of whom played wild games in the meadow out back—mown now, Georgia noted. Ada had asked a few people, and several of Georgia's old schoolmates had come, including Bill March and his fiancée, who was awkward with Georgia at first but then perfectly pleasant to talk to. She and Bill were both full of stories of the university, of people Georgia had known in high school and had thought she would always know, people whose names were like foreign words to her now.

The house grew crowded and hot and they all brought chairs into the side yard and the women took off their hats and the men their jackets and they sat in the dancing shade under the old maples and drank the punch that Mrs. Beston had made. When the children started a game of tug-of-war, several of the young men and women, including Ada, joined in, but Georgia sat with the adults and watched. It all felt curiously flat to her, though she could tell it was a success and that Mrs. Erskine was pleased. For herself, though, she missed the sense of structure to such events at the san, where there would have been music, or poetry, or a film at the heart of things. That, and the feeling of wildness, of a kind of abandon among the adults that she'd gotten used to. That sense of maleness and female-ness in the air, of what she supposed must be thought of as perver-sity. The thing that had made it possible for her to become Seward's lover, to lie down with him shamelessly, over and over.

Sitting here now, hearing her own voice among the others cheering on Ada and Freddie and Bill March and one of the Simp-son children, she found it difficult to believe in that other world, in what she had become and done at the san. And yet she could hardly believe in this world either, she felt so cut off from it now. As though this life, these events, were a dream she was living through. When someone spoke to her, when she answered, she half expected bubbles to rise from her mouth, she felt so underwater, she felt she was moving so slowly and thickly through this day.

Would she ever outgrow this? Would her own life become famil-iar and comfortable to her again, as life in the san eventually had? Or had she made herself unfit for it, with all she'd done, all she'd learned? The shade had deepened as the shadow of the house grew long in the yard.

Of course, she was thinking, it wasn't her own life anymore, not as she'd known it. Maybe that was all that was the trouble. Maybe it was just a matter of getting used to Mrs. Erskine and the way the house would be run. She looked over at the older woman. One of her nieces was on her lap, facing her with her legs straddling her aunt's, playing with Mrs. Erskine's necklace. Mrs. Erskine's hands met around the child's bottom. She was talking in her bell-like voice to Mrs. Mitchell, whose chair was next to hers. Both women laughed. Mrs. Erskine's head tilted back slightly in pleasure. Now the niece's hands reached up to her aunt's face. The little girl cupped Mrs. Erskine's cheeks for a moment, as if to summon her attention. Mrs. Erskine looked down at her, smiled, and bent her head slightly to drop a kiss into one of the little girl's small palms before she turned back to Mrs. Mitchell.

A nice woman. An organized woman—that would certainly make life different from what it had been! A woman who would be friendly with the neighbors, who would have parties, play bridge and mah-jongg.

Georgia sighed.

"Are you weary, dear?" Mrs. Erskine said, instantly attentive, and Georgia had to perk up and say no, no, of course not, and then try to seem to listen once more.

Late in the afternoon, people began to carry their plates and cups in. Then their chairs. They left, two, three at a time, and suddenly all at once, and the house was quiet again. Mrs. Erskine put on one of Fanny's old aprons and began walking around, picking up and talking to Mrs. Beston—whom she called Ellen—about which cookies, which sandwiches had been most successful. Georgia and Ada helped, silently, listening to the older women chatting with comradely pleasure as they moved around the kitchen. "I think that on a hot day like today the cucumber just doesn't stay crisp enough to make it worthwhile," Mrs. Erskine said.

"Yes. And then you always have to worry about the dressing too," said Mrs. Beston animatedly. "All them eggs."

Georgia's first letter from Seward came almost two weeks after the party, forwarded on from the san. It described the train ride out, his arrival in Denver, his moving to the boardinghouse his sisters had arranged for him at the edge of town. He had been dizzy and sleepy on account of the altitude at first, he wrote her, but was slowly getting used to it, and he could feel that the hot thin air was soothing to his lungs.

> I wonder whether you will be leaving the san soon, and when the wedding date will be set. I feel it's our wedding date as much as it is theirs, and I'm impatient for it, though a little time will allow me to recover my strength.

He spoke of his desperation when he'd had to leave without finding her to say goodbye and of how much he thought of her.

> My life here is not as I'd pictured it because I'm still so tired much of the time, but the place itself is everything it promised to be, and once you've come, we can begin to make all of our imaginings come true. Only tell me when. I will be waiting, thinking of you and the places we went together—the woods and also the shed.

Reading this, Georgia felt the strange disappointment that comes when the writer isn't as electric on the page as he was in the flesh. What did she miss? Of course, the sense of him physically. But also the vibrancy of his illness, his frantic feverishness. His greed for her. In the letters he was merely ill; in the flesh he had been alive with it, as though it were a current charging him.

But she wrote back sweetly and, she thought, boringly. About Mrs. Erskine:

> She is, I think, much more refined in many ways than my mother, who grew up, after all, an only child in a farm family. Mrs. Erskine is a person who belongs to clubs and who knows what kind of tea sandwich to serve for what occasion. I do

like her, and she is lovely with my father, but I am not used
to her.

About Ada:

> I cannot find my old comfort with Ada. She was like my echo,
> my heartbeat, part of me, and she isn't anymore. It may simply
> be that she's grown up, it seems overnight, but it feels very
> unsettling to me.

She talked about the way she spent her days, cooking again, cleaning, shopping. And sewing clothes for herself, as none of hers fit
her, and for the wedding, which was set for September.

> I will stay on to take care of Fred and Ada and the house while
> they honeymoon. They have the use of a friend's cabin on
> Green Lake for two weeks. And then I will be free to set my own
> course.

She didn't say she was coming, because she couldn't imagine it, but
she knew he would read what she wrote as though she had, and she
felt a certain sense of falseness as she folded the paper and sealed it
into the envelope.

He wrote back almost right away, a short letter. He'd been quite
ill, hemorrhaging again, and his landlady was insisting he go into a
san there; she wasn't prepared to care for someone so sick. He
would write more when he was rested, when he was better.

Georgia was neither surprised nor truly grieved by the news,
though she felt pity to read it. Her own coldheartedness appalled
her. Did she not love him?

She had loved him then, she knew that, but she had begun now
to think of that time as a kind of trance, an enchantment, fed by her
forced idleness, her fear, her despair. And Seward's attachment to
her had been so quick and absolute that she could see it now only as

born of his desperate need. Why, in all likelihood he saw her as he saw his sisters—as someone to care for him, to center her life on his. Now, busy as she was, taken up as she was by the myriad details of the wedding and her chores, she thought of him as she would think of someone she'd invented, a beautiful boy in a fairy tale. Only he was more like the princess, the sleeping beauty, she mused. And she, more like the prince who was supposed to wake him.

> I am thinking of you, Seward dear, [she wrote]. All that's impor-
> tant right now is that you take good care of yourself.

She and Ada wore silk dresses, midcalf length, of a pale orchid color. Each had a low waist and a draped sash over the hip. Mrs. Erskine—Grace to them now—gave them each a long strand of pearls to wear too, her wedding present to them. Their shoes were gray silk, the softest shoes that had ever held Georgia's feet.

Grace herself wore a satin dress of pale brown, the color of richly creamed coffee. It was ankle length and had a lace panel down the front. On her head she wore a small cap of the same lace. No veil. She carried lilies, lilies from which Georgia had carefully cut each powdery pistil early that morning, so their vivid dye wouldn't stain anything.

After the service, they all walked slowly back across the green to the house, the bride and groom at the head of the parade. Here and there the maples were turned already, cerise, orange, yellow. The wedding and the party afterward were just for family and close friends, but the neighbors came out onto their porches and waved and called out their greetings as they ambled across the green.

It had been cool the night before, but the day was warm, and the house grew warmer as the party went on. Georgia and Ada and Mrs. Beston were in charge this time, with two hired girls to serve and clean up. There was a wine punch and little sandwiches and fruit salad and, of course, the cake.

When everyone seemed settled, Georgia went out to the front porch for a few minutes to cool off, to be alone. Just as she closed the screen door behind her, Dr. Holbrooke, who'd had to park his car all the way around the corner on Main Street, turned into the walk.

He was late because he'd been at a difficult birth where he'd finally had to perform a cesarean section. In the car on the way over, it had seemed to him he still smelled of blood, though he could see none on his hands or clothes. He'd been up since two in the morning, and he was exhausted. He had told himself he'd just stop by the wedding party for a few minutes and pay his respects. He'd been surprised, actually, to be invited; but then, he thought, Rice had no reason to think he felt anything but friendly toward him, and every reason to be grateful for his daughter's good health.

And here she was, just turning from the screen door, flushed, wearing a long glamorous dress, a flower pinned in her hair.

"Dr. Holbrooke!" she cried. "But you completely missed the service."

"I'm sorry," he said. He was standing on the lowest step now, looking up at her just above him. Her face was damp with heat, little coils of her thick hair stuck to her forehead.

"Oh, don't be sorry. Come in! I, for one, am very glad you're here." This sounded so true, so heartfelt, that he was startled by it—by the sense of her pleasure at seeing him.

It was heartfelt. Seeing him so abruptly, Georgia had the sense of him as someone who knew her *as she was,* who understood what had happened to her life, who'd been part of it, in fact, as it changed. There was an extraordinary sensation of relief for her in this, she had felt so solitary and isolated up to now. So *false* somehow.

He followed her in, watching the motion of the long clinging dress against her body as she walked ahead of him. She found her father and introduced her new stepmother, and while he stood there talking to them she fetched him a glass of the punch. When he thanked her, she smiled, her head lifted slightly back, as though she were as thirsty as he in some other way and were drinking his very words.

He stayed the afternoon, until after the cake was sliced and served, until the bridal couple went upstairs to change, until they came back down, running across the front porch and the walk between the guests who pelted them with rice. He moved around and talked, always trying to locate Georgia—across the room, or on the stairs, or darting back into the kitchen. He often caught her eye or found her looking at him. It was as if they had an agreement: first you look, then I will. Even when he couldn't see her, he was aware of her fine, bright laugh, ringing out perhaps just a little too loudly, with too much nervous energy. He could be sure of nothing, of course, but he felt that something had changed in her feelings toward him, that she was suddenly seeing him not as an older man, not as her doctor. He felt absurdly energetic and happy.

She came out onto the porch with him again to say goodbye. There were a few guests still left inside, and the low hum of conversation followed them.

"This will make enormous changes in your life, I imagine," he said, as they stood in the cooling air. "This wedding. This marriage."

"Oh, my life!" she said dismissively. "I'm tired of thinking about it." She had drunk three glasses of the wine punch, and she felt light-headed and carefree.

He was so startled he couldn't answer for a moment. "You're very young to say a thing like that," he said finally, gently.

Her chin lifted. "I'm not so young as you think." And at once she seemed terribly young, a defiant child.

He was amused. He smiled at her. "And what do you imagine I think?"

"You think I'm a girl. Nothing but a sweet little girl. Isn't that so?"

"No. It's not. Even when you were a sweet little girl, it was not."

She was holding on to the porch post, swinging herself slightly from side to side. The fabric of her dress swayed slowly against her legs. There was a burst of laughter from in the house. "I *was* sweet, though, wasn't I?" she said suddenly.

"I imagine you still are."

"No," she said. "No. I wouldn't say that."

"But surely that's for others to say."

She laughed, a surprisingly hard sound. "Well, *they* wouldn't either."

"I would," he said.

There was a long silence. "Would you," she said. She seemed moved somehow.

"I wonder," he said now. "I wonder if I could ask you to come out for a ride tomorrow. It's likely to be a beautiful day, a good day for motoring."

"No, I couldn't," she said. Her hand lifted from the post. "You're ... you're just being nice."

"I assure you, I'm not being nice. I'm not nice." When she didn't turn her face to his or answer for a few moments, he said, very softly, "It would give me great pleasure."

Now she looked. Studying her face, he saw some odd emotion there he couldn't have named. She took a step backward, but she said, "Well, then, it would give me pleasure too." She laughed abruptly. This time the sound was carefree and light. "What time?" she asked.

Ten

Imagine it: the long, difficult birth. The baby unable to be turned. The mother, finally incapable of any control at all, given over simply to screaming. Then the ether, the cutting, and the rich metallic smell of blood and amniotic fluids. The child, limp, too still and grayish at first, then, with the shock of air, squalling into purple life—a boy, his genitals absurdly swollen, his body slick with matter and blood.

Then his arrival at the party, still wearing his dark work suit, still carrying in his mind the astonishment of the birth, and somehow, he felt, the scent of blood. The wave of voices from within the house, the lovely girl turning to him in a dress the odd color of her own lips as they curved into her mouth, the sudden plunge into talk and laughter and celebration.

And through it all, her face lifting to his over and over, as though she had never truly seen him before. Hello. Hello again. Once they bumped into each other and she turned and said "Oh! It's you!" in a way that made him feel she had been waiting for him forever. For him.

Imagine it: the bachelor approaching middle age, whose need to earn his way through college and then medical school had kept his young life austere and straitened; called to a half-rural practice in Maine, part surgery, part obstetrics, part nearly worthless medicine, part commiseration. He was grateful—and then ashamed of his gratitude—to ether, to morphine, to laudanum. His patients were grateful too, even when he could do virtually nothing for them. "Doc" they had called him, from the time he was less than thirty, and it made him feel old and prematurely sorrowful.

Imagine joining the army, being sent to France—the base hospital—full of a shameful eagerness and sense of adventure (for how could this be his freedom, his liberation, this war that had brought catastrophe to Europe and death to thousands and thousands of boys so much younger, so much less liberated than he?), only to find his first task to be uselessly ministering to the scores dying of influenza, drowning in it as it swept through the confined quarters where they lived together. To feel, even as he began his work over there, how powerless he was to be.

Imagine it: the talismanic memory that comes to him from time to time through all of this, the memory of an early evening in Maine, weighted already, even then, with the sense of what he cannot do, with the growing sense of what medicine itself cannot do, parking his motorcar outside the Rices' home. He is late; this is his last stop before he goes to his own empty house, this stop to give Fanny Rice a shot of morphine that will, perhaps, let her sleep through the night. He dreads it, what she's been reduced to: her greedy, cawing voice, the way she weeps sometimes in relief as the drug releases her. As he gets out of the car, his eye is caught by the sense of motion, by a pale dancing glimmer on the deeply shadowed front porch. Ah! it's the oldest child. Georgia. She's heard his car and come out to greet him. But for a moment, standing there in her blue dress, drying her hands on a dish towel, her long ribbon of hair falling over her shoulder, she looks like a young woman, not a child; and he is struck, having had the image of Fanny in his mind as he reached across in the car for his bag (Fanny: weightless, skeletal, her flesh yellow and dried)—he is struck by her solidity, her mobile, youthful beauty, the sense of a contained vitality in her. His heart lifts as he steps into the shadow of the house—he can help *her* after all, even if he can't help her mother—and it almost seems to him for a moment that the girl, this sturdy, grave child, must have intended this gift to him, must have known how he needed it.

But no, she is just relieved. "I thought you'd never get here!" she cries impatiently.

"But you were wrong, weren't you?" he answers, and his reward is the surprised, wide smile—she likes to be teased—and then the light way her hair and her dress bell away from her as she turns to lead him in.

Georgia: she has already been with him through so much.

He died when I was nineteen, a freshman in college, and my grandmother's grief was surprising and almost frightening to me. She had seemed so well used to his being old, so tough-minded about it, so gently mocking of all his foibles as well as of their long history together, that I thought she had a great distance on everything. I had, in fact, presumed his age to be a kind of burden to her and his death to be expected, even counted on.

I came home for his funeral, all the way across the country from California. The house was crowded. Her children, the two who were still alive, had come home too, Rue from France, my uncle Richard from New York. They took Lawrence's and my bedrooms, and we slept downstairs, he on a cot in my grandfather's office and I on the couch in the front parlor. We all foraged for ourselves at breakfast—my grandmother didn't come down until midmorning. It was this, almost more than anything else, that let me know how acute her sorrow was.

She tried to hide it from us. Three or four times each day, when she felt it overwhelming her, she'd go to her room and close the door. There was never a sound from behind it—I actually listened once, to my shame—but when she emerged, her eyes would be red-rimmed, her voice hoarse, dried out.

The service was in the Congregational church on the green, a memorial service, since he'd been cremated. We walked up slowly, and ahead of us as we turned onto Main Street we could see others, dressed in their somber clothes, walking in the same direction. It was still mud season, and those who had come farthest wore galoshes or boots with their Sunday clothes. The air smelled of wet earth. As we approached the green, we saw the cars lined up, completely surrounding the square, some pulled up onto the grass. They left deep ruts that were slowly filling with water.

The minister was young, new, and it was clear he hadn't known my grandfather well. But he kept his part of the service short. It was an old friend, another retired physician, who delivered the eulogy, which was warm and funny. Then we all sang the familiar songs, my grandmother's thin soprano strong through them, and walked back again to the house for the collation.

The house was full at the start, and it had the feeling of a party, people who hadn't seen each other all winter catching up with one another's news. There was no great shock to my grandfather's death, of course—he was eighty-eight—and that made it easy for people to move quickly from consolation to news and gossip.

After an hour and a half or so, though, we were winnowed down to the family and to about twenty people who'd known my grandparents well. Ada and Fred were both there, sitting on the couch in the back parlor, she looking like a fatter and somehow more smug version of my grandmother—who sat quietly most of the time in her favorite chair, speaking only when someone spoke directly to her. Others in the room had pulled dining room chairs in here as the party thinned, and a few people were standing, holding coffee cups or drinks. Who was it who started the stories—Dr. Butler, who'd taken over my grandfather's practice after he retired? or

George Hammond, who fished with him? or Ada, who could tell tales of the early part of her sister's marriage: of the day my grandfather marched Georgia down to the bank and set her up with her own account, for instance—the only woman Ada knew for years and years who could claim to have her own money.

I could have told my own stories too, of course. I could have spoken of my grandfather's funny language for food, designed just to please me, I thought as a child: eggs "done to the death," fried potatoes "smashed to smithereens" and doused with "gobbets of gooey gravy."

I could have described how he'd taught me to drive on the dirt road that ran by Miller Pond, calmly and unflappably reading as I fumbled through the gears and stalled out repeatedly, as I lurched to the shoulder or narrowly missed trees; calling out loudly only if the car began to falter or cough, "It's gas what makes the car go, Cath: *gas, gas, gas!*"

During those lessons, we'd sometimes stop and picnic on the promontory where they later built a summer camp for boys. He would open what my grandmother had prepared with an eagerness that seemed to me to transcend hunger—that had to do, I always thought, with the connection he felt to her, through this food she'd made. Afterward, stuffed, I would sunbathe on the old khaki blanket and he would fetch his fishing rod from the trunk of the car and move around the edge of the lake, casting off out beyond the lily pads. Sometimes I watched him, or waded, feeling the sunfish brush my ankles or nibble at my bare feet. And then we'd drive again. I think now he probably had instructions to keep me out of the house all day so my grandmother could reclaim her solitude. Could nap.

I could have described the long letters he wrote to me at college, reminiscing about his own undergraduate days, calling me back to my wavering purpose—the life of the intellect, wasn't it?—by remembering his with such clarity and fondness. Once he wrote:

There was a secondhand bookstore a few blocks off campus which I used to haunt with friends. You can imagine my pleasure at finding a first edition of Carlyle there one day. I spent almost a full week's wages on it.

I could imagine no such thing, of course, but it made me aware, momentarily, of wishing I were the sort of person who could.

I could have said he was always the one who tended to me when I was sick, arriving at my bedside before I called out for him sometimes, with cold water to drink and cool cloths to wipe my face, my hands and forearms. That he didn't believe in aspirin for a fever unless it got dangerously high. He'd look at the thermometer and shake it down, saying, "Good for you, Cath, you're burning the bugs up."

I didn't say any of this, I think because they felt too dear to me, too private, these memories; and my grandmother said nothing either, perhaps for the same reason.

When I came, at age fifteen, to my grandparents' house to stay, I couldn't have fathomed what it might have meant to them to have me there—as their child, as it were, their last real child having left home so many years before. I assumed their love, I assumed my welcome. I romanticized myself: I assumed, I think, that they would actually take some comfort from me, that I would be their consolation for the death of my mother. And I'm happy for myself—for that other version of myself—that I was able to do so, to be so thoughtlessly self-centered that I didn't for a moment consider that my presence might have been inconvenient, or a burden, or in any way painful.

When I arrived for good, my grandfather had been more or less retired for a decade or so, though people in town still called him for the occasional emergency—when there was a farm accident or a child ran a high fever in the middle of the night—and he kept his black bag ready; he always went when he was called. Aside from that, their lives were ordered and seemed bland to me.

Now they don't. Now even the order seems a matter of will and strength, a way of meeting life energetically, a way of turning away from what had been hard and disappointing to what could be mastered or learned. But I didn't know then, of course, that anything had been hard or disappointing. Oh, there was my mother and her illness, yes, but surely she was my tragedy more than theirs. This, anyway, was how I saw it. I didn't think of what her fragility, her strangeness, might have cost them as she grew up, especially in that time when child-rearing had just become a science and a troubled child a sign of some failure in the great experiment of parenting—which wasn't even a gerund yet.

I knew nothing, either, of their daughter Ruth's—my aunt Rue's—angry estrangement. And though I did know of Lewis's death in the Second World War, that seemed heroic and enlarging to me, almost enviable.

I didn't know anything of what they'd done to each other or forgiven each other in order to make their regulated life. And I shared that life completely without really even being grateful for it, without noticing what I was taking from it, how it was encircling me and comforting me. Though I noticed *them* more than I had before, on summer visits. Then I think it was hard to see around my mother, she so preoccupied us all. Now I saw them. How my grandfather often seemed amused by me, and by Gran. How much she always needed to be busy, to have a project.

Sometimes I felt I provided that for her. She was anxious, I think, about what my mother might or might not have taught me about life and took it upon herself to fill in what she imagined were the gaps. How to knit, for instance. Or the arrangements of knives and forks at a place setting. Sewing a coat button on tight enough to stay, loose enough to be workable. Making egg salad.

Had Dolly—my mother—spoken to me about sex? she asked one day.

My heart sank. "Sort of," I said.

"You know about it anyway, I suppose," she said.

"Yes," I said. I didn't look at her.

"Good." She went on for a few minutes with what she was doing, mashing potatoes for supper. "Still, the relevant information is how natural it feels, I would say. Though when you think about it much, it seems it wouldn't. As natural as breathing or walking." She added butter and began to beat it in. She said, "And if it doesn't, then *some-one* doesn't know what he's doing."

When I came to live with my grandparents for good, I wasn't a happy girl. Of course, part of my unhappiness had to do with my mother's death; but I was also unhappy because I was—I had been—an oddity in my high school in Evanston. A loner. A girl who didn't know how to talk to others. How could I have been otherwise, growing up as I did? With a mother who didn't know how to talk to me?

I think I saw my move to Vermont as offering me the opportunity we all seek at some time in our adolescence to start over. It worked. I suppose I was still a bit of an oddity, but I felt myself here to be a superior oddity, and so I was more comfortable than I'd been at home. And that comfort was what made me acceptable.

It was easy to get to know the kids around me. We rode a bus together to the regional high school, which was, by urban standards, small—only about three hundred pupils. There were around twenty of us who took the bus from West Barstow, another thirty or so from Barstow itself. On the return trip in the afternoon, there were eight or ten stops near town where kids got off, but as the weather warmed—and I had arrived only a month or so before that long, hesitant process began—more and more of them chose to ride past their own stops to get off at the green. The green: my stop. They would hang around there for half an hour or an hour and then even longer than that, as the days grew warmer.

I started to linger too, to hang around with them. We shed our coats. We formed and reformed clusters, sitting perched on the backs of the benches provided (it would not have been cool to sit on the slatted seats). Someone would wander up to Grayson's for Cokes or Slim Jims or small bags of potato chips or candy. The tougher kids smoked. Over the long spring, the hour at which we dispersed to chores or music lessons or television got later and later.

For many of the girls, the point of all this was the cars, the older boys driving by in cars or pickup trucks. They cruised the town green slowly, their radios loud, their voices pitched louder over the music. They'd pull up along the curb in front of the monument and talk and smoke and call the girls over by name, mostly the juniors and seniors. The girls went; they stood bent over with their elbows resting on the window openings, shifting their weight uncomfortably from one foot to the other, their bottoms waggling slowly from side to side in their long straight skirts.

In all of this I was an observer rather than a participant, but I was accepted as an observer. Sought out, in fact, to receive commentary and explanations. There were girls who liked explaining their world to me, who liked the role of guide, initiator. So while I wasn't really a part of things, I wasn't entirely left out either, that first spring.

Then, one morning early in the fall, Sonny Gill got on the bus just outside of town. I'd seen him in school the spring before. He was a year ahead of me, a senior now, and therefore in none of my classes, which was convenient or even perhaps necessary for me: I didn't have to know at first how badly he did in school. What I knew instead was how astonishingly beautiful he was. He had curling blond hair and perfectly even, perfectly shaped features, nearly female in their delicacy.

It's all I saw on this day as he made his way toward me down the aisle between the worn leather seats, nodding to one or another of the sophomore or junior boys who respectfully greeted him. As he passed me, he pointed his forefinger at me and slowly lowered his arched thumb down to it, a shooting motion. My breath stopped.

That was all it took, that gesture. He was beautiful, he was older, and no one in my life had ever claimed me so simply. Had ever claimed me at all.

That afternoon, he sat next to me on one of the bench backs on the green, smoking. He'd wrecked his car, he told me. (Thus his appearance on the bus, which few seniors rode.) He hadn't really minded, though, because he thought I must ride the bus, so he guessed he'd run into me.

"You seen me around, didn't you?"

I said I had.

"You interested?"

I looked away. I couldn't bear to have him see me say *yes*.

"That's it then," he said. "I'll talk to you when the car's fixed. We'll go somewhere."

These were the things that appealed to me about Sonny: he was older than I was—eighteen to my just-turned sixteen. His hands were perpetually grimed with oil, because his father ran a garage at the end of town, and Sonny helped him there in the afternoon and on weekends. He smelled of Old Spice, which I found almost unbearably attractive. He walked with a kind of sashay. He was beautiful. He smoked. He wanted me. It was all I needed.

He began to drive me home after school, though home is not where we went. Mostly we'd drive the winding two-lane or one-lane roads, the trees a rush of deep green around us, the air cooling rapidly as the afternoon grew longer. I sat in the middle of the wide front seat and, when he took curves, felt the thrill of leaning for a moment against him.

For a while it was easy enough to hide our relationship from my grandparents. It took place mostly at school, after all, or in his car. It was a matter of talk, of teasing each other, of standing or sitting next to each other, close enough for our hips or our arms to be touching.

But then we wanted to date, to go out, and I needed their consent.

To my surprise, my grandfather was the one who objected. What, exactly, he wanted to know, would we be doing?

A movie.

What time would it be over?

Nine-thirty.

So, he could expect me home by, perhaps, ten-thirty at the latest?

Well, we might drive around or get something to eat.

Drive around.

Yes, the way Lawrence and I had last summer.

Ah, well, as it happened, he knew Lawrence rather better than he knew Mr. Gill. And, as it also happened, Lawrence was my brother.

"John," my grandmother said.

He turned and smiled a frosty smile at her. "I'm all ears," he said.

"It's time she went out with someone *besides* Lawrence."

So that was that.

But that was also the nature of their postures toward Sonny that year—toward the notion of him and me together. It startled me, to the degree that anything outside my relationship with Sonny registered on me at all. I had always understood my grandfather to be the easygoing one, the one who took what there was to take in his stride, and my grandmother to be the more careful, the more noticing.

He picked on small things. He thought Sonny should get a shorter haircut—he didn't like his curls. He didn't like Sonny's father. "The man's a buffoon," he said vehemently.

"That doesn't mean the son is," my grandmother said.

He didn't like his name. "What's his *real* name?" he'd ask over and over, pretending an unwillingness to believe someone could actually be named *Sonny*. He was offended by the noise that Sonny's car made. That kind of thing. It seemed odd, uncharacteristic, to me.

I slept with Sonny, of course. The first time just after Christmas. I'd gone to my father's in Oak Park for the holiday. I called Sonny the evening I got back, and he picked me up. His grandmother was staying at his house for the holidays, and he drove me three towns over, to her empty place. He knew where the key was, and we let ourselves in. The heat was turned down, and the air was damp and cold inside. Cats meowed and stirred around us, and their smell was overwhelming. We went into her bedroom and shut the door. We lay down together, grabbing and unbuttoning and unzipping all at once. It hurt, but I didn't mind, because Sonny seemed so power-less. So in *my* power, really. Afterward, shivering, dressing quickly again, I was astonished, as young women often are, that I felt no dif-ferent, that I hadn't been transformed somehow.

But that night marked a change for both of us. From then on, that was what he wanted, more and more, and what I began to want less and less. I was still thrilled by my power over him, by how much he desired me. But I wasn't thrilled by *doing it*. Doing it began to seem actually boring to me.

And then, slowly, Sonny himself began to seem boring. I began to notice the ways in which he wasn't bright—the jokes he didn't get, the small circuit of his interests. When I learned that Lawrence was coming to Vermont for his spring break, I realized I didn't want him to, because I didn't want him to meet Sonny. I imagined Sonny through his eyes, clearly, and felt ashamed.

I lied to Sonny. I said we were all going to take a trip together. And when afterward he said he'd driven by my grandparents' house and seen that we were there, I lied again and said my grandmother had gotten sick so we stayed home. It seemed impossible in the face of our diverging feelings to tell the truth to him—about anything. I was always trying to evade him now, to find reasons not to go out, not to make love.

He claimed to be more in love with me than before. He wanted us to marry after I'd graduated—he'd wait a whole year, he said, because he loved me so much. How could I say, Well, as a matter of fact, I've stopped loving you? As a matter of fact, I probably never did. As a matter of fact, I'd like to be able never to see you again.

In late May, he began speaking of a plan he had for the night of his senior prom. A lot of the kids were going to an all-night party afterward, arranged by the Lions Club at a lakeside retreat. If I could get permission to go, we could leave the party early and spend the night together at a motel. The whole night. We'd wake in the morning next to each other. We could make love again, in the light. To hear him say these words, *make love,* revolted me. When he proposed it—in his closed-up car in my grandparents' driveway, excited and eager and smelling of cigarettes—I could feel a kind of sick breathlessness overtake me. But as he went on, I began to relax. I listened and nodded and outlined slow circles on the fog of the passenger window. What I was realizing was that this was something my grandparents would never approve of. I could afford enthusiasm, I could escape the need for truth once again, because they would say no. They would rescue me.

I almost didn't ask them. I thought I might just tell Sonny that they'd refused without bothering to go through the whole charade. But I was scared that it might come up between them—he did sometimes come in and exchange a few awkward words with them when he picked me up—so I broached it one evening.

I broached it as though I was sure they'd say no. I was trying to signal them by this that I wouldn't fight about it, that I wouldn't be upset at their response.

To my surprise, they—or she, anyway—seemed open to the possibility.

"Are there other girls from the junior class going?" she asked. We were sitting in the back parlor, that earlier version of the back parlor, deep and dark and comforting. It was the first warmish night of late spring. My grandfather had had the radio on to a ball game, and at first, he'd just turned it down. Now it was off. The windows were open. The curtains puffed. We could hear voices yoo-hooing up on Main Street.

"I don't know," I said. "Not very many, anyhow."

"But it's all organized and supervised." She looked up from her knitting. "By whom? Teachers, I suppose?"

"Yes. And some parents too, I think."

"And what do you *do* all night, I wonder?" A deep line came and went between her eyebrows.

I shrugged. "Dance. Maybe swim. I don't know. There's food there. Maybe there are games."

"I've never heard of anything so idiotic," my grandfather said. He was in shirtsleeves, rolled up to his elbows. He wore striped suspenders.

She looked at him. "Oh, now, perhaps you have," she answered.

"*Few* things," he was saying, but she'd already turned back to me and started another series of questions. Would we be going with anyone else? Was there some other parent she could call, just to get a sense of the whole thing?

No, I said. No, we were going alone. And I didn't want them to call anyone—please, it would be so embarrassing. "I mean, it's the *Lions Club* that sponsors it," I said. This was going to be my last shot, I told myself. After this, I'd cave in.

My grandfather snorted.

"*John,*" she said. "The girl would like to go. It's what they do, apparently."

"The *girl*," he said, "doesn't necessarily know what's best for her."

There was a long silence then, and just the creaking of my grandmother's rocker filling it. Her chin lifted and the creaking stopped. Her hands were still now. She said, very softly, "Who does, then? You, I suppose."

I was shocked at the deep, controlled anger in her tone. What was that about? Where was it coming from?

He looked at her, waited for her to look back at him. She didn't. Wouldn't.

Finally he said, "You're right, my dear. I'm sorry." He turned to me. "I'm very sorry, Cath."

My grandmother stood up and carefully put her knitting in its basket. She set the basket on top of the piano. Everything she did was tight and tidy and neat. "We'll speak of this later," she said, and left the room. After a moment, we could hear her footsteps on the stairs as she ascended.

My grandfather and I sat for perhaps a full minute in deep embarrassment, not knowing what to say to each other.

Then it occurred to me. "I *do* know what's best for me," I said.

He seemed to come back from a great distance. "*Do* you?" he answered.

"Uh-huh." I waited a moment. "It would be best if I didn't go."

He looked at me sharply. He said, "You mean, it would be best if we said no to you?"

I nodded.

He nodded back. After a few seconds, he smiled. He said, "Well, it's set then. You may not go. And I don't want to hear another word about it." He spoke like a bad actor reading his lines, cheerfully. When I returned his smile after a moment, he reached over and turned the radio back on. It was the eighth inning. The signal was beginning to fade as it usually did at this time of night, and he bent his head in concentration to try to hear the score. The Red Sox were trailing, 3–2. "Damn it to hell," he said.

After I'd gone to bed, I heard him come upstairs too, and then the murmur of their voices in the bedroom, just the slow back and forth, an old deep rhythm that trailed off, finally, into the silence of the ticking, moaning house.

We never spoke of it again. Sonny was disappointed but not truly surprised, and we went on as before.

I had begun by now to worry about the long summer ahead, the possibility of either having to fend Sonny off or have sex with him two, or three, or four nights a week instead of just on Saturday— the only night we had together now.

The weekend before school let out, my grandfather took me fishing, something we occasionally did together, the pleasure for me being the opportunity to drive the car; I had my license by now. We were going to a lake more than an hour away. I got to choose the radio station because I was at the wheel. Rock 'n' roll, the whole way. He never protested, but then, it was he who'd made the rule: *driver chooses.*

When we got there, we stood in the clearing that comprised the parking area, swarms of delicate insects dancing in the patches of sunstruck air, and covered all our exposed skin (not much: hands, neck, ears, face) with bug repellent. My grandfather loudly sang, as he always did while we did this, "Shoo fly, don't bother me." And then, inspired by his own voice, he continued to sing as we lifted the canoe off the car and lowered it into the water, as we loaded in his equipment and our packed lunch. He sang a song about Mussolini eating spaghetti off his thumbs, about black socks, and how they never got dirty ("the longer you wear them, the stronger they get"), he sang "Clementine," all the verses. Then, as I paddled out, he started assembling his rod and fell silent in concentration.

I'd brought a book, *Ethan Frome.* I had to write a final school paper on it. I leaned back and read when he didn't need me to paddle. But as I would tell Samuel all those years later, I hated *Ethan Frome,* so I often set it down and just drowsed. I pretended this could go on and on, that I wouldn't have to go home and wash off the pleasantly strong chemical smell of 6-12 and get dressed to go out with Sonny. The lake was still, the air windless and cool. I leaned over the side of the canoe and let my fingers trail on the cold water.

And then I saw something, something deep under the surface. I leaned over the edge of the canoe. "I think there's buildings down there," I said, after a few moments.

My grandfather made an assenting noise.

I rose up, kneeling. "I think it's a town," I said.

"Well, it *is* a town, Cath," he said. "It was, anyway."

I looked over at him. He was unsurprised. He'd known this. "But what happened?" I asked. "Was there a flood?"

He laughed. "A dam, my dear. They dammed up the river and submerged the whole damned thing."

I looked down again. It came and went under the moving water, the sense of what was there. There were long moments when I couldn't quite get it, when it seemed I must have imagined it. But then there it was again, sad and mysterious. Grand, somehow. Grand because it was gone forever but still visible, still imaginable, below us.

"How could they do that, though?" I asked him. "What about the people who lived there?"

"I don't suppose there were many left by then. And when the dam went in, the ones who *were* left had to leave."

"But that's so terrible, to see your town down there. All the places that were yours, that meant something to you."

"I imagine it would have been," he said.

"It's so . . . weird." I leaned over and watched the shifting images. "But it's kind of magical, really, isn't it? And sad."

"Well, of course you're right. It is. Sad, and beautiful too. As many sad things are."

I looked for a long time. Behind me I could hear the occasional slow ticking of my grandfather's reel as he gently pulled the line this way or that. "Think of it, Grandpa," I said. "Think about the fishes swimming through the places where people used to live."

"Yes."

It made me think of my mother somehow—the lostness of the world down there, the otherness of it. It was like being able to look at memory itself. I felt a kind of yearning for everything past, everything already gone in my life.

Behind me my grandfather said, "What would you think about going away on a kind of adventure this summer, Cath?"

I turned and sat up. "An adventure? What do you mean?" I was so absorbed in what I'd been looking at that his words seemed connected with the shimmering buildings, the sense of what was lost. For a moment it was as though he were offering me the equivalent of entering that underwater world, of going somewhere it was almost impossible to go.

He cleared his throat. "Well, what I mean is France, actually. I've written to your aunt Rue to ask about it. It turns out she has friends who would like an English-speaking sitter for the summer." He had laid his fishing rod across his lap. "You wouldn't be an au pair," he said (at the time I had no idea what this meant, what he was speaking of). "You'd live with Rue. But you'd baby-sit for this friend's children, and get paid, for about twenty hours a week."

France. A way out. A new life. I almost couldn't answer, I was so grateful. After a moment, I said, "I'd love it. I'd absolutely love it. I'd love to go."

I looked at my grandfather. His eyes were steady on me, and what I felt was that he saw me. Saw me as I was, as a person, even at that confused, unformed age. Saw my life and how I didn't know what to do with it; saw that I was special. That France, or the equivalent of France, was the only answer for a person like me.

On the way home, I peppered him with questions about France. When I would go, how long I'd stay, whether anyone would speak English, what Paris looked like. He told me a little of his memory of France from the First World War; he'd been billeted with a family in the village where the base hospital was, but he got to Paris once, after the armistice.

"I stayed in an old hotel—well, damn it, every hotel was old. But it was cheap, and I had to get up in the middle of the night and sit in a chair: bedbugs!"

"Ugh!" I said.

"Still, I thought it was the most beautiful place I'd ever seen." And then, as though it were connected, not a change of subject at all, he said, "Did you know I'd been your grandmother's doctor before I was her husband?"

"No," I answered.

"I was. When she had TB. And before that I was her mother's doctor, too. So you see what an old, old man I am."

I laughed. I was very happy. *France!* I thought.

"It gave me, I think, too much power in her life."

I looked over at him then. He seemed tiny to me all of a sudden, hunched over and shrunken. His trembling hands were lying uselessly curled up on his thighs. What was he talking about? The notion of his having power, power of any kind, seemed absurd to me. It made me uncomfortable to hear this. I didn't know what to say. I turned away quickly, back to the road.

He must have sensed my feelings. I felt him stir and straighten up. After a moment he said, "What do you think, Cath?"

"About what?"

"Why, about the power one person has over another. Should we resist it?"

I looked at him for a moment, mouth open.

"Should I mind my own business, for instance, and let *you* decide what to do with your summer? Because it may be, for all we know, that this trip to France will change your life for good or ill. One day perhaps you'll think, 'Oh, that damned old man, why couldn't he just have let me *be*?'"

"Oh, no!" I said. "I'll *never* think that."

"No?" He sounded amused. I looked over. He *was* smiling.

"No. I *want* my life to change."

"Yes," he said, it seemed to me sadly. "Yes, I know you do."

The rest of the way into town, we rode silently. I think my grandfather fell asleep.

Eleven

I suppose the truth was that I was sent away. Perhaps my father had indicated that he couldn't take me for as long that summer as he had the summer before. Perhaps my grandparents felt they needed a rest, some privacy. But certainly, and naturally, they did want to separate me from Sonny. I had as much as asked them to send me away from that situation.

Sent away was not how I felt, though. I felt liberated. I felt deeply and permanently *set free*, mostly from myself.

Rue lived in a deep, narrow apartment on the Right Bank. If you leaned carefully out the opened windows at the front you could see the Eiffel Tower on the other side of the Seine. These words, *Eiffel Tower, Seine,* had the power to stir me profoundly, maybe even more than the reality of the places themselves did.

My bedroom was at the back of the apartment, overlooking the inner courtyard, which had once, perhaps, been elegant but was now always full of parked cars and the noise of the concierge's television set, turned on all day and into the night to what sounded like game shows: you could hear the emcee's frantic high-pitched voice, the joyless mechanical hysterics of what must have been a studio audience. I had two windows that opened out over this space, and I spent a lot of time, particularly in the evenings, sitting at them and watching the life unself-consciously being acted out in layers in the apartments across the way.

My aunt—the Duchess, was like an older, more elegant, and certainly more stable version of my mother. By the time I saw Rue each morning, she was, as my grandmother always was, carefully dressed—in Rue's case, though, wearing Chanel knockoffs and thick ropes of gold and pearls around her neck and wrists. We had breakfast together in the dining room, served by the Moroccan maid, Claude, who alone among us seemed at ease; she wore bedroom slippers and shapeless clothes to work in and sang as she moved around the apartment.

Each morning, over our coffee and bread and fruit, Rue told me what her day was to be and what time she would come back to get me for whatever cultural excursion we were to undertake that afternoon.

My days were orderly too. In the mornings I took care of the three American Pierce children. I had lunch with them and settled them down for their rest. I came home immediately to a French lesson with Mme. Georges. Then I was free until the agreed-upon hour with Rue. Several times a week I went back to the Pierces' in the evening to baby-sit, but I was paid extra for this and was allowed to refuse if Rue and I had something planned.

I didn't like Rue, but I admired her. Her escape itself, to France, to Paris, to her apartment. Her way of dressing. Her way of seeing the world. All this seemed exotic and remarkable to me, given the little town in Vermont she'd come from, given that she was my mother's sister. Of course, it had arrived in her life step by step. She'd been a nurse, and she came to Europe in the Second World War. She'd met her husband in France just after it ended. He was a businessman, from a stuffy bourgeois family, and she gave me to understand that marrying her represented his rebellion, his defiance of them. This seemed unlikely to me at the time, for wasn't her life, in its way, as stuffy and bourgeois as anything imaginable? She was full of strictures—how to sit, how to eat, how to wear one's hair, how, differentially, to address the people we encountered daily. Rules, endless rules, most of which I'd never heard of before. She meant to make a difference in my life—she had *taken me on,* that was clear—and she did. Mostly in the ways she intended, but in other ways too.

She announced her intentions, not to me but, in my presence, to her friends. In French. But over the course of the summer, even though my own speech in French was always laboriously composed in my mind before I uttered it, I came to understand bigger and bigger chunks of her conversations. And so I knew what she thought of my life: "So extremely narrow, you wouldn't believe it." She spoke of my mother: "Completely deranged, but also capable of a kind of small controlled daily life." Of my father, foolish and pathetic, though loyal, one had to give him that. And of my grandparents, trying their best, of course, but at their age, how could one expect them to have the energy necessary for the job? And my grandmother! Well, one noted she'd already raised a child of her own so disturbed she ended by taking her own life. What more need one say, after all?

And where, in all of this, she would ask dramatically, raising her glass, or her cup, or her cigarette, was there the smallest chance for this poor little one (me) to experience life, culture, art, as one was meant to? I was a pathetic creature. Culturally I might as well be completely orphaned.

Once, when one of her friends protested her speaking of me this way within my hearing—and of my parents and family—she said, "*Ffft.* If you speak at all rapidly, she understands nothing." It was the first whole sentence that I was aware of taking in without the internal process of translation.

I had been lost in myself before this—a defense, I suppose, against my mother's illness and death as well as, to some degree, an intensified version of that particular stage of adolescence. Now

I began to see myself, my *story*, through Rue's eyes. I saw, in fact, that I had a story. But not only that. I saw myself, the embodiment of that story, through French eyes too, I saw myself as I was seen, physically moving around in Paris. Rue gave me this: self-consciousness. Before her, I had been invisibly at the center of my world. But the world grew larger for me now, and I became visible in it. To myself, most of all. Even the Pierce children helped me gain a distance on myself. Nathalie, the oldest, announced to me one day that I was their *second* favorite sitter. I was not, she said, as funny as Lene, the Danish au pair who took care of them in the winter, but I was sweeter, kinder, and at certain times prettier.

Instantly I understood that I was too somber, not witty enough; and I swore to myself I would change.

This became the meaning to me of my stay in France: I would change. I could change. I would come back a different person, ready for a different life. I traipsed after Rue and took in her comments on architecture, on art, on clothes, on manners and food— things I'd never conceived that you thought about, I'd never understood that there could be good or bad versions of. I watched the way French people sat in restaurants and cafés, the elaborate facial expressions and gestures they made as they spoke or listened. So much energy! So much concern! Just about words, ideas. I studied and copied the way the French girls dressed and moved and talked, the light rhythm of their speech. I had my hair cut like theirs. I lost weight. With the money I earned at the Pierces', I bought new shoes, new clothes. I felt pretty, glamorous, unfrightened for the first time in my life. In my room, with the lights out and the windows open, I smoked cigarettes I'd stolen from Rue, tilting my head back glamorously, watching the languor of my arms in the mirror.

But there was another aspect to my stay, another change in perspective being offered me. For Rue had her own vision, too, of my grandparents' lives together. It emerged, it bubbled up in all her talk about them: a clear disdain for my grandmother, a sense of her as untrustworthy, and a deep, jealous adoring of my grandfather. It was the kind of thing, I think now, that my mother, if she'd been like other mothers, if she'd been able to talk to us normally about her family, might have easily explained. She might have said, "Oh, Rue. She was half in love with Daddy. No wonder she always found fault with Mother."

To my own credit—and because of my love for my grandmother—I understood some of it that way anyway, though I couldn't have been so easily dismissive or so amused as this theoretical mother of mine. But I sensed there was something off in Rue's notion of things. I may have concluded this in part because of the way Rue saw my mother's illness: as something my grandmother had caused. This was, of course, the way the world understood it then, the educated world in particular. And Rue had had medical training. She knew her Freud—or at least the distortion of Freud that held parents, mothers in particular, accountable for all pathology in their children.

Even at that age, though, I knew that what had happened to my mother had nothing to do with anyone in our family—with anyone else at all. If I had learned one useful lesson from living with a person so disturbed, it was that some illnesses—and to me, palpably, hers—are driven by something internal, something that goes profoundly and horribly awry. My mother, I could have told you, was just *different* when she was ill. Things were deeply, chemically disturbed in her in a way that even the most misbegotten parenting couldn't have produced. And I didn't understand my grandmother's parenting—even Rue's version of it—to have been that misbegotten.

The tone, then, I ignored or dismissed. I knew it was wrong. It was one of the many ways I slowly understood Rue to be wrong. (I *could* hear in French, and I held it against her that she hadn't guessed that—and that she continued to speak about me long after I could understand almost all of what she was saying.)

It was harder, though, to dismiss the story she told me—that my grandmother had had an affair in the sanatorium—and Rue was the first person who explained anything about the san to me, the notion of being sent away, the sense of another, discrete culture there. That the man had abandoned her and gone somewhere out west. That my grandmother had turned then to her doctor, my grandfather, and won him over ("You've seen the pictures of her then, she was a very pretty girl") by pretending to be what she was not: sweet and naïve. An innocent. "It made all the difference in the world in those days," Rue said. "You know, for a girl of her background to have had any sexual experience at all....Well, it put her quite beyond the pale." She inhaled deeply on her cigarette. We were sitting opposite each other in the darkened dining room. Rue rarely smoked when she was alone with me during the day, and of course never on the street, but after dinner she allowed herself two cigarettes—strong, unfiltered French cigarettes that smelled like my grandfather's cigars.

"And Daddy, of course, knew nothing of it until after the fact."

"After what fact?" I asked.

"My dear, after they were married."

"But she wouldn't *trick* him! I don't believe that."

Rue raised her eyebrows but said nothing.

"Besides, he loves her," I said. "So what does it matter?"

She made a face, a moue.

"Who told you this?" I asked.

"It's well known in the family," she said. "Everyone knew it at the time."

"But who told you?"

"My dear." She was irritated. "Ada did," she said, after a moment. "My aunt. Your great-aunt. Her sister."

"But how did she know?"

"Your grandmother left her journal lying around. And there were letters, letters which came from the man in question even after the wedding. Aunt Ada saw them."

"So she *read* her *diary*?"

Rue tossed her head impatiently. "Which do you think is the greater wrong: to deceive a man you are about to marry or to read a journal left lying around?" I didn't answer. "You are young, my dear. You are offended at the childish slight you can imagine. Later you will be able to imagine the other kind of injury. You will see the far greater wrong in it."

There was finality, judgment in her voice, as there so often was, and I didn't ask her any more questions. Whenever I thought of this story, though—and I thought of it often, of course, and puzzled and picked at it—I remembered it in the moment it was told to me. The gathering twilight of Rue's dining room (though the sky was still yellow above the rooftops out the bank of windows behind her); the wine, of which I was always allowed one glass; the hard crumbs on the table I ran my hand over; the pungent smell of Rue's cigarette; the sounds of Claude in the kitchen, singing softly in her own language and washing dishes; and the bitter pleasure Rue took in the telling, the way she crushed and crushed and crushed her cigarette until no smoke from it trailed any longer. I thought of how horrible her fingers must smell.

Rue was wrong, it turned out. The diary reads:

December 5: Sunny today, and the snow turned to shining ice on the ground. John called late this afternoon and we sat in the parlor for a little while. I found the courage to tell him I was damaged goods. He said it did not matter to him.

December fifth was a week to the day since my grandfather had asked my grandmother to marry him, since she'd told him that she needed time to think about it. He was traveling by sleigh that afternoon—the back roads were snowed in too deeply for a car—and he'd had several calls to make. One in Newport for a child with a fever and sore throat, one in Corinna for an old patient who'd begun to die, and one in St. Albans to change the dressing on a leg injury, a farm accident that hadn't healed and, he suspected now, was never going to heal. In spite of the bright sun—almost blinding as it struck the frozen surface of the snow—he was in a dark mood. As he drove through Preston on his way home, he decided on impulse to stop in at the Rices'. He'd been staying away from Georgia for the last week in an honorable attempt to grant her the time she felt she needed to make her decision, but he told himself as he drove up that he would stop just for a few minutes. He'd use the excuse that he couldn't let the horse cool down to keep himself to his word.

The sight of her opening the door affected him as it always did, with a deep anticipatory pleasure—of what she might say or do, a story she might tell him, some lively gesture she might make that would amuse or delight him. She blushed as she snatched off her apron. She'd been in the kitchen working with her stepmother, she said apologetically. Christmas cookies. He was aware, suddenly, of that familiar buttery, sweet smell. She led him into the parlor, where there was a slow fire going in the fireplace.

There seemed to be something hushed in the air as they sat down together. At first he thought it was just the day, the shocking cold outside and the sense of being closed up in here. But then he realized that wasn't it—that it was, somehow, in *her*. She was different. Subdued and a little awkward.

She spoke to him, not quite meeting his eyes. "You know I have nothing to tell you yet." She had sat down opposite him in a low lady's chair.

"That's not why I'm here."

She tilted her head and looked at him. "Then why *are* you here?"

"I thought it would lift my spirits to see you. And it has."

"Your spirits needed lifting then?" Her voice was lighter now. Teasing a little.

"Apparently they did."

"Well, then, I'm pleased to have been of use." He could see that she was smiling—in spite of herself, it seemed. As if to hide that, she got up and went to the window, her back to him. When she turned to the room again after a moment, the light was so bright behind her he couldn't clearly see her face. "What was it that was discouraging you?" she asked.

"As much as anything, not having seen you."

"If I believed that—" She raised her hand dismissively.

"If you believed that, you would instantly consent to marry me."

She turned quickly back to the window. "I've said I'm not ready to answer that question."

"I'm sorry, Georgia." He was watching her back as intently as if it could tell him something about how she felt. "I was making a joke and that was wrong, when you're still ... struggling with your decision."

"I am. But it's only because ... I'd like everything to be very clear between us if we married."

"Of course. I would too."

Her heard her sigh, impatiently. "You answer me so quickly, John. You always do. Sometimes I wonder if you're really listening to me."

"I am. I am listening." He got up and crossed to her, stood just behind her at the window. He could smell her: sachet and the characteristic strong animal odor of her hair. It had been trimmed again recently, he thought. Her neck seemed long and white. "What needs to be clear?"

"Well. First, I would have to learn to love you better."

He understood that what she was saying was that she didn't love him now, and for a moment everything stopped for him. But he had known this, hadn't he? When he had proposed, when he had spoken of his love for her, she had smiled but hadn't answered in kind. After a few seconds he was able to say, "Do you think that's possible? That you might?"

Outside, the horse shook its bridle, as if to remind him he couldn't stay much longer. The jingling was a faint musical sound from in here.

"I'm in hopes," she said.

In spite of the pain this caused him—this caution on her part—it also made him smile. Her scrupulous honesty. "Then I will be in hopes too," he said gently.

"And then, you know"—her voice got smaller, and he had to lean toward her to hear what she was saying—"I'm...I'm damaged goods. That's all." She was so close to the window that her breath made a cloud on the glass.

He thought she spoke of her illness, of the shadow on her lungs, and he felt such an absurd lifting of his heart—this was all it was!—that he had to control himself not to laugh or cry out somehow in his pleasure and joy. It was evidently so terribly important to her, understanding how he felt about this, that he dared not make light of it. But he had to reassure her, on the other hand, that it didn't matter to him. That nothing could have mattered less. "That's of no importance to me," he said, a little too loudly. "None at all."

She didn't speak for a few moments. What she was wondering was whether he had somehow known already about Seward. Had someone at the san gossiped about her to him? Could it really be he didn't care? That he could know this about her—he could hear this—and love her anyway? She touched her fingertips to the icy glass, so cold it burned. Finally she said, "You sound so sure of that."

"I mean to sound sure. I am sure." He was looking steadily at her face in profile.

She could feel his eyes on her again. She was thinking that his greater experience of the world (when she thought of *the world* she thought of the war, and death, and also certain photographs she'd seen of Paris) must somehow have given him a sense of life broader and wiser than that of the young men she'd known. That he understood her, that he forgave her. It moved her to think he was a person capable of this.

"So if that's all, if that's truly all, I hope you'll have your answer for me soon," he was saying, in his gentle voice.

"That is all," she said. For a long moment she seemed lost in thought. Then she looked at him gravely. She said, "And I will. I will have an answer soon."

When he left, a few moments later, she followed him silently into the cold front hall, where Mrs. Erskine—Mrs. Rice—hearing them, came out from the kitchen to greet him and say goodbye. Her dog, a large mixed breed, brown and white, followed her possessively, his nails clicking on the wooden floor. When Georgia opened the door, he barked wildly at the sight of the horse, and Mrs. Rice had to hold him by his collar while Holbrooke made his exit.

The next day, Georgia accepted his proposal. Three weeks after Christmas, they were married in the small ceremony she had wanted, with just their immediate families present. They went to Boston on their honeymoon. There was a blizzard the second day they were there, and the city seemed, for the remaining two days they stayed, a little like the small town in Maine they'd left behind. Traffic stopped. Stores and offices were closed, and people spoke to each other cheerfully as they passed on the sidewalks. They walked single file through the deep snow to the public library to look at the new murals there by Sargent, whose work Georgia's new husband admired. They went to the river and watched the sun set. They had tea every afternoon at the Parker House Hotel. Before bed each night they had a glass of sherry in their room.

When they lay down together, he touched her everywhere, gently and thoroughly, as though the touching itself were the point. He said as much. He told her she had knees that broke his heart. That her ankles utterly mended it. He said they could wait, wait until she felt ready.

But his touching made her ready. Made her eager. She was curious, too—if his touching was so different from Seward's, would the sex act itself be different? Perhaps there were varieties to that also.

It *was* different—slow and luxuriant. It helped Georgia that it was always dark when they lay down together. It helped her that in the overheated hotel they wore so little clothing. It helped her that his gentleness left room for her to touch him too, to be the aggressor, even the hurried one. She learned to speak his name on those warm nights.

If he was startled by her appetite, by her curiosity and ease, he said nothing. Certainly he guessed nothing. He felt, simply, lucky. He felt that her responsiveness might be part of what was unusual about her in other ways: her straightforward approach to life, her touching honesty, her eagerness to learn.

They went back to Maine, to a small frame house they'd found to rent just outside Pittsfield, and she seemed taken up with the business of making a home—of sewing curtains and slipcovers, of cooking, of writing thank-you letters for the many presents they'd received.

She had asked him before they married for a piano instead of an engagement ring. He had given her the ring because he wanted to, a small moonstone surrounded by chip diamonds. Once they were settled, though, he bought her also an upright piano. With earnest determination, she began lessons with a teacher he'd found for her, someone recommended by one of his patients.

Their life together started to move in its own rhythms. On the weekends, they usually went to visit her family, or her father and stepmother came to them. Often they had Ada, or Ada and Freddie, for the day or overnight. They began to have invitations as a couple: for bridge, for teas. One of Georgia's high school friends lived in Pittsfield, and she and Georgia visited back and forth. In the spring, after the roads had dried out, John began to teach her to drive.

Once during this period, as he approached the house in the early evening, he heard her playing one of her beginner's piano pieces, repeating the same simple phrases over and over. It seemed so emblematic to him of her determination, her strength of character, that he stopped in the walk as though suddenly confused about where he was, overwhelmed with love and pity and desire for her.

．　　　　．　　　　．

They had planned a picnic for the third Saturday in July. They would go to the Saco River and spread a blanket along its banks. He was going to take fishing gear with him—this was the ostensible reason for the trip—but what he really looked forward to was driving up with Georgia beside him in the car. Was spreading the blanket between them, and watching her unpack their lunch. He imagined the way she would set the dishes out, her wrists turning, her hands opening. The way her arms would move, quick and graceful. He loved her! He loved her more now than he had when they married. Their sex was like an unspoken secret between them, a deep pleasure running underneath everything else that he wouldn't have dared to hope for. He felt its promise in her every rushing, impatient step in the house, in the tilt of her head when she greeted him, in each gesture she made.

The house was silent when he entered it, which surprised him. She was not in the kitchen or the living room. The bedroom door was closed.

Was she sleeping? Was she ill? He knocked gently.

"Yes," she said.

"Georgia?"

"Yes. Come in."

She was sitting in the chair by the bed. Perhaps she'd been looking out the window, watching his approach. But her face, he saw as she turned to him now, was reddened, her eyes swollen.

"What is it?" he said. *Her father,* he was thinking. "My darling, what's wrong?"

"Oh…don't," she said. She'd raised a hand to stop him. "John, it's…I'm so sorry. It's just my own—"

"Your father's all right."

A sad, startled little laugh emerged from her. "Yes," she said, and shook her head no. "Yes, everyone at home is fine. It's just—*acch!*" She gestured vaguely. "Ada and Daddy stopped by. She had a letter that had come for me." He saw it then where her hand had suggested, the torn-open envelope lying on the blue coverlet.

"It's about my friend," she said. And, when he didn't respond, "The young man from the san. His death. It's...it's upset me."

"I'm so sorry, my darling."

"Oh, John, I'm sorry. I'm sorry too."

He was kneeling by her now, holding her, but she was inert in his arms, unresponsive, and after a moment he let her go, confused. He sat back on his heels. He asked, "Which young man was this?"

"The young man I spoke to you about. You know."

"I'm afraid I don't remember this. When did you speak to me about him?"

"John, you must remember." She frowned down at him. Seated in the chair, she was taller than he was.

"I don't. I'm sorry. I don't."

"When I spoke to you...before we were married. I *told* you. I told you, of my relations with him." He seemed puzzled still. She looked down at her hands in her lap. "When I told you I wasn't...a virgin."

He turned sharply away, as though she'd struck him. The word shocked him on her lips. It seemed crude. He got up, almost stumbling. He was stunned, and then also trying to recollect the moment she was speaking of.

He did, he did remember it—how she had looked in profile, her lips opened, and the fleeting mist of her breath on the clear glass. He remembered the smell of her hair, the bright sun, a sheen on the snow outside, and the horse tossing its head impatiently.

Damaged, she had said.

No: *damaged goods.* Yes. The jargon of gossips, the ugly phrase that would be used of her, his wife, by others. Yes. Damaged goods. She had said that.

And he had heard it the way he wished to. He had thought—*because he was a fool,* because he was besotted—he had thought she meant her lungs.

Her lungs, which had probably healed themselves before she even entered the san. Before she met her lover. Her paramour. The man who had fucked her before he did. Who damaged her. Whom he had heard of before and understood nothing about.

She was speaking now. "You were so extremely generous and forgiving then. I hope . . . you can be now, too. For a moment, anyway. Because my grief—my sorrow—is temporary, I assure you." Her voice was apologetic now, formal and apologetic. She thought he was hurt. Hurt by her sorrow for someone else. "It will pass, I know."

He stood with his back to her, his elbows resting on the top of the tall bureau, his hands fisted together at his mouth. Around him on the dresser scarf were the odd things he'd left there: coins, a stack of folded handkerchiefs he hadn't put away yet, pressed into neat squares by Georgia, his silver-backed brushes, a set that had been his father's. He didn't see them.

"John," she said. "It has nothing to do with you and me."

"I'm afraid it does." His voice was priggish and chilly; he couldn't help himself.

"No, John. I swear to you, it doesn't." There was a little fear in her voice now. She was startled by his response. She had thought he would be more understanding. He, who by her lights had understood so much.

She stood up. "I will put it behind me, John. Of course, you're right. You're right. I have no right to such grief."

Still he didn't answer, lost as he was in his own amazement and pain.

"We'll . . . we'll go on our picnic, John." She had come to stand next to him. Her hand moved up his back tentatively and lightly gripped his shoulder. "John, look at me. I've put it behind me. I've forgotten it already."

He shrugged her away. "Don't say that. You don't need to say that."

She stood there a moment before she said, "But what am I to do, John? You're angry, I can tell."

"If I'm angry... I *am* angry, you're right. But only with myself." She had been honest, after all. She had made no excuses. She had used those ugly words about herself. *Damaged goods*. It was not her fault he had misunderstood her.

"John," she began. He could see her hands rising again. To touch him.

"Georgia, you must let me *be*!" he burst out.

She stepped back from him. She was white. "Of course," she said. "I only meant—"

"I just need to think this through." He put his head in his hands for a moment.

"Of course. Only—"

"No. Georgia." He turned to face her. "You misunderstand me. It's not you I'm angry with. I've been stupid. I've... heard only what I wanted to hear. I—I didn't take in what you were trying to tell me the day you spoke of this young man."

"But I said—"

"I know what you said. I remember it well. And I misheard it. This is what I'm telling you. I misheard it then. I misunderstood you. I didn't realize until just now that you had had... a lover, before me. Before we were married."

She sat down now on the edge of the bed. "But I *said* so, John," she whispered. "I was at pains to tell you."

"Georgia, I know. It was my own wish to... believe something else that kept me from hearing you correctly."

"But you were so... wonderful. So forgiving. What did you think I was speaking of?"

"Your illness. Your lungs. Your damaged lungs. Which of course are hardly damaged at all."

"You thought I spoke of my tuberculosis?"

"Yes."

She laughed suddenly, a single harsh cry.

"Yes," he said.

Her eyes were unfocused for a moment. Then she looked sharply at him again. "So it wasn't your . . . you didn't understand me then. You didn't forgive me."

"I don't know. No. Not then. I didn't. I need to think this through, Georgia."

There was a long silence in the room. Outside someone walked by, cheerfully whistling off key. Georgia felt lost in herself, in confusion. She felt dizzy. She remembered him that day, how she had begun to love him at that moment—when he forgave her.

Finally she spoke. "Did you know how lovely I found you then, John?" she said. "How . . . wise and lovely?"

After a moment, still not looking at her, he said, "I know what you're saying. You're saying I wasn't. That that wasn't me. And you're right. I understand that. I am not lovely. I've never been wise."

His face was so full of despair that she turned away from him. For a while she watched her own fingers, opening and closing on the blue bedspread, on its bumps and ridges. Finally she said, "Do you want another chance, John?"

"Another chance?"

"Yes." She sat up straighter. "Another chance to say whether or not you find my being damaged goods of importance to you."

"You are my wife, Georgia. Whether it's of importance or not no longer counts for anything."

She stared at him. "How foolish you sound," she whispered.

"I feel foolish."

They remained in miserable silence for perhaps two minutes, looking fiercely away from each other. The breeze lifted the curtain at the window. *I wish I could die,* Georgia thought. *I wish I had died in the san. I wish I had been consumed by TB.*

And then she said, "What did you mean, John, that my lungs are scarcely damaged at all?"

He sighed. He was leaning against the wall now, his arms folded over his chest. He said, "Just that you're well, really."

"Now."

"Yes, now. Probably then too."

"Then. When you sent me into the san."

"Probably. You probably had tidily encapsulated lesions even before you arrived."

"But you're not saying I needn't have been there?"

"In strictly physical terms, probably not. But you did have the disease. And it seemed, given the strains on you at home, the wisest course. You needed a rest, or you might have gotten truly ill. The san provided it."

"But that isn't what you said to me." Her voice was fraying. "You said I had TB. You said I *was* truly ill."

"And so you did. You weren't truly ill, but you did have TB. You had had it."

"But I didn't need to go, really."

He felt, in his grief and shock, that she was off on a tangent, belaboring an entirely irrelevant point. "This is of no importance now, Georgia. Why harp on it?" He sounded impatient. "You rested at the san, and you gained some strength. It did you no harm, and I suspect it did you a lot of real good."

"But it changed my *life*!" she cried.

He thought she was referring to her young man, to her affair. That she was blaming him—him!—for that. He looked at her coldly, and she answered his look.

"You had no right to do that," she said slowly.

He turned away.

"John. You had no right."

"I was your *doctor*, Georgia." His fists hit the bureau at the word. "I needed to do what was best for you."

"But surely I should have had some say in the matter."

"If you had had your say, you would have stayed at home with your father and worked yourself to the bone."

"Yes! and what's wrong with that? That was my *job*."

"Ah, Georgia."

"I would have stayed home, and my father wouldn't have married, and I would never have met Seward or married you, and I would have my life back." She thought of it now; she yearned for it, the way it had been, her solitary, queer life in her father's house, the long nights alone reading, just sitting, the melancholic striking of the old clock every quarter hour, the strong sense of herself as at the center of everything.

"And is that what you want? Your old life back?"

She was weeping now. "It is," she wailed. "It's what I want!"

She wept, on and off, for nearly two days, sometimes not sure what she was weeping over. Everything. Everything that was lost to her forever. Her home, her family. Seward, and his terrible solitary dying. John, who was not who she'd thought he was. Herself: the person she'd felt herself to be before all this started—this muddle that was her life now.

John stayed away the whole first afternoon, driving around the countryside. When he came home, it was after dark and the bedroom door was shut. He undressed and slept on the divan, under the afghan his mother had crocheted for their wedding present. In the night, he opened his eyes to the strange light, the unfamiliar shapes. What had waked him? Then he heard it: the high animal keening, small and pathetic, from behind the door. He didn't go to her.

The next morning, when he went in to dress for church, she was huddled under the covers with the pillow thrust over her head. She didn't move or speak to him the whole time he was in the room, though he didn't try in any way to muffle his noise.

He sat in the last pew, alone, the red hymnals set out evenly next to him on the unoccupied spots. The service was boring, the sermon vague and useless. He left quickly afterward, barely greeting

Dr. Scott. He drove to Empson's Hotel in Ellsworth, as he had often done before he was married, and had a long slow lunch: pea soup with Parker House rolls, roast chicken and potatoes with giblet gravy and string beans, vanilla ice cream for dessert. He tried to tell himself he was enjoying this, but every now and then he would stop chewing and stare into some middle distance, stunned at his bad luck. His and Georgia's, he reminded himself—for she had been mistaken in him too, after all.

Afterward he sat in the hotel lobby smoking a cigar and trying to read the paper, some long article about Sacco and Vanzetti. In the late afternoon he drove back to his office for a while and sat think-ing, his feet up on his desk. Once or twice, he fell asleep briefly and had miserable and confused dreams. In the last one, he saw Georgia as she'd been as a girl, standing in the meadow in the sun when he went in to her mother—so sturdy and brave and pure—and he woke feeling as empty as if she'd died.

And then he swung his legs down and slammed his fist on his desk in a rage at himself. She *was* brave and pure. She'd been utterly truthful, scrupulously so. It was he who'd been the liar—about her illness, and then about his own magnanimity. It didn't matter that it was unintentional. And if she'd lost her virtue in the san, well, who had sent her there? Who had thought he knew what was best for her? Who had behaved as though he were God in His heaven, push-ing mere mortals around, rearranging their lives to suit His whim?

Georgia. He thought of how she had looked the day he had examined her here in his office, her shoulders curved forward to hide her breasts, her long strands of hair straying over her back. The way her flesh had felt, dry and hot with fever under his fingertips.

Then he saw her lying with a faceless male figure. He thought of certain ways she had touched him—he had been so grateful, so surprised!—and imagined her doing that to someone else. Made himself imagine it, carefully and thoroughly.

And then hated himself for that. Where was his magnanimity now? his forgiveness?

He loved her. He loved her, did he not? She was exactly who she had always been.

He went home after dark again. Again the bedroom door was shut. He slept in the living room. In the morning, he woke to her noises in the kitchen. He smelled brewed coffee. He got up and carefully shaved and dressed. When he went into the kitchen, he saw that she had set his place for breakfast. She had poured him orange juice and coffee. She was at the stove, her back to him.

"Good morning, John," she said.

"Good morning," he answered. He noticed that the purple hollyhocks just outside the window were about to burst into tissuey bloom. A fat bee knocked against the screen. She turned slightly and asked him how he wanted his eggs.

"Scrambled and done to the death," he said, and saw her faint quick smile.

They didn't speak of their quarrel again for a long, long time.

Twelve

Samuel Eliasson knew my magical lake, he told me. The Quabbin. The Quabbin Reservoir. It was in western Massachusetts, almost due south of us. The towns that had been flooded were the very towns he was writing about, towns that had disappeared when they dammed up a meandering river called the Swift. They had been sacrificed so that Boston—ever growing, ever thirstier—could have a ready supply of drinking water. It was their sad stories he was telling in his essays.

This was in November. We were celebrating the end of the football season with a fancy dinner I'd cooked, the first complicated entertaining I'd done in West Barstow. I'd had to shop for some equipment at an expensive kitchen store in Rutland: a good sharp chopping knife, individual soufflé dishes, and wineglasses. I'd invited Leslie too, and her husband, and one of the women I'd come to know in my reading group at the library, Lydia Porter. She was lively and near Samuel's age. It seemed to me he might like her. It was an odd number, but Joe always used to say that odd was good at a dinner party—less predictable.

I'd spent the better part of two days cooking. It reminded me of all the meals Joe and I had made together, and the sense of our life then as an ongoing festive celebration of wine and food and friendship. It made me remember the relief I'd slowly come to feel about all that after it was over and food had become simply fuel again, as it had been earlier in my life, when getting the kids fed and on to their homework was my only goal in making a meal. But here I was, chopping, sautéeing, simmering a stock, all with a pleasure I thought I'd left behind me.

They were dazzled—or they claimed to be, anyway. Actually I was dazzled myself, and pleased I could still do it. I ate more ravenously than my guests.

Afterward we sat around the table drinking coffee, the lights dim, the fat white candles burned low, the empty dessert plates pushed aside. Prodded by Leslie, by her curiosity about the house and my grandparents, I was talking about how I'd come to live here. I began reminiscing and found myself telling the tale of the mysterious underwater village my grandfather had taken me to, and of how I had somehow thought of France as being connected to it—a place, anyway, as dreamy and remote and promising.

And Samuel said he knew it.

I was delighted. I wanted to go. Would he take me there?

Of course, he said. It would be his pleasure. He made a little bow with his upper body. And so much easier than a football game. "Except," he said, "you should prepare yourself. There are no buildings."

"What do you mean?" I asked. "The buildings are the whole point."

"Well, the buildings are the whole *myth*," he said. "People talk about them and write about them and imagine they've seen them, but they're not there. They don't exist."

"But *I* saw them. I'll never forget how they looked. You can't invent such a thing. I saw them."

"So you say."

I leaned forward on the table. "Are you telling me I imagined it?"

"I wouldn't dare do a thing like that."

"You are, though."

He turned his cup in its saucer. "Look, here's the story, Cath," he said. "It's a *reservoir*—that's what you have to remember. The water is used for drinking. It has to be pristine. They couldn't leave the buildings there to rot. There were pollutants. Lead pipes. Lead paint. Refuse. Chemicals—from liveries and tanneries and cattle. They even had to scrape the topsoil away. Everything was razed and burned. It's gone. Oh, they saved a church or two. Moved them. They dug up the cemeteries and reburied the dead. But the rest is just not there. Not anywhere."

"But I've heard it too, what Cath says," Leslie broke in. "That you can see buildings on a clear day if the water's still. Haven't you heard that?" She turned to her husband, a large, mostly silent man: Sid.

He wasn't quick enough. "We've all heard that," Samuel said, "because, I suspect, it's such a great story. It just doesn't happen to be true."

I shook my head. "I swear I saw it. That we both saw it, my grandfather and I. We *talked* about it. I remember."

"But that's the way memory works," Samuel said. "We supply the picture demanded by our imagination. And slowly, over time, it becomes *what was*. This is a big problem for historians." One of the candles sputtered suddenly, the flame wavered, and the shadows shifted on all our faces.

"Lord," Lydia said after a moment. "Can you imagine the stink that would be raised if they tried to submerge Barstow? What's amazing to me is how on earth they were able to get away with it."

Samuel raised his hand and rubbed his thumb against his fingers. "Money," he said. "The government bought them out, of course. And the towns were moribund anyway. The whole area was moribund. People desperately needed the money that the government offered." His face, in the candlelight, was lively with the pleasure of telling his tale; the dots of candlelight danced in his eyes. "Enough people, anyway, needed the money. They wanted it. They wanted to go somewhere else and start over. That old American story. So there wasn't a lot left to defend for those who were so inclined. Though there were some who didn't want any part of it. Much anger. Much bitterness. People who said they'd stay, you know, they'd choose to drown in their homes. Attempted sabotage, even, of the dam. All to no avail, of course. The die was cast by then." He leaned back in his chair. "And in a certain sense, all those towns had already been abandoned anyway. Really, all of New England had."

"No they hadn't," I objected. "I was here. My grandparents were here."

"Well." He smiled at me. "We'll adjust for that. But really, the period of the actual flourishing of New England—that was very short. The minute the railroads opened the Midwest, the population in all these little farm villages started to drop. You can trace it in the town rolls, just watch it happen year by year all over New England. As economically viable entities, they were dying very soon after they were born. What we think of as New England is really mostly just memory. Nostalgia for what had been. What, actually, in the grand sweep of time, had *barely* been."

He shook his head.

"No, once the middle of the country was easy to get to, there was no point in trying to squeeze a living out of these hilly, rocky fields, and most people of ambition or gumption figured that out and moved on. So there was a way in which, for the folks in those towns around the Quabbin, it was just the coup de grâce. To be expected."

"Still. Imagine. It must have been so hard." This was Lydia.

"I'm sure it was," he said.

We sat in silence for a moment.

"Damn it!" I said. "It's what I remember. I hate to admit I could be so mistaken."

Samuel's voice was gentle. "Don't we sometimes *want* to believe things? Want it so badly that we actually feel we've experienced them?"

I looked at him. His head was tilted a little, looking at me. I smiled. "That's a coercive *we* you're using, Samuel," I said. "I've been a teacher too, you know. You can't trick me so easily." I shook my finger at him.

He smiled back. "All right," he said. "All right, we'll go. We'll look. Then we'll argue again. And you'll concede that an old man may sometimes be right."

"Oh, an old man! What a posture!" I looked around, to make the others join me in my amusement, and realized that they were watching us. Watching Samuel and me together. Taking us in.

I felt flustered, suddenly. But Samuel had sat up, he was talking again, talking to the table at large. Had he noticed too? Was he trying to deflect their attention?

"It's a fascinating saga, really, even if it doesn't have the buildings. The idea of that submerged lost history. I find it fascinating, at any rate. Full of its own compelling detail. For instance, there are roads, old local roads." He turned to me. "We can see them when we're there. And they just run down under the water. Trail off, as it were." He crooked his finger slowly inward. "Beckoning." He'd made his voice creepy too.

Leslie laughed. "Come, come to me," she croaked.

"Exactly," he said.

Samuel left with the rest; he'd offered to help me clean up but I said I'd rather do it on my own. I could imagine the other three standing outside if he stayed, talking and laughing about it before they got in their cars. "Well, *that* was certainly interesting!" "A little something going on *there*!" They would talk eventually anyway, I knew that, but perhaps with not quite as much assurance if Samuel left with them. They'd have to be more speculative, more curious about the possibility.

But I found myself, as I was cleaning up, thinking again about the possibility too. Samuel? Samuel and me? It seemed clear to me now that he *was* interested. Was I?

It wouldn't be so strange. Many couples had such an age difference between them, especially later in life. And what was the age difference, after all? Twenty or twenty-five years, perhaps?

I thought of Joe, marrying someone fifteen years younger than he was. We'd joked about it in the end, he and I, and then the kids and I, but it didn't seem so preposterous to anyone but Fiona. She, of course, was deeply offended by everything about it.

Did it seem too preposterous to me? I didn't know. As I slid the dishes into the soapy water, I let myself try to imagine how it would be to—I suppose—*date* Samuel. To be involved with him. I thought, of course, of sex too. But I must confess, it was the Samuel in the book jacket picture I saw then moving with me in some abstract space, not the real Samuel, the Samuel who reminded me of my grandfather.

Quabbin wasn't my dream lake. Vast, choppy that day, it seemed oceanic compared to my memory of the quiet green body of water, so much of it visible, that my grandfather had taken me to. Mountainous dark islands rose in this lake's midst, and the water stretched away blue and cold-looking as far as the eye could see. The moment I saw it I felt a sense of disappointment that I connected, unfairly I knew, to Samuel. I think I had somehow imagined coming again upon my magical pond in his company and . . . what?

I wasn't sure. Just that I had wanted our relationship to be connected with that moment in my life, in my past. I had thought of it as affirming in some way what seemed to be beginning, what seemed to be possible, between us.

No, I said. No, this wasn't it at all.

Samuel wouldn't accept my denial. He argued with me. He thought we just needed to find an inlet, a cove, a smaller, more sheltered corner, and then I'd see that he was right. We drove along the shore, Samuel talking, me silent and resentful, I suppose. We stopped here and there. We came to one of the disappearing roads he'd spoken of. We parked and walked down toward the water. Next to the road there was a grove of naked birches, the papery white trunks slender and lissome. Our feet made a rustling noise on their fallen yellow leaves as we walked. The water lapped at the road where it disappeared into the reservoir.

"Now," Samuel said. "You were probably in some protected inlet like this, don't you think? Something that made it feel smaller, more...lakelike." The wind pushed against us. Samuel's nose was red. Mine also, I suppose. He wore a bright red scarf too, knotted around his throat, and its ends danced and flapped at his shoulders.

"No." I shook my head. "This just isn't it."

He smiled at me and then turned away. We stood side by side for a moment, looking out over the water. "You are a very stubborn woman, aren't you, Cath?" he said then.

Don't, I wanted to say. Don't. "I wouldn't have said so, no," I answered miserably.

"I would." He waited.

Or I think he was waiting. Waiting for me to concede. To agree with him. And a part of me wanted to, just to have it over with. Because I knew suddenly that he wouldn't give up. Give in. There simply wasn't a chance of his acknowledging that I might know what I was talking about. It seemed to me to connect with his age— this assurance on his part that he had to be right, that my denying what he felt to be true had to be a kind of childish, womanish resistance to him. I thought of his wife, the sense he had that she'd disapproved of him somehow. Maybe that was what she'd come to, having been lovingly bullied this way, over and over. Withdrawal. We all know the meanness possible in it. The *disapproval*.

I kicked at the yellow leaves. "It's so beautiful here," I said. It was my offering. And it *was* beautiful. The deep green of the pines on the islands, the bright light fractured and sequined on the moving water, the carpet of glowing leaves underfoot here, turning the air around us buttery and golden. Wasn't this enough? Couldn't we both let go?

"Yes, let's agree on that," he said, with a chilly smile, and I turned and started to walk up to the car.

We parked twice more and walked to the water's edge. At the last stop, we walked across the long dam holding the water back. We looked over the vast expanse of flooded valley off to its side. We didn't speak much, and I thought he must be feeling it too, the sense that something that had seemed possible at the start of this day didn't feel that way any longer.

In the car on the way home, we tried—I could feel us both trying—again. Samuel told me a long story about a dance they'd had in one of the town halls the night before it ceased to exist officially. He was planning to include it in one of his essays.

"It's a very dramatic tale, very touching, actually. It was a fireman's ball, complete with orchestra. They stopped the music just before midnight to listen to the clock striking twelve, and the accounts say you could hear sobbing everywhere in the room as the hours tolled."

"God," I said, eager to jump in. "This is something the movies could do, you know. There'd be sweet violin music"—I lifted my arms to bow an imaginary instrument—"and shots of the dancers in the town hall alternating with images of the water rising inexorably in the night."

We had found something healing, something that worked, and we used it to move away from what we'd disagreed about. All the way home we talked. We talked about his book. We talked about my grandparents. We talked about Thanksgiving; he was going to his daughter's in Chicago. We talked about my daughter Karen, and what books might interest her as she lay imprisoned in bed, gestating. Neither of us mentioned the reservoir again, but its brooding splendor, its massiveness, stayed with me, like a chill I couldn't shake off, a tone I kept hearing under the words we spoke to each other.

It was dark as we drove into West Barstow. Samuel asked me if I'd like coffee or a drink at his house—the Gibsons'. He said I could warm up and see it for the first time. I think he hoped—I think both of us hoped—we could somehow bring things around. I did anyway. It's why I agreed.

Yes. A drink, I said. "A drink and a viewing."

Inside, the house was high-ceilinged and spacious-feeling. The furniture was dark and ornate, old-fashioned. Oriental rugs so worn as to be nearly uniformly gray, their patterns almost a matter of the imagination, were scattered everywhere on the wooden floors. After the cold outside, the dry heat of the house felt good, and the gentle, dim light from the old lamps with their shades stained tea-color with age was somehow reassuring.

In the living room, the furniture was pushed back against the walls, each piece as far away from the others as possible, as if to discourage any possible human interaction. But Samuel had pulled one chair up to a round coffee table where papers and books were stacked, and now he slid another one up near it.

We sat down together. There was a floor lamp next to his chair. A yellow pool of light from it fell over his lap and his hands. His face was slightly shadowed. His hands looked gnarled under the light. I looked at my own hands. Gnarled too, of course.

He thought I was looking at my nearly empty glass. He lifted the bottle from the table. "More scotch?" he asked.

"Of course," I said, and held my glass out. He filled it, and I sat back and sipped. "But how about you?" I asked.

"Oh, no, I think I'd better not," he said.

"You're so cautious," I said.

"I suppose I am, but it gives me crazy dreams," he said.

"I don't mind the odd crazy dream," I answered. "My life is uneventful enough to welcome craziness wherever it comes from." Abruptly I thought, what was I doing? Flirting? Beckoning him?

For what? I scolded myself. For what? Surely there was a perversity in this behavior on my part, when I was feeling so distant from him. Cut it out, I said to myself.

"Let's not get into a contest about the uneventful life," he was saying. "You haven't got a prayer of winning that one."

"Oh, I don't know," I said. I wanted to change the subject. "Anyway, define *event*."

"Define *life*," he answered.

"I asked first."

There was a long pause. "Event," he said. "Children," he offered. "A job. Sex." His voice was tinged with sadness, I thought. I was glad I couldn't see his face more plainly.

"No fair," I said, trying to keep my voice playful. "I was going to use all those to define *life*."

He swallowed the last of his drink and sat holding the glass. "How would *you* define *event* then?" he asked.

"Oh, I suppose the accidents that happen to us. War or illness. Hurricanes. Floods. Pestilence." I smiled at him. "Children," I said. "Sex."

He leaned forward. The light struck his face now, harshly. His skin looked white and papery. He was frowning. "But don't you think—wouldn't you agree—that there comes a time in life when even those—the accidents—happen less often?"

"How could that be?" I said. "How could that possibly be? Accidents always happen."

He shrugged. "One is removed, I suppose." He sat back again. "One has less at stake, and so it seems that these things really do happen more to others. Without some urgency, it's hard to feel an event personally." He set his glass down with a little *thunk*.

"Is that how it seems to you?" I asked, finally.

"It is," he said.

I thought, at that moment, that he was asking me for something. That he was asking me to happen to him. I felt I had a choice. I could set my glass down too and cross to him, cross to him and touch him, kiss him, lead him upstairs. Be his event, like the prince who comes to wake the princess.

Or I could do nothing and this moment would pass, and we

would be two people talking a little sadly at the end of a pleasant enough day.

I did nothing. And it wasn't that I didn't find Samuel attractive, because I did—though it may be that seeing that photograph of him in his prime had helped me with this. But it was over. I felt it then. The moment of promise, of suggestion was gone. Because of everything. But mostly, yes, because of his insistence that I had imagined the buildings I remembered seeing, because of his insistence that his enormous reservoir was the country lake I'd paddled my grandfather across. His insistence that I was wrong. A small mean thing like that.

I thought about both of my husbands then and wondered if it had been like this for them, if at some point, as a result of some small thing that suddenly seemed a large thing, an unbearable thing—lipstick on my teeth as a reminder of my slovenliness maybe, or some begging quality to my voice, or a stupid remark in public—they turned; they nearly involuntarily made a decision: this is *over*. I cannot live another day with this person.

Though they had, of course. Lived another day with me. And another. Each of them had, until a larger and a larger and a larger thing had happened. Until the bad thing that we could fight over, separate over, happened.

Maybe I should be grateful, I thought, that this little bad thing had happened now and would make unnecessary bigger and uglier ones between Samuel and me.

We sat there for a while more, talking. He wondered if I was interested in taking on the writing of the basketball columns; the editor had offered it to me. I asked him about his current essay. We discussed tax policy in Vermont. It was easy, partly because I was a little looped by now—two big scotches on an empty stomach.

When I stood up to go home, he stood too and said he would drive me.

"What? It's a five-minute walk!"

"Ten," he said.

"Seven and a half," I said. "Never let it be said I'm incapable of compromise." I moved toward the front hall. "No. No, I need the air," I said.

He was following me. "It's dark and cold," he said. "I'll drive you."

I turned around to face him, and we nearly bumped into each other in the narrow hallway. "Samuel, I don't want a ride," I said. "You cannot force me to take a ride."

He had stepped back. Now he opened the closet door and handed my coat to me.

"If you try to, I'll scream," I warned him.

"Oh, come on, Cath."

I screamed. Once. "See? I mean it," I said. My hand rose involuntarily. I had hurt my throat a little.

He stood frozen in the act of reaching for his own coat. Then his arms dropped. "Apparently you do." His voice was hurt and chilly.

"Come on, Samuel," I said. "Don't be pissed. I'm a grown woman. A grown person. I know what I want. I want to walk home. Alone. And sober up and smell the night air."

"I must accede to that, apparently."

"You must. You absolutely must." My coat was on by now. Samuel was still standing by the closet. "Good night," I said, gently. "Thank you."

He seemed to hear the apology in my voice, the sadness for both of us. He came over to me and held my hands for a moment. "Good night," he said.

I stumbled down the uneven front walk and stepped onto the paving. I made myself turn and wave to Samuel, who was standing behind the glass storm door. His hand lifted in response, and then he stepped back and shut the inner wooden door.

It was cold. Starless. Moonless. I had a certain pleasant numbness brought on by the scotch. Even so, I buttoned up my coat and then fished in my pockets for the hand-knit mittens I'd bought a week or so before at a church bazaar. If I was going to stay, I'd need a hat soon, too, and a decent winter coat, not just the wool one I had on. But was I going to stay? I didn't care at the moment. All I felt was a child's shallow excitement at what seemed like an escape.

From what? I wasn't sure. Something safe. Something too rooted and confining for me. I felt giddy, drunkenly pleased with myself. I was walking fast against the cold, my steps jolting on the uneven, buckled sidewalk, my own fogged breathing loud inside my head. Main Street was busy, fifteen or so cars parked in front of Grayson's, and people coming in and out with bags of last-minute things they'd need for dinner that night, calling greetings or good night to each other. I saw a woman I knew from the newspaper getting out of her car, and we waved and called out *hi*.

There were no street lamps on my grandmother's street, and the sudden darkness felt inky, like a texture. No lights on at the house either; it looked cold and empty. I slowed as I crossed the yard.

I stood on the porch for a minute before I went in, looking at the dull night sky. I could feel my exhilaration drain from me, though nothing else came to replace it, just an odd blankness, a hollowness. It lingered with me even as I moved around inside, turning on lights, making dinner. It was with me when I lay down alone in my grandmother's bed, and it was still with me when I woke, quite early the next morning. I had coffee and then breakfast. I watched the gray squares of the window lighten to reveal the world outside. When I thought it was late enough, I called my Boston lover, Carl, at his office.

He wasn't there. His voice mail said he was out of town all week.

I didn't leave a message. It was so much a desperate whim, my sense of needing him, of wanting him, that it was gone as soon as he wasn't there to answer it. Because it wasn't Carl that I really wanted anyway. No, I think what I wanted was what Samuel had seemed to want the night before: I wanted to escape myself. I wanted to feel overwhelmed and disrupted. I wanted something—an event—to happen to me, to sweep me up and change my life.

Unexpectedly, from another quarter, it did.

Thirteen

The call came in the night, as these calls always seem to. You're jolted from sleep, you fumble toward where the noise, the alarm, comes from, you shake off whatever world you've been in to get to the one you're being summoned to.

It was Karen's husband, Robert. Her labor had begun again, unstoppable and urgent this time. They'd had to deliver the baby early; there had simply been no choice.

I moistened my mouth. "Is she all right?" I asked.

"The baby?"

"Well, Karen, I meant. And the baby, of course. It's a girl?"

"Yes." He laughed sorrowfully. Behind him I could hear voices and a binging noise, the busyness of a hospital. "Yes, a tiny little girl. Named Jessie."

"Oh, I love that name," I said. I turned the bedside lamp on and squinted into the harsh light.

"And Karen's okay. She's . . . she's fine, really." I waited. "Things are really a mess here, Cath," he said finally, his voice suddenly private and close.

"But the baby's *okay*," I insisted.

"The baby—I don't know. Yeah, they say she'll likely be okay. But she's *so* banged up. It was a really messy birth, I guess. They had to kind of *vacuum* her out. And she's unbelievably tiny, and they've got her hooked up to all this stuff. It's really...I don't know. It's awful. It's just godawful. This tiny little girl, full of tubes. Christ, she's got a *blindfold* on."

"Oh, Robert."

He told me she'd been born three hours earlier. Karen had come to the hospital the day before, because she started to have contractions again and they hoped they could get her under control. And they were still thinking they would be able to when he left at about ten o'clock to get some sleep. But the phone was ringing when he opened the door at home. He went back down to his car, drove to the hospital, and went straight up to the delivery room.

Karen was resting now. The baby was struggling to live, chemically forced to rest, pumped with air she couldn't yet draw on her own. He was making phone calls. His parents. Me. His siblings. Karen's. Their closest friends.

"Shall I come?" I asked.

"I don't know. It's up to you. Karen is...well, I'm not sure how long she'll be in here. I guess she's kind of cut up inside too. And nothing's ready at home. I'd been planning to get to it one of these weekends."

There was a long pause. Clearly he hadn't imagined this, what came next for him and Karen and the baby. Then we both spoke at the same time.

"Yeah, come," he said. "I'll come," I said.

Of course I'd thought of Karen often through the fall, especially after she was sentenced to bed with the pregnancy. I e-mailed her almost daily, and sent her regular care packages: books and baby things and, once, a pretty nightgown I saw in a store window in Rutland. But I hadn't *worried* about her. Partly, I suppose, because I'd known other people who'd spent good portions of their pregnancies in bed and delivered more or less on time, and partly because Karen herself seemed so unworried, so blasé about it. I should have known better.

Of my three children, Karen was the one most hurt—most damaged, I would say—by my divorce from Peter. But of course I would also say that she was the one most likely by temperament to have been hurt. To receive his departure as pain.

She'd always been a grave, sober child. She was bright and quick, but she somehow also felt that life was serious business. All of the tasks of childhood—now she rolled over, now she sat up, now she walked, now she spoke her first words—were accomplished by her with a labored earnestness; unlike Fiona, whose achievements at these same kinds of tasks seemed to *happen* to her—she greeted each one mildly, with good humor, with grace, with a sense of pleasant discovery—and unlike Jeff, whose impatience and frustration with himself meant we all rushed to help him and thus made everything more difficult. For Karen, each was a milestone, methodically worked for, struggled at, *done*—and then she'd move directly on and begin her struggle with the next.

For a while after the divorce, what she worked at was getting Peter back. Dressed neatly in what she thought of as her prettiest outfit, she'd be ready for his visits long ahead of time. As I chased Jeff down to get him clean and ready, I'd see her sitting on the windowsill in the living room, watching for her father's car, and my heart would ache for her. It didn't help that I still wanted him back then too. That, just like her, I dressed carefully before he was to come over, that I always hoped, as she clearly did, that he'd see me and be flooded with yearning for everything he'd turned away from.

He told me that she tried more than once to persuade him to let her live with him. She made a distinction between herself and Jeff and Fiona. They were little; she was big. They didn't know how to be good, how to be quiet. She did. She also knew how to make peanut butter and jelly sandwiches and she was learning how to wash the dishes. When he told me this, I felt such sorrow for her that I almost wept.

But what was there to be done? Peter and I had failed. It was finished. My fault. His fault. Not hers. I told her that over and over. I explained how the divorce simply meant she couldn't have us both at the same time anymore. But as it turned out, she could hardly have him at all.

It actually seemed to get easier for her, though, as Peter withdrew from all their lives, so that when he got a better job in Arizona and took it, I was grateful. Coward that I was, I suppose I preferred those slow wounds I didn't have to see to her sharp, visible pain at his every arrival or departure.

But that carefulness, that observant, noticing quality, that wish to please, remained with her as she grew up. She was *nice*. Too nice. As though if she stopped being perfectly pleasant for even a moment, you'd leave. And she attached herself to Joe with an intensity that frightened me.

Though when we separated, she didn't get angry or upset with him. No, as I've said, it was Fiona who swore and stamped and behaved horribly. Karen, Karen was nice even here, sympathetic and understanding to Joe. To me too, of course.

What I told myself was that this was to be expected. She was older. She was married herself. It mattered so much less to her now.

And all that was true. She did seem sealed off and protected from many of the bumps of life by her marriage to Robert. But I suspect that she was also being careful with Joe and me about this. Careful, lovable, risking nothing.

We fucked up, I sometimes wanted to say to her. I fucked up. You have a right to be mad. Get mad.

But I didn't. Again, I was grateful, too grateful, for her kindness, her carefulness and calm. And of course, by now they were indelibly who she was, anyway. There was no longer the possibility of an alternate Karen. A Karen who would have said to me about this pregnancy, "I'm scared, Mom," or "I need your help."

She was sleeping when I came into her room, though her door was open and there was the standard hospital traffic and noise in the hallway. I stood at the foot of her bed and watched her for a minute. She looked done in. She hadn't been outside in months, and it showed in her face, which was as white as her hospital johnny, white as the sheets draped over her. White, with dark smudges of fatigue under her eyes. Her mouth was slightly open, her breathing deep. No makeup. She looked like an exhausted child except for the full swell of her belly and breasts under the sheets.

One bare foot stuck out from under the sheet, long and gracefully arched, the bottom of it a little grimy, the bright nail polish almost grown out, a little stripe of color at the tip of each toe. I wanted to touch her. I wanted to hold her foot. Watching her breathe, I had that feeling I think most parents get when their children are suffering, no matter what their age—the sense that we should have protected them, that somehow it was our failure that caused them to have to feel the pain of the world—even while we know this is ridiculous.

After a few moments I set my flowers down on her tray table and left the room. I asked the first nurse I saw where the neonatal intensive care unit was.

I thought I was prepared for Jessie. I wasn't.

She was incredibly tiny. Not just small—that I'd thought of—but scrawny, her angry red flesh draped loosely over her miniature bones. What I could see of her face and shoulders was mottled with ugly purple bruises. She looked like a newly hatched sparrow, fallen out of the nest. Fallen very hard out of the nest.

She lay on a small chest-high platform crib under bright lights, naked except for a diaper and a tiny pink knitted cap. Plastic tubes or lines of different sizes ran from her everywhere—her navel, her foot, her mouth—to a machine that reminded me of nothing so much as the stand in a dentist's office, the stand that holds the fountain, the lamp, the armature for the drill. Plastic wrap lay suspended about six inches above her. She was blindfolded, as Robert had said, and somehow this seemed more terrible than anything else. Her arms and legs swam vaguely and spasmodically in the air.

A sign by her station said PLEASE BE QUIET. I'M TRYING TO REST. A monitor above her gave what I suppose were her vital signs, pulse being the only one I could understand. The nurse who'd been sitting next to her had stood up when I approached. Now she whispered, "You're the grandma?"

I nodded.

She whispered, "She's doing so well, really. Would you like to touch her?"

"Can I?" I said.

"Of course," she said. "Gently, it goes without saying. Here, I'll shift the cover." She lifted the plastic and I reached in and lightly laid my hand on Jessie's belly, just above the tube strung from her umbilicus. It looked immense, my hand, a giant's ugly, veined mitt descending onto her. Under my fingers she felt hot and dry, but her flesh quivered with life, and her arm motion speeded up.

"Ooo, she's excited," the nurse whispered, looking at the monitor. She was young and pretty, her long hair pinned back. She wore a vividly printed medical smock.

"Is that okay?" I asked.

"Well, a little goes a long way," she said.

I quickly pulled my hand back, and she redraped the plastic.

"What's that for?" I whispered.

"The plastic?"

"Yes."

"It's so she won't dry out under the lights."

"And the lights are on to keep her warm?"

"No, actually, they're for the bruises. The light helps her body absorb the blood waste from them."

"So is that what's wrong with her?"

"Well. That's one thing. She can't breathe on her own yet. And she had a bleed too, did they tell you?"

"No, I just got here. I don't know anything."

We'd moved over by the door, but the nurse was still whispering. Everywhere in the large twilit room—and there must have been ten or twelve stations or insulettes where babies lay and nurses or parents hovered—there was a hush. Even the babies were hushed. No one cried. The noises were mostly electronic—the beeps and dings of monitors and machines keeping the babies alive.

"A bleed," I said.

She nodded. "A head bleed."

"Christ!" I said.

"No," she said, touching my arm. "No, it was over very quickly. It's not necessarily something to worry about."

"But will she need surgery?"

"Oh, no. No. We just wait. We wait and see. Most of the time, it just resolves itself. A lot of what's wrong with these guys resolves itself. Particularly when they're as big as Jessie is." There'd been a sudden sharper beeping as she spoke, and her head turned away and then turned back to me, as though she took it all in, interpreted it, and dismissed it—whatever was happening to whatever child— all in those few seconds.

"She's *big*?" I said.

The nurse grinned. "She's a *mother* by our standards," she said. "Yeah. She's big."

When I turned to go, she was already making her way back to Jessie.

Karen didn't wake until another nurse, a tired-looking overweight young woman, came in and loudly announced that she needed to draw some blood. I'd been sitting in the chair by Karen's bed for more than an hour then, trying to conjure what I'd say about the baby when she opened her eyes.

But I didn't need to say anything. Her eyes filled with tears when she saw me, and I leaned forward to gather her in. "Mom," she said, into my shoulder.

"I can come back later," the nurse said.

"Could you?" I said. "That'd be great."

"*Pas de problème,*" she said. She pronounced it *paw*.

But Karen had turned away from me already; she was fumbling for the box of tissues on her bedside stand. "Oh, *fuck*!" she said. "I was not going to cry again. Fuck *me*." She blew her nose, at length, and her breathing slowly evened out. Finally she said, "Thanks *so* much for coming, Mom."

"Oh, hon. I wanted to. Don't say thanks."

"Did you see the baby?"

"I did."

"I won't ask what you think. You think what we all think. 'God, how awful.' 'God, she's so tiny.' 'God.'"

"I think she's beautiful, too. She's terribly beautiful."

She was wiping her eyes rapidly, alternating: one, then the other. Her mouth was open.

Finally she closed it. She leaned back.

"I can't wait to hold her," I said. "Have you held her yet?"

The wrong question. Her eyes welled again.

"Don't ask me that," she said.

"Oh sweetie, I'm sorry." I watched her for a moment, trying to stay in control of herself. "Karen," I said. "You *could* cry. God knows I wouldn't mind."

"I would," she said fiercely. She looked suddenly like the child she'd been: determined, single-minded. "I would mind a lot." She sat up and blew her nose again. "We have a daughter. A wonderful little girl. I will not cry. What a betrayal. It does her … it does no one any good at all."

"You do have a wonderful daughter. But she's in big trouble. She's having to work terribly hard just to stay alive. And that's sad. That's awful, how hard she's having to work. Worth crying over—especially because you love her. That's not a betrayal, Karrie. None. Surely."

"I know. I know," she said. She ran her hands through her hair. It was lank and dark. She needed a shampoo. "But what I'm afraid of, Mom, is that if I begin I'll never stop. And then I'll just be . . . useless. As useless as I've been lying around all these months."

"What do you mean, useless! You've been gestating! You've been making it possible for Jessie to be born."

"And you see what a very good job I did." She smiled angrily.

"Karen."

Her face shifted. She fell back against the pillows and said, "Oh, I don't mean any of it. Don't listen to me. I don't. I'm tired. I'd like a good stiff drink."

"Oh, well. Now I know what to bring instead of flowers next time."

She laughed. And then wiped her eyes again.

I couldn't go to my own house, of course. My tenants with their three teenage boys were there until just before Christmas. I would stay at Karen and Robert's apartment on Montgomery Street, at least until she got home, sleeping on the pull-out couch in the study. Late that first afternoon, Robert met me at the hospital and took me to get my car from the neighbor's garage where I'd left it. We drove back separately to their apartment, and before he left to say good night to Karen and Jessie, he showed me where the bedding and towels were and pulled the couch out for me. I was asleep before he got home.

The next day, he went in to the hospital early, leaving before I was up, though I heard him in the distant reaches of the apartment, showering, drying his hair, opening and shutting drawers, the tinny bark of early-morning news on the radio.

I cleaned the house before I went out. It was a mess. The sheets needed washing, there were dishes in the sink, crumbs and dried-up spills on the table. The shelves in the kitchen were almost bare. Robert and Karen had been living a kind of reduced, catch-up purchasing life since she'd been confined to bed—buying corner-store-sized containers of Tylenol or Advil, two rolls of toilet paper at a time, getting lots of take-out food. I stopped at a supermarket on the way to the hospital and bought big. When I got home, I filled their shelves and closets with food and paper goods and drugstore supplies. The next day I went shopping again before I went in to see Karen—baby things this time: the tiniest T-shirts and gowns and sleepers I could find, which even so would swim on Jessie. And blankets and crib sheets. Rubber pads, a mobile, some soft toys.

Both days I got to the hospital around midday and stayed for three or four hours, sometimes sitting with Karen, sometimes with the baby. When I got back to the apartment, I fell asleep for more than an hour; it was somehow so exhausting just being in the hospital, always waiting to hear from one doctor or another, or for this or that test to be run or this or that result to come in.

Karen felt it too. "I'm going crazy in here," she said on the second day. "Let's do something dumb to pass the time. Maybe they've got some cards down in the gift shop."

Of course they did, and for her last two days there this became part of our routine too. Each of us would sit with Jessie, whisper to her and carefully stroke her, and then we'd come together in Karen's room for a cutthroat series of games of gin rummy, which, maybe because we needed to be taken away, took us away completely. She frowned and grimaced as she played. She kept up the steady, insulting patter the children had always used with one another as they competed in games: "Very cle*vair*, m'sieur, but nowhere *near* clevair enough." "Watch it, smarty-pants, I'm comin' after you."

Sometimes, as she slammed her cards down on the Formica tray table in vindictive pleasure and announced she was going down or ginning, I felt I was being useful to her at last, in a way she'd rarely left room for, growing up.

Jessie, meanwhile, was doing well—or so they said. It was hard for me to tell. She still couldn't breathe on her own, though they'd administered a drug to help her, a surfactant, and they were steadily lowering the level of oxygen she was getting. On the third day when I went in, they'd taken her off the bright lights and put her in an isolette. This meant she didn't have to wear eye protection anymore. Suddenly I could see most of her little bruised face, her lashless lids. Her eyes didn't open often, though, because she was tranquilized. Babies on ventilators, I had learned, usually were.

When I sat with her, I sang very softly or held her minuscule hand between my fingers and whispered to her. I willed her to hear me, to feel my touch, and it seemed to me she did, actually. Sometimes her hands seemed to squeeze my finger with the most delicate of pressures. And the nurses agreed. They said her signs— the signs they monitored so carefully—calmed down when I was there.

The head bleed preoccupied me; just the idea of blood leaking in her brain seemed so dangerous. I talked to her doctor about it one day when I was there without Karen. He was reassuring. It had been a brief episode, he said. Her heart rate had gone down slightly, and her blood pressure up, but they got everything adjusted very quickly. She'd had no seizures, no signs of damage. All these were good, good signs.

I wanted to believe him. He was a small, gentle man. Hispanic. He spoke with a lovely accent. He called her "Chessie," and it made her seem a person in the world to me, to have someone have his own version of her name.

My fourth day back—the day before Karen was to come home—I bought a plastic carry chair and a crib. The chair I brought up to their apartment myself and unboxed. When Robert got home from the hospital, late in the evening, he helped me unload the big, heavy flat box containing the crib from the car. We lugged it up and into the baby's room by stages, resting often for my sake, and cut the box open there.

Robert was methodical assembling it, utterly different from Joe in this regard. He gathered all the tools he thought he'd need ahead of time. He read through the several pages of instructions before he began. My job, he told me, would be to hold things in place while he tightened bolts and nuts. He was still wearing his work clothes, though he'd taken off his tie and jacket and rolled his sleeves up. His shirt was a pale blue, clearly expensive, his suit pants dark and elegant. How beautiful he was! I thought, watching his strong, slender hands at work, watching the corded muscles in his forearms leap and shift. Beautiful in a way none of the men I'd ever been involved with had been. Expensive, handsome, coiffed, reassuring. Not, I had thought, Karen's type.

I had felt he and Karen were marrying too young. I had thought Robert wasn't special enough for her—though that's not how I put it. But a student lawyer! I said. A boy with such a predictable, safe life ahead of him. Karen understood that, but he was exactly what she wanted. What she said was, "I know that all my life Robert will be there for me, he'll take care of me."

I was appalled. "But you don't need anyone to *take care* of you, Karrie."

"I know I don't. I sure don't." Her laugh was almost bitter. "But that's exactly why I *want* it."

While we worked, Robert and I talked in the easy way that's possible when something else is taking up much of your attention. We talked about Jessie a little, about how worrisome, or not, the bleed was, about when she might come off the breathing tube, about what this doctor had said, or that one. He told me he'd already "crossed over"—that was how he put it. That Jessie was just who she was, to him, and whatever happened to her, he loved her and wanted to be sure she had the best version of her life she could have. And then he said, "But I still think she'll be fine." His brows were knit in concentration as he tightened a screw. "She's a fighter, you know."

"I do know," I said. And it seemed to me that she was. Even drugged, Jessie *worked* so much of the time. She swam and swam.

We talked about the likelihood that they'd move within a year or so, to some place with more room, maybe a yard. We talked about Karen, about how long it had been since she'd been able to work, about how important it was to him to guarantee that she get back to her music as soon as possible.

"Maybe she won't want to for a while, though," I said. "Children—a child—can be mighty distracting. And Jessie . . . well, she'll be especially distracting, I would think."

"That's fine too, of course," he said. "But she should get to choose, that's all."

He asked, and I talked about myself a little, about my life in Vermont.

"What's the verdict, do you think?" he asked.

"I don't know, honestly. Now that I'm back here, even though I'm not in my own home, it feels light-years away. It's as though one world sort of negates the other. I can hardly believe in any of it."

We pushed the crib into its corner and dropped the mattress in. I ripped open a package of crib sheets and made up Jessie's bed, while Robert untangled the musical mobile I'd bought—little wooden orchestra figures, in honor of Karen—and attached it to the headboard. Then we took the cardboard and the trash down to the garbage bins and stuffed them in. It was after eleven when we said good night. "You use the bathroom first," I said. "You're the one who has to get up in the morning."

I went into the study and pulled the curtains on the twinkling lights of the city. I changed into a nightgown, thinking about how companionable Robert and I had been in our project, thinking about how pleasant it was to live with someone, thinking about how I'd missed it, even though there were things I enjoyed about my solitary life.

While I was taking my turn brushing my teeth I heard the phone ring, and when I went past Robert's bedroom door, I could hear that he was talking to Karen—gently, reassuringly. From the study as I drifted into sleep, I could hear the faraway intermittent rise and fall of his voice, and it seemed I was somehow a child again, hearing my grandparents talking below me in the kitchen.

When Karen came home, the routines shifted. I moved out, for one thing, over to the guest room at my old friend Ellen Gerstein's house. Now I had a daily nighttime or breakfast dose of gossip about the Frye School to listen to: the other teachers' doings and the girls' lives: who'd applied to what college, whose parents were getting divorced, who'd been caught smoking or drinking or illegally off campus.

I went in with Ellen one day, just to look around, just to make myself begin to think harder about what I was going to do. It was early in the morning, and the long locker-lined halls were empty; the girls were all in chapel. The English room was a mess, the chairs out of line and the blackboards unerased. On the board at the back of the room were several attempts to diagram a sentence, and on the one in front, behind the teaching desk, one of the girls had scrawled in large sloppy print, IF THIS IS AN OBJECTIVE TEST, GUESS WHAT??!!! WE OBJECT!!!

I was looking through the file drawers for some of my papers when I heard someone call my name in the hallway, and then suddenly five girls had surrounded me, squealing. "Miz Hubbard, ohmygod, you're back! Ohmygod, Ohmygod!" They smelled of soap, of cologne, of coffee and hair spray and cigarette smoke. I sat down for a moment at the desk and they swarmed me, talking too fast, berating me for abandoning them in their last year. Someone leaned against my back, someone touched my face to get my attention—Lizzie Lanier. She had a recommendation she wanted me to write. It would be late, but I *had* to do it, I just *had* to, it was like Fate that I was here today, it was so, like, *perfect*.

I thought of Jessie then, of Jessie being this age, being a pest, applying to college, smelling like this, touching me.

My dreams at Ellen's house were disordered, as so often happens when you're sleeping in a strange bed, when your life has been turned upside down. Usually, I could tell, they were of Jessie, based on the haunting vision of her I carried with me everywhere. In my dreams, though, she took different forms. Several times she was one of my own children. Once Jeff, frantically ripping out the tubes, trying to free himself; once Fiona, comatose or dead. In these dreams I was useless, helpless—but frantic too. Often I woke up from them with my fingers scrabbling in the bedding around me, my heart lurching desperately in my chest.

I stayed on because they needed me. There was almost no time in their lives for household chores, for cleaning up and shopping and fixing meals, and those were the things I took on myself, that was what I could do for them, and I did it with as much attention and care as I'd given to the fancy meal I'd cooked in Vermont, as I used to employ cooking for friends and restaurant people with Joe.

I met Karen each day at a little café near the hospital for lunch. Then I went in to sit with Jessie for a while so Karen could take a walk or go home for a nap if she felt like it. It was only when she came back that I left, to shop and then to head to her house to make dinner.

Robert usually stopped in at the hospital on his way home from work and lingered for a little while after Karen left, to have some time alone with Jessie. Karen and I often had a glass of wine together while we waited for him. Sometimes I left when he got home, to give them time alone together; sometimes they insisted I stay on and eat with them. Often one or the other of them was leaving when I was, after the meal, to say good night to Jessie, to hold her and beckon her toward her life with them one last time for the day.

For they could hold her now. She'd come off the ventilator, though she still had apnea, that momentary periodic forgetting to breathe that happens to premature babies because they have to learn how too soon, before their bodies are programmed to do it. But they could hold her—they were exultant, almost dizzy with it when they were finally allowed to.

And I was too, of course. The night after she'd been extubated, I went in alone after we'd all eaten. It was around nine, and the only other visitors were a young couple—parents of a new preemie—and two fathers I'd come to know over the long days. We all waved to each other in greeting, old hands in the neonatal unit.

Jessie's nurse grinned at me. "I know what you're here for," she whispered.

"Damn straight," I said.

They'd set a rocker by her isolette, and the nurse gestured me into it. She opened the side hatch and expertly slid Jessie out and into my arms. She still had a little oxygen tube in her nose, and an I.V. line in her arm, but her face was open and free for the first time: no tube in her mouth, no white tape like a milk mustache on her upper lip holding it there.

She weighed nothing in my arms and against my body, but she curled into me, and I bent over her and touched her face. Her eyes flickered once. She gave a little gasp and shook herself and then relaxed again.

I sat with her until the nurse said it was time to go, rocking her slowly and singing very softly all the songs I'd sung to my children, all the songs my grandfather had sung to me. She woke at one point, but without startling, and lay back across my forearm, her opaque dark eyes wide in the twilit room, her face frowning and concentrating on me, as if taking me in, as if really seeing me for the first time and recording me slowly and permanently into her memory.

Fourteen

I didn't move into my own house until just before Christmas, when the renters left. By then I'd been to Vermont and back again. I stayed for just four days—to pack everything up, to say goodbye, to let Samuel know he could take over the house again, to return the rental car—because it was settled. I was going back. Back to my old life, and also my new life, in San Francisco—that strange city where it seems everyone has come in flight from somewhere else. Not just from Italy or China or South America but from the narrowness of the East, the flatness of the Midwest, the constrictions of the past.

For me, though, it felt less like a flight this time than a beckoning. I thought of myself as moving forward, I suppose into the future. It seemed to me that Jessie's presence, her simply being alive, had changed the terms of my life, was calling me away from what might have been in Vermont and returning me to a realer and messier and more ambiguous world.

I barely saw West Barstow this time, so focused was I on getting home. The real event of each day for me was the late-afternoon call to hear how Jessie was doing. Her progress was slow, but it was progress. They had moved her to a room for less critical babies, so though she still had apnea she was now officially a "grower and feeder." She had begun to nurse a little. When Karen told me this, she cried for a moment on the phone. We spoke of when Jessie would come home, though she had a long way to go to the five-pound cutoff. We spoke of Christmas, of my next semester back at the Frye School.

I had dreaded seeing Samuel, worried, I suppose, that something of the tension and sorrow of our last encounter would remain between us—maybe even be all that was between us. But he arrived with flowers and determined good cheer. We were not having a drink at my house, he said. Too banal. We were going to the Babcock Inn.

I went upstairs and changed out of my jeans. We drove the two towns over and sat in a dim corner of the wood-paneled bar and ordered burgers and fries and a raw-tasting Chianti.

Samuel announced that he had turned seventy-three in my absence. We were celebrating, he said, and we clinked glasses.

"What'dja get?" I asked him.

"Ha!" he said. "One tasteless card, signed by both my children. So it goes for us oldies."

"Well, who wants the *stuff* anyway? I get knickknacks now. That's how I know I'm over the hill. And I never know what to do with them. *Display* them? I'd sooner shoot myself."

"Yes. The knickknack. It metamorphoses into the card, eventually."

"I'll be grateful, honestly," I said. I drank some Chianti. "I'll confess I got peanut brittle last year," I offered.

"That's really a *kind* of knickknack, isn't it?"

I laughed. We talked about age—the upside: Jessie, his grandchildren. The downside: knickknacks. Pain. Being humored.

We talked about the house, which I was still unsure about selling. He could wait a little longer, he said. He'd be grateful just to be

living there again. "In part, of course, because it comes with memories for me too. Of Margaret."

We talked about gas mileage with snow tires, about his essays,
about the political campaigns. We finished the bottle of wine and
he drove me home, walked me to my door.

"I won't ask you in," I said, and was starting to explain—the
packing I hadn't done, the hour I had to leave—but he said, "No,
please don't," and smiled in a way that made me laugh. And then he
stepped forward and kissed me. It was a two-armed, thorough, and
accomplished kiss that pressed the length of my body against him
and tasted of wine and left me breathless.

After a moment, he let me go and stepped away. "There!" he
whispered, as in *Touché.*

"Oh," I answered.

He walked away across the snowy lawn in his boots, and I
opened the door and stepped into the house, just so he wouldn't see
me standing there looking sad and goofy, which is how I felt.

I sat down with my coat still on in the darkened front parlor and
listened to him start his car and drive away. If he'd wanted to make
me feel what I might have had, what I'd turned away from, it
worked. I felt emptied out and very alone.

I'm not sure how long I sat there, but finally I got up. Without
much thinking about it, I went outside. I walked, up to Main Street
and then to the town green, as I'd done the first day I was here in the
early fall. There were lights on in the houses—in Samuel's too—
and in the church. I could hear singing as I passed; they were having choir practice. I made myself take it all in, and then I walked
slowly home to pack. Everything, everything seemed lovely and
lost and precious to me, now that I knew I was going.

Fiona met me at the San Francisco airport; she'd gotten in the day
before. She said the house looked fine to her and that some of my

boxes had arrived. She'd been to see Jessie twice, she said, and sat with her in her arms for a while, "trailing her finery—all those *tubes*."

When we stepped outside to walk to the parking lot, the warmth, the moisture in the air, the greenness of the hills around us, all startled me anew. There had been patchy, crusted snow on the ground in Vermont. I took a deep breath. "Ah, winter in California," I said.

"I know," Fiona answered. "I arrived in a *parka*."

"Well, it'll be handy when you rearrive, back in New York."

In the car, we talked about Jessie. Fiona hadn't wanted to ask what her prognosis was.

"I'm glad you didn't, actually," I said. "I think it's hard for them to talk about. Not that she seems much at risk. But she had a little head bleed. And then...I don't know. It took her a little while to breathe when she was first born. Things like that. I think, honestly, no one knows."

I watched the traffic for a moment. Then I turned to her.

"Well, some things they know. I mean, she's doing well. Really well. But some things they just can't know about. And they won't, until they see how she does what she does."

"That would drive me totally crazy," she said, banging the steering wheel for emphasis.

"Would it?" I realized that it didn't drive me crazy; it didn't even bother me anymore. Not at all. As Robert had said to me about himself, I'd *crossed over*.

"Yes. Are you kidding?" She looked over at me. "Not to know?"

"But she's going to live, Fee. She breathes on her own. She nurses. She looks at you and responds. And a while ago they were afraid about all that stuff. So they're glad. They see her as vastly accomplished. And she is. For her age? She shouldn't be *breathing* now. She's a miracle!"

"Still, Mom."

"Oh, Fee. I know what you mean, of course I do. But you never know anyway."

"What do you mean?"

"Oh. Just... well, *you*, for instance. Actually any of you. You could have been schizophrenic. Don't you think I worried about that, with my mother as crazy as a loon? Or you could turn into a... junkie, let's say. Any second now." She waved her hand dismissively, making a face. "Okay, let's get more ordinary," I said. "You could come to hate me for some reason or other and we'd be forever estranged. Or Jeff. He could stay on in South America and we'd never see him again."

"Not likely," she said.

"No, but you know what I mean. It's just, I guess, that it's all so unknown anyway, what becomes of one's children. What *we* become, for that matter. It's really... I mean, now that she's *here*, it doesn't seem any harder to me not to know about Jessie than not to know what will become of each of you."

"*Any* harder?" She looked at me again, eyebrows raised. "Any harder, Mom?"

"Well, maybe a little harder. But only a little. Really."

"Yeah, yeah, yeah." She shifted her weight and hunched forward over the wheel. After a moment, she said, "You're such a..."

"What?"

"I don't know. Such a *mother*, I guess."

I smiled, remembering that this is what the nurse had called Jessie. "Why, thanks, my dear," I said.

When we pulled up outside the house, I saw that Fiona had put a tree up. Its tiny white lights glowed in the living room window.

"Oh, Fee," I said. "It's like coming home."

"What do you mean, you big jerk? It *is* home."

We got out and she lugged my bag in. She'd bought the tree the day before, she said, and gotten just the lights on by herself. She'd waited to do more until I was back. So after I'd unpacked and changed my clothes, I made myself some coffee and we went to work on it together, pulling the old ornaments out of their damp-smelling boxes. Fiona cried out with delight, as she did every year, to see certain familiar shapes: the teapot, the Santa, the tin angel.

We talked off and on as we worked. At one point Fiona said, "You're gonna stay, right?"

"Here, you mean?"

"Yeah."

"Yes, I am."

"Good," she said. She hung a gilded pear up with elaborate care. Then she said, "Though I thought Samuel was mighty nice."

"Well, of course he was. He is."

When I looked up at her, she was grinning.

I shrugged.

We were stepping back from the tree now before we hung each ornament, to see where the few remaining empty spots were.

"Are you sad to be back?" she asked.

"No," I said. "Not at all."

"I just wondered. I mean, seriously, what . . . whether you felt you could have lived there. You know, made a life there."

"Did you think I should?"

"I dunno. I mean, in a way it seemed . . . I mean, like even Samuel, like some kind of replication of your grandmother's life. Like getting really, really old, really really fast. Getting ready to *die* or something. You know what I mean?"

I said I did.

"But then I'd think no, no, it was just the opposite. That it was brave of you to think about starting out all new again in a different place." She had flopped down on the couch. "I don't know," she said, chewing her nail. "I guess I just kind of stopped trying to figure it out, I was, like, so totally confused."

I sat down opposite her. The window had darkened, and the tree lights filled the room with their aimless light. Fiona's eyes looked almost teary reflecting them.

"On the other hand," I said, "it occurs to me that maybe it's more like getting ready to die to come back here."

"What do you mean?"

I looked at her.

"Well, here is where I really *am* a grandmother. You know, first in line for the Reaper, when he comes. The buffer between him and all of you. 'Excuse me, sir.'" I pointed to my own chest. "'Over here first, please.'"

"Oh, come on."

"No, really. I feel that. I do. Especially because of Jessie. It's just *important*, her life, in a way mine isn't anymore."

She snorted. "Please!"

"No, really, Fee."

"Really, nothing. Here is where you stay young forever. This is *California*, remember? You have permission for everything. Wanna be a dancer now? At—what, fifty-two? No problem. Wanna...I don't know. I mean, look at Joe. Wanna begin again, and again and again?"

"But maybe I don't."

"Don't what?"

"*Don't* want to begin again."

She waved her hand. "That's just un-American. Forget that. Grow up. Live in the real world, Ma."

I shrugged. "It is how I feel, whatever world it is."

We sat for a while, not talking, looking at the glittering ornaments and the white lights.

Fiona went out to see friends after supper. After she'd gone, I turned out all the lights except for the ones on the tree, and put on a CD of Annie Fischer playing Schubert and Liszt. I lay down on the couch. The lights cast fractured, crazed patterns over the ceiling. I was tracing them with my eyes, listening to the music, and then I noticed something else up there. Smudges. A pattern to them, too. I got up and turned the light back on.

They were footprints, barefoot footprints, faint and gray.

My inventive acrobatic adolescent tenants, clearly. The prints seemed to run across the ceiling to the front window, and then they disappeared. The piano surged dramatically and I laughed out loud.

For a moment I wondered why they'd done it. Probably no answer. Because it was fun. Because it was so unlikely. Because it would make me, the stodgy owner, wonder how they'd accomplished it, this mad reference to a world turned upside down. Or maybe to the idea of escape. Or maybe to precisely nothing. I turned the lights off again and lay down. You could always paint them over, I thought.

Though you'd have to be crazy to do that.

None of us had done much of anything for each other for Christmas, Fiona because of exams, I because I'd been moving around so much, Karen and Robert because of Jessie's birth. All of us, though, had somehow found time to get presents for the baby, and Jeff had sent a box of things from South America, which had arrived while the tenants were still in the house. So we opened Jessie's gifts—stuffed animals, clothes, books—and Jeff's box, full of odd-smelling weavings and cheap, beautiful jewelry. And then we made a trip to the hospital, taking a couple of the toys with us. Everyone else with babies in the neonatal unit had had the same idea, of course, so we had to take turns going in. We left Robert there after an hour or so and came home to fix dinner.

He had just come back in the early afternoon, we were all standing around in the kitchen doing last-minute things to the food, when I looked out the window and noticed the sun slanting across the backyard, making everything seem lush and green. "Look!" I called out. "How pretty it is!"

"Let's get a picture," Karen said. "I'd like to have a record for Jessie of her first Christmas. We can take turns taking them."

"Her first Christmas, and already she's spending it away from home," Fiona said. "What a model modern girl!"

"It'd be nice to have some to send to Jeff too," I said. "Make him sorry he wasn't here."

We all put on coats and trooped into the backyard. Robert was the photographer first. He arranged us in a line coming down the back stairs, one hand on the railing.

"This is so hokey," Fiona objected.

"Hokey's the very thing in the family photo," he said.

We moved over by the olive trees. Fiona and then Karen took shots of us sitting in a row. Then Karen set the timer and we all stood in the horizontal late-day light and squinted at the camera. She took about three this way, dashing back each time to get in the frame, and then suddenly the sun was gone, and the air felt chilly and damp. As we headed back in, I heard Karen ask Robert, "Did she seem okay when you left?" and I recognized that for her the divided life had begun, that life always half lived elsewhere, always ready to be claimed and summoned. I felt a curious pang for her— some combination, I suppose, of compassion and envy.

I still have those pictures. They're not kind to any of us, because of the low sunlight and the way our faces look squinting into it, but I love them anyway. Karen presented my copies to me the week after Christmas. By then the boxes had arrived from Vermont, and I'd unpacked them. I'd set the badger and the great blue heron out, the bird on top of the piano, the badger in the kitchen, as if rooting around on the floor. I'd put the diaries in a row on the shelf above my desk, and when Karen gave me the pictures, I arranged five or six on the same shelf.

Fiona was looking at the pictures one day late in her stay when her eye fell on the cloth of the old bindings. "Oh, here they are, all those diaries of Gran's," she said.

"Yes. I'm not quite sure what to do with them."

She splayed her fingers and wiggled them spookily. "Any deep dark secrets?"

"A few."

"Yeah, but it all came out happily in the end, right?"

"Happily enough," I said.

It had actually taken me a while to piece together the last chapters of the story. I hadn't, in fact, until late on the last night of my stay in Vermont, when I sleeplessly went downstairs for hot milk. It was the evening I had dinner with Samuel, the evening he kissed me good night and made me want him. I was restless and upset, full of the sense of loss and self-doubt. In that mood, I wandered back into my grandfather's study. I sat down and flipped through the first diary to the page that confused me each time I read it: a single reference, very late—long after his death and my grandparents' reconciliation—to Seward Wallace again. This was it:

March 18: Sleet. A muddy, cold day. Terrible drive to Bangor to say a last goodbye to SW. Even worse on the way home. I told John the whole story tonight. It seems settled at last. *Happy*.

I simply couldn't understand it. How could there be "a last goodbye" now? Seward had died the summer before, in Colorado. And how odd this switch to initials for him seemed. Though it occurred to me as I sat looking at it that night that she'd used them for Seward somewhere before. I just wasn't sure where. I flipped backward through the diary to the section where she met him, to her life in the san, but in every other reference she used his name: Seward, Seward, Seward, Seward. Where had I seen it then? *SW*. Where was that the way she referred to him?

Then I remembered. It had been in the ledger. In her accounts. I opened that outsize book and went to the same period of time, the middle of March. And then, because I saw nothing but the usual list of names, I backed up through the weeks and months of recorded purchases and expenses.

And there he was, starting in January: *SW.* Among all the other initials and names that came up weekly or monthly: *Mrs. B,* the piano teacher; *LG,* the iceman; *Mr. P,* chimneys cleaned. There was *SW.* Moving slowly back farther, I saw that listed next to him each week was usually around $5 or $6. The last of these notations occurred in October. Before then, nothing. I turned the pages forward again, to January. A week or so after the last deduction by Seward's initials, I found the entry *Miss Wallace* and noted by her name the astronomical sum of $65.

I sat there for a while, and then I turned back to the diary again to try to figure out what it meant, what had triggered the squirreling away of this money in Seward's name after he died, and why she'd given it in the end to someone—I presumed—in Seward's family: *Miss Wallace.* I found it in an entry I'd read through many times before without really noticing it.

Fifteen

October 12. A splendid day. John out driving around from dawn till dusk. The younger Miss Wallace came by this pm. The older is ill now too. She asked for help to bring the body home. I promised to try. It will be difficult, though John takes no notice of these things.

Easy enough for me to translate now. Miss Wallace is Seward's sister, of course. She wants his body home, in Maine, back from wherever he'd been hastily buried in Colorado. Back to his sisters, the older and the younger Misses Wallace, the older one now dying too.

By *these things* in the last line of the diary entry my grandmother means money, of course. The household expenses. Of which she did take notice. From the time of her marriage on into the late twenties, she kept her books carefully, with records of even the smallest expenditure: *collar stays 25¢, bluing 70¢, 4 yds dimity $1, knives sharpened 35¢, LG for ice $3.* All recorded in now-fading ink, all tallied up at week's end. And from October 12 forward for those three months there is the weekly amount deducted beside the letters *SW* in her books. It varies some over those months—certain expenses, like tithing, could not be reduced to accommodate what amounted to her embezzlement, so she could not always control how much she had to set aside—but at the end of that time she was able to give the Wallace sisters their money. It must have felt strange, writing down such a huge expenditure, especially to a person whose life was usually meted out in such tiny increments.

Imagine it, the daily awareness of the sacrifice, achieved in butter, needles, yarn, cloth, shoes. Things denied herself. Things, perhaps, denied him too—my grandfather. Though maybe she had rules for that as she clearly did for tithing. Maybe she felt only she should pay for Seward's return. There's no recorded discussion with herself about this, of course—no introspection on the subject anywhere—so it's impossible to say.

It does seem my grandparents' lives went on normally during this period. The diary made note of their trips to Pittsfield or Bangor, or to Georgia's father, or John's mother. There were occasional evenings out, and a good deal of the calling back and forth that women did, to visit or to help with household chores. (This, in fact, was why I hadn't noticed Miss Wallace's visit earlier; the diaries were sprinkled everywhere with women's names, women who called or were called on; were ill or had gotten well or had had children.)

Throughout these months she recorded how at night my grandfather read aloud and how, every now and then when she had a new tune she'd mastered, she would play the piano for him. During this time he got a one-tube radio and began a lifelong habit of spending some time in the evenings playing with it. Duly noted.

She had begun by now to help him in his office sometimes too, and those often traumatic episodes were reported as part of her routine.

My first tonsillectomy today. Horrible. So much blood. John praised my steadiness with the ether.

One gets a sense then of harmony and routine. Of increasing mutual dependence.

The other undiscussed, undisclosed reality of her life during this period was that she was pregnant. Nowhere was it explicitly mentioned in the diary, but as I was looking through this material, I suddenly remembered that the date when the initials *SW* appear in the diary after his death and long absence was very close to the date of my mother's birth. I counted back seven months or so from my mother's birth to the period when my grandmother might first have guessed or known that she was going to have a child, and found this entry:

September 15: A cool, foggy day. Not well this morning, but in the afternoon I let out two dresses and mended John's socks and some old trousers. He is very happy with my news. We will celebrate Sunday with dinner at Empson's.

Counting back farther, to nine months before my mother's birth, the time when she would have been conceived, I came to the weeks directly after my grandmother got the news of Seward's death, to the time my grandparents had their painful confrontation about that. They started a child then, in that tender, raw period after my grandfather learned that my grandmother had had a lover before him; in the time right after she learned that her lover had died. After she understood that all the changes in her life had been set in motion by my grandfather's interference in it. Thinking of it, their making love then, I felt sorry for them and envied them at the same time—I remembered that sex so well: the sex that both binds us and reminds us of our estrangement. The urgent sex that makes us cry out and then weep afterward. The powerful sex that combines anger and desire and sorrow and finally becomes itself a form of forgiveness and healing.

Out of all this had come my mother, it seemed; and so, I suppose, finally me too.

How odd it must have been for Georgia, this period of discretion, of secrecy in so many things. And how strange it is to read her record of it, knowing all that stays unmentioned, knowing all that was truly going on. Each day is "grand" or "lovely," or "foul," "gray." Once "dismal." Their daily accomplishments are recorded, and mention is made occasionally of one of her endless rounds of chores; but the only references to the pregnancy are oblique: "Knit 2 prs cunning booties." "Knit a bonnet with pale green ribbon running through." And the only note made of the stolen money is the weekly amounts recorded in the ledger next to the initials *SW*.

But perhaps it isn't so strange. The life of a pregnant woman is so private, so secret anyway: the sense of deep solitary fatigue for those early months; the first flickering motions of the swimmer within so light that you aren't even sure they have happened; the later lurches and kicks that only you know of, while your life outside your body goes on as usual. You smile, you respond: all of this is so inward-turned that perhaps the secret of the money, of Seward's body coming home, was just like one more thing she was pregnant with, the twin to the growing baby.

She was almost eight months into her pregnancy when he was brought back. The day he was to return she took my grandfather's car and drove to Bangor in order to meet the train with Seward's sisters.

It was cold and rainy, the height of the mud season, when the ice deep under the unpaved roads released its grip on the frozen dirt and turned it into a thick muck. Driving was difficult. Twice she got mired in the mud. Once a farmer behind a team of horses pulled her out, and once she got out herself, taking the board John carried for just such emergencies and pushing it under the tire that was spinning uselessly. She had allowed herself plenty of time for just such an event, though, so in spite of the delays she arrived ahead of Seward's sisters at the station.

There was a fire going in the big cast-iron stove in the waiting room. She sat close to it, trying to warm her wet feet, her hard, stiff fingers. The windows had completely steamed over but for the trails of moisture running like tears down the panes, silvering a clear streak here and there.

She hadn't told John where she was going, just that she had errands to attend to.

Couldn't they wait for a better day? he'd asked.

No, she said. No, they couldn't.

And he acceded, as he always did when she was absolute, though he asked her to ring him during the day, to set his mind at ease. She didn't do this. She forgot all about it in her hurry, in her guilt.

In the waiting room an odd sense of timelessness overtook her, a sense of suspension, of living in the interstice between at least two worlds. In some way she almost forgot where she was or what she was doing there. It felt a little like dozing, but she was keenly aware of everything—the conversation of the ticket seller and someone else behind the shiny brass grille, the tick of the station clock, the occasional stutter of the telegraph, the hiss and pop of the fire within the stove. These seemed to her in her drowse like the consoling elements of song.

She was startled when Seward's sisters came in, two tall women, dark-haired, as he had been, followed by a man wearing a black suit. She only knew the younger sister, the one who called on her and shamefacedly asked for her help—they'd found her notes, she said, in Seward's things and thought ("it was our last hope, really") that she might be willing, for sentiment's sake, to loan them something to help them bring him home.

The other sister seemed initially an elderly woman. Both of them were dressed in black, and in the old-fashioned way, the very way Georgia had dressed until only a little while earlier, in fact; the way only old women dressed now. But while the younger one was recognizably still youthful on closer examination, the older one was clearly ill, with the fever-flushed pallor Georgia knew so well.

As the younger sister began her breathless introductions, Georgia stood up. Her pregnancy was, of course, instantly apparent, and Miss Wallace fell silent for just a beat and then went on. She introduced Georgia to their pastor, the Reverend Winter, who had been kind enough to drive them. She chattered. Her voice was fluty, her elocution precise and careful. She thought the train should be coming any moment. They could not, by the way, speak of their gratitude, only hope one day to repay her, and also hope it had not caused hardship in her own life to be so generous to them. They hadn't realized, she started to say, and trailed off.

No, Georgia said. *It hadn't caused hardship.* For how could she speak of her little privations as hardship to them—who had suffered, who were suffering, such enormous, unthinkable losses?

When they heard the bell of the train approaching the station, they went together to the door to the platform and stepped outside into the March cold. The wet, raw rain slapped at them all, and the younger Miss Wallace stood closer to her sister, as though to take the brunt of the blow. The stationmaster had come out too, and now he spoke to Georgia, almost shouting in her ear. He told her the baggage cars would be near the end of the train. He pointed. When they all looked in that direction, down the platform, they could see that beyond it, a horse-drawn hearse was waiting, black and ominous in the thick drizzle. Georgia heard the older Miss Wallace's quick, shallow gasp.

The train loomed up out of the mist now, its bell clanging, and then it was upon them like a huge dark animal, so noisy they didn't bother trying to speak. The steam hissed, the doors clattered open, and suddenly the platform was crowded with people getting off the train, gathering their luggage, being greeted, calling back and forth. Georgia and the Wallace women continued to walk slowly through them, against the tide of buoyant life, making their way to the red baggage cars at the end of the train, where the porters were already stacking boxes and suitcases onto their trolleys. They worked fast—the train was going on—but even so it was startling to have the coffin appear so suddenly, carried off the train by four men. To have it set down matter-of-factly on its own trolley when they were still some distance from it, to have one of the porters call out, as he turned from it, "Zat everything?" and someone else laugh before he leaned from the door of the train and shouted, "Ayp!"

The undertaker and several helpers were approaching them from the other end of the platform. They reached the trolley first and waited. Only one of them stepped forward to greet the Wallace women. They spoke for a moment in hushed tones. Then the older sister turned and set her hands on the coffin. "Now it's really true, isn't it?" she said, to no one in particular.

Her sister gripped her more tightly and bent her head toward hers. Georgia felt herself to be an interloper, an intruder. Her presence here was nothing but ugly, she thought.

The four of them stood watching at the end of the platform, as the trolley was wheeled down the ramp, as the undertaker's men lifted it off—it seemed no strain to them—and slid it into the back of the hearse, as they closed the doors and went to the front of the carriage. When the horse had clopped off, the sisters turned. The younger one said to Georgia, "Shall you follow us then, in your automobile?"

Georgia said she would and walked slowly back up the platform, just behind them, next to Dr. Winter.

"There's to be no service," he said abruptly, as though compelled to speak of something to her. "Just a prayer."

"I see," she said.

"The Wallaces had a service earlier, just after he died. A memorial service. Quite moving."

"Yes," she said.

"But perhaps you were there," he said.

"No," she answered.

"Ah," he said in agreement. He held the station house door open for her. Ahead of them the sisters moved slowly across the waiting room to the outer door. "Someone played the pipes," he said. "Bag-pipes," he explained. "Such a mournful sound."

"It is," she said.

"I don't think I'd ever heard them before. It was stunning." When she didn't answer, he said, "I understand the young man was a piper himself. If that's what you call it."

"Yes, he was," she said.

Now he opened the entrance door to the rain again. The sisters stood by his car under their umbrella. "Well," he said, quickly lifting his hat. "We shall see you there."

"Yes," Georgia said. While she went to her automobile and set the spark and throttle, he helped the sisters into his car. Then he noticed her, starting to crank the car, and came over to help her. She got back behind the wheel and, as soon as the engine caught, set the spark and throttle back and leaned out the window to thank him. He lifted his hat ceremonially and went to start his own engine.

The two cars caught up to the hearse within three or four blocks and then drove slowly behind it. Georgia watched the car in front of her, the high black hump jolting through the mist. There was a part of her that wanted to flee, to take this turn or the next one and avoid the ceremony, such as it would be, and the cold, rainy day. To go back to the real world, where she lived.

But how could she? Seward had had so little, and she was so little of that, how could she not do this small thing for him?—watch him lowered into the earth, say goodbye one last time?

She tried to make herself think of him, lying in his black suit in the coffin in the hearse. She tried to remember him alive. She called up specific things in her effort to conjure him: the dry fever heat of his body when he lay with her, his long, slightly spatulate fingers.

The baby kicked and moved. She felt the glide of a tiny fist or a knee along her arm where it rested on her belly. She was flooded, suddenly, with the memory of the dreams she'd had earlier in her pregnancy—dreams in which she gave birth to Seward. In one dream she'd had over and over, he lay sleeping and she was filled with an unspeakable joy as she bent over his bed. In another, he was as she'd most often seen him in life—wearing his black suit, talking and gesturing with assurance. But *well*, she saw. No longer ill. And in the dream, she understood that she had achieved this for him by carrying him inside her for so long. That this was the cure he'd been searching for.

She was happy. Though when she woke, she tried to put the dreams out of her mind quickly. They seemed wrong to her. Bigamous. Obscene.

She remembered, abruptly, that she was to have called John. Her hand rose to her mouth.

But then she thought of Seward again, Seward saying, "Let's try it this way. You go, I'll stay."

Well, I have, Seward. I've gone on. I've changed. And you have stayed. Where you were, as you were. You are the past, Seward, and I have traveled forward, away, into another country, into the future.

They stood under the pelting rain—it had almost turned into sleet at this point—and watched as the undertaker and his men leaned back against the pull of the ropes and the coffin jolted and slid into the deep hole. When it was seated, when the muddy ropes had been pulled up and coiled and tossed casually into the back of the hearse, Dr. Winter said the Twenty-third Psalm. Isolated under her umbrella, Georgia strained to hear his voice. It was almost inaudible under the clamor of the storm. He began the Lord's Prayer, and after the first few words, Georgia heard the sisters join in, though she heard it more as a thickening of the sound than as additional voices. She murmured the words too. She felt like an actress speaking lines.

For a few seconds after the amen, no one seemed to know what to do. Georgia felt it wasn't her place to make the first move. To make any gesture, really. Though she was cold. Cold, and her feet were wet, her thin dress shoes soaked through. Finally the younger Miss Wallace stepped toward her.

"Won't you come back to our house and warm up before your trip back? Our mother would so like to meet you. Have some tea with us, please, or coffee, and something to eat. We are all so grateful...."

No, Georgia said. No, she wanted to try to get home before dark. It had been a hard ride over—all this mud.

Oh, she knew, said Miss Wallace. They'd certainly brought Seward home in the worst weather possible, but she had felt some urgency, her sister was so ill.

Oh, yes, Georgia said. She understood.

At the autos, they said their farewells. Again Dr. Winter helped Georgia start her engine. She drove away before he'd begun to crank his, waving over to the dark shapes within his car as she passed.

It was night, prematurely night, by the time she stopped the car next to the house. The last half an hour or so she'd driven in a terrible state of tension, anxious about where the edges of the road were, anxious about the rutted mud she sometimes slid through, powerless to steer the car at all. The windows of the house were dark; John was still at work.

Inside, she turned on the kitchen lights and started a fire in the cookstove. Then she moved around the tiny house, turning the other lights on too, so it would look cheerful to John as he came up the walk. She changed out of her dark clothing, her wet shoes and stockings. She toweled her hair dry and brushed it into its neat shape.

It is strange what you think of when you're trying not to think of something else, and my grandmother's mind that night was very busy, thinking and yet not thinking. She saw herself making a hash with the leftover roast beef and the beets she'd put up, and potatoes. She pictured exactly the steps involved. She saw herself washing the potatoes, drying them, grinding the meat into a bowl. She remembered, too, how she'd made the ketchup she would serve with the hash. It had been a hot day late last summer, and the air in the kitchen was thick with the rich sweet-sour smell of vinegar and sugar and overripe tomatoes. She thought of how sick she'd felt, how she'd blamed the heat, blamed the smell, not yet knowing she was pregnant.

She thought again of the baby and rested her hands on her belly. Boy or girl? she wondered, as she often did, picturing each—not naked, not genitally, but as she would dress them. Dolly, they'd decided, if it was a girl—Dorothy. If a boy, they weren't sure. A boy, she hoped. A boy for John.

John. She saw his face. His dear face. And then abruptly she remembered the way it had looked when she told him about Seward. His disbelief. His angry confusion. His mouth that funny pulled-down line. Bitter, as though he'd bitten a lemon. She'd seen then how old he was, how much older than she.

She got up quickly and poured what was left of her tea down the gurgling drain. She fetched the potatoes from the bin in the pantry and began to rinse them off. She started to hum "Where E'er You Walk." The water in the pot bubbled silver and then started to roil, releasing its thin cloud of vapor. She dropped the potatoes in. The windows slowly turned opaque with steam.

When John came home, ruddy-cheeked, wet, he started to scold her—why hadn't she called, he had been so worried—but she went to him and embraced him. She kissed him so passionately, so reck-lessly, that it took his breath. He felt himself stir and harden in response to her, and he had to turn away to gain control of himself.

While he washed up and changed his jacket for dinner, she reheated the hash, warmed the green beans, and poured their glasses of milk. Over the meal, they spoke only desultorily. He told her something of his day, tidbits he'd saved that he thought might be of interest to her. She hardly spoke at all, but when she lifted her eyes to his, there was a sort of stunned devotion in them that he found startling. She looked almost dizzy. He actually wondered, once, if her labor was perhaps starting, but he didn't want to ask her such a question.

They stood next to each other to do the dishes, leaving the serving pieces to dry in the rack. He hung the wet towel on the wooden bar. She turned off the light.

In bed, they lay side by side for a while. He could feel the thrum of something alert and tensed in her.

"You're awake, dear?" she whispered.

"How can I sleep, next to a machine that won't turn itself off?" he said.

She laughed. Her hand found his and held it briefly. "I want to tell you something, John. Something terrible and wonderful at the same time."

"Yes," he said, suddenly alert himself.

"And I want you to hear me out, to listen to all of it before you say one word. John?"

"Yes," he said.

"Really to listen," she said.

He waited.

"Seward Wallace came home today. His body. His coffin. From Denver. I went to meet it and see him buried."

He didn't answer. His heart had begun to pound, heavy thick beats he could feel in his throat.

"His sisters, they had wanted him back, to be buried with the family, and I agreed to help them. I did help them. With money, John. Money from household accounts. So I've known about it for a long time, you see. About his coming back. I should have told you, I know. But somehow, I couldn't. That's why I went to Bangor today. Not for errands for myself, but for Seward."

She had turned and he could hear her voice close to his ear. He could feel the heat of her breath.

"John, I didn't know what I would feel. Whether... I just didn't know. But what I felt was... oh, I'm not sure I can explain it! I felt so far away from all that. I felt it had all happened in another world somehow. And that I had gone on, I'd gone forward. I felt, I think, with the baby, that a claim had been made on me that makes me live in this world. The baby, and you too, of course. I belong here, John. I belong with you."

John didn't answer her. He was afraid to. He was grateful and glad, but he was angry too, and he didn't want her to know that. Her voice was so charged, so alive with this gift she felt she was giving him that he felt to question her, to question it, would be to wound something vital in her that connected them. That *could* connect them if he just left it alone. He had failed her once before in a similar moment. What he knew was that he could not fail her now. He had to be as generous as she so carelessly assumed he was.

But he felt it, her appalling carelessness. The sense of something youthful and cruelly insensitive in her. Something missing. He had known this about her, he realized in this moment. That she was like this, that this was who she was. It was part of why he had fallen in love with her, though he couldn't love it, this hard part of her that failed to see beyond herself. He had a momentary, quickly suppressed thought, a worry about what she'd be like as a mother. He pushed it aside. He pushed all this aside: She was his valiant girl. His scrupulously honest Georgia.

And even though it was later than he recommended it to his patients, even though he had felt a kind of constraint for months, the embarrassing constraint (he couldn't help this perception) of the baby as a witness, or even, somehow, a participant in their lovemaking, he turned to her now and began the purposive touching that signaled his desire for her.

Georgia too had sometimes had the thought that the baby was part of their intimacy, but it only deepened her pleasure. As John rocked gently in her, she held his hands to her swollen belly, she made him feel the moving life there; and when she reached her climax, she sent her cries out into the night, as though she wanted him, far off in the future, still to hear her joy.

Sixteen

The next day, the day after Georgia told him "the whole story," my grandfather came home at noon and told her to put on a coat, he had a surprise for her. A coat, and gloves too, he said. It was cold out.

Georgia took off the smock she was wearing. She pulled on the only coat she could still wear at this stage in her pregnancy, the navy wool, still damp from the rain yesterday. She buttoned the one button, at the very top of her belly, that would close. She pinned on her hat. He helped her into the car and went around to the driver's side.

"Am I to guess?" she asked gaily when he got in. She was relieved. He had seemed quiet at breakfast, pensive, and she had worried that he was brooding over her confession of the night before, over Seward. She had wanted to speak to him, to comfort him, but she decided not to. Sometimes, she had thought, it's better just to wait and see.

"No," he said now, and smiled over at her. "No, you are to be utterly surprised and, I hope, utterly delighted."

She had thought then that maybe he was planning to buy something for the baby. Perhaps a crib—they still didn't have one, only the cradle that had been John's when he was an infant. And so she was startled when they stopped in front of the bank. Startled, and then a little frightened. It suddenly occurred to her that they were going to make some kind of ceremony of putting the stolen money back. Oh, surely, she thought, he wouldn't be so unkind.

She followed him into the building, nodding as people greeted them. They all knew John. He led her to the back, to a door marked VICE-PRESIDENT. She had the thought that perhaps John was going to speak publicly of her shameful behavior to this authority. He introduced her to a horrible greedy-looking person, Mr. Blake. She sat down. John and Mr. Blake sat down. Mr. Blake rubbed his plump white hands together. "Well, what may I do for you today?" he asked.

When John said, "We are here to start an account in the name of my wife," Georgia felt such a rush of relief that she actually laughed aloud, and Mr. Blake, whose rubbery chops quivered with his every move, turned quickly to her and glared, his whole face trembling.

"If looks could kill," she told me later. But he turned back to John and said, with what seemed strained politeness, "Of course."

It was a nearly formal occasion. Mr. Blake's secretary was called in and then sent out again to fetch the records of my grandfather's account. When she was seated once more, Mr. Blake explained to her what they were doing.

"My goodness!" she said, and looked at my grandmother with something like admiration.

It was difficult for Mr. Blake to accept the terms being described by my grandfather. The account was to be in his wife's name only. No, Dr. Holbrooke did not need to know, indeed, did not wish to know, when she made deposits or withdrawals; that was exactly the point. Yes, her signature alone would suffice on all the documents. Yes, the money to start it would come from Dr. Holbrooke's savings account. Yes, five hundred dollars. Yes, he knew what that left him with. Yes, he was quite certain. No, he did not wish for account summaries or statements to be sent to him.

When they were done, when they were back in the noisy car once again and on their way home, where he wouldn't have time to eat the lunch she'd carefully prepared, she turned and said to him, "I never would have guessed that, John."

He looked over at her. She was smiling like a child in her pleasure. It made him feel old and somehow sad, but he smiled back. He said, "Well, I'm glad to be able to surprise you still from time to time."

I remember that when my grandmother first told me this story—or the part of the story she felt was fit for my ears—I was unimpressed. So he started a bank account for her. So what? It was only much later that I realized how extraordinary a thing this must have been and, realizing that, felt the sense of difference, of distance, between my grandparents' world and my own.

What she said to me when she told me the story was that she'd secreted money away for her own purposes. "It was early in our marriage, and I was still, I suppose, feeling sometimes as though I wanted to be my own person. To have some privacy for this and that. You know, some things you like to keep to yourself." She never mentioned Seward to me, she never spoke of what the money was for.

So that was the way I had understood it. Simply that my grandmother, innocently enough, squirreled away some of the money my grandfather gave her so she could have the sensation of independence—the sensation that she'd had far more, peculiarly, when she was someone's daughter than she did now as a wife. And it made sense to me, that the young woman who'd once been the solitary girl staying up late in her father's house just to feel her aloneness, her ownership of her own world, should wish for some private corner in her new life. Should steal it, if she had to.

In this version, as in life, she eventually told my grandfather. But in this version, of course, she confessed just to taking the money, not to using it as she had. "And do you know what he did?" she asked me. We were picking blueberries on Bald Mountain, and the light pinging of the berries in our buckets was an almost musical accompaniment to her tale.

No, I didn't.

"Well, of course, at first he was shocked, I think. Surprised that I would have felt it necessary to do such a thing. You know, anything I wanted, your grandfather would have given me. But that was the point of it, of some of it anyway, for me. I didn't want to tell him every single little thing I wanted. I didn't want everything to be a gift from him to me." Her hands moved rapidly over the low bushes, and the berries seemed to fall eagerly into her bucket, in groups. I plucked mine more laboriously, one by one.

"But he understood all that, without my ever saying it, don't you know. He understood me so well. And the next day he *marched* me down to the bank and we sat down across the desk from a horrid-looking fat old man named Mr. Blake." She looked up at me, smiling. "I can see him now, all jowls and muttonchops. Anyway, we set it all up. And not a word to me about whether he thought what I'd done was wrong. To this day I don't know if he thought so." Then she stood and moved farther away, to a fresh patch.

Had she come to believe this version herself over time? That her worst crime, her worst insult to her marriage had been theft? Had she forgotten by the time she told me about it that she'd stolen for *Seward*? That the theft itself was perhaps the least of it for my grandfather?

Of course, the point of the story as she passed it along to me was to praise my grandfather for his generosity, and even in her version he was certainly generous enough. And after all, why would she tell a child—or even an adolescent—the other version? The version in which my grandfather's generosity included his acceptance of, his forgiveness of, her love for Seward Wallace and her affair with him.

Her entry for that day reads:

March 19. Clear all day today. At noontime, John took me to the bank to get my own account. Mr. Blake could scarcely believe his ears. It took so long that John had no time to eat! I napped this pm and Susie Morrell came to tea. Stew for dinner. I hemmed a blanket this evening.

This was who he was then. Betrayed, robbed by his wife, he tried to understand the reasons why she might have felt it necessary to do either and to arrange their lives so she'd never have to do it again.

Maybe that was it. Maybe that was why he made her this unexpected gift.

But maybe he understood her better than she understood herself. Maybe what he saw even then was that he *had* had too much power in her life, that it could only make her want to rebel against him unless he released her, unless he gave her some kind of freedom from him.

Or it might have been that he understood that their quarrel over Seward, over his having sent Georgia to the san, wouldn't be over, couldn't be over, until some equity had been established between them. Maybe he saw that her embezzlement was her way of evening up the balance between them, and he was acknowledging the justice of it by making sure it was never again necessary.

Of course, it might all have been simpler and less personal than that. After all, women had just gotten the vote. Maybe her embezzlement caught him up and made him realize how old-fashioned their arrangement was. Maybe they stepped together into the modern world when they entered Blake's office.

I can't know. All I can say is, no matter what he put aside in himself, no matter what he hid, his doing this in response to her theft seemed to me utterly characteristic of him. And when I pieced together the final bits of what we might call his story, sitting in his transformed study late at night, I wept for everything that must have been painful for both of them in all this. I wept for their hardwon triumph.

If that's what it was.

. . .

It would seem that their marriage was ready at this point for its true beginning. All the false assumptions had been cleared away, all the false starts had played themselves out. It was only a little less than a month after this that my mother, Dolly, was born, "fat and healthy," Georgia notes in her diary. (Her diary, which ends eight months after this, though by then she has become so inconstant a journalist that it might as well have ended with the birth.)

Why is it, then, that only five months after Dolly's birth, they move? They leave Maine, which my grandmother never stopped calling *home*, and go to a little town in southern Vermont not very different from the one they left behind.

My grandmother used to offer a joking explanation for it sometimes, years later, when she was teasing my grandfather in front of us. She'd say, "Oh, your grandfather! He couldn't bear to share me with anyone, not even my own family, so he whisked me off—well, it might as well have been to the ends of the earth in those days, it took so long to get from here to there." But there was not, in this topic, ever the note of true anger or bitterness that came up over the issue of the san, of the control he'd exerted at that only slightly earlier time in her life. And clearly he felt the difference. He was at ease with this joke, as he wasn't with the other. He would smile abstractedly at her, his part of the ritual.

Of course, the simple answer is they left because he was offered a job. Someone was retiring from his practice or had died, I can't remember if I ever knew which. It was certainly a better job—the annual income higher, the town a little bigger, the roads (and that was so important) a bit better and better maintained.

But might there not have been too the wish to leave certain things behind? To put away the pain of the past and start anew?

What things?

Well, their difficult beginnings, for one. Of course, the reminders of Georgia's illness, and all the people who'd known about it.

Maybe even her father and all he had once meant to her, and her old home, which was Mrs. Erskine's now. Mrs. Rice's. Grace's.

And then Seward. Seward, white and cold and young forever, never changing, in his grave; and the things she'd done, the money she'd stolen, to bring him there.

All this past, all these memories, they abandoned. They became simply a part of the place left behind. They became a story they told to us in bits and pieces. And by the time I was old enough to want to go back and find the place—to put the story together with what was left of it—everything had changed. The san was the tasteful conference center. Preston, the little town where Georgia and Ada and Fred grew up watching their mother's death, was a nameless crossroads with a few sagging buildings clustered together. The graveyard where Seward and his parents and at least one sister lay buried was overgrown and vandalized, many of the old stones stolen or knocked over and their names made almost indecipherable anyway by acid rain and time.

But what lasts, after all? What stays the same through the generations? Boundaries shift, refugees die or flee with what they can carry, the waters slowly fill in behind the dams, and what was once there is lost forever, except in dreams and memories.

Of course, my dreams and memories were of Vermont, the place that wasn't quite home to them, the house they fled to, their new start in their new world. This was the past I had decided to live in exile from. This was what I dreamt of: the village, the house itself. Its smell of wood ash and damp and oranges and rosewater. The stillness that fell over it in the afternoons when my grandmother napped, and the yearning I felt in the summers during that stillness, when I could hear, rising and ringing from elsewhere in the village, the sounds of life. I dreamt of the tangled lilacs by the front door. Of the raspberry patch behind the house and the iridescent Japanese beetles that gathered on the fruit. Of the smell of jam boiling after we'd picked the berries, of fireflies glinting in the summer dark, of snow lightening the nighttime winter sky.

Most of all, I dreamt of my grandparents living there—as though they always had—with their habits, their rituals, their ways of speaking. With the illusory sense I had as a girl, when my own world was so fragile, that they always *would* be there. That they would always welcome me and care for me. That they were a place I could always go. A homeland.

In mid-January, Fiona went back to New York. A few days later, my classes began again at the Frye School. Suddenly my life, which had been my own to shape for so many months, seemed frantically full. I was still visiting Jessie daily, still helping Karen and Robert with meals, but now I added my regular workload to all that. Often I didn't get home until nine or later, and I was up by six, preparing for the long day.

Arriving home late one night, I stepped over the mail in the front hall and shed my coat. When I bent down, I saw that I had one personal letter, the address typed on an old-fashioned typewriter that did odd things with several letters. It was from Samuel. I took it with me back to the kitchen, where I fixed myself a sandwich, poured a glass of red wine, and then sat down at the table to open it.

> Dear Cath,
>
> I've just about settled myself back into your house, and grateful I am, every day, for being here. I think of you often as I move through the rooms, and wonder how things are for you, and for your daughter and her baby. May she flourish.
>
> We are in the midst of real winter here. A lot of snow, a lot of ice, a lot of cold. I've just about given up driving for the nonce (too old to negotiate all of that), but before I did, I made a trip to a little reservoir I'd heard of not too far from here. I couldn't go out on the water, but it seemed to me it looked much as you had described the lake you went to with your grandfather. Here's what the guidebook says of its creation: "The river was dammed

near Wilmington, and a mill complex was built on the reservoir that resulted. This industrial area, which once had about three hundred residents, became known as Mountain Mills. The once-thriving community, including a three-story building, is now submerged beneath the Harriman Reservoir. Portions become visible only in time of low water."

So now I'm afraid I must eat crow. This reservoir, so much smaller, so much closer by than Quabbin, and with buildings intact underwater, must be the one you went to, wouldn't you think? It does exist then, that world below the water you thought you saw.

My apologies, therefore, for my too-forceful assertions to the contrary, and all good wishes to you in this new year and new century. (Doesn't it feel strange to be living in the future?)

Yours as ever,
Samuel

I sat in my glamorous kitchen and thought of him in my grandmother's house. Samuel. It all seemed far away now, that moment when I might have moved toward him, that moment when he kissed me. His letter, though, stirred me. It brought back to me suddenly the way the buildings had looked through the shifting mirror of the water, the way the world below was there and then not there and then there again, and the way I had felt that day looking down into it, dizzy with my sense of yearning and loss for what was gone, and somehow for all that would ever be gone, in my life.

And I remembered too that when I'd come into the house that afternoon—by myself; my grandfather had stayed outside to clean his fish—my grandmother was waiting. She wanted to know whether my grandfather had spoken to me about France and what I thought about going. When I told her yes, yes he had, and yes, I was going to go, she said, "This will be good for you, Cath. An opportunity," in a tone that suggested I might be reluctant, might need persuading.

I remember that I tried to tell her that I *wanted* to go, that I was *meant* to go, but somehow she couldn't hear that; at cross purposes to me now, she kept on buoyantly arguing with some phantom reluctant granddaughter. *Sometimes we needed to do things that seemed difficult, to challenge ourselves.* It was only much later that I realized that she, like my grandfather, must have been making a connection between my trip and her parallel voyage as a young woman into the sanatorium; and that she was telling me it had been worth it, it had been good for her. That it had opened her and changed her as she hoped France would open and change me. This was the only time ever, in my memory—this day when she needlessly tried to persuade me of the necessity of my going away—that she spoke unequivocally positively about her own going away, about her going into the san, that she directly acknowledged what was good about the changes it made in her life.

The rains had started by now in San Francisco, the wild sweeping lashes of water off the ocean that were our version of winter. At night I lay in my own bed and listened to them rolling across the roof. Everything felt damp, even my clothes when I put them on in the morning. The ground underfoot was utterly saturated; your print was filling with water as you lifted your foot.

Late one afternoon, I stood by a parking meter outside the butcher shop I liked near Robert and Karen's apartment in North Beach, the stem of my umbrella tucked under my arm, the top of it resting on my head like a huge ribbed hat the rain was using for a drum, while I frantically rooted around in the change part of my wallet for the right coins. And then I realized: I was thumbing past the quarters looking for some other coins, coins I didn't have, francs or pesos or soles or rials. Who knows? Dream coins, in any case. I laughed at myself for a second. "The quarter will do," I said aloud.

"What?" a girl shouted at me from under her umbrella as she walked by.

"Ah, nothing," I said, but she was gone.

When I got over to Karen and Robert's, I told her the story. I blamed it on the rain. I said I must have thought I was in monsoon country.

"Well, take heart," she said. "It'd be worse if you'd stayed in Vermont. I heard on the news that it was snowing in New England—a big storm."

Snow. As I moved around my daughter's kitchen helping to fix the meal, I saw it in my mind's eye, falling on my grandmother's house. And then I had the sudden memory of a time going home years before, going home in a snowstorm to visit my grandmother as she lay dying.

When the family friend who'd taken charge of things for us then called me, she said she thought it was going to be an easy death, that my grandmother was just sleeping more and more of the time. It might even be a few weeks, she thought, but if I wanted to say goodbye, it would probably be best if I came now, when she might still be able to take me in, to speak to me.

My life was complicated. I was married to Joe, I was teaching, of course, but that was the least of it. Mostly it was the kids. They were teenagers then, each with an elaborate schedule, each with activities I was supposed to attend and applaud. My daybook was full of destinations and arrows and times. It would be hard to arrange getting away.

I tried to muster the reasons for not going. Maybe I *didn't* want to say goodbye. We had said goodbye over and over, actually, at the end of every visit for years, my grandmother holding my hands after our kiss and saying, "I want to take a good long last look at you now. You never know."

But I went. Of course I went. I had to go. Joe said he'd drive out to Jeff's big basketball game. He'd cook and decorate a sheet cake for Fiona's class party. These were the things he loved about our life together anyway. He was glad to do them, he said, and I knew that was true.

I flew east into a snowstorm, though our sky so high above the earth was sunny and blue the whole way. We came down into clouds and darkness. We landed in Hartford and I rented a car there. It was truly night by the time I set out, and still lightly snowing. I drove north on the blanketed interstate at about forty miles an hour, sometimes stuck for long stretches behind a slowly moving plow.

The thick flakes coming out of the dark at the windshield, the steady shuddering slap of the wipers, the vehicles looming ahead of me on the road—all this was hypnotic. When I pulled into my grandmother's driveway and turned the engine off, I sat for some long moments in the silence that followed, trying to relax and at the same time prepare myself for what was to come. The flakes landed silently on the car and melted with the engine's heat. The windows on the first floor of the house glowed with light, light that fell into the yard and made the steadily falling snow seem thicker and heavier than it was.

I looked at myself in the rearview mirror. I smoothed the flesh under my tired eyes, patted my hair into place. I put on some fresh lipstick—as though it mattered what I looked like. But I didn't know what to expect of this goodbye. I'd never seen death or a dying person before. The event had always happened offstage in my life. Everything about what I was getting ready to go through frightened me. And I suppose I wanted something from it, though I wasn't sure what. Some moment of recognition from her of me. Some gesture. Some final words to take with me back into my life. I couldn't have imagined that there would be anything she would want of *me*.

When I opened the car door, the air was still and, oddly, not cold. The walk hadn't been shoveled, and my shoes filled with snow in the short distance to the house. I knocked and opened the door almost simultaneously—of course it wasn't locked—just as the hospice nurse emerged from the back of the house. We'd spoken frequently on the phone in the last weeks, but I'd never met her. She was young, maybe in her early thirties, with rosy freckled skin and no makeup. She wore jeans and a flannel shirt and big green puffy slippers. As she took my coat, as I heeled off my shoes, she fussed over me—the terrible driving, the treacherous conditions. Some news or talk show droned on in the kitchen.

And then she said, quite simply and terrifyingly, "Go right on in. I told her you were on your way, and I think she's expecting you."

Georgia was asleep, propped up in the hospital bed that had replaced her own bed in the front parlor. She was thin, which she'd never been in my memory, and this more than anything else shocked me. It had caved her face in and made her nose prominent. Her hair had been cut very short too, as short as a boy's. Her ears stuck out a little. She wore an old familiar nightgown, buttoned neatly up to her neck. Her knobbed hands rested on the smoothly folded back sheet as though arranged there.

My feet in their wet socks had made no noise as I crossed to her, so I spoke in a whisper and touched her very gently—her hands first, and then her face. Her skin, which I'd been afraid of, was soft as a baby's.

Her eyes blinked a few times and then opened: brown, brown flecked with green. Why had I never noticed that before? She seemed to focus on me, to take me in, so I spoke again. "It's Cath, Gran," I said. "I'm here to sit with you awhile."

What was it about my gestures then, or my face, what confusion of association or of physical resemblance made her take me for someone else? For my grandfather, I think: her prince, come to wake her. Made her face lift in pleasure, made her hands swim vaguely toward me, made her cry out with delight, "Oh! *Here* you are at last!" Her smile was radiant. "Now you can take me home!"

And what gift of love or sympathy made me able to be what she needed in that moment, made me able to act my part, to give her back to her world? Made me able to answer her, "Yes"?

"Yes, of course I will."

The World Below

Sue Miller

A Reader's Guide

A Conversation with Sue Miller

Michelle Huneven is the author of two novels, Round Rock *and* James-land. *Sue Miller and Michelle Huneven have been friends for seventeen years.*

Michelle Huneven: What was the germ for this book, the first glimmer you had for it? Where and when did your find the evocative title?

Sue Miller: I think the initial impulse came from some diaries I inherited years ago from my grandmother's grandmother. They were written in 1869 and 1870, and they document her daily life with her husband on a farm in Maine. The entries are each only a few sentences long, and they concern primarily the weather and the work that got done on a given day, and who came to call, or whom they called on. There's a kind of fascinating boredom to the document as a whole. And then, on a day in June 1869, there's an entry that reads:

"It has rained all day. I washed in the morning and worked on Mrs. (illegible)'s dress in the afternoon. I am doomed to be disappointed in everything that I take pride in. I sometimes wish I was under the sod sleeping the sleep that knows no waking."

Nowhere else is this feeling expanded on, nowhere is the context for this cri de coeur discussed, and the next entry is back to the routine pattern—the waters having folded over it. I was moved by this, by the notion of a life of deep feeling running under the surface of this life of daily achievement and steady labor. By the idea of an unacknowledged world living below the world of the mundane. This was part of the germ for the book, and certainly the source of the title.

MH: This book seems to be about losses—the loss of ances-
tors, grandparents and parents, the loss of children, marriages, ways of life, and even parts of ourselves. Cath is at a
time in her life when she can actually face her losses—isn't
that what she's doing by going back to her grandmother's old
home? Is there a value to facing losses?

SM: I think it's not clear that that is Cath's intention in going
back—her motives seem more confused than that to me—but
from the start of her visit, with her arrival at the altered house,
that's what she's dealing with. And certainly once she begins to
face the reality that Georgia's life also held such enormous loss,
Cath finds a kind of consolation for her own, and a way to live with
them.

MH: There is much talk of starting over in this book, and
of the idea that people can re-create or change their lives—
Georgia going to the san, Cath going to Vermont (several
times: as a child after her mother's death, after both divorces)
and to France. Do you think people really can start over?

SM: I think there may be a few times in life, times when you're not
really formed, as in adolescence, when you can consciously redi-
rect it. And maybe sometimes later, in times of great crisis, when
you actually learn or see something about yourself that you hadn't
known or recognized before, that access of consciousness may
make some small changes and shifts possible. But I do think we are,
largely, who we are, once we're adults. It's difficult to do more than
change certain behaviors.

MH: Do you think that divorce happens now, whereas in the
past couples used to have to be more resourceful and find ways
to live together and begin again?

SM: Certainly once divorce becomes a possibility, becomes a socially viable alternative to marriage, it undercuts the sense that one must work things out, no matter the personal costs. And that's no doubt both bad and good. I used to love to read the "Can This Marriage Be Saved?" column in my mother's *Ladies Home Journal* when I was a kid, and to think about the compromises recommended to the couple in trouble—whether I could make them, whether it seemed to me they ought to be made. And this is a question I've asked fictionally more than once, too. The enduring marriage is a mystery. Not always a happy mystery. But a mystery.

MH: *The World Below* also concerns itself with secrets—family secrets and how they eventually surface, and also how they're resisted. John, when he's told Georgia's secret (about Seward), actually hears something else—something far easier for him to assimilate. The times that Georgia tries to talk about her experiences in the san to Cath, Cath can't draw her out—she doesn't want to know so much about her grandmother. And yet, you seem to say that there comes a time when knowledge is necessary and illuminating . . . ?

SM: To take up Cath's resistance to understanding her grandmother's story, I'd argue that she has a deep emotional stake in wanting to see her grandparents' marriage in a certain way, as that image of their gathering the laundry together in a storm suggests. And it's a mark of her growth, I think, that she accepts the complexities and compromises they've made, and is able to imagine some of the cost to each of them in that. So, yes, pushing through to knowledge and understanding of the emotional truths that surround us can be important.

MH: Because I know you always have strong opinions about your characters as you are writing them, I'm curious to know how you felt about Cath, Georgia, and John.

SM: Cath was certainly less clear in my mind at the start of my writing than the others were. In a certain sense, she was my lens, my way of looking at the others. About them my feelings were clearer. I saw Georgia as a strong, rather fixed person, a person who has needed to be authoritative and in charge from a very early age, and has lost, to a degree, the ability to consciously register certain feelings on that account—though they are there, and surface from time to time. John I saw, and wanted to draw, as more open, more flexible. I wanted to have him growing and learning and asking questions all his life. I love the scene in which he offers Cath the trip to France, and then openly speculates about whether it's a good thing or not that he's interfering in her life. This kind of questioning, his openness to it, endeared him to me as a character.

I learned more about Cath as I went along, as I recorded the subtle shifts and changes in her that occurred as she discovered the truth about Georgia and John's life.

MH: **There are several moments that really hit me hard. The one that really lingers is when Joe can't believe that Cath has been happy in their relationship when he's been so restless. Was Cath wrong to feel content?**

SM: I don't know whether she was wrong or right. It was certainly part of who she was that she saw and understood a serene domestic surface as enough—so disordered was her early life in her own family, and so troubled her first marriage. And her model for happiness, of course, was what she understood about her grandparents' marriage, which had that same apparent quality of serenity, contentment.

MH: **So what about marital happiness and contentment? Georgia and John's marriage was held together by mutual respect and history, but also by rituals and an almost formal** structuring of the days that is far less common in today's hectic world. Is ritual an ingredient for marital happiness?

SM: I do think that one can signal a great deal with ritual, and this certainly happens in that breakfast scene after Georgia and John have their terrible moment of recognizing the errors they've both made in coming together. So I think you're right to suggest that ritual—some rituals—and people's ability to share them may actually make their sense of happiness together stronger. May bind them, in a variety of ways.

MH: Memory is another theme in the book—its reliability, its emergence, what it offers us. Cath and Samuel's possible romance breaks down, in part, over their differing views of memory. Samuel sees memory as hopelessly subjective and self-serving. Cath, however, believes in the truth of her memory.

SM: I think the issues between them are less important to their romance breaking down than the way each of them approaches the issues. Each is bothered by the other's insistence on his/her own infallibility about this. Probably Samuel is *less* bothered—it seems clear he would wish to continue to be involved with Cath, in spite of what he sees as her stubbornness. But for Cath, his absolutism is fatal to the possibility of a romance between them, partly because she sees it as connected to his age, to a kind of rigidity born of age; and perhaps partly because she connects it to an attitude toward women born of the period Samuel grew up in and was part of. I thought of myself as pushing the reader to think a little about the differences and similarities between Cath, as a "modern" woman, and Georgia, as an "old-fashioned" one, when confronted with this kind of assertiveness on the part of the older man each is involved with. And perhaps, too, to think of the differences between John and Samuel.

On the other hand, Cath implicitly learns a great deal about memory from talking with Samuel; and perhaps part of her being able to imagine the passages in the book about her grandparents is a result of thinking with Samuel about history and its meaning—the imaginative entry we need to make into it to understand it.

MH: You make numerous references to books the characters read or are given—Willa Cather and Edith Wharton are both mentioned several times. I know you're not suggesting that the reader of *The World Below* read these books, but if he or she did, what ties or connections might be seen? (Except, of course, with the dreaded *Ethan Frome*.) What does it say about Georgia that she loved *Song of the Lark*?

SM: I hoped that it would suggest that she was thinking of the possibility of a more expansive life for herself; that this experience in the san had opened her to the notion of a life lived on terms different from the ones she has understood up until now to be the necessary ones.

As for *Ethan Frome*—well, maybe all that needs to be said is that I dislike that book intensely. I think that Wharton is particularly heavy-handed in that book about the inescapability of one's lot—though this is often her theme. And in a sense, it is the theme here, though I'd argue that the tone is quite different.

MH: *The World Below* seems a very natural progression from your last book, *While I Was Gone*, which was also about memory and marital happiness, but this book is more introspective, quieter in content. In your body of work (six novels, one book of short stories)—where does this book sit with you? If someone loved *The World Below*, which of your books would you have them read next?

SM: I do think of this book as quieter, as you suggest, than some others—mostly about an internal process in Cath triggered by "the story" of Georgia's life as it gets revealed. In that sense I feel it's different from *While I Was Gone*, which is very dramatic, very plot driven—as *The Good Mother* was, too. So I think I'd suggest perhaps *Family Pictures* to someone who liked this book. Or perhaps *The Distinguished Guest*. Both of them have less "action," more dwelling in thought.

MH: I understand that after finishing *The World Below*, you finished a memoir of your father that you had been working on for years. Did writing *The World Below* give you any clues or help in finishing that book?

SM: I think it was rather the reverse: writing and thinking about that book—I had been working on it between and among novels for years—fed this book. In part with the sense that I had of learning about my father, changing in my thinking about him, long after his death.

MH: Any new novels on the horizon?

SM: I am beginning to make notes. I hope truly to launch myself this summer (the summer of 2002). I haven't written any fiction in over a year now, and I feel as though I've been deprived of some nearly chemical processes in my brain—the way, perhaps, people deprived of REM sleep are said to feel.

Reading Group Questions and Topics for Discussion

1. Soon after Catherine arrives in Vermont, a real estate agent approaches her about showing the house to prospective buyers. The realtor compliments her on the house and adds that she is also enamored of the house's "story"—"in the family for generations, both your parents living here into their old age, and so forth." Catherine recoils. "The truth was I didn't want to think of any of us that way—my grandparents, my mother, me. Or to have our life here used as a selling point—all that pain and sorrow and joy—to make the house itself more appealing. We weren't the house's *story*, none of us." Catherine is objecting, in part, to the fact that the story is more complicated than the realtor could possibly know—more complicated than any of them could possibly know, in fact. What does she mean? How is this notion advanced throughout the novel?

2. Miller writes that as Dr. Holbrooke examined nineteen-year-old Georgia he was "already beginning to think in terms of rescue." Yet in the same chapter he reflects on the arbitrariness of fate—of death in particular—and of the bewildering weight of his power in relation to both. How do you think Dr. Holbrooke squares his discomfort with his decision to have Georgia sent to the san? How do you think the author views his actions?

3. Catherine speaks of rescue, too, in the scene in which she first meets Joe. "What shall I say of Joe? That I felt rescued by him from something I hadn't been conscious of needing rescue from? That I trusted him? Both were true. I never considered that I might be rescuing him." How does this differ from Dr. Holbrooke's rescue of Georgia? To what extent are all relationships, especially romantic ones, a form of rescue?

4. As young women, both Cath and Georgia felt a deep sense of shame; both of them, early on, came to believe that they were failures. Why? Discuss the parallels in their lives.

5. Shortly after receiving the news that her father is to be remarried, Georgia cuts her hair. Is this transformation an act of empowerment or of self-punishment? "She unpinned her hair and let it down—*your crowning glory* her mother had called it—and watched as the long bolts of it slipped and whispered to the floor." What is Georgia rejecting? What is she embracing?

6. In chapter eight, Catherine invites Samuel Eliasson back to her house, and they have a conversation about the past. Eliasson, a historian, says that he views himself as an anthropologist, of sorts; he compares the past to "another culture, another country." What does he mean? And how is this notion of the past reflected in the novel as a whole?

7. In this same conversation, Samuel describes his wife's religious devotion as "the central invisible fact of her life." He continues, "You could write her life's story without including it if you didn't know specifically about it, it was simply underneath everything." How does this idea of a "central invisible fact" come into play elsewhere in the novel? What is the central invisible fact of Georgia's life? Of Dr. Holbrooke's? Of Catherine's? What is the central invisible fact of your own?

8. The novel takes its name from the image of a town submerged beneath the surface of a lake. Catherine glimpses this world one day while fishing on the lake with her grandfather: "I looked down again. It came and went under the moving water, the sense of what was there. There were long

moments when I couldn't quite get it, when it seemed I must have imagined it. But then there it was again, sad and mysterious. Grand, somehow. Grand because it was gone forever but still visible, still imaginable, below us." Discuss this image in relation to the novel's themes. How has the author woven it into the novel's narrative and the narrative of its individual characters? What is the "World Below"?

9. Catherine expresses a desire to begin life anew at various points throughout the novel—when she arrives with her young children on her grandparents' doorstep, after separating from her first husband; when she arrives in Vermont to make a decision about whether to sell the house or stay on; when, as a teenager, she is offered the chance to live with Rue in Paris for a summer. Each of these moments offers her, or seems to offer her, the possibility of inventing a new self. Is this kind of self-invention possible? Discuss the author's views on identity.

10. Discuss the question above in relation to Georgia's life. Look, in particular, at Georgia's thoughts after leaving the san, and at her first conversation with Dr. Holbrooke at her father's wedding. To what extent is it possible for other people to act as a bridge between our past and future selves?

11. In chapter eleven, Georgia and Dr. Holbrooke have a heated argument in which it unfolds that their marriage has been built on a misunderstanding. Can true love ever emerge out of a falsehood, even an accidental one? How does the author shape our perception of their marriage through the course of the book?

12. During Georgia's argument with Dr. Holbrooke it is also revealed that Georgia did not have TB at the time she was

sent to the san, and that Dr. Holbrooke misled her about the condition of her lungs. Dr. Holbrooke claims that he was justified in lying to her because her time at the san was beneficial—she rested, she gained strength, she was relieved of the daily burdens of caring for her family. "But it changed my *life*!" Georgia cries in response. What is your view of Dr. Holbrooke's decision to have her sent away? Was this an act of mercy, or a misuse of power, or both? Do we have the right to change one another's lives?

© Marion Ettlinger

About the Author

Sue Miller is the bestselling author of *While I Was Gone*, *The Distinguished Guest*, *For Love*, *Family Pictures*, *Inventing the Abbotts*, and *The Good Mother*. She lives in Cambridge, Massachusetts.